UTAH BLAINE
&
SILVER CANYON

Bantam Books by Louis L'Amour
ASK YOUR BOOKSELLER FOR THE BOOKS YOU HAVE MISSED.

NOVELS

Bendigo Shafter
Borden Chantry
Brionne
The Broken Gun
The Burning Hills
The Californios
Callaghen
Catlow
Chancy
The Cherokee Trail
Comstock Lode
Conagher
Crossfire Trail
Dark Canyon
Down the Long Hills
The Empty Land
Fair Blows the Wind
Fallon
The Ferguson Rifle
The First Fast Draw
Flint
Guns of the Timberlands
Hanging Woman Creek
The Haunted Mesa
Heller with a Gun
The High Graders
High Lonesome
Hondo
How the West Was Won
The Iron Marshal
The Key-Lock Man
Kid Rodelo
Kilkenny
Killoe
Kilrone
Kiowa Trail
Last of the Breed
Last Stand at Papago Wells
The Lonesome Gods
The Man Called Noon
The Man from the Broken
    Hills
The Man from Skibbereen
Matagorda
Milo Talon
The Mountain Valley War
North to the Rails
Over on the Dry Side
Passin' Through

The Proving Trail
The Quick and the Dead
Radigan
Reilly's Luck
The Rider of Lost Creek
Rivers West
The Shadow Riders
Shalako
Showdown at Yellow
    Butte
Silver Canyon
Son of a Wanted Man
Taggart
The Tall Stranger
To Tame a Land
Tucker
Under the Sweetwater Rim
Utah Blaine
The Walking Drum
Westward the Tide
Where the Long Grass
    Blows

SHORT STORY
    COLLECTIONS

Beyond the Great Snow
    Mountains
Bowdrie
Bowdrie's Law
Buckskin Run
The Collected Short Stories
    of Louis L'Amour
    (vols. 1–5)
Dutchman's Flat
End of the Drive
From the Listening Hills
The Hills of Homicide
Law of the Desert Born
Long Ride Home
Lonigan
May There Be a Road
Monument Rock
Night over the Solomons
Off the Mangrove Coast
The Outlaws of Mesquite
The Rider of the Ruby
    Hills
Riding for the Brand
The Strong Shall Live
The Trail to Crazy Man

Valley of the Sun
War Party
West from Singapore
West of Dodge
With These Hands
Yondering

SACKETT TITLES

Sackett's Land
To the Far Blue
    Mountains
The Warrior's Path
Jubal Sackett
Ride the River
The Daybreakers
Sackett
Lando
Mojave Crossing
Mustang Man
The Lonely Men
Galloway
Treasure Mountain
Lonely on the Mountain
Ride the Dark Trail
The Sackett Brand
The Sky-Liners

THE HOPALONG CASSIDY
    NOVELS

The Riders of the High
    Rock
The Rustlers of West Fork
The Trail to Seven Pines
Trouble Shooter

NONFICTION

Education of a
    Wandering Man
Frontier
THE SACKETT COMPANION:
    A Personal Guide to the
    Sackett Novels
A TRAIL OF MEMORIES:
    The Quotations of
    Louis L'Amour,
    compiled by
    Angelique L'Amour

POETRY

Smoke from This Altar

Utah Blaine
&
Silver
Canyon

Louis L'Amour

BANTAM BOOKS

UTAH BLAINE / SILVER CANYON
A Bantam Book / March 2008

Published by Bantam Dell
A Division of Random House, Inc.
New York, New York

Photograph of Louis L'Amour by John Hamilton—Globe Photos, Inc.

Bantam Books and the rooster colophon are registered trademarks
of Random House, Inc.

ISBN 978-0-553-59182-8

Printed in the United States of America
Published simultaneously in Canada

www.bantamdell.com

OPM   10 9 8 7 6 5 4 3 2 1

UTAH BLAINE

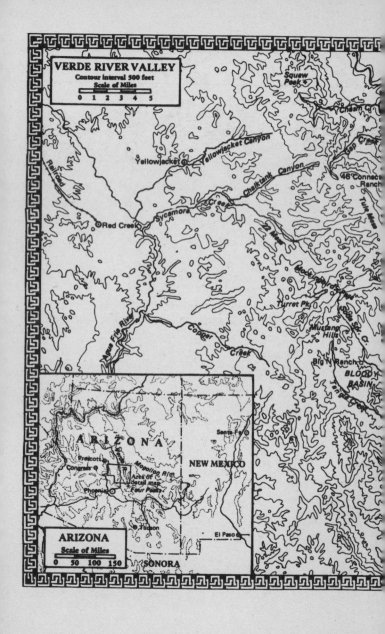

Map by William & Alan McKnight

CHAPTER 1

HE WAS ASLEEP and then he was awake. His eyes flared wide and he held himself still, staring into the darkness, his ears reaching for sound.

He could smell the dry grass on which his blankets were spread and he could smell the night. And then he heard again the sound that had awakened him. It was the stir of hoofs on the dusty trail some thirty yards away—not the sound of one horse alone, but of several horses.

Carefully, he lifted himself to one elbow. This was strange country and he was unarmed. What motives might inspire whoever was out there he could not guess, but large groups of riders do not move silently along midnight trails without adequate reason.

This was no celebrating bunch of cowhands headed for the home ranch. These men were quiet, and their very stillness was a warning. No stranger to trouble, he lay perfectly still, feeling the muscles back of his ears tighten with suspense.

They had stopped. A horse moved nervously, and then there was a voice. "Right above your head." There was a pause. "That's it."

Another and deeper voice spoke. "Lead his horse over here." There was movement, a click of hoof on stone. "Hold it."

Saddle leather creaked, easily heard in the still night air. Then that second voice came again. "There!"

The word held satisfaction, a gloating born from some dark well of hatred and rolled on the tongue as if the speaker had waited long for this moment and wished to prolong it.

"Easy with that horse!" There was harsh impatience. "Don't let him drop! Ease him down! I want him to know what he's gettin'!"

"Hurry it up!" The voice held impatience and obvious distaste. "Do it, if you're goin' to, an' let's get out of here!"

"Take it easy!" There was a snarl in the deep voice. "I'm runnin' this show an' I've waited too long for this chance. How d'you like it, Neal?"

The voice that spoke now was that of the man being hanged. He spoke coldly. "You always were a double-crossin' rat, Lud, an' you ain't changed any."

There was the sharp crack of a slap, and then the same voice spoke again. "Lucky my hands are tied, Lud. Old as I am I'd take you apart."

There was another blow, and the sharp creaking of leather that implied more blows. The man in the blankets was sweating. He eased from the blankets and grasped his boots, drawing them on. Then he stood up.

"Hurry it up, Lud! It'll soon be light an' we've miles to go!"

The listener held himself still. To be found here would mean certain death, and he was utterly defenseless. Against one man, or even two, he might have taken a chance, but without a gun he was helpless against this number.

This was no committee of honest citizens but some dark and ugly bunch out to do business that demanded night and secrecy. They could not afford to be seen or known.

"All right," Lud's voice was thick, irritated, "lead his horse out easy. I want this to last."

A horse moved and the listener heard the creak of a rope taking strain; then he heard the jerking of it as the hanged man kicked and struggled. The listener knew. He had seen a lynching before this.

"Never thought I'd live to see the day," the first speaker said. "After Neal the rest of them will be easy. This was the one had me bothered."

"Huh!" Lud grunted. "You leave it to me. This was the one I wanted. Now we'll get the rest. Let's get out of here!"

There was a sudden pound of horses' hoofs and the listener moved swiftly. Yet it was a movement without sound. Like a shadow he slid into the brush, the branches not even whispering on his clothing.

The chance was slight, but there was a chance. The last few feet he ran soundlessly on the thick leaves and grass. He went up the tree with swift agility and with a quick slash, he cut the rope and let the body tumble into the dust. Grasping the branch he swung out and dropped lightly beside the body, then bent swiftly and loosened the noose. Almost at once the man began to gasp hoarsely.

So far as could be seen the trail was empty, but this was no healthy place. Picking up the older man as if he were a child, the rescuer went quickly through the brush to his bed and placed the man on the ground. Then he loosened the man's shirt and got his own canteen. Gasping painfully, his neck raw from the manila rope, the man drank. Then he sank back on the blankets.

Restlessly, the young man paced, staring up the trail through the brush. One of the riders might come back, and the sooner they got away from here, the better. He knew the folly of mixing in other people's business in a strange country.

The old man lay on the ground and stared up at the sky. His fingers fumbled at the raw flesh of his throat and came away bloody. His gray eyes turned toward his rescuer. "Fig...figured they...had me." His voice was thick and hoarse.

"Save the talk. Only reason you're alive is that Lud hombre. He wanted you to choke slow instead of break your neck with a drop."

The old man rolled over to his elbow and sat up. He stared around, looking at the two worn blankets, then at the canteen. He took it in trembling hands and drank slowly. Then he said, "Where's your horse?"

"Don't have one."

The older man stared at him. The young man's possessions appeared to be nothing but the blankets and canteen. The flannel shirt he wore was ragged and sunfaded, the jeans did not fit him, and he had no hat. His only weapon was a Bowie knife with a bone handle. Yet beneath the ragged shirt the shoulders and chest bulged with raw power and the man's face was hard and brown, his green eyes steady. Moreover there was about him a certain undefined air of command that arrested the older man's curiosity.

"My name's Joe Neal," he volunteered. "Who are you? What are you?"

The big man squatted. He reached for a piece of brown grass and snapped it off. "What's this all about?" he jerked his head at the trail. "Who were they?"

"Vigilantes," Neal's voice was still hoarse. "That's the devil of it, stranger. I helped organize 'em."

He stretched his neck gingerly. His face was brown and seamed with wrinkles. "My brand's the 46 Connected. The country was overrun with rustlers so we got them vigilantes together. Them rustlers was well organized with spies everywhere. Nobody ever knew who was behind 'em until Lud Fuller turned it up that Gid Blake was the man. I'd never have believed it."

"They hung him?"

"Nope. He got him a gun first an' shot it out. Fuller handled it."

"Blake a gambler?"

"Lord, no! He was a rancher. The B-Bar, almost as big as my outfit."

The man got to his feet. "If you're up to it, we better light out. Is there anywhere near we can pick up horses?"

"The nearest is over by the lava beds. The Sostenes's outfit."

"Sostenes? A Mex family?"

"Uh huh. Been here a long time."

They started walking, heading back up a draw. When they reached a ledge of rock the stranger stepped over to it. "Better keep to this. They'll trail us. Sounded like they wanted you mighty bad."

Neal's muscles were still jumping nervously from

the shock of hanging. Sweat got into the raw flesh on his throat and smarted painfully.

He scowled as he walked, feeling with his brain for the answer to the problem that confronted him. Why had they done this to him? He had never dreamed that Lud might hate him, although he had always secretly despised the big man. The vigilante notice had come to him shortly before midnight and he had answered it all the more promptly because he felt it was time to disband. He was not at all satisfied about the hanging of Gid Blake and he knew the community had been profoundly shocked. He had joined the riders at their rendezvous and had been promptly struck over the head from behind. By the time he shook himself out of it, he was tied and they were taking him to the tree.

He turned and glanced at the big man who walked behind him with an effortless ease that he could never have hoped to match. Not even, he reflected, as a young man.

Who was the fellow? What was a white man doing with no more outfit than a digger Indian?

After awhile, Neal stopped. "Better take a blow." He grinned wryly. "Never was no hand for foot travel, not even when I felt good. And it's a distance yet."

"Got any plans?"

"No," Neal admitted, "I haven't. This thing has been a shock to me. Can't figure why they did it. One of the men in that outfit was my foreman. Now I don't know who to trust."

"Then don't trust anybody."

"That's easier said than done. I've got to have help."

"Why?" The big man leaned back on the ground. "Folks who want to help mostly just get in the way. This here's a one-man job you got."

Neal felt gingerly of his neck. "I'm not as young as I used to be. I don't want to go back there an' get my neck stretched."

"You aim to quit?"

Neal spat. "Like hell, I'll quit! Everything I've got is back there. You want I should give up thirty thousand head of cattle?"

"Be a fool if you did. I figured you might send me."

"You?"

"Sure. Give me papers authorizing me as ranch manager, papers the banks will recognize. Let me work it out. You're up against a steal, and a smart one."

"I don't follow you."

"Look, you organized the vigilantes to get rid of some crooks. Then all of a sudden when you aren't with them the vigilantes hang this Gid Blake. He was a big rancher, you said. What happens to his outfit?"

"What happens? His daughter runs it."

"Can she?"

"Well, I don't know," Neal admitted. "She's mighty young."

"Was her foreman a vigilante? I'm bettin' he was. I'm bettin' somebody got smart down there and decided to use the vigilantes to get possession of your range and that of Blake. From what they said they have others in mind, too. I'm bettin' none of your range was filed on. I'm bettin' that with you gone they just move in. Is that right?"

"Could be." Neal shook his head. "Man, you've

struck it. I'll bet that's just it." He shook his head. "I can't figure who would boss a deal like that."

"Maybe nobody. Maybe just two or three put their heads together and got busy. Maybe when the job is done they'll fight among themselves.

"Who would stop it? Is there anybody down there who might try?"

"Tris Stevens might. Tris was marshal once, years ago, and he's still right salty. Ben Otten might, he's smart enough. Blake, Otten, Nevers and me, we were the big outfits. Lee Fox was strong but not too big. It was us decided on the vigilantes, although I was the ringleader, I expect."

They got up and started on, walking more slowly. "Well, like my proposition? You go back there now they'll kill you sure as shootin'. Send me in an' you'll have 'em worried. They won't know what's become of you, whether you're dead or alive."

"I'd have to be alive to send you down there."

"No, not if you predated the order, say two months or even a couple of weeks. Then I could move in and they would be some worried."

"What's to stop 'em from killin' you?" Neal demanded. "You'd be walkin' right into a trap."

"It wouldn't be the first. I'll make out."

They walked on and the sun came out and it grew hotter, much hotter. Joe Neal turned the idea over in his mind. He was no longer a youngster. Well past sixty, with care he might live for years. But he wasn't up to fighting a lone hand battle. While this fellow— he liked his looks.

"I don't know who you are. Far's I can see you're just a tramp without a saddle."

"That's what I am. I just broke jail."

Neal chuckled. "You got a nerve, stranger. Tellin' me that when you're askin' me to drop my ranch in your lap."

"The jail was in Old Mexico. I was a colonel in the army of the revolution, and the revolution failed. They took me a prisoner and were fixin' to shoot me. The idea didn't appeal very much so I went through the wall one night and headed for Hermosillo, then made it overland to here."

"What's your name? I s'pose you got one?"

The young man paused and mopped the sweat from his face. "I got one. I'm Utah Blaine."

Joe Neal stiffened, looking up with startled realization. "You . . . you're Utah Blaine? *The gunfighter?*"

"That's right."

Joe Neal considered this in silence. How many stories had he heard of Blaine? The man was ranked for gun skill with Wes Hardin, Clay Allison and Earp. He had, they said, killed twenty men. Yet he was known as a top hand on any ranch.

"You took a herd up the trail for Slaughter, didn't you?"

"Yeah. And I took one up for Pierce."

"All right, Blaine. We'll make a deal. What do you want?"

"A hundred a month and an outfit. A thousand dollars expense money to go in there with. I'll render an account of that. Then if I clear this up, give me five hundred head of young stuff."

Neal spat. "Blaine, you clear this up for me and you can have a thousand! A permanent job, if you want it. I know how to use a good man, Blaine, and if you were good enough for old Shanghai Pierce you are good enough for me. I'll sign the papers, Blaine, makin' you ranch manager and givin' you right to draw on my funds for payrolls or whatever."

They came up to the Sostenes ranch at sundown. For a half hour they lay watching it. There were three men about: tall old Pete Sostenes and his two lanky sons. It was a lonely place to which few people came. Finally, they went down to the ranch.

Pete saw them coming almost at once and stood waiting for them. He glanced from Blaine to Neal. "What has happen'?" he asked. "You are without horses! You have been hurt."

Inside the house, Neal explained briefly, then nodded to Blaine. "He's goin' back there for me. Can you get us out of here to the railroad? In a covered wagon?"

"But surely, Señor! An' if I can help, you have only to ask."

Four days later, in El Paso, they drew up the papers and signed them. Then the two shook hands. "If I had a son, Utah, he might do this for me."

"I reckon he would," Blaine replied, "an' I've got a stake in this now, Neal. You want your outfit back, and I want to start a little spread of my own."

The dust from the roadbed settled on his clothes. Come hell or high water, Blaine thought. But he knew it was foolish to make promises. It was action that mattered, and now he was ready for action. He liked the feel of the gun in his waistband, and the knowledge of the other guns in his bag and the cased Winchester beside him.

Red Creek was the name of the town. First he had to hit Red Creek, then head for the 46 Connected. Utah Blaine slumped in the train seat and pulled his new hat over his eyes. He had better rest while he had the chance.

CHAPTER 2

UTAH BLAINE REACHED Red Creek at high noon and helped unload his horse from the baggage car. Persuasion supplemented by ten dollars had assured the passage of the stallion.

It was a lineback dun with a black face, mane and tail. Short coupled and powerful, the horse showed his Morgan ancestry in conformation but there was more than a hint of appaloosa or other Indian stock in his coloring, and in a few other characteristics. From the moment Utah glimpsed the stallion he had eyes for no other horse.

When he had the horse off the train he saddled up with his new saddle and bridle, then slipped his Winchester into the scabbard and mounted. He walked the horse up the street to the livery stable, aware that both he and the stallion were being subjected to careful examination.

It was a one-street town with hitching rails before most of the buildings. The bank was conveniently across from the livery stable. Beyond the stable was the blacksmith shop, facing a general store across the street. There was a scattering of other buildings and behind them, rows of residences, some of the yards fenced, most of them bare and untended.

Blaine stabled his horse and came to the door of the building to smoke. Two men sat on a bench at the door of the stable facing the water trough. They were talking idly and neither glanced his way although he knew they were conscious of his presence.

"... be fighting for months," one of them was saying, "an' we all know it. Nobody around here could buck Lud Fuller, an' I don't reckon anybody will try."

"I ain't so sure about that," the other man objected. "The 46 Connected is the best range around here. Better than the B-Bar or any of them. I wouldn't mind gettin' a chunk of it myself."

Utah Blaine stood there in the doorway, a tall, broad-in-the-shoulder man with narrow hips and a dark face, strong but brooding. He wore a black flat-brimmed flat-crowned hat and a gray wool shirt under a black coat. His only gun was shoved into his waistband.

He stepped to the door and glanced briefly at the men. "If you hear talk about the 46 bein' open range," he said briefly, "don't put any faith in it. Joe Neal isn't goin' to drop an acre of it."

Without waiting to see the effect of his remarks he started diagonally across the street toward the bank. Even the dust under his feet was hot. Up the street a hen cackled and a buckboard rounded a building and came down the street at a spanking trot. A girl was driving and she handled the horses beautifully.

Blaine threw his cigarette into the dust. Stepping into the coolness of the bank building, he walked across toward a stocky built man with sandy hair who sat behind a fence at one side of the room. On the desk there was a small sign that read: Ben Otten.

"Mr. Otten? I'm Blaine, manager of the 46 Connected. Here's my papers."

Otten jerked as if slapped. "You're what?"

His voice was so sharp that it turned the head of the teller and the two customers.

Blaine placed the packet of papers before Otten. "Those will tell you. Mr. Neal is taking a vacation. I'm taking over the ranch."

Ben Otten stared up into the cool green eyes. He was knocked completely off balance. For days now little had been talked about other than the strange disappearance of Joe Neal and its probable effect on Red Creek. There wasn't a man around who didn't look at the rich miles of range with acquisitive eyes. Ben Otten was not the least of these. Neal, it had been decided, was dead.

No body had been found, but somehow word had gotten around that the vigilantes had accounted for him as they had for Gid Blake. Not that it was discussed in public, for nobody knew who the vigilantes were and it was not considered healthy to make comments of any kind about their activities.

At first, two gamblers had been taken out and lynched. Others had been invited to leave town. That, it was generally agreed, had been a good thing—a move needed for a long time. However, the attempted lynching and eventual killing of Gid Blake had created a shock that shook the ranching community to its very roots. Still, Blake *might* have been involved in the rustling. Then Joe Neal vanished, and the one man who had questioned the right of his disappearance had been mysteriously shot.

Another man, a loyal Neal cowhand, had likewise been killed. Nobody mentioned the reasons for these later killings but the idea got around. It was not a wise thing to talk in adverse terms of the vigilantes.

Despite this, Ben Otten had been giving a lot of thought to the vast 46 range and the thirty thousand head of cattle it carried. After all, somebody was going to get it.

Otten was aware that Lud Fuller imagined himself to be first in line, and Nevers, while saying little, was squaring around for trouble. Information had come to Otten that Nevers had quietly eased several hundred head of his cattle to 46 range and that his line cabins nearest to the 46 were occupied by several men to each cabin. Nobody was going to get that range without a fight. And now this stranger had come.

Opening the manila envelope Otten took out the papers and examined them. There was a letter addressed to him, advising that Michael J. Blaine had been appointed manager of the 46 holdings with full authority to sign checks, to purchase feed if necessary, or any and all things appertaining to the successful management of the ranch.

There was a power of attorney and several other papers that left no doubt of Blaine's position. Otten knew the signature well, and there could be no doubt of it. Joe Neal was alive. Moreover, he scowled, these papers were dated some weeks prior to this day.

Otten looked up. "These seem to be in order, but I'm afraid I don't understand. Where is Joe?"

"I left him in El Paso, but he's not there now. In fact, he told me he wanted a vacation. I doubt if he'll be back here for several months, or even a year."

Otten leaned back, chewing on his cigar. "Have you got any idea what you're steppin' into?"

"More or less."

"Well, let me say this. You'll have few friends. Neal was a well-liked man, but there was envy around. When he disappeared nearly everybody began maneuvering to get a piece of his spread. Some of them have been counting on it pretty strong, and you'll have trouble."

"I'm no stranger to it," Blaine said quietly, "but I'm not huntin' it."

He picked up a letter from among the papers. This informed all and sundry that Blaine was manager of the ranch with complete authority to hire, fire or purchase. It was signed by Neal and two witnesses, both of them known locally as prominent El Paso businessmen.

"Get the word around, will you?" Blaine suggested. "I'm going out to the ranch in the morning. I hope there'll be no trouble."

"There will be."

Blaine turned toward the door and then stopped. The girl who had driven the buckboard was coming through the door, walking swiftly. As she walked she peeled the gloves from her hands. She was about five feet and four inches and very pretty. Her eyes were deep blue, her hair red gold. She was apparently angry.

"Ben, have you heard anything from the capitol? Are they sending a man up here to investigate my father's murder?"

"Now, Mary, you know they can't be sendin' men all over the state to look into ever' little squabble. We're all sorry about Gid, but it just ain't no use to fret."

"Another thing. I want you to find me a new foreman. Miller is getting completely out of hand. He's even claiming the range now. Says I'm a woman and can't hold range."

Otten got up. His face was square and brown. He looked more the successful cattleman, which he was, than the banker. He was worried now, but obviously uncertain as to what course to adopt. "There's no law says a woman can't hold range, Mary, you know that. But I reckon it won't be easy. You'll have to fight for it just like Blaine, here."

She turned sharply and seemed to see Utah for the first time. "Blaine? I don't know the name. What are you fighting for?"

"He's manager for Joe Neal, Mary. Come from El Paso to take over."

"Manager for Joe Neal?" She was incredulous. "I don't believe it! What would Joe want a manager for? Anyway, Joe Neal's dead, and you know it as well as I do. If this man says he's Neal's manager, he's lying."

Utah smiled from under his eyebrows. "Those are hard words, Ma'am. An' Joe Neal is alive—and well."

"He couldn't be!"

"Sorry, Ma'am, but he is."

"But I was told—!" she broke off sharply. Then she said, "We heard the vigilantes got him."

"He's alive and I'm his manager."

She looked at him scornfully. "Maybe you are. Go out an' tell that to Lud Fuller. If you get back to town alive, I'll be inclined to believe you."

"Thank you, Ma'am," he smiled at her. "I shall look forward to seeing you when you've decided I'm not a liar. I sure hate to have such a right pretty girl think so hard of me."

He turned and walked out and Ben Otten looked after him, mightily puzzled. There was a quality about him . . . Otten was reminded vaguely of something. For an instant there, as the man spoke and then as he turned away, Otten had seemed to smell the dust of another cowtown street, the sound of boot heels on a walk; but then the memory was gone, and he saw Mary Blake turn on him again. He braced himself to meet her anger.

It was strangely lacking. "Who is he, Ben? Where did he come from?"

Otten picked up the letters and stacked them together. "His credentials are in order, Mary. Joe Neal is alive. At least," he amended, "he was alive when these papers were signed. Nobody in this world could duplicate Joe Neal's scrawl. And those witnesses are names to swear by."

"But who is he?" she persisted.

"His name is Michael Blaine. I reckon we'll just have to wait and see who he is. Names, Mary," he added, "don't account for much. Not out here. It's action that tells you who a man is. We'll see what kind of tracks he makes."

"Mighty small ones after he meets Lud. I'll bank on that."

Otten fumbled the papers into the envelope. That faint intangible memory was with him again. It caused him to say, "Don't be too sure, Mary. Never judge a man until he's showed himself. Unless I miss my guess, that man has smelled gunsmoke."

Gunsmoke! That was it! The day that Hickok

killed Phil Coe in Abilene! That was the day. But why should it remind him of this? This man was not Hickok, and Coe was dead.

The afternoon was blistering hot. Utah squinted his eyes against the sun and walked up the street. By now the two loafers at the livery stable would have started their story. By now all eyes would be looking at him with speculation. Yet it was unlikely that anybody in Red Creek would know him. Most of these people had been around for several years. This was a settled community and not a trail town or a wide-open mining camp. They would have heard of Utah Blaine. But there was very little chance they would guess who he was—for awhile.

He carried his new saddlebags in his left hand and he walked up to the hotel and pushed open the door of the long lobby. The clerk turned and looked at him from under the rim of an eyeshade. Stepping up to the desk the clerk turned the register. "Twelve," he said, "at the end of the hall upstairs."

Blaine pulled the register closer and wrote in a quick, sure hand, *Michael J. Blaine, El Paso, Tex.*

The clerk glanced at it, then looked up. "Be with us long, Mr. Blaine?"

Blaine permitted himself a smile. "There seems to be a difference of opinion on that subject. But I'll tell you—I'll be here a lot longer than some of them that figure otherwise."

He took his saddlebags and went up the steps. Inside the room he doffed his coat, placed the new six-shooter on the table beside him and proceeded to bathe and shave. As he dressed again, his thoughts returned to the girl. She was something, a real beauty.

He grinned as he recalled her quick challenge and accusation. She had fire, too. Well, he liked a girl with spirit.

Glancing from the window he saw a man come out of the saloon across the street and stare up at the hotel. Then the man started across, little puffs of dust rising from his boots. He was a tall, slightly stooped man with unusually high heels. They gave him a queer, forward-leaning movement. He paused in the street and stared up again, something sinister in his fixed scrutiny.

Blaine turned from the window and opened the carpetbag he had brought with him. From it he took a pair of holsters and a wide gun belt. He slung the belt around him and buckled it, then took from the bag two beautifully matched pistols. They were .44 Russians. He checked their loads, then played with them briefly, spinning them, doing a couple of rapid border shifts and then dropping them into their holsters. Suddenly his hands flashed and the guns were in his hands.

He returned the guns to their holsters and, with strips of rawhide, tied them down. Once again, despite the heat, he put on the black coat. There was a sudden hammering on the door.

"Come in," he said. "It isn't locked."

The door slammed back and the man from the street stood in the doorway. He was even taller than Blaine, but he was stooped and his jaws were lean, his cheeks hollow. He stared at Blaine. "You ain't goin' to get away with it!" he flared. "I'm tellin' you now, stay away from the 46!"

"You have rights there?" Blaine asked gently.

"That's no affair of yours! We'll have no strangers hornin' in."

"My job is not to horn in," Blaine said. "I'm to manage the 46. That's just what I intend to do."

"Bah!" The man stepped farther into the room. "Don't try to throw that guff on me! Lee Fox is no fool! Neal's dead, an' you damn' well know it! An' I ain't sorry, neither. He cornered that range when he first come into this country and he hung onto it. Now he's gone an' the rest of us have a chance. Believe you me, I'll get mine!"

"Fox," Blaine said it quietly, "regardless of what you may think or hope, I am manager of the 46 Connected. As such I will warn you now, and I shall not repeat it later, that I want none of your stock on 46 range. Nor do I want any branding of mavericks on our range. Every foot of it, every inch, is going to be held. Now that's settled."

"You think it's settled! Why, damn you, I—" His eyes caught the rawhide thongs about Blaine's legs and he hesitated, his voice changing abruptly, curiously, "Gunman, hey? Or do you just wear 'em for show? Better not be bluffin', because you'll get called."

"Fox," Blaine's voice was even and he was smiling a little, "I do bluff occasionally, but I can stand a call. Don't forget it. Any time you and anybody else want to call, they'll have sixes to beat."

CHAPTER 3

THE STALLION WAS fretting in his stall when Utah came down to the stable the next morning. Saddling him up, he led the dun stallion outside and mounted; then he rode up to the eating house. Despite the early hour, two other horses were tied at the hitch rail before the cafe.

Both men looked up as he entered. One of them was a slender young fellow with an intelligent, attractive face. He had sharply cut features and clear gray eyes. He nodded to Utah. "How are you, Blaine? I recognized you from the descriptions." He held out his hand. "I'm Ralston Forbes. I own the local newspaper."

Blaine shook hands gravely. "First I've heard of a paper," he said. "You take ads?"

Forbes laughed. "You wouldn't ask that if you knew the business. Advertising is the lifeblood of the business."

"Then take one for me. Just say that Mike Blaine has taken the job of manager for the 46 Connected and in the absence of Joe Neal all business will be with him."

Forbes chuckled. "If I didn't need the dollar that ad will cost you, I'd run it as news, because it will be the worst news some of these ranchers have had in years. All of them liked Joe, but they liked his range better. In a free range country you know what that means."

"I know." Blaine was aware that a subtle warning was being conveyed by the editor. He also noticed that the other man was not saying anything, and that Forbes expected him to. However, they didn't have to wait much longer.

The man was short and blocky with a beefy red face and hard gray eyes. He stabbed a slab of beef and brought it to his plate. "Have your fun," he said, "while you're able. You won't last long."

Blaine shrugged. "Two ways to look at that."

"Not hereabouts. These folks don't take kindly to no brash stranger comin' in here tryin' to run a blazer on 'em. Joe Neal was hung. He got his neck stretched nigh two weeks ago."

Blaine's voice was soft. "Were you there, friend?"

The blue eyes blazed as the man turned his head slowly. "No. But I've got it on good authority that he was hung." He slapped butter on a stack of hot cakes. "I'll take that as true. The gent who told me should know."

"It wouldn't be Lud Fuller, would it?"

The man did not look around this time. He kept spreading butter. "What makes you mention Lud? He was Neal's foreman."

"I know that. I also know he was there." Blaine filled his cup again. "And, friend, I'll take an oath on that."

Both men stared at him. The only way he could swear to it would be if he saw it. If he had been there, in the vicinity. The short man shrugged it off and cut off a huge triangle of hot cakes and stuffed them in his mouth. When he could talk again, he said, "You go on out to the ranch. You tell that to Lud. Better have a gun in your hand when you do it, though. Lud's fast."

"Is he?" Blaine chuckled. "I've known a few fast men."

Rals Forbes was suddenly staring hard at him. He slammed his palm on the table. "I'm losing my mind," he said excitedly. "What's the matter with me? You're Utah Blaine!"

The stocky man dropped his fork and his mouth opened. He took a deep breath and swallowed, then slowly his tongue went over his lips. The feeling in his stomach was not pleasant. A tough man, he knew his limitations, and he did not rank anywhere near the man as Utah Blaine was reputed to be. Nor, he reflected, did Lud Fuller. There was only one man, maybe two, in all this country around who might have a show with him.

"That's right," Utah replied, "I'm that Blaine."

He got to his feet and Forbes walked to the door with him. There Forbes hesitated briefly and said, "By the way, Blaine, if you make this stick you could do me a favor. There's a girl homesteading on your range. Right back up against the mountains. Her name is Angela Kinyon. Joe let her stay there, so I hope you will."

"It's still Joe Neal's ranch."

Forbes looked at him carefully. "All right, leave it that way. Angie's all right. She's had a hard time, but she's all woman and a fine person. Just so she stays, it doesn't matter."

"She'll stay."

"And watch your step, Utah. Not even you could stop this bunch if they get started. Every man in this country has been poised and ready to jump at the 46 range. They'll have it, too. I doubt if even Joe's being alive will stop 'em now. They've wanted it too long, and this is the first excuse they've had. It would take a hard, gunfighting outfit to hold it now, and even then it would be a question. One man could never do it."

"Any of that crowd that could be trusted?"

"I doubt it. When you ride onto 46 range, you ride alone."

Riding up the trail to the crest of the Tule Mesa, Utah Blaine rolled a cigarette while studying the country. His knowledge of this land might mean the difference between life and death, and he was too competent a fighting man not to devote time to a study of the terrain.

The trail went down off the mesa and into the coolness of a pine forest before cutting through some cedars and down into the valley itself. There were rich green meadows close along the streams, and along the streams there were cottonwoods, willows and sycamore trees. The ranch itself lay in a grove of trees, most of them giant sycamores.

Large and ancient, the ranch house occupied a small knoll among the trees with the barns and corrals below it. As Blaine rode up to the yard he saw a man come out of the bunkhouse with a roll of bedding under his arm and start up the hill toward the house. The sound of his horse stopped the man, who turned to stare at him.

Utah glanced once at the bunkhouse. Another man had come from the door and stood there leaning against the door jamb, a cigarette in his lips. Blaine walked his horse toward the man with the bedding. This, he rightly surmised, would be Lud Fuller.

Fuller was a big man, thick in the waist, but deep in chest and arms bulging with muscle. He was unshaven and had cold, cruel eyes.

Blaine drew up the horse and swung down, trailing the reins. "Are you Fuller?" he asked.

"What d' you want?" Fuller demanded.

Blaine smiled. "My name is Blaine. I'm the new manager of the outfit. If you're the foreman, we'll have business to discuss."

Fuller was astonished. Of all the things he might have expected, this was certainly not one of them. It took him a minute to get the idea and when it got across to him he was furious. "You're what!" He dropped his bedding. "Look, stranger, I don't know what you've got in your skull, but if that's a sign of it, you're breedin' a mighty poor brand of humor."

"This is no joke, Fuller. Joe Neal appointed me manager. I've visited the bank and Otten agrees my papers are in order. You'd better take that bedding back to the bunkhouse—unless you're quitting."

"Quittin', hell!" Fuller stepped over his bedding. "Neal's dead, an' this here's a crooked deal!"

Blaine's eyes were cold. "No, Lud, Neal isn't dead. He is very much alive. Does that signature look like he was dead?"

Blaine handed the letter to Fuller who glared at it, too filled with fury and disappointment to speak. He was scarcely able to see. Yet the signature was there, and it was Joe Neal's. Nobody could ever write like that but Neal himself.

"You can't get away with this!" Fuller's voice was hoarse.

"I'm not trying to get away with anything, Fuller." Blaine kept his voice calm. "I've been given a job, and I've come to take over. From here out you'll be subject to my orders."

"Like hell!" Fuller snarled. "I'm boss here and I'll stay boss. There's something rotten about this!"

"You're exactly right. It's a rotten deal when a man's friends turn against him and try to hang him for nothing except that they want to steal his ranch. Now get this into your skull, Fuller. You take orders from me or get off the ranch! And you can start right now!"

Fuller was beyond reason. Unable to coordinate his thoughts and realize what had happened, his one instinct was to fight, to strike out, to attack. Despite the fact that he had himself put the rope on Neal, he knew that signature was genuine. But this curbed none of his anger.

Men were coming from the bunkhouse. Only minutes before, Fuller had rolled his bedding and told them he was moving into the big house. They had looked at him, but said nothing. Like himself they wanted to get something out of this new situation. But most of them wanted to strip the ranch of cattle, sell them off and skip. They were men Fuller had hired himself, for Neal had left most of the hiring in his hands. Only Rip Coker had spoken up. He was a hatchet-faced cowhand, tough, blond and wicked. "I'd go slow if I were you," he had said, "the old man might show up."

"He won't."

"You seem mighty sure of that. Maybe you made sure he won't."

Fuller had glared, but something in him warned that Coker would be no easy task in a gunfight. With his hands—well, Lud Fuller had never been whipped with fists. But the lean, wiry Coker was not the man to fight with his hands. Therefore Fuller had merely turned and walked up the hill with his bedroll. Now he was stopped and he could hear them coming, Coker among them.

"Joe Neal," Fuller persisted, "is dead. I'm takin' over."

Blaine shook his head. "Sorry to tear down your dream house," he said, "but you're just a little previous. Get back to the bunkhouse with your bed or load up and get off the place."

Blaine turned to the seven men who had come up the hill. "I'm Blaine, the new manager here. I have shown my papers to Fuller. Before that I showed them to Otten. They are in order. Any of you men who want to draw your time can have it. Any of you that want to stay, you have a job. Think it over. I'll see you at chuck."

Deliberately he turned his back and started up the hill to the house.

Fuller stared after him. "Hey! You!" he yelled.

Blaine kept on walking. Opening the door to the house, he stepped inside.

Rip Coker chuckled suddenly. "Looks like you should of took my advice, Lud. You jumped the gun."

"He won't get away with this!" Lud said furiously.

"Looks to me like he already has," Coker said.

"Don't you try buckin' that hombre, Lud. He's out of your class."

Lud Fuller was too angry to listen. Slowly, the men turned. There was muttering among them, for several had already been spending the money they expected to get from the stolen cattle. Now it was over. Coker looked toward the house with a glint in his eyes; then he began to chuckle softly. The situation appealed to him. It had done him good to see the way Blaine turned Fuller off short. But what was to happen next?

Wiser than Fuller, Coker had complete appreciation of the situation in the Red Creek country. Fuller might grab the ranch, but he would never keep it. He was only one wolf among many who wanted this range; and his teeth were not sharp enough, his brain not keen enough. In this game of guns, grab and get, he would be out-grabbed and out-gunned.

Rip Coker rolled a smoke and squinted at the blue hills. There would be some shuffling now. It seemed like one man against them all, and the odds appealed to Rip. He chuckled softly to himself.

Lud Fuller walked back to the bunkhouse and slammed his bedroll on the bunk. He glared right and left, looking for something on which he could take out his fury. Then he stalked outside and walked toward the corral. He would ride over and see Nevers. He would see Clell Miller, on the B-Bar. Something would have to be done about this and quick.

Coker watched him saddle up and ride out; then he turned and walked up the steps to the house. He was going to declare himself. As he reached for the door, Blaine pulled it open and stepped out. He had his coat off and he was wearing his two guns low. Rip Coker felt a little flicker of excitement go through him: this man was ready.

"My name's Coker," he said abruptly. "Been on this spread about four months. I'm the newest hand."

"All right, Coker. What's on your mind?"

"Looks like you're in for a scrap."

"I expected that."

"You're all alone."

"I expected that, too." Blaine grinned briefly. "Tell me something I don't know, friend."

Coker finished rolling his smoke. "Me," he said, without looking up. "I always was a sucker. I'm declaring myself in—on your side."

"Why?"

Coker's chuckle was dry. "Maybe because I'm just ornery an' like to buck a tough game. Maybe it's because I don't like fightin' with a gang. Maybe it's just because I want to be on your side when you're pushed."

"Those are all good reasons with me." Blaine thrust out his hand. "Glad to have you with me, Coker. I won't warn you. You know the setup better than I do."

"I figure I do." Coker nodded toward the north. "Up there are about thirty land-hungry little ranchers. They are tougher'n boot leather, an' most of them have rustled a few head in their time. The B-Bar has a foreman named Clell Miller. He's a cousin of one of the old James's crowd and just as salty. He's a whiz with a six-gun and he'll tackle anything. He's figurin' on ownin' the B-Bar when the fight's over. And he figures on having added to it all that land between Skeleton Ridge and the river—which is 46 range."

"I see."

"Then see this. Ben Otten's friendly enough, a square man, but range hungry as the rest. If the thing breaks up, he'll come in grabbin' for his chunk of it."

"And the rest?"

"Fuller, Miller and Nevers are the worst."

"What about Lee Fox?"

Coker hesitated. "I don't figure him. He's poison mean, killed two of his hands about a year ago. Nobody figured him for a gun-slick, but when they braced him he came loose like a wildcat and he spit lead all over."

"Any others?"

"Uh huh. There's Rink Witter. He's Nevers's right hand."

"Heard of him."

"Figured you had. He's hell on wheels."

"How about these men to the north? Who's the big man up there?"

"Ortmann, and he's a hard man."

Blaine chuckled suddenly. "Sounds like I'm buckin' a stacked deck. You still want in?"

"You forget, I've known this all the time. Sure, I want in. I wouldn't miss it for the world!"

CHAPTER 4

MARY BLAKE SWUNG down from her mare, stripped off the saddle and bridle, as she turned the horse into the corral. There was no one in sight when she started toward the house and she reflected bitterly that for all her father's training, she was not showing up so well as owner of a ranch. Not with a foreman like Clell Miller. But how could you fire such a man? She knew he would not go and she had no desire for a showdown until she was ready. Right now she had nothing to back her play. All she could do if he refused to go would be to shoot him from the house, and that went against the grain.

She felt lost, trapped. Two or three of the old hands would stand by her, she knew that. Kelsey and Timm would not fail her, and both were good men. But they were only two against so many, and she was too shrewd to risk them in a pointless struggle. They provided backing she had to keep in reserve until the likely moment came.

As she went up the steps, Miller came around the corner of the house. He was a tall, well-built man and good looking. He had a deep scar, all of three inches long, on one cheekbone. It was his brag that he had killed the man who put it there, and he liked to be asked about the incident.

"Back so soon?" His manner was elaborately polite. "Did Otten offer to send his men over to help?"

"I need no help."

He looked up at her impudently. "No? Well, maybe not. Looks to me like you're out on a limb."

She could see the danger of this sort of talk and swiftly changed the subject. "Joe Neal's alive."

Clell Miller had looked away. Now he swung his head back, swift passion flushing his face. "What was that? What did you say?"

"I said Joe Neal is alive."

"He's back in town?" Miller was incredulous, but had a lurking suspicion that she was telling the truth. Fury welled up within him. That damned Lud! Couldn't he do anything right?

"No, he's not back. He's in El Paso. He sent a manager down here. A man named Blaine."

"Blaine!" Miller's dark features sharpened suddenly and his eyes were those of an animal at bay. "What was his other name? What did they call him?"

Surprised at his excitement, she shrugged it off. "Why, his first name is Michael, I think. Do you know him?"

"Tall man? Broad shoulders? Green eyes?" Miller was tense with excitement.

"Why, yes. That sounds like him. Why, who is he?"

Miller stared at her, all his animosity toward her forgotten with this information. "Who?" he laughed shortly. "He's Utah Blaine, that's who he is, that hell-on-wheels gunman from the Nueces, the man who tamed Alta. He's killed twenty men, maybe thirty. Where did Neal round *him* up?"

Utah Blaine! She had heard her father talk of him

so much that his name had been a legend to her. Mary remembered her father had been driving north right ahead of Shanghai Pierce's big herd when Utah was trail boss. Gid Blake had been stopped by herd cutters and she knew every word of that story from memory, how Blaine had faced them down, killed their fastest gunfighter, and told them to break up and scatter. Her father had gone through without trouble, although at first he was sure he was going to lose cattle. Somehow she had expected Utah Blaine to be an older man. It was strangely exciting to realize that her girlhood hero was here, taking over the 46 Connected.

Clell Miller was excited and for the moment he had forgotten his troubles. Miller had never faced a gunfighter of top skill, but he knew that many rated him right along with them. There were those who said he was faster than Hardin. But he knew nobody was faster than Hardin, not anybody at all. Nevertheless, it would be something to kill Blaine! Something inside him leaped at the thought. To be the man who killed Utah Blaine! He walked off without a further word, bursting with excitement and the desire to talk.

Mary went on up the steps and closed the door carefully behind her before crossing the porch. When she entered the large room decorated with Navajo blankets the first person she saw was Tom Kelsey. He got up quickly and stepped toward her. He was a solid, square-built man, a top hand in any crowd, and he was, she knew, in love with her—not that he expected anything to come from it.

"Ma'am," he said quickly, "I think Miller's fixin'

to drive off some cows. He's got maybe a hundred head bunched in Canyon Creek."

"Where's Dan Timm?"

"He's watchin' 'em, Ma'am. We figured I'd best come back an' tell you."

"Thanks, Tom, but there's nothing we can do. Not right now, anyway. We'll have to let it ride. We can't risk a showdown."

Tom Kelsey twisted his hat in his fingers. This he knew perfectly well, but it griped him. He wanted to do something. But while a fair hand with a gun, he was not in Clell Miller's class and knew it. Nevertheless, to let him get away without a fight went against the grain.

"We may have a chance now, Tom. I want you to do something for me. Ride back and get Timm. Send him to me. I want one of you to stay in this house from now on. I don't trust Clell or any of that crowd. But after you have started Timm back, I want you to ride on over to the 46. Utah Blaine is there."

"Are you sure? What's he want there?"

She explained, her eyes watching the bunkhouse through the window. "I want you to tell him I want to see him. And talk to him alone."

When he had gone she walked into her own room and began to comb her hair. She was a slim, boyish girl with beautiful eyes and lips. Her figure, while only beginning to take on the shape another year or two would give her, was still very good. She looked at herself in the mirror, her not too thin lips, good shoulders and nice throat and chin.

For the first time since her father's murder she thought she saw a way out. She had Timm and Kelsey.

If they could get together with Blaine, they would have the beginning of a fighting outfit. Not enough, but such a man as Blaine was a man to build around.

As Mary Blake pondered the problem of concerted action against those who would split up the range of the two large outfits, Lud Fuller was whipping a foam-flecked horse down the trail to the Big N outfit of Russ Nevers.

Within him burned a dull rage that defied all reason. Joe Neal, whom he had hated during all the time he worked for him, was alive! He did not stop to think how he was alive, or what had happened—all he could think of was that fact. Not even the appearance of Blaine had hit him as hard.

His hatred for Neal was not born of any wrong Neal had done him, for Neal had always been strictly fair with his men, his foreman included. That hatred was something that had grown from deep within the fiber of the man himself, some deeply hidden store of bile born of envy, jealousy, and a hatred for all that seemed above him.

To any other man but Lud the grievances would have been trivial things but during long hours in the saddle or lying on his bunk, Lud's slow mind mulled over them and they grew into festering hatred and resentment.

Nevers looked up as Lud rode into the ranch yard. "Neal's alive!" Fuller burst out, his eyes bulging. "He ain't dead! He sent a man—"

"Shut up, you fool!" Nevers stepped toward him, his voice cracking and harsh. "Shut that big mouth! I know all about it! What I want to know is what

you're doin' here? Roust out your damned vigilantes
now and hang him!"

"Neal?" Fuller asked stupidly.

"No, you fool! Blaine." Angrily he stared at the
big foreman. "Don't stand there like a fool! Get busy!
Let him alone for a few days and he'll get set. Hang
him! Hang him now! His rep is bad enough so there'll
be an excuse! Get busy!"

Lud Fuller was half way back to the ranch before
he began to get angry at Nevers.

CHAPTER 5

ALL THE HANDS were at table when Utah Blaine walked in and seated himself. He felt like hell and didn't care who knew. He hated checking over books and that was what he had been doing for half the night. The first thing, of course, was to find out just what it was he was managing, and he discovered it was plenty.

Thirty thousand head, Joe Neal had said. Well, the ranch would carry more, and some of those were ready to sell. It was time the ranch was worked over but good. There was water and there was grass. He considered that with a cold, clear brain and liked what he decided. It was time some new elements were injected into this game.

Coker had stated it clearly the night before, and he decided he liked Coker. Also, there had been that talk with Tom Kelsey. Mary Blake wanted to talk to him, but she had little to offer. Kelsey had said she had two loyal hands. Still, that made four of them if they worked together, and Kelsey, while not as salty as Rip Coker, was a solid man. The sort that would have staying power. He would talk to Mary Blake.

Lud Fuller was there, his big jaw swinging up and down as he chomped his food. "Lud," Blaine said, "there's a lot to be done on this outfit. Take four men and head for Squaw Peak. There will be some of our stuff up there. I want everything wearing our brand thrown back across the river."

Fuller started to object angrily. Squaw Peak? Why, that was away north! There would be no chance for him to organize any vigilante meeting up there! He started to object, but the logic of the move appealed to him. Those nesters were always cutting out 46 stock and butchering it.

"You givin' up that range?" he looked up from his plate.

"I'm givin' up nothing. From what I hear Ortmann an' his boys up there are makin' mighty free with our stock. Well, we'll throw our beef back across the river until we get a chance to clean them out of there."

All eyes were on him. "We'll clean them out," he said, "or make believers of them."

"That's a sizeable job," the speaker was a long-eared man with sparse red hair. "They'll fight."

"I've tackled sizeable jobs before," Blaine said shortly, "and they fought."

There was no answer to that for they all knew the story of the mining town of Alta where three marshals had lasted a day each, and then Utah Blaine rode in and took the job. Four men had died the first week he was on the job. The leader of the bad ones going first, on the first night. Twenty-two men had been jailed that night, and two had gone to the one-room hospital with cracked skulls.

Alta, where there had been a killing every night, and where sixty-two men had been buried in Boot Hill before one townsman died of natural causes. The town where there were seven thousand belted men headed straight for the doors of hell, and every one of them packing a gun. Two thousand miners and five thousand to rob them—and Blaine had tamed the town. It was there they started calling him Utah.

"Like I said," he continued, "take your men and move up there. Work well back up in all the draws. No stock but our own, but start it for the river. Nobody works alone, work two or three together and hit both heads of Chasm Creek. Check the head of Gap mighty careful because I've an idea when they take our beef it goes over from Gap into Chalktank. Then work south. It will be slow, but throw the beef back over the river."

"You aim to talk to Ortmann?" Red asked.

"When I'm ready."

The other hands waited expectantly. "Coker, there's a busted stall in the barn and that corral needs work. That's for you." He looked beyond the hatchet-faced warrior. "The rest of you work south along the edge of the mesa to Skeleton Ridge. You do the same thing. Throw the cattle back across the river!"

He finished eating and took a final swallow of coffee. Abruptly, he got to his feet. As he picked up his hat, he let his eyes go over the crowd. "I'm new here. New to you and you're new to me. If any of you ever have any kick coming, you come and make it. But get this between your ears. I'm runnin' the 46 and I'm goin' to run it smooth. If it gets rough, then I'll smooth her out. You boys won't have any trouble as long as you do your jobs."

He stepped out and closed the door behind him. Coker stuffed his mouth with a chunk of beef to keep from laughing. Fuller was flabbergasted. Obviously, he didn't know what to do. As poor a foreman as he was, he knew sensible orders when he heard them. Throwing the cattle back across the river would undoubtedly save a good many head from rustlers. From the ranch house a man with a glass could watch the river, and see the whole length of it as it crossed the range. Nobody could possibly drive off cattle which were to the ranch side of the river.

Coker could see the idea penetrating Fuller's thick skull and could see Fuller's grudging appreciation of the tactics it implied. Coker could also see that Blaine's promise to face Ortmann had aroused the men's admiration. Moreover, what Blaine had done most successfully was to take the play away from them. Fuller had to obey orders or be fired. Once off the range Fuller was useless to the others and they would cut him out of the gang that expected to split the spoils of the ranch. Fuller was shrewd enough to appreciate all this.

While Coker disliked the work around the ranch, he also appreciated that Blaine was keeping the one man he could trust close at hand.

———

As SOON AS Fuller had left him, Nevers saddled up and rode for the B-Bar. He met Clell Miller when he was halfway there. Clell pulled up his sweating horse.

"Lud played hell!" Nevers burst out. "Neal's alive, and now when this Blaine shows up he runs to me instead of doin' somethin' about it."

Miller curled his leg around the saddle horn. "What you aim to do, Nevers?"

"I ain't goin' to see no outsider jump that range!"

"You think Neal is dead?"

"How should I know? If he ain't, he's gonna be, believe you me!"

Miller looked at Nevers thoughtfully. "That's an idea," he said, "a good idea."

"Look," Nevers came closer, "Neal may or may not be alive. If he's dead, we've got to know it. If he's alive, he's got to be killed. I ain't gonna be cheated at this stage of the game."

"Blaine ain't no cinch," Miller said.

"Afraid?"

"You know better than that."

Nevers nodded. "Yeah, I do. Forget it. I'm jumpy myself."

"What about Neal?"

"Don't let it bother you. Just you think about Blaine."

Clell Miller looked down at the older man. So that was the way it was? You never knew about a man until you got into a deal with him. This was a steal. Miller was making no bones about that with himself, and he would not hesitate to kill if somebody got in the way. But everybody knew what he was and who he was. However, they had never exactly known about Nevers. They thought they knew, but ... Miller got out the makin's. "Where's Rink?"

"Never you mind about Rink. He's got his own work to do."

So that was it! Rink had gone after the old man, Joe Neal. Well, there wasn't a better man for the job. Little leather-faced Rink with his cold eyes and his remorseless way. A fast hand with a gun and ready to kill—a sure-thing operator. He would make no mistakes.

That meant the 46 Connected range was going to be thrown to the wolves, all right. "What about Blaine?" he insisted. "What if he won't stand still for it?"

"He won't have to," Nevers said. "We're going after Blaine. We're going to corner him. No gunfights, Clell. We can't take the risk. We're all going in. You, me, Lud—all of us."

"Otten?"

"Otten's out of it. I mean, he will be after we do all the dirty work. If he tries to get in we'll cut him off at the pockets. Far's that goes, we might as well split his range too if he gets ornery."

Clell Miller looked thoughtfully at the end of his cigarette. Nevers was like a bull. Once started nothing would stop him. Clell considered the matter. With anyone but Blaine the steal would seem like a cinch. "Why don't we steer Blaine into Ortmann?" he suggested. "Let 'em kill each other off?"

"Too slow." Nevers liked the idea, though. Clell could see that. "But we might try it. Get rid of one of them, anyway. If he uses guns, Blaine will kill him. If Ortmann ever got his hands on Blaine it would be the end of Utah."

"He'd never let him. Blaine's no fool."

"Get your boys together," Nevers advised. "I'll put a bug in Ortmann's ear. Maybe we can get them together. If we don't succeed we'll move in fast. Your outfit and my outfit, and we'll pour cattle all over that range and hit Blaine from every direction at once. We'll cut him out of the herd, get him alone, and then kill him."

"What about Mary Blake?"

"Settle that when this is over. She's nothing to worry about."

"A couple of the boys will side her: Kelsey and Timm."

"Kill 'em. Get them out of it tonight. You hear, Clell?"

Riding back to the ranch, Clell considered that. Nevers was right. There was no use giving them a chance to side her. Get them now. Kelsey was a good man. Too good a man to die, yet that was the way it had to be.

With Lud out of the way, Blaine left Coker in charge and rode swiftly to meet with Mary Blake. The place of the meeting was designated as a spot called Goat Camp, beyond the river. As he neared the Bench, Utah glimpsed a spot of green back under the very shadow of the cliff. There, among some ancient cottonwoods and sycamores was a small cabin. With sharpening curiosity he realized this must be the cabin of the girl, Angie Kinyon.

He glanced at the sun. There was time for him to see Angie. He swung the horse from the trail. Before he reached the house, he saw the flowers. The place was literally banked with them, and he looked around with real pleasure. The house was shadowed by the cliff and the giant trees, and a small stream trickled past the house. Alongside the house were several fenced patches of crops. All showed careful attention and considerable appreciation for beauty as well as necessity. He rode up under the trees and swung down.

A door slammed behind him and he turned. The

girl had stopped on the steps, a girl with dark hair and large soft dark eyes. She came down the steps quickly and he swept off his hat. "I'm Blaine," he said, "the manager of the 46. You'd be Angie Kinyon."

She gave him sharp attention, seeming to measure and gauge him in one swift, comprehensive glance. "I hadn't heard there was a manager."

He explained, taking his time and enjoying the coolness after the heat of his ride. She was a tall girl, but beautifully formed, and her voice was low and throaty. As he talked, he wondered at her presence in this far place.

"You've a beautiful place." There was a note of wistfulness in his voice. "You must have been here quite awhile."

"Three years. It doesn't seem long."

She watched him, all her womanly curiosity turned upon this tall young man with the grave face and the slow smile. She had noted the two tied-down guns. She was far too knowing not to realize what they meant. Immediately she connected them with his name. She also knew better than most what an impact his presence must be making on the valley ranchers and their riders. Long before Joe Neal had any warning of what was coming, she had tried to warn him. She had watched the cattle of the 46 fattening on the rich graze and plentiful water, and she had seen the men from other ranches lingering hungrily around the edges. Their range was not bad, but it is not in many men to be satisfied with less than the best—when the best seems available.

Angie told Blaine this, of how stubborn Joe Neal

was. He had wrested his range out of Apache country. Nobody would chase him from it.

"He told me he came here in '60," Blaine marveled. "How did he get along with the Indians? Surely there were a lot of them?"

"He talked peace when he could, fought when he had to. Twice all his men deserted but one, but he stayed on and fought it out."

"One stayed?"

"Yes." Angie Kinyon turned and indicated a stone slab at the head of a mound of earth under the sycamores some thirty yards away. There were flowers on the grave. "He lies there. He was my father."

"Oh." Utah looked at her curiously, this tall, lonely girl with the leaf shadows on her face. "You were here? Through all that?"

"My mother died in Texas before we came west with Joe. I grew up here, through it all. Never a week went by that first year without a raid of some kind. The second year there were only three. Then there were years of peace, then more fighting as the Apache began to fear the soldiers and wanted to kill all white people."

"You never left?"

She looked at him quickly. "Then they haven't told you about me?"

"No. They told me nothing. Forbes told me you lived here."

"You've seen him?" The quick smile on her lips brought Utah a sharp twinge of jealousy that surprised him. Was that it, then? Was she in love with Forbes? "He's fine. One of the finest people I've known."

She was silent for a few minutes and he began

thinking of his meeting at Goat Camp. "I'd better go."

She followed him. "Be careful." She put her hand on his sleeve suddenly. "Utah—do be careful! They'll all be after you, every one of them. There's not one you can trust."

"Maybe we can work something out. Mary Blake has two good men, and Coker is going to stand with me."

"Mary . . . then you've met her." Her eyes searched his face. "You're going to meet her now."

"Yes. To work out a plan of battle."

"She's selfish." She said it quickly and it surprised him. He had not expected her to speak ill of another woman. "She's been spoiled."

"I wouldn't know." Despite himself his voice was cool. "She only seems to want to protect her ranch."

Angie nodded seriously. "You didn't like what I said, did you? Perhaps I should only have said something nice. It would have been wiser for me, but of no use to you." When he did not respond, she added, "Mary is lovely, and she is like her father. Nothing existed in this world but the B-Bar for Gid. Mary is the same way. She is strong, too. They are underrating her, all of them. To keep that ranch intact she will lie, steal and kill."

"You really think that, don't you?" He put a foot in the stirrup and swung up. "Sometimes one has to kill."

She acknowledged that. "There are ways of killing. But remember what I have said. If she thought she could save the B-Bar by selling you out she would do it without hesitation."

He turned the dun stallion. "Well, thanks," he said, "but I think you judge her too severely."

"Perhaps." Her eyes were large and dark. She stood there in her buckskin skirt and calico blouse, looking lonely, beautiful, and sad. "I would not have said that, Utah Blaine, but I know the man you are, and I know you ride for Joe Neal, and for something stronger and better than all of them."

She turned abruptly and started for the house and he looked after her, a little puzzled, but captured by her grace. She turned suddenly. "When it happens that they are all against you," she said, "and it will happen so for I know them and they are wolves... when it happens, come to me. I will stand beside you as my father did beside Joe Neal."

CHAPTER 6

MARY BLAKE WAS waiting impatiently beside a spring at Goat Camp. There was nothing there but a dark and gloomy hut with a roof so sunken that only a midget could have used the old cabin. A stone corral and a shed thatched with branches loomed in the background.

She walked to Blaine quickly as he came up. "You're late. You've been talking to that girl."

"Angie? Yes, I have."

"She's beautiful." Mary said it shortly and Utah repressed a grin as he swung down. No love lost here, that was certain.

"Yes," he agreed cheerfully, "I believe she is. Now what's this proposition?"

"You may have guessed. I've two good men. Kelsey and Timm. Neither are gunmen but both will stick. They'll fight, too, and both are tough men. You have yourself. Together we can make a better fight than alone, and you—well, your name should draw some help to us."

"I've one man," he admitted, "Rip Coker."

She was immediately pleased. "Good! Oh, fine! He's the best of that lot on the 46, and as a fighting man he's worth two of my men. Good. And we can get some more. There's lots of them drifting into the Junction."

"Not them. Paid warriors."

"Aren't they all? Aren't you?" She flared at him, then she swept off her hat and shook out her hair. "Don't mind me, Utah, I'm upset by this thing. I'm snapping at everyone."

"It's understandable. I get a little upset at times."

She looked at him critically. "I doubt that. Were you ever upset by anything? Or anyone? You look too damnably self-sufficient, like you had ice water in your veins."

"All right," he brushed off her comments. "We've got four men and they had, as you suggest, better operate together. The 46 is the center, and we could fort up there."

Her face changed swiftly. "And leave the B-Bar? Not for a minute. I thought you'd come over to my place. I could cook and I have Maria, too. I couldn't leave her alone."

You mean you couldn't leave the ranch alone, he told himself, then immediately felt guilty. After all his irritation at Angie he was adopting her viewpoint. "What we had better do," he said, "is ride into town and have a showdown with Otten. Swing him to our side."

"It won't work. He can gain nothing that way. He'll stay neutral as long as he can, then join them." She moved closer to him. "Utah, help me. On the 46 you'll have Ortmann on one side and the others to your south. You'll be between two fires. Come to the B-Bar and we can present a united front, with only enemies from one direction."

There was some logic in that, but not much. His own desire was to move right in, to take the bull by the horns. He said finally, "Tomorrow I'm riding to see Ortmann. I'm going to talk him out of this if I can, then I'll tackle the others."

"He won't listen to you."

"He'll have his chance."

She shrugged, then smiled at him. "Oh, I shouldn't argue! You're probably right. Only...only...only I'd feel safer if you were over there with me. Maria is wonderful, and I know she would die for me, and so would Kelsey and Timm, but neither of them could face Clell. He frightens me."

He looked at her quickly. "You don't think he'd bother you?"

"I wouldn't put it past him. Or the others." She was not being honest and she knew it. Clell—well, he might—but she doubted it. He liked telling her off, he liked being impudent because she had been boss so long, but Clell for all his killing and the innate vicious streak he undoubtedly had, was always respectful to women. Even, she had heard, to bad women.

Yet she could see her suggestion had influenced Utah. He was disturbed, and she set herself to play upon this advantage. He was handsome, she told herself. And the first man she had ever seen whom she could really admire. It would be pleasant to have him at the ranch.

"It seems so silly," she said, "you and Rip Coker down there batching when you could be having your meals with us. I can cook and so can Maria. And you know how foolish it is to divide our forces."

"I'll see Ortmann first," he said. "Then I'll come back this way and I'll bring Coker."

They left it at that.

ALL WAS QUIET on the ranch when Blaine rode in, and none of the men were back. Rip walked out from the house with a Winchester in the crook of his arm. Briefly, Blaine explained the plan. Coker shrugged, "Well, it gives us some help we can use. I know those boys. One thing about them, they'll stick."

"All right," he said, "first thing tomorrow I'm heading for Ortmann's bunch. I'm going to try to swing him my way."

"You won't do it."

"We'll see, anyway. Want to come along?"

Coker chuckled. "I wouldn't miss it. I want to see your expression when you see that gent. He's bigger'n a horse, I tell you."

The next morning they were on their way. The trail led back to the rim of Tule Mesa and ran along the Mesa itself. It provided Blaine with a new chance to study the country and he took time to turn and look off to the southeast toward the Mazatzals, twenty-five miles away to the southeast. It was all that had been implied from the looks of it, a far and rugged country.

Rip rode without talking, his eyes always alert. They had reached the Yellowjacket Trail before he spoke.

"Neal's got me worried. What if something happens to him? I mean, what happens to you?"

It was a good question, and it started Utah thinking. He had come with the backing and authority of Neal, but if Neal died or was killed, he would be strictly on his own. His lips tightened at the thought. "No need to worry about that. Cross that bridge when we come to it."

"Better think of it." Coker shifted his seat in the saddle. "I'll bet Nevers has."

"What about Nevers? You know him?"

"Yep. He's one o' those gents who puts up an honest front but who's been mixed in a lot of dirty stuff. He's got guts, Utah, an' he's a wolf on the prowl, a hungry wolf. He's strong, tough, and smart. He's not erratic like Fox. He's no gunman, but he's been in a lot of fights. He'll be hard to handle."

Blaine shrugged and swung his horse into Yellowjacket Canyon. "None of them are easy."

Almost at once he saw the shacks. There were at least twenty of them. Not more than half of them were occupied, and the others were in varying stages of ruin. There was a long building with a porch on which was a sign that informed the wandering public that here was a saloon and store. Several loafers sat on the edge of the porch, legs dangling.

Blaine drew up. "Howdy, boys. Ortmann around?"

One of the men jerked his head. "Inside."

Utah dropped to the ground and Coker glanced at him, his eyes faintly amused. "I'll stand by," he said, "an' keep 'em off your back."

Utah grinned. "Keep 'em off yours," he retorted. Turning, he walked up the steps. The loafers were all hardcases, he could see that. They eyed him warily and glanced curiously at the hatchet-faced blond man who leaned against the watering trough.

There were three men inside the store and one of them was Lud Fuller.

Blaine stopped abruptly. "What you doin' over here, Lud?"

Fuller shifted his feet. He hadn't expected to meet Blaine and was confused. "Huntin' cows," he said bluntly.

"You'll find some back near the end of Chalktank," Blaine told him. "We rode past a few on the way up."

He turned then to look at the big man who sat on the counter. Blaine was to learn that Ortmann always sat on the counter because he had no chair to fit his huge size. He was the biggest man Blaine had ever seen, wide in the shoulder with a massive chest and huge hands. That he stood at least eight inches over six feet, Blaine could believe, and all his body was massive in proportion to his height.

"You're Blaine." Ortmann said it flatly and without emphasis.

"And you're Ortmann." Neither man made an effort to shake hands, but sized each other up coolly. Blaine's two hundred pounds of compact rangerider was dwarfed by the size of this man.

"I'm in a fight, Ortmann." Blaine had no intention of beating around the bush. "Neal is out of the state and I'm in charge here. It seems that everybody in this country has just been waitin' for a chance to grab off a chunk of 46 range."

"Includin' me," Ortmann acknowledged. His face was very wide and his jaw and cheekbones flat and heavy. He wore a short beard and his neck was a column of muscle coming from the homespun shirt. The chest was matted with hair.

"Includin' you," Blaine agreed. "But I'm goin' to win this fight, Ortmann, an' the fewer who get hurt the better. You," he said, "size up like a tough chunk of man. You've got some salty lads."

"You biddin' for our help?" Ortmann asked.

"I want no help. I'm askin' you to stay out. Let me handle the big outfits. I don't want you on my back while I'm tangling with the others."

"That's smart." Ortmann turned his glass in his fingers. He drank from a water glass and in his huge hand it looked like something a doll might use. "That's smart for you. Not so smart for me. That there range is free range. As long as a man uses it, he's got a rightful claim. When he steps out, it falls to him who can hold it. Well, me an' the boys want grass. We want plowland. It lays there for us."

"No." Blaine's voice was cool. "You will never have one acre of that ground unless by permission from Joe Neal or myself. Not one acre. I say it here and now, and it will stick that way.

"Nor will anybody else. I'm saying that now and I hope you spread it around. All the ideas these would-be range grabbers have, they'd better forget. The 46 isn't givin' up anything."

"You talk mighty big. You ain't even got an outfit."

Utah Blaine did not smile. He did not move. He merely said quietly, "I'm my own outfit." Despite himself, Ortmann was impressed. "I don't need your help."

"In answer to your question." Ortmann got to his feet. "No, I won't lay off. Me an' the boys will move in whenever the time's ripe. You're through. The 46 is through. You ain't got a chance. The wolves will pull you down just like they pulled down Gid Blake."

Utah Blaine's eyes grew bleak and cold. "Have it

your way, Ortmann," he said flatly. "But if that's the way you want it, the fight starts here."

For an instant the giant's eyes blinked. He was startled, and felt a reluctant admiration for this man. There was Ortmann, a giant unchallenged for strength and fighting fury. There were twenty of his men within call, and yet Blaine challenged him.

"You think you can kill me with that gun." Ortmann placed his big hands on his hips. "You might do it, but you'd never stop me before I got my hands on you. And then I'd kill you."

Blaine laughed harshly. "You think so?" He turned his head slightly. "Rip!" he yelled. "Come an' hold my coat! I'm goin' to whip the tallow out of this big moose!"

"Why, you damn' fool!" Fuller burst out. "He'll kill you!"

"You'd better hope he does," Blaine replied shortly. "I'll settle with you afterward."

As Coker came through the door, Blaine stripped off his guns and handed them to him. "Ortmann," he said, "my guns would stop you because every bullet would be in your heart. I can center every shot in the space of a dollar at a hundred yards. You'd be easy. But you're too good a man to kill, so I'm just goin' to whip you with my hands."

"Whip *me*?" Ortmann was incredulous.

"That's right." Utah Blaine grinned suddenly. He felt great. Something welled up inside of him, the fierce old love of battle that was never far from the surface. "You can be had, big boy. I'll bet you've never had a dozen fights in your life. You're too big. Well, I've had a hundred. Come on, you big lug, stack your duds and grease your skids. I'm goin' to tear down your meat house!"

Ortmann lunged, amazingly swift for such a big man, but Utah's hands were up and he stabbed a jarring left to the teeth that flattened Ortmann's lips back. A lesser man would have been stopped in his tracks. It didn't even slow the giant.

One huge fist caught Blaine a jarring blow as he rolled to escape the punch. But with the same roll he threw a right to the heart. It landed solidly, and flatfooted, feet wide apart, Utah rolled at the hips and hooked his left to Ortmann's belly. The punches landed hard and they hurt. Blaine went down in a half crouch and hooked a wide right that clipped Ortmann on the side of the head.

Ortmann stopped in his tracks and blinked. "You—you can hit!" he said, and lunged.

CHAPTER 7

ORTMANN PUNCHED SWIFTLY, left and right. Utah slipped away from the left, but the right caught him in the chest and knocked him to the floor. Ortmann rushed him, but Blaine rolled over swiftly and came up, jarring against the counter as Ortmann closed in. Utah smashed a wicked short right to the belly and then a left. Burying his skull against the big man's chest, he began to swing in with both fists.

Ortmann got an arm around Blaine's body and held the punching left off. Then Ortmann smashed ponderously at Blaine's face. The blows thudded against cheekbone and skull and lights burst in Blaine's brain. Smashing down with the inside of his boot against Ortmann's shin, Blaine drove all his weight on the big man's instep. Ortmann let go with a yell and staggered back, and then Blaine hit him full.

Ortmann went back three full steps with Blaine closing in fast. But close against the counter the big man rolled aside and swung a left to the mouth and Blaine tasted blood. Wild with fury he drove at Ortmann, smashing with both fists, and Ortmann met him. Back they went. Ortmann suddenly reached out and grabbed Blaine by the arm and threw him against the door.

It swung back on its hinges and Blaine crashed

through, off the porch and into the gray dust of the
road. Following him, Ortmann sprang from the
porch, his heels raised to crush the life from Utah. But
swiftly Blaine had rolled over and staggered to his
feet. He was more shaken than hurt. He blinked.
Then as Ortmann hit the ground, momentarily off
balance, Blaine swung. His fist flattened against
Ortmann's nose and knocked him back against the
porch. Crouched, Blaine stared at him through trickling sweat and blood. "How d' you like it, big fella?"
he said, and walked in.

Ortmann ducked a left and smashed a right to
Utah's ribs that stabbed pain into his vitals. He staggered back and fell, gasping wide-mouthed for air.
Ortmann came in and swung a heavy boot for his
face. Blaine slapped it out of line and lunged upward,
grabbing the big man in the crotch with one hand and
by the shirt front with the other.

The momentum of Ortmann's rush and the pivot
of Blaine's arms carried the big man off his feet and
up high. Then Blaine threw him to the ground.
Ortmann hit hard, and Blaine staggered back, glad
for the momentary respite. Panting and mopping
blood from his face, he watched the big man climb
slowly to his feet.

Blaine had been wearing a skin tight glove on his
left hand, and now he slipped another on his right,
meanwhile watching the big man get up. Blaine's shirt
was in rags and he ripped the few streamers of cloth
away. His body was brown and powerful muscles rip-
pled under the skin. He moved in, and Ortmann
grinned at him. "Come on, little fella! Let's see you
fight!"

Toe to toe they stood and slugged, smashing blows that were thrown with wicked power. Skull to skull they hit and battered. Ortmann's lips were pulp, a huge mouse was under one eye, almost closing it. There was a deep cut on Blaine's cheekbone and blood flowed continually. Inside his mouth there was a wicked cut.

Then Blaine stepped back suddenly. He caught Ortmann by the shoulder and pulled him forward, off balance. At the same time, he smashed a right to Ortmann's kidney.

Ortmann staggered, and Blaine moved quickly in and stabbed a swift left to the mouth. Then another. Then a hard driven left to the body followed by a right.

Blaine circled warily now, staying out of reach of those huge hands, away from that incredible weight. His legs felt leaden, his breath came in gasps. But he circled then stepped in with a left to the head, and setting himself, smashed a right to the body. Ortmann went back a full step, his big head swaying like that of a drunken bear. Blaine moved in. He set himself and whipped that right to the body again, then a left and another right. Ortmann struck out feebly, and Blaine caught the wrist and threw Ortmann with a rolling hip-lock.

Ortmann got up slowly. His eyes were glazed, his face a smear of blood. He opened and closed his fingers, then started for Blaine. And Blaine came to meet him, low and hard, with a tackle around the knees. Ortmann tried to kick, but he was too slow. Blaine's shoulder struck and he went down. Quickly, Utah rolled free and got to his feet.

Ortmann got up, huge, indomitable, but whipped. Blaine backed off. "You're whipped, Ort," he said hoarsely, "don't make me hit you again."

"You wanted to fight," Ortmann said, "come on!"

"You're through," Blaine repeated. "From here on I'd cut you to ribbons, an' what would it prove? You're a tough man, an' you're game, but you're also licked."

Ortmann put a hand to his bloody face then stared at his fingers. He looked disgusted. "Why," he said, "I guess you're right!" He mopped at his face. Then he stared at Blaine, who was standing, bloody and battered, swaying on his feet, but ready. "You don't look so good yourself. Let's have a drink."

Arm in arm the two men staggered into the store and Ortmann got down a bottle and poured two big drinks, slopping the liquor on the counter. "Here," Blaine said, "is to a first class fightin' man!"

Ortmann lifted his glass, grinning with the good side of his mouth. They tossed off their drinks, and then Blaine turned abruptly to Lud Fuller who had followed them inside. "Lud, you're fired. Get your stuff off the place by sundown and you get out of the country. You tried to hang Joe Neal, tried to hang him slow so he'd strangle. You tried to double-cross me. If I see you after sundown tonight, I'll kill you!"

Lud's face grew ugly. "You talk big," he sneered, "for a man who ain't wearin' a gun! I've got a notion to—" his hand was on his gun.

"It's a bad notion, Lud," Rip Coker said, "but if you want to die, just try draggin' iron. Blaine ain't got a gun, but I have!"

Lud Fuller stared at Coker. The blond man's face

was wicked in the dim light of the door. He stood lazily, hands hanging, but he was as ready as a crouching cougar. Fuller saw it and recognized what he saw. With a curse he swung out and walked from the room.

The return to the 46 was slow. Twice Blaine stopped and was sick. He had taken a wicked punch or two in the body and when he breathed a pain stabbed at his side. Rip Coker's eyes roved ceaselessly. "Wish Fuller had gone for his gun," he complained bitterly. "As long as he's alive he's a danger. He's yella, an' them kind worry me. They don't face up to a man. Not a bit."

Miles away, on the B-Bar, Timm paced restlessly while awaiting the return of Kelsey. He should have been back by now. Some of the crew were down in the bunkhouse and drunk. Where the liquor had come from he did not know, but he could guess. With Kelsey around he wouldn't be worried, but this was too big a house for one man to defend. Maria came in and brought him coffee. When at last they heard a rattle of hoofs, Timm ran to the door. It was Mary.

"Gosh, Ma'am!" His voice shook. "I sure am glad to see you back! I been worried. Tom ain't showed up."

"Is Clell out there?"

"I don't figure so. He rode off an' I ain't seen him come back." Timm walked restlessly from window to window. "You better eat something. Did you see Blaine?"

"Yes. He's with us. And Rip Coker is with him."

That was good news to Timm. Utah's reputation was widely known, and while he knew little of Rip Coker, it was sufficient to know the man was a fighter. Nevertheless, knowing Tom Kelsey as he did, his continued absence worried him.

"When's Blaine showin' up?" he asked.

"He wanted to see Ortmann first. He thinks he can talk him out of butting in until the fight is over."

"Ma'am, where could Kelsey go? This ain't right. He was to start me back for here, which he done. Then he was to see Blaine. An' as Blaine met you, he sure enough did that—but where is he now?"

HOWEVER, TOM KELSEY was not thinking of Timm. Nor was he thinking of getting back to the B-Bar. He was lying face down in the trail atop Mocking Bird Pass with three bullets in his body and his gun lying near his outflung hand.

Kelsey lay there in the road, his blood darkening the sand. A slow cool wind wound through the trees. Leaves stirred on the brush. His horse walked a few feet away, then looked back nervously, not liking the smell of blood. Then it walked into the thick green grass and began to crop grass. Kelsey did not move. The wind stirred the thin material on the back of his vest, moved his neckerchief.

Utah Blaine and Rip Coker found him there just at sundown. The best route from Yellowjacket to the B-Bar lay over 22 Mesa and through Mocking Bird. They switched horses at the Rice place on Sycamore. Rice was a lonely squatter who gardened a little, trapped a little, and broke a few wild horses he found in the canyon country. He was neutral and would always be. He took their horses without comment, glancing at Blaine's swollen and battered face with interest. But he asked no questions. "Take good care of that stallion," Blaine said. "I'll be back."

On fresh horses they pushed on, holding to a rapid gait. Things would begin to break fast now; they knew that. There was no time to be lost. Dusk was well along before they pushed into the Pass. Blaine was riding ahead when suddenly he reined in and palmed his gun. "Horse ahead," he said hoarsely. "No rider."

Rip grabbed his Winchester out of the bucket and spurred forward. Alert for an ambush, they glimpsed Kelsey's body almost at once. "Man down!" Rip said, and swung from the saddle. Then he swore.

"Who is it?" Blaine dropped to the ground.

"Kelsey. He's shot to doll rags. How he stayed alive this long, I don't know."

Blaine turned abruptly into a small copse and began breaking up dead dry branches. Swiftly, he built a fire. Making a square dish of birch bark, he began to boil water. Then he helped Coker carry the injured man to the fire. Coker stared at the bark container.

"Hell," he said, "why doesn't it burn? I never saw that before."

"Water absorbs the heat," Blaine explained. "Don't let the flames get above the water level. It's an Injun trick."

Working swiftly, they removed enough of Kelsey's clothes to get at the wounds. All were bad. Two were through the stomach and one right below the heart. There was, and both of them knew it, not one chance in a million.

Blaine bathed the wounds with hot water and then bandaged them. Kelsey stirred on the ground and then opened his eyes. "Blaine," he muttered. "Got to see Blaine."

"I'm here, Tom," Utah said. "Who shot you?"

"Blaine!" he groaned. "Blaine! You got to run! All of you! Get out! Mil—Miller told me. Neal's dead. Killed. They are all comin' after you."

Coker swore. Crouching over Kelsey's body, he demanded quickly, impatiently, "Tom—you sure?"

"Rink... Rink killed him."

"Rink," Coker straightened to his feet. "That tears it. If Rink went after Neal, then he's dead. That means you're out, Utah."

"Like hell." Utah was still working over the wounded man. "Take it easy, Tom."

"It ain't what you think I'm talkin' about," Coker protested. "It's them. With Neal dead you've no authority. The lid's off an' they'll come like locusts. An' they'll hunt you—us—like animals."

"Maybe." Utah's jaw was set, his face grim. Suddenly, he was tired. He had tried, but now Neal was dead. That good old man, murdered by Rink Witter.

Rink... well, that was something he could do. "I'll kill Rink," he said quietly.

"If you stay alive long enough." Coker was pacing the ground. "God, man. They'll all be after us! We'll have a real fight now!"

"Clell Miller did this?" Utah asked.

Kelsey was growing weaker. "Yes," he said faintly. "Don't mind me. I'm—I'm—finished. Ride. Get out."

He started a deep breath and never finished it.

Utah swore softly. "Good man gone," he said,

unconsciously speaking his epitaph. "Let's get out of here. Timm will be alone at that ranch."

"Take his guns. We'll need 'em. I'll get his rifle and start his horse home."

They mounted again and rode off in silence, leaving behind them the body of a "good man gone."

When they crossed the ridge near Bloody Basin they could see, several miles off, the lights at the Big N.

"There they are," Coker said bitterly. "Gettin' ready for us."

Utah's comment was dry. "What you kickin' about? You asked for a fight."

"You stickin' it out?"

"Sure."

Coker smiled. This was his kind of man. "You got a partner," he said quietly. Then he added, "You take Rink. I want Clell."

CHAPTER 8

RINK WITTER HAD come upon Neal at Congress Junction. Witter, under orders from Nevers, had started for El Paso to find and kill Joe Neal. He arrived at the Junction in time to see Joe Neal get down from a cattle train, and Witter swung down from his horse and walked up the platform. Neal did not see him until they were less than twenty feet apart.

"Hello, Joe," Rink Witter said, and shot him three times through the stomach. As the old man fell, Witter walked up to him, kicked away the hand that groped for a gun and shot Neal again, between the eyes. Then he walked unhurriedly to his horse, mounted and rode back to the Big N.

The news swept the country like wildfire. Neal was dead. Blaine, therefore, no longer had any authority. The few who had lagged now saw there was no longer any reason for delay. As one man they started to move. Nevers began at once to gather his forces. He wanted to be on the 46 range in force before any opposition could arrive. Then he could dictate terms.

Otten worried him none at all despite the man's political influence over the Territory. Nevers figured they could buy Otten off with a few square miles of range which he would accept rather than enter a free-for-all fight. There would be trouble with Ortmann, but with Clell and Fuller's men that could be handled.

It was Lee Fox who worried Nevers—far more than he would have admitted.

Fox, at Table Mountain, was between Nevers and the bulk of the 46 range. Moreover, Fox was a highly volatile person, one whose depth or ability could not be gauged. He was given to sudden driving impulses, and reason had no part in them. If he went into one of his killing furies the range might be soaked with blood within the week.

Nevertheless, Nevers fully appreciated the strategic value of the accomplished fact. If he were sitting at Headquarters on the 46, his position would be strong and he could dictate terms. Moreover, because of his affiliation with the hands of the two big spreads, he far outnumbered the others.

———

WHEN CLELL MILLER reached the ranch house on the 46 he found it almost deserted. A few of the hands were around and they told him that neither Utah nor Lud were around. Fuller and some of his men had been sent off to work the north range and had not returned. Rip Coker was riding with Blaine.

Clell considered that while he built a smoke. Coker was a tough hand. If he had decided to ride with Blaine, they would make a tough combination to buck. Alone he couldn't tackle them. He turned his horse and rode south, heading for the river and the easiest route to the Big N.

Clell Miller was a man at odds with himself. For the first time a killing was riding him hard. The memory of the falling of Tom Kelsey, and the memory of just how good a man Kelsey had been nagged at him and worried him. He could not shake it off, and that had never been true before. An old-timer had told him just what would happen, and that was years ago. "You're fast with your guns, Clell," he had said. "But someday you'll shoot the wrong man an' you'll never rest easy again."

Hunching his shoulders against the chill, Miller stared bitterly into the darkness. The night seemed unusually cold, and suddenly he felt a sharp distaste for going back to the Big N, for seeing those hot, greedy eyes of Nevers, the dried-up, poison-mean face of Rink Witter.

———

UTAH BLAINE RODE up to the B-Bar and swung down. Then he said to Rip, "We'll have a showdown with the crew, right now."

He walked swiftly to the bunkhouse. Coker heard Timm come to the door. "Stay where you are, Timm. We'll handle it." He walked after Blaine who threw open the door of the bunkhouse and stepped in.

Five men were there. The other hands were off somewhere. One of those was dead drunk and snoring on a bunk. The others looked up when Blaine stepped in. Coker followed and moved swiftly to the right.

"Showdown, men!" Blaine spoke crisply. "All cards on the table. Neal's been murdered by Rink Witter. Clell Miller has killed Tom Kelsey, shot him down up on the Mocking Bird. Now you declare yourselves. If you're with us, fine! If you're not, you ride off the ranch right this minute, just as you are. If you want to call, shuck your iron and let's see how many of you die game!"

Nobody moved. Not a man there but had used a gun. Not a man there but who had been in fights. So they knew this one, and they liked nothing about it. With those two men facing them even their numerical superiority would not help. Several men would die in those close quarters and none of them wanted to die. Each seemed to feel that Blaine was directing his full attention at him.

"Always wanted a shot at some of you," Coker said easily. "Suppose we settle this fight right now. If you boys want it, you can have it."

A short, squat man with a stubble of coarse beard and a bald head spoke. "We'll ride out. We ain't afeerd, but we ain't buckin' no stacked deck. Do we take our guns?"

Blaine laughed. "Why, sure! I'd never shoot an unarmed man an' some of you rannies may need killin'! Take 'em along, but remember this: if I ever see any one of you east of Copper Creek or north of Deadman again, he'd better be grabbin' iron when I see him."

"My sentiments," Coker agreed. "Any of you feel like takin' a hand right now? Utah figures we should give you an out. Me, I'd as soon open the pot right now."

The bald man stared at him. "You wait. You'll get yours. You ain't so salty."

"Want to freshen me up?" Coker invited. "I think we ought to shorten the odds right here."

The man would say no more, but a tall, lean man in long underwear looked at Blaine. "Don't I get to put on no pants?" his voice was plaintive.

"You look better that way. I said you ride the way you are. If you hate to lose your gear, blame it on double-crossin' your brand."

The men trooped out, taking the dead drunk with them. One after another they rounded up their horses, mounted and rode off. There were no parting yells, nothing.

Mary Blake was standing in the doorway. Timm got up from where he had been crouched by the window with his Winchester.

"Utah! You're back! I was so worried!" she cried.

"Seen Tom?" Timm asked quickly.

Blaine hesitated, feeling how well these men had known each other. "Tom won't be back," he said quietly. "Clell Miller killed him on Mocking Bird."

Timm swore softly. "I was afraid of that. He was a good man, Tom was." He rubbed a fumbling hand over his chin. "Rode together eight years, the two of us. I wish," he added, "I was a gunslinger."

"Don't worry," Coker promised, "I'll stake out that hide myself."

Blaine walked restlessly across the room. He had never liked being cooped up when a fight was coming. It was his nature to attack. Nor did he like the presence of the women. Bluntly, he explained the situation to Mary. "The stage for hesitation is over now," he said quietly, "and all the chips are down. You'd better go."

"And leave you to fight them alone?" she protested. "I'll not go."

"It would be better if you did," he told her. "We may have to leave here, fight somewhere else."

Coker took his rifle and went outside, moving off

into the night, and heading away from the house. Timm walked out on the porch and stood there, lighting his pipe. He felt lost without Kelsey. It seemed impossible that Tom could be dead.

"Mary," Utah said it quietly, "I wish you would go. Red Creek if you like, or over east of here, to that Mormon settlement. You might be safer there. All hell's breakin' loose now."

She looked at him, her eyes serious. "What will you do? What can you do now? Against them all, I mean? And without the backing of Joe Neal's authority?"

He had been thinking of that. The murder of Neal cut the ground from beneath his feet. Neal had no heirs and so the range would go by default. He might, of course, claim it himself. Had he the fighting men to enforce such a claim, he might even make it stick. But he had no such men nor the money to pay them.

Nor could they hope to hold out long against the forces to be thrown against them. "We've got to get out." He said it reluctantly but positively. "We've got to move. We'd be foolish to try to hold them off for long, but I will try. If we fail, then we'll run."

Coker had come back to the door. "Riders headed this way. What do we do?"

Utah turned to the door. "Better ride out, Mary. This isn't going to be nice."

"Are you quitting?"

He laughed without humor. "You're the second to ask me that question in the last few hours. No, I'm not quitting. A man killed Joe Neal. Another man ordered it. I've a job to do."

Rip Coker was leaning against the corner of the

house. He looked around as Blaine walked over to him. "Quite a bunch. Timm's bedded down by that stone well."

"All right. Hold your fire unless they open the ball. If they do, don't miss any shots."

"Who's goin' to miss?"

Utah Blaine walked slowly down the trail. The moon was up and the night was bright. As the riders neared they slowed their pace. Blaine moved forward. "All right, hold it up!"

They drew up, a solid rank of at least twenty men. "That you, Blaine?"

"Sure. Who'd you expect? You murdered Joe Neal."

There was a short, pregnant silence. Nevers replied, his rage stifled. "All right, so Neal's dead. That finishes you on this place."

"I'd not say so. If Neal had lived he might have fired me. As it is, he can't. I was given a job. Nobody has taken me off. I plan to stay."

"Don't be a fool!" Nevers burst out. "I've twenty men here! I'm takin' over this spread right now."

"I wouldn't bet on it," Blaine replied quietly, "an' if you do take over, Nevers, you'll have fewer men than you've got now. And also," he paused slightly, "I'll be back."

"Not if you die now."

Blaine lifted his voice. "Boys, you're backin' this gent. Let's see what kind of an Injun he is. Nevers, I'll take you right now, with any man you pick to side you. I'll take the two of you right here in the moonlight, Nevers. Come on, how much guts have you got?"

It was the last thing in the world that Nevers had

expected. Moreover, it was the last thing he wanted. With nerve enough for most purposes, he had no stomach for facing a gunfighter of Blaine's reputation—not even with a man to help him. He knew, just as Blaine had known he would, that Blaine's first shot would be for him—and it wouldn't miss.

Yet he knew how much depended on courageous leadership. Men, particularly western men, do not follow cowards. He had been fairly called, and his mind groped for a way out, an excuse.

"What's the matter, Nevers? Not ready to die?" Utah taunted. "Don't worry too much. My hands aren't in the best shape right now, an' you might have a chance." He was stalling for time, trying to turn their attack, or at least to dull its force. "They took quite a hammering yesterday when I whipped Ortmann."

"When you what?"

That was somebody back in the crowd, one of the silent riders who waited the outcome of this talk.

From off to the left, Rip Coker spoke up. He wanted them to know he was there, too. "That's right, boys. Blaine gave Ortmann the beating of his life. Called him right in his own place of business and whipped him good. Although," he added, "I'd say Ort put up one hell of a scrap."

"Did you hear that?" One rider was speaking to another. "Utah Blaine whipped Ortmann—with his *fists*!"

"Wish you gents would make up your minds to die," Coker commented casually. "This here Colt shotgun is loadin' my arms down."

Rip Coker was carrying a Winchester, but he was well back. He knew all they could see was light on his barrel. A Colt revolving shotgun carried four shells and no man in his right mind likes to buck a shotgun. It was a shrewd comment, well calculated to inspire distaste for battle in that vague light.

"Yeah," Timm's voice came from the well coping. "You hombres make a right tempting target. This Spencer sure can't miss at this range!"

All was quiet. Nobody spoke for several minutes. Nevers held himself still, glad that attention was off him for the minute. He had no desire to meet Blaine with guns now or at any time, yet he knew of no easy way out of the situation he was in. He had been neatly and effectually out-guessed and it infuriated him. Moreover, with a kind of intuition he knew that the men behind him had lost their enthusiasm for the attack. Blaine was bad enough, but that shotgun . . . a blast from a shotgun did awful things to a man, and this gun held four shells. And there was the possibility of reloads before they could get to him.

The Spencer .56 was no bargain either.

"All right!" Blaine stepped forward suddenly, gauging their hesitancy correctly. "Show's over for tonight. You boys want this ranch, you take it the hard way. Let's start back."

Nevers found his voice. "All right," he said evenly, "we'll go. But come daylight, we'll be back."

"Why sure! Glad to have you!" Blaine was chuckling. "Room enough on this place to bury the lot of you."

Slowly, those in the rear began to back off. None of them seemed anxious to push ahead. Reluctantly, stifling his frustration and fury, Nevers followed his retreating men.

Rip Coker walked over slowly. "It'll never be that close again," he said sincerely. "I had goose flesh all over me there for a minute."

"That shotgun remark was sheer genius, Rip," Blaine said.

Coker was pleased. "Just a trick idea. I sure wouldn't want to buck a shotgun in the dark."

"What's next?" Timm had walked up. "I was listenin' for Clell, but I don't think he was with this outfit."

"We wait for morning," Blaine said, "and just before daybreak we'll pull out."

"Hell!" Rip said. "We've got 'em stopped now, why run?"

"The object," Blaine said, "of any war is to destroy your enemy's fighting force. With superior numbers and armament the British couldn't whip Washington because they couldn't pin him down. He always managed to pull out and leave them holding the bag. That's what we do now.

"They'll never own this ranch," he said, "or the 46 as long as we're alive and in the country. We can let 'em have it today, an' we can take it back when we want it!"

CHAPTER 9

AT DAYBREAK THEY started east. Mary Blake, accompanied by the fat Maria, was to ride to the Mormon settlement. Later, they would return to Red Creek and do what might be done there toward retaining title to their land. Blaine, accompanied by Rip Coker and Timm, took to the rugged country to the south.

The sun was hot and the three rode steadily, circling deeper into the hills. With them they had three pack animals loaded with food and ammunition.

"Maverick Springs," Timm told them. "That's the best place for us. She's 'way back in the hills in mighty rugged country."

Blaine mopped the sweat from his face and squinted through the sunlight toward the west. From the top of the mesa they could see a long sweep of the valley and the river. Table Mountain was slightly north of west from them and they could see riders fording the river.

"Lee Fox," Coker said. "Nevers won't have it all his own way."

"Nevers's place is beyond, in Bloody Basin, if I recall," Blaine said thoughtfully. "I figure we ought to pay him a visit after we cache these supplies."

"Now you're talkin'!" Coker agreed.

"An' we'll make three separate caches. No use havin' all our eggs in one basket."

They turned down into the canyon back of Razorback and made one cache at the base of Cypress Butte. They rode on through the tall pines, the air seeming cooler in their shade. There was the smell of heat, though, and the smell of dust. They took their time, anticipating no pursuit and not eager to tire their horses. Blaine thought several times of the stallion. He missed the fine horse and would pick him up in the next few days.

They rode at last into a secluded glen shielded on all sides by ranks of pines and aspens. Scattered among these were a few giant walnut trees. They were now close under the Mazatzals which Blaine had observed from the faraway rim of Tule Mesa.

At daybreak, they moved out following Tangle Creek up to the Basin where they found the Big N standing alone. The only man on the place was the cook, who came to the door with a rifle. Utah stopped. "Where's Nevers?"

Coker had been bringing up the rear and at the first glimpse of the cook he had turned his horse sharply left and circled behind the house while Blaine stalled.

"Ain't none o' your business!" The cook retorted harshly. "Who 're you?"

"Blaine's the name." Utah saw Coker slip from his horse and start toward the back side of the house. "You tell Nevers to stay off the 46 and the B-Bar or take the consequences."

"Tell him yourself!" The cook retorted. He was

about to amplify his remarks when the sharp prod of a gun muzzle cut him off short.

"Lower that shotgun mighty easy," Coker said quietly. "You might miss but I can't."

The logic of this was evident to the cook. Gingerly he lowered the shotgun and Coker reached around and took it from his hands. "What you goin' to do to me?" the cook demanded.

"You?" Blaine laughed. "We've no fight with you, man. Get us some grub. We've had a long ride and we ate a light breakfast. You just tell Nevers we were here. If he tries to grab any piece of the 46 we'll burn him out right here. You tell him that."

"There's only three of you," the cook objected, going about fixing the meal. "You won't have a chance."

"Well," Coker said cheerfully, tipping back in his chair, "you can bet on this. If we go, our burials will come after that of Nevers. Take it from me."

NEVERS WAS UNHAPPY. His men had closed in on the B-Bar ranch house only to find it deserted and empty. He was no fool, and he knew that there would be no safety for him or for anyone else on either the B-Bar or the 46 as long as Blaine was alive and in the vicinity.

Clell Miller rode in, unshaven and surly. Nevers went to him quickly. "Where's Blaine? You seen him?"

"No." Miller dismounted wearily. "An' I don't want to."

"Losin' your nerve?" Nevers sneered.

Miller turned sharply around and Nevers stiffened.

"No," Clell spoke slowly, "but I don't like this. It looked good, but I don't like it now."

Nevers could see the man was on the ragged edge and he knew better than to push him. "What happened?"

"I met Tom Kelsey up on Mocking Bird," he said, "an' killed him."

"Oh." Nevers had liked Kelsey himself, and at the same time had known the man stood between them and the possession of the B-Bar.

"Blaine got away," he said, "with Coker an' Timm."

"There'll be hell to pay then," Miller was gloomy. "Nevers, let's call it off. I'm sick of it."

"Call it off?" Nevers's rage returned. "Are you crazy? The biggest deal ever an' you want to call it off. Anyway," he added practically, "nobody could stop it now. Even if we backed down the rest of them wouldn't."

"That's right." Clell Miller studied Nevers. "I wonder what will happen to you for the Neal killin'."

Nevers jerked around. "I didn't kill him."

"Witter killed him at your orders. But now what? Neal had friends, Nevers. Friends down at Phoenix, friends in Tucson. Some of them will ask questions. Far as that goes, Neal told me one time he helped Virgil Earp out of a tight spot. The Earps stand by their friends. Look how they stuck with Doc Halliday."

Nevers shook himself irritably. Despite his bluster, he was worried. Had he gone too far? But no—this was no time to waver and it was too late to turn back—much too late.

He scowled at the thought, then shook himself impatiently. "We'll run Blaine down. We'll have him in no time."

"Think he'll wait for you to come after him?"

Nevers turned his large head. "What do you mean?"

"Just this. I think he'll hit us an' hit hard. Have you forgotten Alta? I haven't. And the bunch he tackled in Alta were so much tougher than most of our crowd there's no comparison."

They stood there, not liking any part of what they felt, knowing there was no way back. Yet there was no stopping. Nevers heard a scrape of heels behind him and he turned. One of his riders was standing not far away with a rifle in his hands. "Riders, boss, quite a bunch. Looks like Lee Fox."

"Fox." Nevers said it aloud. There was that, too.

A tall man rode up on a yellow buckskin. He pulled up sharply and looked around him. "Moved right in, Nevers? Well, you keep it. I'm headin' for the 46."

"Nobody's made any claim yet." Nevers held himself in. "I want the 46 an' part of the B-Bar. You can have the rest."

Fox smiled. It was not a pleasant smile. Nevers had the feeling that he had had before. This man was riding the borderline of insanity. "Got it all figured, have you? What about Ben Otten?"

"He's out of it."

"Tell him that. You've got to take him in or he'll go to Neal's friends."

Grudgingly, Nevers admitted this. Where all had been simple, now all was complication. Maybe Miller wasn't getting weak-kneed after all; maybe he was just getting smart. "Go on up to the 46," he said. "We can settle it later."

Fox did not move. "We can settle now if you like."

Nevers was a bulldog. His big head came up slowly and he stared at Fox. "That makes no sense, Fox. No sense in killin' ourselves off." He turned slowly. "Lud, open that keg of whiskey. We might as well celebrate."

Fuller got up heavily. He had been profoundly shocked by Blaine's swift and brutal cutting down of Ortmann. It was something long believed impossible, yet the slashing power of Utah's fists had been a shocking thing. It had been soon apparent to all that Blaine had been the faster of the two, and he had hit the harder. Despite Ortmann's huge size, his blows had shaken Utah. They had failed to keep him down. By his victory, Utah Blaine had seemed invincible, then on top of this he had fired Fuller and had told him to get out of the country.

Fuller had said nothing about the fight. The news was around though, and while the men gathered to empty the half of whiskey, talk swung to it. "Never would have believed it if I hadn't seen it," Fuller said.

All eyes turned to him. Miller stepped forward, quick with interest. "You *saw* it?"

"Yeah." Fuller straightened up from driving the spigot into the keg that sat on an outdoor table. "Blaine ruined him. He cut him down like you'd cut up a beef. Ortmann was rugged but he never had a chance."

There was silence, and then a cool voice interrupted: "Am I invited?"

They turned swiftly. Utah Blaine stood there, his feet apart, his green eyes hard and ready beneath the flat brim of his hat. Beyond him, still astride their horses, were Rip Coker and Timm. Each held a shotgun taken from the Big N.

Nevers's face turned crimson. "You? *Here?*" His voice was thick.

"Why, sure." Utah let his eyes go slowly from one to the other and finally settled on Lud Fuller. The face of the 46 foreman turned white. "Don't let it get you, Lud. I invited myself here. You still got time to leave the country. But don't let me meet with you again."

"What do you want?" Nevers demanded.

"Want? Why, I saw you fellas were openin' a keg so we thought we'd come down." Blaine turned his eyes slowly to Nevers. "You sure make a nice target through the sights of a Winchester, Nevers. I come darn near liquidatin' the stock of the Big N."

Nevers stared at Blaine, hatred swelling within him. Yet even as it mounted, a little voice of caution whispered that he should go slowly. This situation was shot through with death.

"Had my sights on Miller, too," Blaine said. "I sort of like the looks of you boys with my sight partin' your eyes. It's a right good feelin'. I might have shot Miller, but I promised him."

Clell's nerves were jumping. "Yeah? To who?"

"Me, Clell," Rip Coker was smiling wickedly. "I asked for you. I always figured you weren't as salty with that six-gun as you figured. An' when we tangle remember it ain't goin' to be like it was with Tom Kelsey. That was murder, Clell."

Clell glared, but his eyes shifted. Timm's glance

met his and Clell felt a little shiver. That quiet man—
square-faced, cool, calm, steady Timm—his eyes held
a kind of hatred that Clell had never seen before.

"Kelsey an' me rode together for years, Clell,"
Timm said.

Blaine stepped forward and jerked the tin cup from
Nevers's fingers. Then he filled it partly. Stepping
back, he looked at Nevers. "I'm goin' to kill you,
Nevers," he said quietly, "but not today. We're just
visitin' today. I promised Coker that I wouldn't kill
you today if he wouldn't tackle Miller."

He turned and walked back, handing the cup up to
Timm, who took a swallow, then passed it to Rip.
Coker laughed and emptied the cup. Utah Blaine
walked back, his spurs jingling. Nobody spoke; the
riders stood around, watching him. Clell felt a faint
stir of reluctant admiration. This man had guts, he
told himself.

Rightly, Blaine had gauged them well. No western
man in his right mind was going to try reaching for a
gun when three armed men, two of them with ready
guns, covered him. One man Blaine was not sure
about was Lee Fox. Fox was a man who might gamble. Yet even as Utah thought that his slanting eyes
went to Coker.

Rip was watching Fox with care. Trust Rip to
know where the danger lay.

"Yeah," Blaine said, "you've started the killing
with two murders, Neal and Kelsey. Both were good
men. The killing can stop there if you back up and get
off this ranch and stay off it and the 46 Connected."

"If you think we'll do that," Nevers replied,
"you're crazy!"

"We won't back up," Fox interjected.

Utah Blaine took another drink and then replaced the cup on the keg. He stepped back. "All right, boys, this goes for every man jack of you. Get off the two ranches by sundown or the war's on. We'll kill you wherever we find you and we'll hang any man who injures any one of us."

"You talk mighty big for such a small outfit."

"Want to try your hand right now, Nevers?" Blaine looked at him from under the brim of his hat.

"Plenty of time," Nevers said.

Utah swung into the saddle. "All right, we've told you. Now it's on your head."

Suddenly his gun sprang to his hand. "Drop your belts!" The words cracked like a whip. "Drop 'em, an' no mistakes!"

As one man their hands leaped to the buckles and they let go their gun belts. "All right," Blaine said. "Turn around!" They turned, and then Blaine said, "Now run! Last man gets a load of buckshot!"

As one man they sprang forward and raced for the draw, and wheeling their horses, the three rode out of the clearing and into the trail.

Hearing the horses' hoofs, Nevers braced to a stop and yelled, "Horses! Get after 'em! I'll give five hundred dollars for Blaine, dead or alive!"

CHAPTER 10

TIMM LED OFF as they left the Basin. Instead of taking the trail for Mocking Bird Pass he swung west into the bed of Soda Springs Creek. Trusting Timm's knowledge of the country, Blaine trailed behind him with Coker bringing up the rear. They rode swiftly, confident their start would keep them ahead without killing their horses.

Timm swung suddenly west over a shelf of rock. He turned up over a saddle in the Mustangs and into a creek bottom. The creek was dry now. Ahead of them loomed the battlemented side of Turret Peak where Apaches had been trapped and captured long ago.

"Fox had me worried. I was afraid he wouldn't stampede." Coker's comment was in line with Blaine's own thoughts. "It'll set him wild."

"Yeah, we're on the run now for sure."

Timm had nothing to say. The older man studied the hills, selecting their route with infinite care, leaving as little trail as possible. They turned and doubled back, choosing rocky shelves of sand so deep their tracks were formless and shapeless, mingling with those of wild horses and of cattle.

"How far are we from Otten's place?" Blaine asked.

"Just a whoop and a holler." Timm turned in his saddle. His face looked strangely youthful now, and

Blaine noticed the humor around his eyes. Timm was taking to this like a duck to water. It probably brought memories of old days of campaigning. "You want to go over there?"

"Sure. As long as we're ridin', let's drop in on him."

"That outfit will be runnin' us," Coker warned.

"I know that. So this may be our last and only chance to see Otten."

Luckily, the banker was at the ranch. He came out of the house when he saw them approaching, but his face shadowed when he identified them. "What are you doin' here, Blaine? You'd best ride on out of the country."

"You'd like that, wouldn't you?" Blaine watched Timm lead the horses to the trough. "We're not goin', Ben. We're stayin'. We're goin' to fight it out."

"Don't be a fool!" Ben Otten was more worried than angry. "Look, boys, you don't have a chance! The whole country's against you. I don't want to see any more killing. Ride on out. If you're broke, I'll stake you."

"No." Blaine's voice was flat. He looked at Otten with cool, hard eyes. "I don't like bein' pushed and I'm not going to run. If I have to die here, I will. But believe me, Ben, they'll bury some men along with me."

"That's no way to talk." Otten was worried. He came down from the steps. "Where's Mary? What happened to her?"

"She's over in the Mormon settlements. She'll be safe if she stays there."

"Where's Tom Kelsey?"

"Then you haven't heard? Clell Miller killed him. Joe Neal's dead, too."

Otten nodded. "I know that. I'm sorry about Tom. Neal should have stayed out while he had the chance."

Utah Blaine stared down at the banker, his opinion showing in his eyes. "Ben," he said frankly, "you've the look of a good man. I hate to see you running with this pack of coyotes! Soon's a man is down you all run in to snap and tear at him."

"That's a hell of a thing to say." Otten kicked dirt with his boot toe. "Where'd you come from?"

"The B-Bar. We faced up to Nevers and Fox over there. Stopped by to tell them what they were buckin'. That's why we stopped here, Ben. You know what this means, don't you?"

Otten looked up, his eyes granite hard. "What does what mean? You're not bluffin' me, Utah!"

"I never bluff, Ben." Blaine said it quietly and the older man felt a distinct chill. "I'm just tellin' you. Run with that pack and you're through. I'll run you out of the country."

Otten's face darkened and he stepped forward, so furious he could scarcely speak. "You!" he shouted. "You'll run me out! Why you ragged-tailed gunslinger! You're nothin' but a damned driftin' outlaw! You stay here an' I'll see you hung! Don't you come around here tellin' me!"

"I've told you." Blaine turned his back on him and gathered up the reins of his horse.

"Let's go, Utah." Timm's voice showed his worry. "They'll be right behind us."

Blaine swung into the leather and then turned,

dropping his glance to Otten. "Make your choice, man. But make it right. You've done nothing against me yet, so don't start."

In a tight group, the three rode out of the yard and Ben Otten stared after them, his hand on his gun. Why, the man was insane! He was on the run and he talked like it was the other way around! He'd...! Ben's fury trailed off and old stories came flooding back into his mind. This man, alone and without help, had walked into Alta and tamed the town.

Otten knew other stories, too. More than once he had heard Gid Blake's story of the trail cutters. He shook himself irritably, and swore aloud, then said, "Why, the man doesn't have a chance!" But the words rang hollow in his ears and he stared gloomily after them. Suppose the man did win? The answer to that was in Blaine's words: he never bluffed. He would do what he promised.

But that was absurd. Utah Blaine wouldn't last the week out. A few minutes later when Nevers and his hard-riding crew raced in, he became even more confident. It was not until he lay in bed that night that he remembered Blaine's face. He remembered those level green eyes and something turned over in him and left him cold and afraid.

———

NOW THE CHASE began. To the three riders it became grim and desperate. After nightfall they came down to the Rice cabin and after looking through the windows, tapped gently on the door.

"Who is it?" Rice demanded.

"Blaine. After my horse and a couple of others."

The door opened and Rice stepped out. He glanced sharply at Coker, then over at Timm. "All right. Better ride your horses back up the canyon. There's an old corral there where they won't be seen. I'll come along."

At the brush corral, he watched them strip the saddles from their tired horses and saddle up afresh. Utah got his kak on the lineback and the stallion nudged him happily with its nose. "You haven't seen us," he explained to Rice.

Rice chuckled wryly. "I wasn't born yesterday. You boys watch your step."

He backed up, holding the gate open for them. As they passed he looked up at Timm. "I s'pose you know you're ridin' with a couple of wolves?"

Timm chuckled. "Sure do," he said cheerfully, "an' you know, Rice, I feel fifteen years younger! Anyway," he added, "I like the company of wolves better than coyotes."

Four days later, worn and hollow-eyed, they rested in Calfpen Canyon. Hunkered over a fire they watched the coffee water come to a boil. Then Timm dumped in the grounds. There was a bloody bandage on Coker's head and all of them were honed down and fine with hunger and hard riding. The horses showed it even more than the men.

"Ridin' with the wolves is rough, Timm," Blaine said.

The older man looked up. The grizzled beard on his jaws made him seem even older than he was. "I like it, Utah." His voice was low. "Only one thing I want. I want to fight back."

"That," Blaine said quietly, "starts the day after

tomorrow. We're goin' to swing wide to the east an', take our time, let our horses rest up from the hard goin' and swing away around to the Big N."

Rip Coker looked up. His hatchet face was even thinner now, his tight, hard mouth like a gash.

"We're goin' to hit back," Utah said, "an' hard. We're goin' to show 'em what war means!"

"Now you're talkin'!" Rip's voice was harsh with emotion. "I'm fed up with runnin'!"

"They haven't seen us for a day now," Utah said, "and they'll not see us again for a couple more. We'll let 'em relax while we rest up."

N EVERS WAS DEAD tired. He stripped off his clothes and crawled gratefully into the blankets. In the adjoining room he heard the hands slowly turning in. There was little talk among them tonight, and he stared gloomily at his boots. The chase, which had started off with excitement, was growing dull for them, and when not dull, dangerous.

On the second day they had caught up with Blaine and his two companions and in the gun battle that followed two of the Big N riders had been wounded, one of them seriously. One of the Blaine group had gone down—Coker, somebody had said. But they had escaped and carried the wounded man with them.

Twice the following day Nevers and his men lost the trail, and then, at daybreak of the next day, it vanished completely. After several hours of futile search they had given up and wearily rode back to the Big N.

Nevers stretched out and drew the blankets over him. There was still the matter of Fox. The Table

Mountain rancher had moved into the house on the 46 and had a rider on the B-Bar. The Big N also had a rider there, and it was believed Ben Otten was to send a man to establish his claim also.

Nevers awakened with a start. How long he had been asleep he did not know, but some sound outside the house had awakened him. Rising to an elbow, he listened intently. He heard the snort of a horse, the crack of a rope on a flank, and then the thunder of hoofs. Somebody was after the horses!

He swung his feet to the floor and grabbed for his boots. In the adjoining room a match flared and a light was lit. Then a shot smashed the lamp chimney to bits and he heard the crack of the shot mingling with the tinkle of falling glass.

With a grunt of fury, Nevers sprang for his rifle, but a bullet smashed the window frame and thudded into the wall within inches of his rifle stock. Other bullets shattered other windows. A shot struck the potbellied stove in the next room and ricocheted about, and somebody yelled with sudden pain. Outside there was a wild yell, and more shots. Nevers grabbed his rifle and got to the window. A shot scattered wood fragments in his eyes and he dropped his rifle and clawed at his face, swearing bitterly.

More shots sounded, and then there was a sudden glare of light from outside. Through his tear-filled eyes, Nevers blinked at the glare. His carefully gathered haystack was going up in flames!

With a roar, he grabbed up his rifle and rushed from the house. Somewhere he heard a yell. "You wanted war, Nevers! How do you like it?" A shot spat dirt over his bare feet, and more glass sprinkled behind him.

Impotent with fury, he fired off into the dark and then rushed toward the barn. The others joined him and for more than an hour they fought desperately to save the barn. The hay was a total loss: ten tons of it gone up in smoke!

Wearily, sodden with fatigue, they trooped back to the house where coffee was being made. "I'll kill him!" Nevers blared. "I'll see him hung!"

Nobody said anything. They sat down, sagging with exhaustion. After the hard ride of the past few days the fight against the fire had done them in, all of them. And they still had to round up their horses.

Only one man had been hurt. Flying glass had cut his face, producing a very slight, but painful cut.

The man wounded in the gunfight during the chase raised up in bed. "That Blaine," he called out, "ain't no bargain!"

"Shut up!" Nevers turned on him. "Shut your mouth!"

All was quiet in the house. Finally, Rocky White got up and stretched. "I reckon," he said slowly, "I'll go to sleep outside." He walked out. Then slowly a couple of the hands got up and followed him.

Nevers stared after them, his face sour. Viciously, he swore. That damned Blaine!

The other hands drifted one by one back to sleep, and then the light winked out. The sky was already gray in the east. Nevers slumped on the bed, staring at the gray rectangle of the window. The bitterness within him was turning to a deep and vindictive hatred of Blaine. Heretofore the gunfighter had merely represented an obstacle to be overcome. Now he represented something more.

There was only one answer. He would get Rink Witter to round up a few paid killers and he would start them out, professional manhunters. Fox would chip in, maybe Otten, too. They could pay five or six men a good price to hunt Blaine, and get up a bounty on his scalp.

Wearily he got to his feet and walked outside. He saddled up and swung into the saddle. One of the hands stuck his head out of the barn. Nevers shouted back, "I'll be back tomorrow! Ridin' to Red Creek!"

———

MARY BLAKE HAD arrived in Red Creek only a short time before the night attack on the Big N. Restive, unable to await results in the Mormon community, she had boarded the stage for Red Creek with Maria. The next morning the first person she met was Ralston Forbes.

"Hello!" He looked at her with surprise. "I heard you left the country."

"I've not gone and I've no intention of going. Have you seen Utah?"

"No, but I've heard plenty. Nevers has been hot on his trail. They had a scrap the other night with honors about even by all accounts. What are you planning to do?"

She smiled at him. "Have breakfast and not tell any plans to a newspaperman."

"Come on, then! We'll have breakfast together." They walked across the street to the cafe just in time to meet Otten at the door. He stared at her gloomily, then looked at Forbes.

"Any news?" he asked.

"Not a word."

They opened the door and stepped into the cafe and stopped abruptly. Blaine, Timm and Rip Coker were seated at the table eating. All were unshaven, dirty and obviously close to exhaustion. Utah looked up, his eyes going from one to the other. They hesitated on Mary, then went on to Otten. He said nothing at all.

"You're taking a chance," Forbes suggested.

"We're used to it," Blaine replied. "Has Ortmann been around?"

"No. He isn't showing his face since you whipped him. What do you want with him?"

"Suppose I'd tell you with one of the enemy in camp?" Blaine asked.

Otten flushed and started to speak, but Rip Coker interrupted him. "Straddlin' a rail can give a man a mighty sore crotch, Ben."

The banker looked from one to the other, his face sour. "Can't a man even eat his breakfast in peace?" he complained.

Utah looked at Mary. "You came back. Why?"

"I couldn't—just couldn't let you do it alone. I wanted to help."

Nobody said anything for several minutes. Utah ate tiredly, and the girl came in and filled his coffee cup. The hot black coffee tasted good, very good.

Rip's bandage was fresh. They had awakened the

doctor for that, and he had bandaged the scalp wound after making some ironic comments about hard heads.

"Anything for publication?" Forbes asked, finally.

Blaine looked up. His eyes were bloodshot. "Why, sure," he grinned suddenly, "say that Utah Blaine, manager of the 46 Connected, is vacationing in the hills for a few days but expects to be back at Headquarters soon. You might add that he expects to return to attend the funerals of several of the leading citizens of the valley—and he hopes their respected banker, Ben Otten, will not be one of them."

Otten looked up, his face flushing. Before he could open his mouth, however, there was a clatter of horse's hoofs and then boots struck the boardwalk and the door burst open.

In the open door, her face flushed from riding in the wind, her dark eyes bright with excitement, was Angie Kinyon!

"Utah! You've got to ride!" She was breathless with hurry. "Lee Fox struck your trail and he's coming right on with a pack of men. Nevers joined him outside of town! Hurry, please!"

Blaine got to his feet, hitching his gun belts. He looked across the table at Angie and his eyes softened. "Thanks," he said. "Thanks very much!"

Mary Blake looked startled. Her eyes went quickly from one to the other. Ralston Forbes was watching her and he was smiling.

CHAPTER 11

WHEN THEY WERE gone Mary Blake looked over at Angie. "It's a surprise to see you here, Angie," she said graciously, but with just the slightest edge to her voice. "You don't often ride to town. Especially at this hour."

Angie smiled gaily, but her mind was not in the room. It was out there on the trail with the galloping horses. Forbes could see it, and so could Mary. "No," Angie said, "I don't often come in, but when a friend is in danger, that changes everything."

"I didn't know you even knew Utah Blaine," Mary said too casually.

"We only met once."

"Once?" Mary was ironic. Her chin lifted slightly. Ralston Forbes grinned. He was seeing Mary Blake jealous for the first time and it amused him.

Angie was suddenly aware. She smiled beautifully. "Isn't once enough?"

"I suppose it is," Mary replied stiffly, "but if I were you, Angie, I'd be careful. You know how these drifting punchers are."

"No." Angie's voice was deadly sweet. "You tell me. How are they, Mary?"

Mary Blake's face went white and she started from her chair. "What do you mean by that?" she flared. "What are you trying to insinuate?"

Angie's surprise was eloquent. "Why nothing! Nothing at all, Mary! Only you seemed so worried about me, and your advice sounded so—so experienced."

Mary Blake turned abruptly to Forbes, but before she could speak there was a clatter of horses' hoofs. A dozen riders swung to a halt before the door. It smashed open and Lee Fox stepped in. "Where are they? Where's Blaine?"

Angie turned slowly and looked at him, her eyes cool. She said nothing at all. Mary shrugged and walked to the window and Lee's face flamed with anger. He stepped into the room and strode toward Angie. "You!" he shouted, his face contorted. "You just rode in! I seen your horse out here, all lathered! You warned him!"

"And what if I did?" Her eyes blazed. "I should stay here and let an honest man be murdered by a pack of renegade land thieves?"

Lee Fox gasped. His anger rendered him speechless. "Thieves?" He all but screamed the word. "You call us thieves? What about that—that—"

"I call you thieves." Angie said it quietly. "Lee Fox, neither you nor anyone else has one particle of claim to that land, nor to the B-Bar. Both ranches were used by far better men who got here first. You've been snarling like a pack of coyotes around a grizzly for years. Now the bear is dead and you rush in like the carrion hunting scavengers you are, to grab off the ranches they built! You have no vestige of claim on either place except your greed. If anyone has a just claim on the 46 it is Utah Blaine."

"Utah?" Fox was wild, incredulous. "What claim would he have?"

"He was left in charge. That is claim enough. At least," she shrugged, "it is more claim than you have." Her tone changed. "Why don't you be sensible, Lee? Go back to your ranch and be satisfied with what you have while there's still a chance? You don't know what you're doing."

Fox stepped toward her, his eyes glittering. "You—you—" His hand lifted.

"Fox!" Forbes barked the name, and Lee froze, shocked into realization. His eyes swung and stopped. Ralston Forbes held a six-shooter in his hand. "You make another move toward that girl and I'll kill you!"

Fox lowered his hand slowly, controlling himself with an effort. "You keep out of this," he said thickly.

"Fox, you've evidently forgotten how people think of Angie Kinyon in this country. If you struck her your own men would hang you. You'd not live an hour."

"I wasn't goin' to hit her." Fox controlled himself, pressing his lips together. "She ain't got no right to talk that way."

"When your common sense overcomes your greed, Fox, you'll see that every word she said was truth. Furthermore," Forbes said quietly, "I intend to print just that in my paper tomorrow!"

Fox's eyes were ugly. "You do an' I'll smash that printin' press an' burn you out! You been carryin' it high an' mighty long enough. There's a new system comin' into bein' around here. If you don't think like we do, we'll either change you or kill you!"

Forbes was tall. He looked taller now. "That's your privilege to try, Fox. But I wouldn't if I were you. There are some things this country won't tolerate. Abuse of a good woman and interference with a free press are two of them."

Fox stared at Mary Blake. He started to speak, then turned abruptly and strode from the room. Then there was a rattle of horses' hoofs and they were gone.

"Thanks, Rals," Angie said. "He would have hit me."

Forbes nodded. "And I'd have killed him. And I've never killed a man, Angie."

"At least," Angie said, "Blaine will have more of a start. They'll not catch him now."

"No."

Mary Blake turned from the window. "What about you, Rals? You'd better not try to fight them. You're all alone here."

"Alone?" Forbes shook his head. "No, I'm not alone. There's a dozen men here in town who'll stand by me: Ryan, the blacksmith, Jordan, the shoemaker, all of them."

————

IT WAS ONLY an hour later that news reached Red Creek of the attack on the Big N. Ben Otten was in the cafe talking to Forbes when a Big N hand came in. They listened to Rocky White's recital of what had happened. Ten tons of hay gone! Although worth twenty-five dollars a ton now, the hay would be priceless before the coming winter was gone.

And the ranch house had been shot up. More and

more he was beginning to realize that once trouble was started anything could happen. He tried his coffee and stared glumly out the window.

Rocky White said nothing for a few minutes. Then he commented, "The Old Man's fit to be tied. He's sure cuttin' capers over this shootin'. I wonder what he figured would happen when he braced Utah Blaine? Lucky the man isn't an out an' out killer. He'd have killed Nevers by now."

"What's Nevers goin' to do?" Otten asked.

"He's importin' gunmen. He's goin' to hunt Blaine down an' kill him. He's sent Witter after some gunslingers. He's goin' to offer a flat thousand for Blaine's scalp, five hundred for the other two. Five hundred each, that is."

"That will blow the lid off. We'll have a United States Marshal in here."

The cowhand got up. "Yeah, an' a good thing, too," he said. "Well, so long." He glanced around. "I'm draggin' my freight. I want no part of it."

———

THE LEAVE-TAKING OF Rocky White created a restlessness among the other hands. Two of Otten's oldest cowhands suddenly pulled out without even talking to him, leaving wages behind. A man quit Fox the same way. In the meanwhile, however, men came in to replace them, five of them were gunfighters.

Now the chase was growing intense. One by one the waterholes were being located and men were staked out near them. Blaine found that Rice's cabin was no longer safe. It was being watched. Even the corral back in the brush had been located and was under constant observation. Blaine struck Fox's Table Mountain outfit at midnight on the third day after the Big N raid. Only two men were at home. They were tied up, the horses were turned loose and driven off, the water trough ripped out and turned over, the corral burned.

Clell Miller and Timm exchanged shots but both missed. Rip Coker came upon one, Pete Scantlin, an Indian tracker working for Nevers's manhunters. The Indian had his eyes on the ground. He looked up suddenly and saw Rip sitting his horse, and the Indian threw up his rifle. His shot went wild when Rip's .44 ripped through his throat. The body was found an hour later. Written in the dust alongside the body were the words:

NO QUARTER FOR MANHUNTERS.
YOU ASK FOR IT, YOU GET IT.

Soon after two of Nevers's gunhands shot up Red Creek while on a drunken spree, wounding one bystander with flying glass. Forbes's paper came out on schedule with a headline that shouted to the world and all who would read:

LAWLESSNESS RAMPANT IN VALLEY.
ATTEMPTED LAND GRAB BY NEVERS,
FOX AND OTTEN LEADS TO KILLINGS

That night men with sledge hammers broke into his printing office and smashed one of his presses. Forbes's arrival with a smoking gun drove them off. His ire fully roused now, the following morning

Forbes mailed copies of the paper, of which only a few had been left unburned, to the governor of the territory, to the United States Marshal and to newspapers in El Paso, Santa Fe and other western towns.

However, following the Fox raid no word came from Blaine. The rumor spread that he was wounded. The death of Scantlin was attributed to Blaine until Rip Coker drifted into town.

He came riding in just before closing time at the Verde Saloon. He pushed through the doors and walked to the bar. His face was drawn, his eyes sparking and grim. He tossed off a drink and turned to face the half-dozen men in the room. "Folks say Utah killed Pete Scantlin. It wasn't Utah. It was me. Utah can stand for his own killin's, I stand for mine. He was huntin' me down like a varmint, so I rode out an' gave him his chance. He lost."

"You better ride, Rip. Clell's huntin' you."

"Huntin' me? Where is he?"

"In his room over at the hotel," somebody said. "But you . . . you better—" The speaker's voice broke sharply off for Clell Miller stood in the doorway.

Miller's face had sharpened and hardened. His eyes were ugly and it was obvious that he had been drinking—not enough to make him unsteady, but more than enough to arouse all his latent viciousness.

"Huntin' me, Rip?" Clell stepped in and let the door close behind him. "I saw you ride in. Thought I'd come down."

"Sure, I'm huntin' you." Rip Coker stepped away from the bar. His thin, hard-boned face was drawn and fine from the hard riding and short rations, but his smile was reckless and eager. "You want it now?"

"Why not?" Clell went for his gun as he spoke and it came up, incredibly fast, faster than that of Rip Coker. His first shot struck Rip right over the belt buckle and Rip took an involuntary step back. Clell fired again and missed, but Rip steadied his hand before he fired. His shot spun Miller around. Miller dropped to one knee and fired from the floor. His second shot hit Rip, and then Rip brought his gun down and shot twice, both bullets hitting Clell in the head. Clell fell over, slammed back by the force of the bullets.

Rip staggered, his face pale. He started, staggering for the door. As he stepped out, a voice from across the street called out. "We get five hundred for you Rip!" And then a half-dozen guns went off. Slammed back into the wall by the force of the bullets, Rip brought up his own gun. His knees wavered, but he stiffened them. He was mortally wounded, but he straightened his knees and fired. A man staggered and went down, and Rip fired again. Bullets struck him, but he kept feeding shells into his gun.

Shot to doll rags, he would not go down. He fired again and then again. Somebody up the street yelled and then another ragged volley crashed into the blond fighter. He fired again as he fell, and one of the killers rose on his toes and fell headlong.

Forbes rushed from the hotel, Mary Blake and Angie following him. Ben Otten and others began to crowd around. Rink Witter pushed through the crowd. "Back off," he snarled. "If this varmint ain't dead, he soon will be!"

Forbes looked at him, his face drawn in hard lines in the light from the Verde window. "Leave him alone, you murderer!" he said. "You've done enough!"

Rink Witter's eyes glittered and he looked down. The doctor had come up and was kneeling over Coker. Coker's eyes fluttered and he looked up at Witter. Suddenly, the dying man chuckled. "Wait! Wait!" he whispered hoarsely. "You're dead, Rink! Wait'll Blaine hears of this! He'll hang up your scalp!"

"Shut up!" Witter snarled.

Rip grinned weakly. "Not—not bad," he whispered, "I got Clell. Nev—figured—I'd—I'd beat him."

The bartender, an admirer of gameness in any man, leaned over. "You can go happy, son," he said. "You got two more to take along."

Rip put a feeble hand on the doctor's arm. "You—wastin' time, sawbones." He blinked slowly. "Clell an' two more! Hell, I don't reckon Utah could of done much better!"

The doctor straightened slowly and looked over at Forbes. "I can't understand it," he whispered. "He's shot to ribbons. He should be dead."

Angie moved in. "Carry him to my room, Doc. He's got nerve enough for two men. Maybe he'll come through."

By mid-morning the story was all over the valley. Rip Coker had shot it out with Clell Miller and killed him. Staggering from the saloon, badly wounded, he had been ambushed by six gunmen, had killed two of them before going down under a hail of bullets. Although shot eleven times, he was still alive!

"He might make it," Forbes told Angie. "Cole

Younger was shot eleven times in the fighting during and after the Northfield raid, and he lived."

"Yeah," the bartender was listening. "I was tendin' bar in Coffeyville when the Daltons raided it. Emmett was shot *sixteen* times in that raid. Hear he's still alive."

———

Utah Blaine had been scouting the 46 range. When he returned to their temporary hideout in The Gorge near Whiterock Mesa, Timm came down to him, his face dark with worry. "See anything of Rip?" he asked. "He took off when I was asleep last night. Never said a word."

Blaine swung down. His jaws were dark with four days' growth of beard, his eyes hollow from lack of sleep. "That damn' fool!" he said anxiously. "He's gone huntin' a fight! Saddle up an' we'll ride in!"

"No," Timm said, "you get some rest. If Rip is still alive now, he'll stay alive. You go down there like you are and you'll be duck soup for whoever runs into you first. Get some sleep."

It was wise advice and Blaine knew it. In a matter of minutes he was asleep. Timm looked down at his face and shook his head. Slowly, he walked out in the sunlight and sat among the rocks where he could watch both approaches to The Gorge. There was small chance of their being found here, but it could happen. He was tired himself, when he thought about it. Very tired.

Far down on the riverbank, an Apache signaled to Rink, motioning him over. "One horse," the Indian said. "He ver' tired—cross here."

"A big horse?" Witter asked eagerly.

"Uh-huh, ver' big."

Blaine's dun stallion, the lineback stallion, was larger than most of the horses around here. Rink Witter rubbed his jaw thoughtfully and squinted his glittering little eyes as he studied the terrain before him. The great triangular bow of the mesa jutted against the skyline some three miles away. It was all of fifteen hundred feet above them, and the country to both left and right was broken and rugged. A man on a tired horse would not go far, and a man who was exhausted, as Utah Blaine must be, would have to bed down somewhere. Nor would he be watching the covering of his trail so carefully.

"Let's shake down those canyons left of the mesa," he said, "I've got a hunch."

Slightly less than six miles away, Timm sat in the warm sunshine. He was very tired. The warmth seeped through his weary muscles, easing them and relaxing them. Below him a rattler crawled into the shade and a deer walked down to a pool of water and drank. Timm shifted his seat a little, but did not open his eyes.

It felt mighty good to be resting. Mighty good. And it was warm after the chill of the night. His eyelids flicked open, then lowered...closed...they started to open...then closed again. Timm was not as young as Rip or Blaine. This riding took its toll. Slowly, his eyes closed tighter and he slept.

CHAPTER 12

THE MOUNTAINS INTO which Rink Witter led his four men were rugged and heavily wooded. Skirting the lower shoulder of a mesa, he headed across an open stretch of exposed Coconino sandstone and swung back toward the river.

Ceaselessly he searched out the possible hideouts that could be used by two exhausted men and their worn mounts. North of the towering wall of the mesa there were a half-dozen deep canyons. Each of these canyons had occasional seeps from intermittent streams where a man might obtain water.

Even without a cache of food there was game back here: deer, elk, bear and plenty of birds. A man could scarcely ask for a better hideout. Rink was in no hurry. Hunched atop his horse, he studied the terrain with his flat-lidded eyes. Trust Blaine to pick a hole with a back way out. Yet if they took their time, Blaine might relax. He was tired. He had to be tired. And after a few minutes he would relax and sink down, and possibly he would go to sleep.

Wardlaw, one of Rink's special men, studied the terrain with care. "Country for an ambush," he commented. "This Blaine ain't no tenderfoot."

It was nearing sundown before they completed an examination of the two canyons to their north and started up the main canyon called The Gorge, which led almost due east. They had gone scarcely a half mile when the tracker lifted a hand. Plain enough for all to see were the marks of a horse crossing a stream.

All drew up. Wardlaw struck a match and squinted past the smoke at Rink. "Figure it's far?"

Rink looked speculatively up The Gorge. "This canyon," he told them, "takes a sharp turn about two miles east. My guess would be they'll be located right up there at the foot of Whiterock Mesa. There's an undercut wall there, plenty of firewood an' good water.

"I say," he continued, "that we take her mighty easy. If we come along quiet we may come right up on them."

———

Timm CAME AWAKE with a start, horrified at what he had done. Hours must have passed for it was already past sundown. He started to move, and then he stopped. Not sixty yards away were Rink Witter and his killers!

They saw him at the same instant. Wardlaw's gun leaped and blazed. The shot sprinkled rock on Timm, and he swung his rifle. His own quick shot would have taken Rink but for the fact that the gelding Rink rode chose that instant to swing his head and the shot took him between the eyes. The horse went down, creating momentary confusion, but Wardlaw fired again, knocking Timm back into the rocks. Rolling over, he started to crawl.

Utah came out of his sound sleep wide awake. He sprang to his feet and threw himself into the shelter of a rock before he realized the shooting was centering about a hundred yards away. Hastily he swung saddles on the two horses and cinched them. Then he threw the packs on. It was the work of a minute for all had been kept ready for instant travel.

He heard another shot behind him and knew that for the moment Timm was doing all right. But Blaine also knew they couldn't hold this spot longer than a few minutes. However, it was, fortunately, close to night. He left the horses standing and raced down the short canyon to the main branch. The first thing he saw was Timm. The older man was crouched by some boulders, his rifle ready, his back stained with blood. That the man was hard hit, Utah saw at once.

Sliding up beside him, he whispered, "Stay in there, partner!"

Timm's face was agonized. "I went to sleep!" he was shocked with the shame of it.

Blaine grinned. "Hell, you couldn't have seen 'em until they were right on you, anyway!" The Apache showed and Blaine burned him with a shot across the shoulder, then slammed a fast shot at a shelving rock that ricocheted the bullet into the shelter taken by the killers. Lead smashed around him.

He glanced at Timm. Hard hit he was, but he was still able to move. "Start crawlin'," he said. "I took time to saddle the horses. Get to 'em, an' if you can, get into the saddle."

Utah shifted left and fired, then shifted back halfway to his original position and fired again. A shrewd and experienced Indian fighter, he knew just exactly what their chances were. The men against them were bloodhounds, and fighting men, too. They would be on the trail and fast, and they were men one couldn't gamble with.

Suddenly, a shot clipped rock near him, and he noticed where it came from. Right up from behind a boulder on a steep slope. The boulder was propped by a small rock while behind it was piled a heap of debris. Snuggling his rifle against his shoulder, he took careful aim at the rock, then fired!

The rock splintered and the boulder sagged. Carefully, Blaine took another sight, and then fired again. He never knew whether it was the first shot or the second that started it, but just as his finger squeezed off that second shot the whole pile tore loose and thundered down the hill!

There was a startled yell, then another. Two men sprang into the open and with calm dispatch, Utah Blaine drilled the first through the chest, and dropped the second with a bullet that appeared to have struck his knee. The rocks roared down, swung sharply as they struck a shoulder of rock, then poured down into the streambed.

Swiftly, before the manhunters would have time to adjust themselves, Utah turned and raced back up the canyon to the horses. Timm was in the saddle, slumped over the pommel. His rifle was on the ground. Picking it up, Utah dropped it in the bucket and they started. He led Timm's horse and went right straight for a dim mountain trail between huge boulders. Beyond it there was brush. The shadows were heavy now and it would soon be dark. With an occasional glance back at the wounded man, he rode swiftly.

Now they climbed through the pines, mounting

swiftly on a winding, switchback trail. Darkness filled the bowl of the valley below and the dark gash of the canyon; it bulked thick and black under the tall pines. Beyond them, far to the south, the sunlight lay a golden glory on the four peaks of the Mazatzals.

With a mile more of the winding mountain trail behind him, he turned into the pine forest and crossed the thick cushioned needles and then took a trail that dipped down into the basin of Rock Creek. Instead of following it south toward their cached food and ammunition, Utah turned left and went up the canyon of Rock Creek itself. Then he crossed a saddle to another creek.

Glancing back, seeing that Timm was still in the saddle, he grimly pushed on. Hours later, and then he sighted his objective: a canyon crossed by a natural bridge of rock. Dipping deep into this canyon he worked his way along it until he reached the caves of which, long since, he had heard described.

When he stopped Timm swayed and Utah reached up and lifted the older man from the saddle. Timm's face was pale, visible even in the vague light near the cave's mouth. "I stuck it, didn't I?" he whispered, then fainted.

There was a sand floor in one of the caves, and Blaine led the horses there. He drew them well back from the entrance and out of sight; then he built a fire. No one could ever find them here.

When water was hot he uncovered Timm's wounds and bathed them carefully. The older man was hard hit, and how he had stayed so long in the saddle was nothing short of a miracle. Carefully, he bandaged the wounds and then sat beside the old man and prepared food.

Outside, the air was damp and there was a hint of coming rain. He listened to the far-off rumble of thunder and was thankful for the shelter of the cave. The rain, if it came, would wipe out their tracks.

On the adverse side, they were far from their caches of food and Timm was in no shape to be moved. Moreover, wherever he was, Rip Coker might be needing them. Timm stirred and muttered, and then moaned softly. He looked bad, but there was no medicine ... suddenly from the dark archives of memory came a thought ... something he had not remembered in years.

Going to the sack of maize carried for horse feed, he took out several cups' full. Making a grinding stone of a flat rock, he crushed the maize to meal and then made a mush which he bound on the wound. This was, he recalled, an Indian remedy that he had seen used long ago. Then he made a like poultice for the other wound. When next he walked to the cave entrance he saw the rain pouring down past the opening. Luckily, the entrance of the cave was high enough so that water could not come into the cave mouth.

The horses pricked their ears at him and he curried them both, taking time out to walk back to his patient. Finally Timm awakened. Supporting him with a raised knee, Utah fed him slowly from a thick hot soup he had made from maize and jerky. Timm was conscious but had no knowledge of where he was.

When finally the old-timer dozed off again, Utah walked to the cave mouth. The stream had risen and was washing down the canyon bottom deep enough to wipe out any tracks made there, and probably it would erase the tracks left on the high ground as well. Seeing driftwood just beyond the cave mouth, Utah gathered some of it and dragged it inside where it would have a chance to dry. Then he returned to his patient and changed the maize poultice on the wounds. Then adding fuel to the fire so that it would continue to give off a low flame, he rolled up in his own blankets and slept.

Blaine prepared some breakfast and used the last of the maize for a new poultice. Timm seemed a little better. He ate some of the grub, and seemed in improved spirits.

"Not bad," he said, grinning. "My old lady couldn't've done better."

"Didn't know you were married, Timm."

"I'm not no more. Amy died . . . cholera."

"Too bad."

Timm said nothing and Utah Blaine got to his feet. "Will you be all right? I want to hunt some herbs that may help those wounds."

"Go ahead."

Blaine started for the cave mouth and then looked back. Timm was staring after him. "Utah," his voice shook a little, "you—you—think we'll ever get back? You think—" His voice trailed weakly off.

"We'll get back, Timm," Blaine promised, "you'll be back on the old job again."

"Reckon I'd rather work for you," Timm said quietly. "I reckon I would."

It was an hour before Utah returned. In his arms he had a stack of herbs used by the Indians to doctor wounds and—he stopped. "Timm?"

There was no reply. Blaine dropped his load and rushed forward. He needed only a glance.

Timm was dead. He had died quietly, smiling a little.

Utah Blaine looked down at him. "I'd like to have had you work with me. You were a good man, Timm. A mighty good man."

Wearily, he gathered up the guns and ammunition. And now he was alone . . . Alone. And somewhere out there they were hunting him. Hunting him like a wild animal.

CHAPTER 13

DESPITE HER WORRY over Utah Blaine, Angie had not returned to her small home. So she was standing in the hotel with Rals Forbes when they saw Rink Witter come in. Two men rode with him, and two more were across their saddles. One of the riding men was wounded. Her face stiff, Angie looked down upon the little cavalcade.

Forbes turned abruptly. "I'm going down there. I'm going to find out what happened."

Angie followed him, walking quickly. Slowly, the street began to fill. Nevers was in town this morning as was Lee Fox. Lud Fuller was also there, his face somber. Fuller never talked these days.

Ben Otten came down the street and stopped beside Nevers. He looked up at Rink, feeling the cruelty in that dark, leather-like face. "No," Witter said, "we didn't get Blaine. He got away an' took Timm with him, but I think Timm was bad hurt. We trailed 'em over Whiterock Mesa but lost 'em near Rock Creek. He was headed south toward the Mazatzals, but he couldn't have gone that far, not with Timm hurt an' his horses tired."

"You lost some men."

Rink Witter turned to Forbes, who made the statement. "Huntin' Blaine ain't no picnic," he said harshly.

"They killed two men for me an' one horse. An' Wardlaw's wounded."

Rink swung to the ground. "Utah's an Injun on the trail," he said flatly, stating a fact. "He don't leave no more trail 'n wolf."

"You think you got Timm?" It was Fox who asked the question.

Witter nodded. "Figure so."

"Then Blaine's alone," Nevers said, "he'll quit."

Lud Fuller stirred. "He won't quit. I seen him fight Ortmann. He don't know what the word means."

Nevers glared at Fuller. Then he turned and moved toward the hotel. "Come in, Rink. We'll make talk."

Forbes turned and looked at Angie. "What can we do?" he said. "It's plain hell to want to do something and have your hands tied. My press is coming around, but I doubt if I'll get more than one paper off before they bust it up again."

"I wish the governor would write."

"He probably threw the paper away."

Mary Blake came down the street, switching her leg with a quirt. She stopped, looking from one to the other. "He's out there," she said. "I'm going looking for him."

"You'd better leave him alone," Angie replied shortly. "That's all he'd need would be a woman leading Rink Witter to him."

"I'll find him. And Rink Witter won't trail me, either. I can lose him."

"Coker and now Timm. He's all alone out there."

"It's not your fight," Mary said quietly. "There's no reason for you to worry."

Angie made no reply, turning slightly to look at

Forbes. She looked down the street. A tall man in black was walking up from the station. He carried a carpetbag in his right hand. He paused, then came on over to where they stood. He was a gray-haired man with sharp, quick eyes.

"How do you do?" he said. "I am George Padjen, attorney-at-law. May I ask to whom I am speaking?"

"I'm Ralston Forbes." Forbes's eyes smiled. "I was the local editor until my press was smashed up." Suddenly his interest quickened. "You're not from the governor?"

"No," the man smiled, "I'm not. I was told that I should be very careful about who I talked to, but your name was on the favorable list."

"May I introduce Miss Kinyon? And Miss Blake?"

Padjen removed his hat with a flourish, then looked at Forbes. "Where's Utah Blaine? Is he on the 46?"

Briefly, Forbes outlined the events of the past few days: the fight with Ortmann, the attack on Blaine at the ranch, the escape and the killing of Kelsey and then of Coker and the probable killing of Timm.

"But you said Coker was still alive?" Padjen objected.

Forbes smiled wryly. "As a matter of fact, he is. However, the man hasn't a chance. The doctor has been expecting him to die ever since he was shot. Somehow he has hung on. But as far as Utah goes, Coker might as well be dead. He's out of the running."

"My news seems to be important then," Padjen said quietly. "Before Joe Neal returned here he came to me and made a will. If anything happened to him the ranch was to go to Blaine."

"What?" Forbes's shout turned heads. "You're telling the truth?"

"I am."

Forbes grabbed his arm. "Come on then!" Quickly he rushed him down to the newspaper office. "This," he said, "I'll set up and run off by hand!"

With both girls helping and Padjen explaining further details, Rals Forbes stripped off his coat and went to work. Quickly, he ran off twenty handbills. They carried the story in short, concise sentences following a scarehead in heavy black type.

!!!JOE NEAL WILLS 46 TO BLAINE!!!

According to a will filed for probate in El Paso, Joe Neal willed the 46 Connected with all cattle, horses and appurtenances thereto to Utah Blaine, to take effect immediately upon his death. THIS DEFINITELY THROWS OUT ANY CLAIMS TO THIS RANGE ADVANCED BY THE ASSOCIATED RANCHERS WHO HAVE ATTACKED AND KILLED HANDS FROM THE 46 AND B-BAR RANCHES.

According to the terms of the will Blaine may never sell, lease, or yield up any rights or privileges of the 46 to any of the ranchers now in the valley. THE LAST SHADOW OF A CLAIM MADE BY THESE RANCHERS IS NOW REMOVED AND IF THEY PERSIST IN THESE MURDEROUS ATTACKS THEY WILL BE OUTLAWS AND MUST BE TREATED AS SUCH!

Padjen grinned and looked up at Forbes. "If you tack these up you'd better barricade yourself or leave town!"

Forbes nodded ruefully. "I've been thinking of that, believe me, I have!" Then he looked up at them and picked up some handbills. "Hell, I asked for it," he said, "here goes!"

Padjen's eyes twinkled. He shifted his gun to the front and picked up a few of the remaining handbills and walked out.

Angie moved slowly from the building and stood on the street. She knew now what would happen. Or she believed she did. For what else could happen? Nevers had gone too far to back up now. So had Fox. They had killed men, killed them unjustly; killed them in a wild grab for range. Now the last vestige of right had been taken from them. They had no shadow of legality to their claims, yet had they ever had such a right where the B-Bar was concerned? And now the 46 Connected was definitely Blaine's.

Somewhere out there in the hills Utah was wandering now, perhaps wounded, certainly hungry. Could Mary Blake reach him without leading Witter to Blaine? No, not even if she knew right where to go. She was not skillful enough. But this was not true of Angie. She did know...she turned abruptly and walked swiftly down the street.

————

FAR BACK IN the hills near the caves, Utah Blaine finished his burial of Timm. Over the grave he said a few simple words, and then he gathered a few flowers and planted them near the crude cross he had made.

He stepped back and looked at the grave. "See you, Timm!" He turned and walked to his horse. Mounting, with Timm's horse behind him, he started southwest down Pine Canyon. For the first time in his life he was going on the hunt. He was going to seek out three men and kill them.

Blaine rode swiftly. When he had covered five miles, he shifted horses and rode Timm's gelding. In this manner he pushed on through the night, holding his gait steady, and averaging a good eight to ten miles an hour over all kinds of country. At daybreak he released Timm's horse, retaining only the old-timer's guns. He now had two rifles, a shotgun and three pistols—all loaded.

Yet he needed food. It had been days since he had enjoyed a decent meal and Angie's cabin was only a few miles north. He turned the lineback north along the river trail. Not more than an hour after daybreak he rode up to the cabin. The first thing he saw was the thin trail of smoke from the kitchen chimney. The second was the saddled horse standing at the corral gate.

Riding his own horse into the pines behind the cabin, he tied it there and then, with the shotgun in his hands, he worked his way forward under the trees. When he reached the big sycamore under which he and Angie had talked, he paused and made a careful survey of all the ground in sight. He found no tracks but those of the girl and her horse. Warily, he looked over the terrain beyond the river. Only then did he walk up to the door. He opened it and stepped inside.

Angie was dressed for riding and she was working swiftly. Only one plate was on the table.

"Got a couple of more eggs, Angie?"

She turned swiftly, her eyes large with shock. "Utah! Oh, thank God! You're here! You're all right!"

"Don't tell me you were worried?" He looked at her somberly. "Were you leaving?"

"To look for you. Utah, Neal's will has been probated in El Paso. He left the ranch to you. Everything to you."

Utah Blaine stared at her. "To *me*? Are you sure?"

"Yes." Quickly, as she put on more eggs, she explained. She gave him the details of the will as she had them from Padjen; she told him what Forbes had done.

Then, "Utah, where's Timm?"

"I buried him at sundown. He was wounded in the Whiterock fight. Have you seen Coker?"

She told him about Rip Coker's desperate fight in town, his killing of Clell Miller and two other men. "And he's still living. He hasn't been conscious for days, but he's alive. The doctor says it isn't reasonable, that he's shot full of holes, and he gave him up days ago—but he still lives."

"You were coming to tell me about Neal's will?" He studied her over the rim of his coffee cup. "What else?"

"Nothing, except—except—Mary's been worried about you, Utah. She was going to ride out." She hesitated. "Are you in love with her, Utah?"

"With Mary?" He was surprised. Angie's back was turned to him and he could not see her face. "Now whatever gave you an idea like that?"

She put eggs and ham on his plate, then a stack of toast. He ate and forgot everything in the wonderful taste of food. For several minutes he said nothing. When he did look up, he grinned, a little ashamed. "Gosh, I was sure hungry! Say, is there a razor in the house?"

"Dad's razor is here. I've kept a few of his things. His razor, his gun—" She went to get it, and while he shaved, she talked.

She watched the razor scrape the lather and thick whiskers from his jaw. It was a long time since she had seen a man shave. She noted how broad his shoulders were. Hurriedly she got up and walked to the door, looking carefully down the trail, then across the river.

"What will they do, Utah? Will they keep after you?"

He turned and looked at her, holding the razor in his hand. For an instant their eyes met and she looked away quickly, flushing and feeling an unaccountable pounding in her breast.

Her question was forgotten. Slowly, he walked over and stood behind her. "Angie..." He took hold of her shoulder with his left hand. "Angie, I think..." She turned, her eyes large, dark and frightened. His hand slipped down to her waist and drew her to him, and then he bent and kissed her parted lips. She gave a little muffled gasp and clutched him tightly. Neither of them heard the sound of the approaching horse. It was the step on the porch that startled them apart. As one person they turned toward the door.

Mary Blake stood there, her hat in her hand, her face flushed from the wind. Her eyes went from Utah to Angie and her nostrils widened a little. "Well,

Angie," she said with an edge in her tone, "I see you got here first!"

"Why—why, I just came home! I—"

"You'd look better," Mary said, "if you'd wipe the lather off your chin, Angie. Or have you taken to shaving?"

"Oh!" Angie gasped and ran for a mirror.

Utah chuckled suddenly. "Hello, Mary. It's rather a surprise seeing you here."

"So I gathered," Mary said dryly. "And if you don't hurry and get out of here you'll get another surprise. Rink Witter isn't far behind me."

CHAPTER 14

"RINK IS COMING?"

"Yes, but Nevers will be here first, I think. Rink turned from the trail to do a little scouting. Wardlaw is with him, and Lud Fuller."

"And with Nevers?"

"A half-dozen of his riders."

Utah Blaine turned and picked up his hat. "Both of you stay here. I'll manage all right."

He walked outside and around the house. When he reached the stallion, he untied it and led the horse through the trees to the house. The horse had been cropping grass and now he let him drink, but only a little.

When he saw the dust cloud he swung into the saddle and rode down to the ford of the river. The river here was some twenty yards wide and, at the ford, about stirrup deep. He stopped in a grove of trees leaving his horse back out of range in a sheltered hollow.

He saw the riders swing around the bend of the river and come toward him. He let them come while he sat on a rock and smoked a cigarette. When the riders were three hundred yards off he propped his knee on another boulder and lifted the rifle, getting his elbow well under the barrel. Nestling his cheek against the barrel he aimed at Nevers. His intention was not to kill the man. Yet at the moment he was supremely indifferent. If the horse bobbed at the wrong time—he fired.

His intention had been to clip Nevers's ear, and he had held Nevers under his sights as the distance closed. Nevers jerked and clapped a hand to his head and Blaine heard his cry of anguish and could see the blood streaming down the side of his face.

Instantly, there was a hail of bullets and men scattered. Blaine began to fire. One man was diving for cover and Utah shot him through the legs. His second put Nevers's horse down and Nevers was pinned beneath it. Then Blaine fired again, kicking dirt into Nevers's eyes.

"Want to die, Nevers? You bring other men out to fight your dirty battles! How do you like it?"

He fired again, deliberately missing but putting the shot close. "Get dust in your eyes, Nevers? This'll be better!" Blaine fired again, his bullet striking into the sand square in front of Nevers's face. Sand spat into the rancher's eyes.

Blaine waited an instant, then called out, "The rest of you stay out of this an' you won't get hurt. One of you pull that man in and fix up his leg! Go ahead! I won't shoot!"

A cowhand ran out and picked up the wounded man and started back. Blaine held his fire. He heard Nevers yell from the ground. "Go get him, you fools!! Get after him!"

Utah laughed. "I never saw you come after me, Nevers! Not without plenty of help!" He threw another shot close to Nevers. "I'll kill the first man who shows himself on the bank of this stream!"

He took his time, his eyes roving restlessly to prevent a flanking movement. He had a hunch none of the hands were too anxious to come across the river under fire. After all, Nevers had gunmen to do his killing—men who were getting paid warrior's wages. Anyway, probably few of them disliked to see their boss pinned down and scared—and Nevers was scared.

Without help he could not escape from the dead horse, and Utah Blaine could kill him any time he wished.

"You had Timm killed," Blaine said conversationally. "You had Coker shot up, an' you've hired murderers to get me. You were one of the lynchers who tried to hang Joe Neal an' by all rights I should shoot you full of holes."

Nevers did not speak. He lay still. Now he was aware that Blaine did not intend to kill him. Frightened as he had at first been, he was remembering that not far behind him were Rink Witter and his killers. They would hear the shooting and would know what to do.

Blaine fired again, and then he faded back into the brush and ran to his stallion. Keeping the lineback to soft sand where he made no noise, he circled swiftly and raced the horse for the river. Crossing it, he headed for the trail to head off Witter. He was coming down the mountain through the trees when suddenly he heard a yell. Not two hundred yards away, fanning across the hillside were a dozen riders! It needed only a glance to tell him that these were Fox and his men.

Snapping a quick shot, Utah wheeled the stallion

and plunged down the trail. He was just in time to intercept Witter—but this wasn't the way he had planned it. The surprise was complete. He charged down the mountain and hit the little cavalcade at full speed. They had no chance to turn or avoid him: his stallion was heavier and had the advantage of speed. With his bridle reins around his arm, Blaine grabbed a six-shooter and blasted.

A man screamed and threw up his arms and then Blaine hit him. Horses snorted and there was a wild scramble that was swamped with dust. Through the group the lineback plunged and Blaine had a glimpse of Rink Witter's contorted face as the gunman clawed for a pistol. Blaine swung at the face with the barrel of his six-gun, but the blow was wide and the back of his fist smashed into the seamed, leathery face. Witter was knocked sprawling, and then the lineback was past and heading for the river.

A shot rang out, snapping past him, and then something hit him heavily in the side. His breath caught and he swung the lineback upstream. Then slowing down deliberately and turning up a draw, he doubled back. Every breath was a stab of pain now, but the horse was running smoothly, running as if it was his first day on the trail, and Utah turned for a glance back. Nobody was in sight. He cut up the hill and crossed the saddle into the bed of the dry wash and rode northwest toward the 46 ranch house. It was more than ten miles away, but he headed for it, weaving back and forth across the hills, using every trick he knew to cover his trail.

Twice he had to stop. Once to bandage his wound, another time for a drink. The bullet had hit him hard and he had lost blood. His saddle was wet with it and so was the side of the stallion. Turning west, he skirted the very foot of the mesa and worked toward the ranch house.

As he rode, he thought. They would know he was wounded. He mopped sweat from his face, and saw there was blood on his hand. He rubbed it against his chaps. They would know he was hurt. Now they would be like wolves after a wounded deer. He had planned to come down behind Witter, to disarm the others, then shoot it out with him. But the arrival of Lee Fox had wrecked his plans and now he was in a fix.

He walked the stallion, saving its strength. He checked all his guns, reloading his pistol and rifle. His throat was dry and before him the horizon wavered and danced. It was hot, awfully hot. It couldn't be far to the ranch.

They were after him now, all of them. Rink Witter would now have a personal hatred. He had been struck down, and Nevers had been frightened to death. All of them . . . closing in for the kill. He tried to swallow and his throat was dry. The sun felt unbearably hot and his clothes smelled of stale sweat, and mingled with it was the sickish sweet smell of blood.

He looked down and saw the ranch close by and below him. It looked deserted. Was that a trail of dust he saw? Or were his eyes going bad on him? The heat waves danced and wavered. He turned the lineback down the trail through the woods, and he slumped in the saddle.

A last stand? No, he needed food for the run he

had ahead of him. He had meant to get some from Angie, but his hunters had come too quick.

Angie...how dark her eyes had been! How soft and warm her lips! He had never kissed lips like them before. He remembered his arm about her waist and then he raised his head and saw that the stallion was walking into the ranch yard. He slid from the saddle. How long did he have? Ten minutes...a half hour...an hour?

They would not expect him to come here. They would never expect that. Suddenly the door on the porch pushed open and a man came down the steps. Utah Blaine stopped and squinted his eyes against the sun and the sweat. He saw Lud Fuller.

"Dumb, am I?" That was Lud's voice, all right. "I figured it right! I slipped away! Knowed you'd come here! Knowed you was bad hurt! Well, how does it feel now? Me, Lud Fuller! I'm goin' to kill Utah Blaine!"

Utah wavered and stared through the fog that hung over his eyes. This man—Lud Fuller—he had to kill him. He had to. He gathered his forces while the foreman blustered and triumphed. He stood there, swaying and watching. Fuller had a gun in his hand. Stupid the man might be, but he was not chancing a draw.

Utah Blaine got his feet planted. He smelled again the smell of his stale sweaty shirt and his unwashed body. He peered from under his flat-brimmed hat and then he said, "You're a fool, Lud! You should have gone when I sent you!"

The strength in his voice startled Fuller. The foreman stared, his eyes seemed to widen, and he pushed the gun out in front of him and his finger tightened.

He never saw Blaine draw. Blaine never knew when his hand went for the gun. There had been too many other times, too many years of practice. Wounded he might be, weary he might be, but that was there, yet, the practice and the past. And the need all deepened into a groove of habit in the convolutions of his brain. It was there, beyond the pain, the sweat and the weakness. The sure smooth flashing draw and then the buck of the gun. Fuller's one shot stabbed earth, and Utah Blaine shot twice. Both shots split the tobaccosack tag that hung from Fuller's shirt pocket. The first shot notched it on the left, and the second shot notched it on the bottom. Swaying on his feet, Utah Blaine removed the empties and thumbed shells into his gun.

He did not look down at Fuller. In the back of his mind he remembered those brutal words when Fuller had tried to make Joe Neal die slow. Back there at the lynching—well, Fuller had certainly died fast.

Utah Blaine went into the house and he found a burlap sack in the pantry. He stuffed it with food, anything that came to hand. Then he walked out and looked in the cabinet and found some shells. He took those and put them in the sack, too. He walked out, avoiding Fuller's body and went to the corral.

A big black came toward him, whimpering gently. He put his hand out to the horse's nose, and it nudged at him. He got a bridle on the stallion and led it out. Then he switched saddles and turned the dun into the corral, but before he let the horse go he took an old piece of blanket and rubbed him off with care.

When he had finished that, and when the sack was tied behind the saddle, he bathed his wound. Still watching the trail, he took off the temporary and bloody bandage and replaced it with a new one. He was working on nerve, for he was badly hurt. Yet men had been shot up much worse and had kept moving, had survived. Nobody knew how much lead a man could carry if he had the will to live.

Somehow he kept moving, and then with the saddle on the black, he crawled aboard and started north. The river swung slightly west, he recalled. He could cross it there and get over into broken country to the northeast. As he rode he tied himself to his saddle, aware that he might not be able to stick it.

Not over three miles from the house he struck the river and crossed. There were two peaks on his left and one right of him. The rest of them were ahead. There seemed to be a saddle in front of him and he started the black toward that. Then he blacked out for several miles. When he opened his eyes again, he was slumped over the saddle horn and the horse was walking steadily.

"All right, boy," he said to the horse. "You're fine, old fellow."

Reassured, the horse twitched an ear at him. The sun had set, but there was still some light. Before them the dark hollows of the hills were filled with blackness, and a somber gray lay over the land. The higher peaks were touched with reflected scarlet and gold from the sunset that still found color in the higher clouds.

All was very still. The air felt cool to his lungs and face. He held his face up to the wind and washed it as

with water. His head felt heavy and his side was a
gnawing agony, but before him the land was soften-
ing with velvety darkness, turning all the buffs, rusts
and crimsons of the daylight desert and mountains to
the quietness of night and darkness. Stars came out,
stars so great in size and so near they seemed like
lamps hanging only a few yards away. Off to his right
lifted a massive rampart, a huge black cliff that he remembered as being in some vague account of the
place told him by Neal when they traveled together.
That was Deadman Mesa.

Dead man...he himself might soon be a dead
man...and he had left a dead man behind him.

Dead man...all of them, Rink Witter, Nevers, Lee
Fox and himself, all were dead men. Men who lived
by violence, who lived by the gun.

Swaying in the saddle like a drunken man, he
thought of that, and the names beat somberly
through the dark trails of his consciousness. Rink an'
Nevers an' Fox...Rink...Nevers...Fox...all men
who would die, all men who would die soon...Rink,
Nevers, an' Fox.

The last light faded, the last scarlet swept from the
sky. The dark shadows that had lurked in the lee of
the great cliffs or the deepest canyons, they came out
and filled the sky and gathered close around him with
cooling breath and cooling arms. And the black
walked on, surely, steadily, into the darkness of the
night.

CHAPTER 15

BEN OTTEN HUNCHED gray-faced in his office chair. The bank had closed hours before, but still he sat there, the muscles in his jaw twitching, his stomach hollow and empty. He had the news, what little there was. The lawyer, Padjen, was still in town. He had been retained by Neal, paid in advance, to stand by Utah Blaine.

The twenty handbills posted by Ralston Forbes had been torn from the walls by the order of Nevers, but that did not end the matter and all knew the news. Forbes was barricaded with his printer in the print shop and both men had food, ammunition and shotguns. This time they did not intend to be ejected or to have the press broken.

Mary Blake was back in town with the story of the fight at the Crossing. Rink Witter was around town with his face bandaged because of his broken nose. The smash of Blaine's fist had done that and Blaine was still alive to be hunted down. But the hunters were not having much luck. They had trailed Blaine, finally, to the 46 Connected, but once there all they found was the body of Lud Fuller, dead hours before.

Clell Miller...Lud Fuller...Tom Kelsey...Timm... how many others? And no end in sight, no end at all.

Nevers and Fox had come to the bank that morning. They had served Ben Otten with an ultimatum.

They were all in it, there was no need for him to say he hadn't been. From the first he had known the score, and from the first he had lent tacit support to their plans. He had taken no active part, but the time had come. Either he came in or he was to be considered an enemy.

The prize was rich. More than three hundred thousand acres of rich range—some of it barren desert range—but the remainder well-watered and covered with grass. And the cattle. On the two ranches there must be fifty thousand head, and it was past time for a shipment. Why, there must be four or five thousand head ready for shipping right now! And a big fall shipment, too! No other range this side of the Tonto Basin would support as many cattle as this, and well Otten knew it.

If the combination won their fight, if they took over the two big outfits, they would all be wealthy men. Already two of the men who could have justly claimed shares had been eliminated. Now, if he came in, and they needed him badly, there would be but three. He could figure on a hundred thousand acres of range—more than four times what he already grazed!

All that stood between them and that wealth was one man. If Utah Blaine were killed the opposition would fall apart at the seams. For after all, Blaine had no heirs; the lawyer's part would be fulfilled, and he might take a substantial payment to leave. Mary Blake could be promised and promised and gradually squeezed out of the country with nothing or a small cash payment, which by that time she would probably need desperately.

He knew about that, for Mary Blake had no more

than three hundred dollars in cash remaining in the bank.

Forbes . . . well, Ralston Forbes could be taken care of. With Blaine out of the way it would be nothing for Witter to do. And then the big melon was ready to be cut—the big, juicy melon.

Ben Otten rubbed his jaw nervously. It was a big decision. Once actively in, he could not withdraw, and he was secretly afraid of Lee Fox. Still, the man was wild, erratic. He might get himself killed, and Nevers might, too.

Ben Otten sat up very straight. Nevers and Fox dead! That would mean . . . His lips parted and his tongue touched them, trembling. That would mean that he might have it all, the whole thing!

How to be sure they died? Of course, with Blaine in the field, anything might happen. He had his grudge against them, and he would be seeking them out soon. Blaine had killed Fuller, even though it was known that he was badly wounded. And if Utah Blaine did not? Otten remembered the cold, deadly eyes of Rink Witter . . . for cash . . . a substantial sum . . . such men were without loyalty.

He got to his feet slowly and began to pace the floor, thinking it all out. There remained Rip Coker, but the man could not live. In a pinch he would see that he did not. Yes, it was time for him to get into the game, to start moving . . . but carefully, Ben, he told himself, very, very carefully!

As he turned toward the door he had one moment of realization. It was a flashing glimpse, no more, but something about what he felt then was to remain with him, never to leave him again. He saw in one

cold, bitter moment the eyes of Utah Blaine. He saw
the courage of the man and the hard, driving, indomitable will of him. And he remembered Rip
Coker, his back to the wall that propped him up,
shooting, shooting and killing until he dropped. And
Rip Coker was still clinging to a thin thread of life.

What was there in such men that made them live?
What deep well of stamina and nerve supplied them?
Coker had been deadly, very deadly, but at his worst
he was but a pale shadow of the man known as Utah
Blaine. In that brief instant with his hand on the door
knob, Ben Otten saw those green, hard eyes and felt a
twinge of fear. A little shiver passed through all his
muscles and he felt like a man stepping over his own
grave.

But the moment passed and he went on outside
into the dark street. The lights from the saloon made
rectangles on the street. He saw the darkness of the
print shop down the street where Ralston Forbes
waited with his printing press. Forbes was not
through ... what would he run off next? The stark
courage of those handbills blasting Nevers and Fox
was something he could admire. Forbes had nerve.

He shook his head wearily and pushed open the
door to the saloon. A man turned from the bar to look
at him. It was Hinkelmann, who owned the general
store. As Otten moved up beside him, Hink asked,
"Ben, what do you make of all this? How's it goin' to
turn out? I can't figure who's right an' who's wrong."

"Well," Ben Otten agreed, "I've thought about it
myself." He ordered his drink. "I've known Nevers a
long time. Always treated me all right."

"Yes," Hink agreed reluctantly, "that's right."

"He pays his bills, an' I guess it rankled to see an outsider, a man with Blaine's reputation, come in here and grab off the richest ranch in the place. Although," he added, "Blaine may be in the right...if he and this lawyer aren't in cahoots. After all, Rink killed Neal, but who put him up to it?"

"He's workin' for Nevers," Hinkelmann suggested uneasily.

"Uh-huh, but you never know about a man like that. Offer them the cash an'...sometimes I've wondered just how hard they were tryin' to find Blaine. Doesn't seem reasonable one man could stay on the loose so long."

They talked some more, and after awhile, Otten left. On the steps he paused. Well, he had started it. There was still time to draw back...but deep within him he knew there was no time. Not any more. He was fresh out of time.

LONELY IN HER cabin on the river, Angie turned restlessly, wide-eyed and sleepless in her bed. Somewhere out there in the night her man was riding... wounded...bleeding...alone.

Her man?

Yes. Staring up into the darkness she acknowledged that to herself. He was her man, come what may, if he died out there alone; if he was killed in some hot, dusty street; if he rode off and found some other woman—he was still her man. In her heart he was her man. There was no other and there could be no other and she had felt it deep within her from that moment under the sycamores when first they talked together.

She turned again and the sheets whispered to her body and she could not sleep. Outside the leaves rustled and she got up, lighting her light and slipping her feet into slippers. In her robe she went to the stove and rekindled the fire and made coffee. Where was he? Where out there in the blackness was the man she loved?

Stories traveled swiftly in the range country and she knew all that anyone knew. She knew of the killing of Lud Fuller, of the bitter, brief struggle that preceded it and how Blaine had ridden, shooting and slashing like a madman, through the very middle of Rink Witter's killers. She had heard of Rink's smashed nose, heard of the man screaming his rage and hatred, and of how slowly Blaine would die when he got him.

She had also heard that Utah Blaine was wounded. They had followed him part of the way by the drops of blood. He had been shot, but he had escaped. Had she known where he was, she would have gone to him. Had she had any idea . . . but it was best to remain here. He knew she was here, and here she would stay, waiting for him to come to her. And so he might come.

In the morning she would ride over to the 46 and get the dun stallion. She would bring that powerful black-faced horse back here, and she would feed him well, grain him well, against the time that Blaine would come for him.

At long last she returned to bed and she slept, and in the night the rains came and thunder muttered in the long canyons, grumbling over the stones and in the deep hollows of the night.

During the day she worked hard and steadily, trying to keep occupied and not to think. She cleaned the house, cleaned every room, dusted, swept, mopped, washed dishes that had been washed and never used. She wanted to sew but when sewing she would think and thinking was something she wanted to avoid. She prepared food, put coffee out where he could find it easily if he came, and banked the fire. Then she put on her slicker and saddling her own horse, started for the 46.

She might have trouble there, but the old hands had drifted away and probably nobody would be there. She would get the dun and bring him back. She would also leave a note, somewhere where only he would be apt to find it.

The rain fell in sheets, beating the ground hard. It was not far to the 46, but the trail was slippery and she held her mare down to a walk. Rain dripped from her hat brim and her horse grew dark with it. From each rise she stopped and studied the country. The tops of the mountains were lost in gray cloud that held itself low over the hills. The gullies all ran with water and caused her to swing around to use the safest crossings.

When she saw the 46 she was startled to see a horse standing there. Even as she saw it, a man in a slicker came from the stable and led the horse inside. From the distance she could not recognize him.

Her heart began to pound. She hesitated. No one must realize that she was friendly with Blaine, and it would not do for anyone to know that she had taken the dun to her place. They would watch her at once if they did know.

Keeping to the timber, she skirted the ranch at a distance, never out of sight, watching the stable to see who would emerge. Whoever it was must soon come out and go to the house. In her mind she saw him stripping the saddle off and rubbing the water from the horse. It would be soon now, very soon.

She drew up under a huge old tree that offered some shelter from the rain. The lightning had stopped and the thunder rumbled far away over the canyons back of Hardscrabble and Whiterock. She watched, smelling the fresh forest smells enhanced by rain and feeling the beat of occasional big drops on her hat and shoulders. Nothing happened, and then she saw the man come from the barn. Careful to leave no footprints, he kept to hard ground or rocks as he moved toward the house. There was no way to tell who it was or whether the man carried himself as if wounded.

The dun was standing with the other horses in the corral, tails to the rain, heads down. If that man had been Blaine she wanted desperately to see him. If it was not Blaine, she did not want to be seen but did want to get the dun out of the corral and away. Instinctively she knew that when Blaine could he would come to her. And when he did come she wanted his horse ready for him.

Whoever the man was, he would be watching the trail; so she started her horse and worked a precarious way down the mountain's side through the trees.

Leaving her own horse she slipped down to the side of a big empty freight wagon. Then from behind it, she moved to the stable's back. Through the window her eyes searched until they located the horse. Disappointment hit hard. Although she could not see the brand, the horse was certainly not the big stallion that Utah Blaine was reported to be riding.

The gate to the corral faced the house. There was no use trying to get the dun out that way. If she could only take down the bars to the corral ... They were tied in place by iron-hard rawhide. She dug in her pocket for a knife and at the same time she called.

The dun's head came up, ears pricked. Then curiously he walked across to her. She spoke to him gently and he put his nose toward her inquisitively, yet when she reached a hand for him he shied, rolling his eyes. She had seen Blaine feed him a piece of bread and had come prepared, hoping it would establish them on good terms. She took out the bread and fed it to him. He took it eagerly, touching it tentatively with his lips, then jerking it from her hand.

With careful hands she stroked his wet neck, then got a hackamore on him. Knife in hand she started to saw at the rawhide thongs.

"I wouldn't," a soft voice said, "do that!"

She turned quickly, frightened and wide-eyed. Standing just behind her, gun in hand, was Lee Fox! His big eyes burned curiously as they stared at her over the bulging cheekbones of his hard, cadaverous face; the eyes of a man who was not mentally normal.

CHAPTER 16

THE BLACK GELDING was sorely puzzled. There was a rider in the saddle but he was riding strangely and there was no guiding hand on the reins. It was the black's instinct to return home, but the rider had started in this direction and so the horse continued on. As it walked memories began to return. Three years before it had known this country. As it sensed the familiarity of the country, its step quickened.

The memory of the black was good. This way had once been home. Maybe the rider wanted to go back. The gelding found its way through a canyon and found a vague trail leading up country between the mesa on the north and the stream that flowed from the springs.

Utah Blaine opened his eyes. His body was numb with pain and stiff from the pounding of rain. He straightened up and stared. Lightning flashed and showed him why the horse had stopped. On the right was a deep wash, roaring with flood; on the left there was the towering wall of a mesa with only a short, steep slope of talus. Directly in the trail was a huge boulder and the debris that had accompanied it in the slide.

His head throbbed and his hands were numb, and the rawhide binding his wrists to the pommel had cut into the skin. Fumbling with the knots, he got his hands loose and guided the horse forward. The narrow space between the boulder and the trail worried the gelding and it dabbed with a tentative hoof, then drew back, not liking it. "All right, old-timer, we'll try the other side."

On the left was the steep slope of talus, yet at Blaine's word the horse scrambled up and around. Suddenly there was a grinding roar from above them. Frightened, the gelding lunged and Blaine, only half conscious, slid from the saddle. In some half instinctive manner he kicked loose from the stirrups and fell soddenly into the trail.

The deafening roar of the slide thundered in his ears, stones cascaded over him and then dirt and dust. He started to rise, but a stone thudded against his skull and he fell back. The dirt and dust settled, and then as if impelled by the slide, the rain roared from the sky, pelting the trail like angry hail. The black gelding, beyond the slide, waited apprehensively. The trail bothered it, and after a few minutes it started away. Behind in the trail the wounded man lay still, half-buried in mud and dirt.

————

WHEN THE RAIN pelting his face brought him out of it he turned over. Then he got to his knees, pain stabbing him. His head throbbed, and he was caked with mud and dirt. Staggering, he got over the barrier of the second slide. There was no sign of his horse and he walked on, falling and getting up, lunging into bushes, and finally crawling under a huge tree and lying there—sprawled out on the needles, more dead than alive.

There was no dawn, just a sickly yellow through the gray clouds. The black pines etched themselves against the sky, bending their graceful tops eastward. The big drops fell, and the wind prowled restlessly in the tops of the pines. Utah Blaine opened his eyes again, his face pressed to the sodden needles beneath the trees.

Rolling over, he sat up. His wound had bled again and his shirt was stuck to his side with dried blood. His head throbbed and his hair was full of blood and mud. There was a cut on his head where the stone had struck him. He felt for his guns and found them, held in place by the rawhide thongs he wore when riding.

Gingerly his fingers touched the cut and the lump surrounding it. The stone had hit him quite a belt. He struggled to get his feet under him and by clinging to the tree, hauled himself erect. His head spun like a huge top and there was a dull roaring inside his skull. Clinging to the tree, he looked around. There was no sign of the black horse.

He braced himself, then tried a step and managed to stay erect. There was a stream not far away and he made his way to the edge of it. For the time being there was no rain and he dug under a fallen log and peeled some bark from its dry side. Then he found a few leaves that were dry and a handful of grass. The lower and smaller limbs on the trees, scarcely more than large twigs, were dead and dry. These he broke off and soon he had a fire going.

When he had the flames going good he made a pot

of bark and dipped up water. Then he propped the makeshift pot on a couple of stones to boil. His side was one raw, red-hot glow of agony, his head throbbed, and his body was stiff and sore. Removing his handkerchief from his neck he dried it over the fire. Then he took out his right-hand gun and cleaned it with care, wiping off all the shells. By the time that was finished, the gun returned to the holster, the water was boiling.

Soaking the bandage off the wound, he studied it as best he could. The bullet had gone through the flesh of his side just above the right hip bone, but it did not appear to have struck anything vital. His knowledge of anatomy was rusty at best. All he knew was that he had lost plenty of blood. The wound looked angry and inflamed. He began to examine the shrubs and brush close about and all he could find was the *yerba del pescado,* a plant with leaves dark on the upper side and almost white on the lower. Nearby, fortunately, he found its medicinal mate, the *yerba de San Pedro.* He ran his fingers through the leaves beneath them and found some that were partly dry. These he crushed together and placed on the wound after he had carefully bathed it. Then he rearranged the bandages as well as he could and felt better.

The sky was still somber, and he lay back, relaxing and resting. After a few minutes he put out his fire, cleaned his second gun, and got to his feet. How far he could go he did not know, but he was unsafe where he was. If the black returned home they would immediately backtrack the gelding.

The mesa towering south of him would have to be

Deadman, if he had kept on his course. There was no hope of escaping from the canyon now. Not with his present weakness. He would have to continue on. Walking on stones, he worked his way slowly and with many rests up along the canyon. He had to rest every fifty yards or so. But despite that, he covered some distance, his eyes always alert for a cave or other place he could use for a hideout.

Reaching a place where the talus was overgrown with brush and grass, he climbed up among the trees and continued on, keeping away from the trail. It was harder going, but he worked his way higher and higher among the rocks. After awhile he became conscious of a dull roaring sound that he was sure was not imagined. It seemed to increase and grow stronger as he pushed farther along.

Coming through the trees he stopped suddenly, seeing before him a clearing with a pole corral, obviously very old, and a log cabin. Beyond it he could see a spring of white water roaring from the rocks. At the corral he could see the black gelding cropping grass. He came out of the trees and walked toward the cabin, his eyes alert. Yet he saw nothing, and when he came closer he could see no tracks nor any sign of life but the gelding.

The black horse looked up suddenly and whinnied at him. He crossed to it, stripping off the saddle and bridle and turning the gelding into the corral. Then he walked to the cabin, broke the hasp on the door and entered.

Dust lay thick over everything. There were two tiers of bunks, each three high, some benches, a chair and a table. In the fireplace there was wood as if ready for a fire and there were some pots and pans.

He walked again to the door and sat down, his rifle across his knees. Had the gelding returned to the ranch his situation would have been exceedingly precarious by now, but having come here, he knew there could be no vestige of a trail after last night's rain. Obviously nobody had been at this hideout in a long time, no doubt several years, and there was no reason to believe the place was even known of. Neal had known of it, but Neal was a close-mouthed man.

After he had rested, he got to his feet and finding an ancient broom, he swept part of the house, then lit the fire and made coffee. He had plenty of food in the pack on the gelding and he ate his first good meal in hours. Then he rested again, and when he felt better, went outside and looked carefully around. Back up in Mud Tank Draw he found another and better built shack and another corral. Farther from the roaring springs, it was also more quiet, and its position was better concealed.

Catching up the gelding, which was tame as a pony, he went back to Mud Tank Draw and turned the gelding loose in that corral, then transferred his belongings to the second cabin and removed all traces of his stop at the springs. By the time he had completed this, he was physically exhausted. Rolling up in his blankets on one of the bunks, he fell asleep.

When he awakened it was night again and rain was starting to fall. There had been an old stable outside, so donning his slicker he went out and led the gelding into a stall and pulled several armfuls of grass for him. Then he returned again to the shack, made coffee and then turned in again. Almost at once he was asleep.

He awakened with a start. It was morning and then the rain was literally pouring down on the cabin. The roof was leaking in a dozen places, but the area around the fireplace was dry. He moved to it, then broke up an old bench to get the fire hot and started coffee again.

He felt better, yet he was far from well. The wound looked bad, although it did not seem quite so flushed as before. There was no question of going out again, so he dressed the wound with some cloth from his pack and sat back in the chair.

For the first time he began seriously to consider his situation. He was wounded and weak. He had lost a lot of blood. He had ammunition and food, but shooting game to add to the larder would probably only attract attention. For the time being he believed he was safe, insofar as there could be any safety with a bloodhound like Rink Witter on his trail.

Aside from the roof, the cabin was strong and he could withstand a siege here. Yet if he were surrounded they would fire the place and he would be trapped. He would have no more chance than Nate Champion had in the Johnson County War. To be trapped in this cabin would be fatal.

For two days he rested and was secure and then on the third day he saddled the gelding and led him back up the draw at a good point for a getaway. His instinct told him that he should move, and he started back to the crevice in the rocks. He was rolling his bed when he heard the horses.

"I tell you, you're crazy!" It was Nevers's voice. "He'd not be up here!"

"All right, then!" That was Wardlaw speaking. "You tell me where he is!"

"Boss," another voice said, "I see tracks! Somebody's been here!"

"Then it's him! Look sharp!"

Utah Blaine was through running. Dropping his rifle and bedroll he sprang into the open. "Sure, I'm here!" he shouted, and he opened fire with both hands. The rider on the paint, whoever he was, grabbed iron and caught a slug in the chest. He let go with a thin cry and started to drop. Nevers jumped his horse for the trees, firing wildly and ineffectively, and Blaine dropped another man. A slug thudded against a tree behind him and Utah yelled, "Come on Wardlaw! Here I am! Here's the thousand bucks! Come an' get it!"

The big gunman slammed the spurs to his mount and came at Utah on a dead run, but Blaine stood his ground and drove three bullets through Wardlaw's skull, knocking the man from the saddle. The horse charged down on him and Blaine, snapping a shot at the remaining man, caught up his bedroll and rifle and sprang to the saddle. He rode off up the draw, hastily swapped horses and took off swiftly.

Yet now he did not run. He circled around to the cliffs above. Three men were on the ground below and two were bent over them. As he watched, rifle in hand, Nevers came from the brush with a fourth man. That Wardlaw and at least one other man were dead, Utah Blaine knew. Now he intended to run up a score. Kneeling behind a flat rock he lifted his rifle and shot three times at Nevers. Yet he shot with no intention of killing. He wanted Nevers alive to take his defeat, at least to see the end.

A shot burned Nevers's back and he swung around staggering as the other bullets slammed about him. One of them burned him again for he sprang away, stumbling and falling headlong. One other man grabbed his stomach and fell over on the ground, and then Blaine proceeded to drive the others into the brush, burning their heels with lead and his last shot shattered a rifle stock for one of them. Reloading, he saw Nevers start to crawl and he put a shot into the ground a foot ahead of him. "Stay there, damn you!" he yelled. "Lay there an' like it, you yellow belly!"

A rifle blasted from the brush and Blaine fired three times, as fast as he could work the lever. He fired behind the flash and to the right and left of it. He heard a heavy fall and some threshing around in the brush. He came down off the little rise and, reloading his gun as he walked, mounted the black and started back for the ranch.

He was far from being in good shape, he knew, but now the running was over.

Utah Blaine rode swiftly, dropping down to find a cattle trail that led to the top of Deadman Mesa. Far ahead of him he could see Twin Buttes and he rode past them. He crossed Hardscrabble and dropped down into the canyon right behind the Bench, from where Angie's ranch could be dimly seen.

Would Angie be there? Suddenly, for the first time in days, he grinned. "It would be something," he told the black gelding, "to see her again!"

He rode slowly down the trail, circled, and came

up through the sycamores. There was no movement at the cabin, no smoke from the chimney. He slid from his horse and slipped the thongs back off his guns. Carefully, he walked forward, up the steps. He opened the door.

The room was empty and cold. He touched the stove. It was cold. Angie was gone. Some of the midday dishes were on the table, and that could only mean she had left suddenly at least one day before, possibly even prior to that.

His stomach sick with worry, he looked slowly around. Her rifle was gone. And her pistol.

He looked at the calendar. It was marked to indicate the 5th was past—this then was the sixth. She had been gone but one night. At least twenty-four hours.

Utah Blaine walked outside and looked down the trail. Beyond the hills lay Red Creek. To the northwest was the 46. Which way?

CHAPTER 17

ANGIE KINYON LOOKED coolly at Lee Fox. Inwardly she was far from cool, for she could see that Fox, always eccentric and queer, was now nearing the breaking point. She realized it with a kind of intuitive knowledge that also warned her the man was dangerous.

Yet Angie had heard stories about Fox. His father had been a hard-working, God-fearing pioneer, his mother a staunch woman who stood by her family. Something of that must be left in Fox.

"I want the horse," she said quietly. "It belongs to Utah Blaine."

"That's why I'm here," he replied, watching her with his strange eyes. "He'll come back for the horse."

"I doubt it. If I believed that, I wouldn't have come for him. I'm taking the horse home to be cared for. This is too fine a horse to be left like this."

Fox nodded, but she could not tell what he was thinking. Then he said suddenly, "What is he to you? What is Utah Blaine to you?"

It was in her to be frank. She looked directly at Lee Fox and spoke the truth. "I love him. I do not know whether he loves me or not. We have not had time to talk of it, but I love him the way your mother must have loved your father. I love him with all my heart."

A kind of admiration showed in the man's eyes. He

laughed suddenly, and with the laughter the burning went out of his eyes. "Then he's a lucky man, Angie. A very lucky man. But let's take the stallion out the gate, no use to ruin a good corral."

It was simple as that. Something she had said, or her very honesty, had impressed Fox. He walked around the corral and roped the dun for her. She put a lead rope on him and mounted up. Fox walked to his own horse. "No need for me to stay here, then. You'll tell him." He mounted. "I'll ride with you. Nevers and his lot aren't the men to be around good women."

They rode quietly, and suddenly Fox began to talk. "You knew about my mother, then? I never knew a woman more loyal to a man. I'd admire to find her like, as Blaine has found you. Maybe after he's dead you will forget him."

"He will not die. Not now. Not of any gun this lot can bring against him."

Fox shrugged. Now he seemed normal enough. "Maybe not, but everything's against the man. Nevers will not quit now. Otten has come off the fence, there's nowhere in this country Blaine can hope to escape. His only chance to live is to cut and run."

"And he won't do that."

"No, he won't."

He left her at the Crossing and turned away, and seemed headed for Red Creek. She sat her horse, watching him go. Would he go far or circle around and come back? That, probably. Lee Fox, sane or insane, was western—a good woman was always to be treated with respect. He might kill her husband, brothers and son, but he would always be respectful to her.

Crossing the river, Angie rode up the far bank and turned toward the cabin in the sycamores. It was as she had left it, quiet and alone. When she had stabled the horses she went inside. Nothing was different, and it was not until she went to her dressing table and picked up her comb that she saw the note. She smiled when she saw it. Leave it to him to put the note in the place she would first come. The note read:

Stay here. Gone to 46. Back later.

"Let me see that!"

She had heard no sound. She turned, frightened, to find Rink Witter standing behind her. His hand was outstretched for the note.

Although she had known his name and his deeds for ten years, she had never seen him at close range. She looked now into the pale, almost white blue eyes, the seamed and leathery skin, the even white teeth, and the small-boned, almost delicate facial structure. She saw the hand outstretched was small, almost womanly except for the brown color. She saw the guns tied low, those guns that had barked out the last sound heard by more than one man.

Rink Witter, a scalp hunter at sixteen, a paid warrior in cattle wars at eighteen, a killer for gamblers and crooked saloonkeepers at twenty. Rustler, horsethief, outlaw—but mostly a killer. He had ridden with Watt Moorman in the Shelbyville War. Deadly, face to face, he would kill just as quickly from hiding. He was a deadly killing machine, utterly without mercy.

She had heard that the wilder the shooting, the hotter the fight, the steadier he became. He was a man who asked for no breaks and gave none.

There was no way out of it. If she did not give him the note he would take it. She would have to give it to him, play for time, watch her opportunity. Without a word, she handed the note to Rink.

He took it, studied her coolly for a minute, then read what it said.

He turned. "Hoerner," he said, "you stay here. Tell the others to head for the 46. Utah Blaine was here and he's headed there. If they don't get him there or lose his trail, they are to head for Red Creek. Tell 'em not to come back here."

Rink crumpled the note and dropped it to the floor. "Make us some coffee," he said abruptly, and then turned and picked up her rifle and pistol and walked outside.

She went to the cupboard and got out the coffee mill and ground the coffee slowly. As she worked, she tried to study this situation out. She was helpless, and getting frantic would not do a bit of good. Her only chance to help Utah was to wait, to watch, and to find some way out.

She kindled the fire and put the water on. Utah would be careful. He was too shrewd a campaigner to take chances. She must trust in that, and in his good sense. Also, he might get to the 46, find the dun gone and see her tracks.

As a matter of fact, Blaine had passed within two hundred yards of them when she was returning to the Crossing with Fox. Utah Blaine stopped under the trees near the 46 ranch house and built a cigarette.

He felt better this morning. His side was sore, but he was able to move more easily. He studied the ranch house for several minutes while he smoked the cigarette. Finally he decided it was deserted. He was about to leave the brush when he saw the small, sharp prints of Angie's boots. He studied the tracks, saw where she had waited under the trees as he was now doing, and then how she had circled to get behind the barn. Somebody had been at the house then.

Cautiously, he followed the trail to the corner of the corral and saw where the knife had scratched the rawhide thongs. He saw the tracks of Lee Fox, but did not recognize them at first.

There had been no struggle . . . they had walked together to the gate . . . the gate had been opened by Fox . . . the stallion led out.

He read the sign as a man would read a page of print, as a scholar or writer would read the page. He saw not only what was there, but what lay behind, interpreting movements, somehow almost discerning their thoughts, their attitudes toward each other.

The girl had mounted here . . . the man had walked to his own horse . . . a tall man or a man with very long legs. Not Witter. Not Nevers. He studied the track of the horse the tall man rode and decided: it was Lee Fox.

They had started away, riding down the trail toward the cabin. So Angie had gone home then. He must have missed them somewhere back along the trail. Or rather, he had missed them because he was not following trails.

He paused to consider this. There had to be a showdown, but he was not anxious to encounter Lee

Fox, not just now. Nevers and Witter were the men he had to meet. With Fox, despite his slightly off-the-trail mind, there was a chance of reasoning. There would be none with Nevers.

Ben Otten did not enter his thinking. Otten had been out of it, and Utah Blaine had no means of knowing he had come in. Or that he could be dangerous.

He knew there was to be no more running. He was through with that now. Right was definitely on his side, and he meant to follow through on the job he had taken. He would ride right into Red Creek and show himself there. If they wanted a showdown they could have it.

He rode slowly, making it easy for the gelding. The sun was hot and dust puffed up from the horse's hoofs. He rode accompanied now by that stale smell of sweat that he would never forget after these bitter days. It seemed he had known that smell as long as he had lived, that he had always been unshaved, always gaunted from hunger, always craving cold, fresh water.

Blaine rode with ears alert for the slightest sound, his eyes roving restlessly. Yet he could not always remain alert. He could not always be careful. His lids grew heavy and his chin dropped to his chest. He lifted his head and struggled to get his eyes open. It was no use.

Turning from the mesa trail he rode down into a gulch and followed it along until he came to a patch of grass partially shaded by the sun. Leading his horse well back into the trees, he picketed it there. He then pulled off his boots and stretched out on the grass. No sooner was he stretched out than he was asleep.

———

Witter's three killers reached the 46 only a little after Blaine left. Fortunately, the three were tired, hungry, and not overly enthusiastic. They stopped to make coffee and throw together a meal from the ample stores on the 46. Only when they had eaten did they decide to pull out.

"Look," said the one named Todd, "Turley, you all stay right here. You lay for him. He might come back thisaway."

Turley had no objection. He was tired of riding. He concealed his horse and then sat down inside the house at a point from which he could see without being seen.

Now, Todd reflected, things were taking shape. With Rink Witter and Hoerner at the girl's cabin, with Turley on the 46, and with men on the Big N, they were slowly covering all the possible points of supply. Yet they lost Blaine's trail not two miles from the 46 and rode on into Red Creek to find Blaine had not been seen there. Todd then reported to Ben Otten.

Otten could see the picture clearly now, and he liked it. He had come in just at the right time. This thing was as good as ended. Fuller and Clell Miller were out of it, and he would place a small bet that either Nevers or Fox would be dead before the shooting was over. That left himself and one other to divide the pot.

"Good idea," he said, "leaving Turley at the 46. Now if Blaine goes back there he's a dead man."

Otten drew a handful of coins from his pocket and slapped a twenty-dollar gold piece in Todd's hand. "Buy yourself a drink," he said genially, "but not too many until this is over."

Todd pocketed the coin with satisfaction and was turning away when Ben Otten said, his voice low, "Might be a good idea, Todd, to remember where that came from. That is, if you'd like some more like it."

Todd did not turn around. "I ain't exactly a forgetful man, Mr. Otten," he said, " 'specially where money's concerned. I'll not be forgettin'. That Peebles, over yonder. He's a good man, too."

Otten drew another gold eagle from his pocket. "Give this to him, and both of you let me know how things are goin'." He hesitated, uncertain just how much to say. Then he added, "I'll want to keep in touch. When a fight like this ends nobody knows just how many will be left who can pay off."

He walked back to the bank, not knowing how much of what he had said had gotten across. Todd seemed reasonably shrewd, and he seemed ready enough to hire himself out. In any event, the forty dollars spent was little enough to insure a little good will. It might prove the decisive element. And it was better than dealing with Rink Witter. Every time he looked at the man he felt cold.

BLAINE'S EYES OPENED suddenly. The first thing he saw was a pair of huge feet and then the knees and a rifle across the knees. He looked up into the battered face of Ortmann.

Surprisingly, the big man grinned. "Man," he said, "you sleep like you fight."

"Where'd you come from?" Utah demanded, sitting up carefully. Ortmann's presence surprised him for he had not given the man a thought since their fight. He knew now that he should have. Ortmann had been giving him a lot of thought.

"Been sort of lookin' around." Ortmann rubbed his cigarette into the turf. "Seen you asleep an' figured I'd better keep an eye on you. Some of Nevers's outfit went by down there, not two hours back."

"You been here for two hours?"

"Nigher to three. Figured I'd let you sleep it off."

Blaine dug for the makings and rolled a smoke. When he touched his tongue to the paper, he looked up. "What's the deal, Ort? Where do you stand?"

Ortmann chuckled and looked at Blaine with faint ironic humor. One eye was still bloodshot. "Why, no deal at all! It just sort of struck me that a man who could lick me was too good a man to die, so I figured I'd take cards."

Utah Blaine stared at him. "You mean," he said incredulously, "on my side?"

"Sure." The big man yawned and leaned back on one elbow, chewing on a chunk of grass. "Hell, I never had no fight with you. I wanted me a piece of good land, an' it figured to be easy to get some of the 46 range. The others figured the same way, although not more than five or six of them really wanted land. Some wanted trouble, some to get paid off.

"They told me you was a gunman, a killer. I decided I'd no use for you, but when you shucked your guns an' fought me my style, stand up an' knock down—Well, I decided you were my kind of folks."

Utah Blaine got to his feet and ran his fingers through his hair. Then he put on his hat and held out his hand. "Then you're the biggest big man I ever saw," he said simply, "the kind to ride the river with."

Ortmann said nothing and Blaine thought about it a minute or so. Then he said, "Now get this straight. I can use your help, but I don't want anybody else. No use getting men killed who don't need to be and sometimes too many is worse than too few. You an' me, well, we make a sizeable crowd all by ourselves." Then he added, "But how many of the others are good solid men?"

"Maybe five or six, like I said. Mostly farmers from back East, an Irish bricklayer—folks like that."

"All right," Blaine drew on his cigarette, "when this fight is over I'll see each of you settled on one hundred and sixty acres of good land. The land belongs to the ranch. You farm it on shares. The ranch will furnish the seed, you do the work. The ranch takes half of your crop. If at the end of five years you're still on the land and doin' your share, the ranch will deed the land to you."

Ortmann drew a deep breath. "Man, that's right fine! That's all right! They'll go for it, I know. And we'll have none but the best of them. I know them, every one." He picked up his rifle. "All right, Utah, where to?"

"Why to Red Creek," Blaine said quietly. "We'll go first to Red Creek."

CHAPTER 18

NO FURTHER MOVE had been made against Ralston Forbes or his paper. Red Creek dozed in the sun with one wary eye open. All was quiet, but there were none here who did not realize that the town was simmering and ready for an explosion. Many of the citizens of Red Creek had come from Texas or New Mexico. They remembered the bitter fighting of the Moderators and the Regulators, when armies of heavily armed citizens roamed the country hunting down their enemies.

The arrival of Todd and Peebles was noticed. Both men were known. Todd had been in the Mason County War, and had escaped jail. He had broken out of jail in Sonora, too. Peebles was an Indian fighter, accustomed to killing but not accustomed to asking questions. Both were cold, hard-bitten men more interested in whiskey than in justice; their viewpoint was always the viewpoint of the man behind their hired guns.

Padjen, from his seat in front of the big window in the Red Creek Hotel, could survey the street. Skilled at acquiring information, it had taken him but a short time to get the lay of the land. He had been paid to handle any legal details about the transfer of the ranch to the hands of Utah Blaine, and he intended to see Blaine seated on the ranch securely before he left

Red Creek. He witnessed the arrival of Todd and Peebles, and he was keenly interested when Todd talked with Ben Otten. He even saw the coin change hands. And he saw Todd cross to the saloon and enter, followed by Peebles.

Casually, and with all the diplomacy he could muster, the young lawyer had been moving about town and he had been talking, getting a line on sentiment and dropping his own remarks. All, he suggested, would profit if the fighting were ended. There was no telling who might be killed next. In any event, the vigilantes had been wrong to start lynching, and had been wrong in their attempts on the lives of Blake and Neal.

Actually, he suggested mildly, it looked like a factional fight in which both parties had done some shooting, but the killing of Joe Neal was outright murder. And slowly, sentiment began to crystallize. Yet as he sat that day watching Todd and Peebles, Padjen knew that the time was far from ripe for action.

Todd was a lean, tall man with a sour face and narrow, wicked eyes. He put his big hands on the bar and ordered a drink. Peebles, swarthy and fat faced, stood beside him. They had their drinks, then a second.

Neither man heard the two horses come into the street. But Padjen had seen them at once, and had come instantly erect. He had seen Blaine and Neal together just once, but the big man in the black hat was not hard to recognize. The huge man with him could be nobody but Ortmann.

Ducking out of the hotel he ran across the back of the building and managed to reach the livery barn as the two pulled up. Some busybody or sympathizer of the vigilante party was sure to rush at once to the two men in the saloon.

Utah Blaine saw Padjen and stopped. But as Padjen drew nearer, he recognized him instantly. "This true about Neal leavin' the ranch to me?" he asked.

"You bet it is, but watch your step or you won't inherit. Two of Witter's killers are in the saloon. Todd and Peebles."

"Bad actors," Ortmann suggested, rolling his quid in his jaws. "Which door you want me to take?"

"We'll try to take 'em prisoners," Blaine said, after a moment's thought. "There's been enough killing."

"Where'll you keep them?" Padjen asked practically. "Look, man, I'm up here to make peace if it can be done, but when you've got a rattler by the tail you'd best stomp on his head before he bites you."

"Makes sense," Ortmann agreed.

Utah Blaine turned the problem over in his mind, then looked at Padjen. "Is Angie Kinyon in town?"

"No," the lawyer said, "she's not. I've never met her but if she was here, I'd know it. Mary Blake knows her."

Had Angie returned to the ranch? If so, where was Rink Witter? Utah considered the possibilities and liked none of them. Not even a little bit. And there was this affair, here in town. "Better get back to the hotel," he advised Padjen. "No use you getting into this."

"But I—" Padjen started to protest.

"No," Blaine was positive, "you'll do more good on the sidelines."

Padjen started back up the street but when he had

gone only a few steps and was crossing the street, Todd came from the door of the saloon. He stood there, one hand on the doorway, staring at Padjen. The innate cruelty of the man wanted a victim, and here, in the person of this city lawyer who had brought the news to Utah Blaine, he decided he had found his man.

"You!" Todd walked out from the awning. "Come over here!"

Padjen felt his stomach grow cold. He was wearing no gun, and had little skill with one. Yet he walked on several steps before he stopped. "What is it?" he asked quietly. "Are you in need of an attorney?"

Todd laughed. "What the hell would I want with a lawyer? I never do no lawin'. I settle my arguments with a gun."

"You do? Then you'll need to be defended sometime, my friend," Padjen smiled. "Unless a lynch mob gets to you sooner."

Todd stepped down off the walk and walked toward Padjen. Behind him a door closed and he knew Peebles had come out. "Run him my way, Todd," Peebles said. "I'll put a brand on him."

Padjen's face was pale, but he kept his nerve. "Better not start anything," he said quietly. "Ben Otten wouldn't like it."

That stopped Todd and puzzled him. This man had brought news of Blaine's inheritance to town. On the other hand, he was a lawyer and it was Todd's experience that lawyers and bankers were thicker than thieves. The change of the gold piece rattled in his pocket and he wanted to do nothing to stop that flow of gold, now that it was started.

"What you got to do with Ben Otten?"

Padjen perceived his advantage. The outlaw was puzzled and a little worried. "That," Padjen said sharply, "is none of your business. If Ben wants to tell you anything, that's his problem. Not mine. Now stand aside."

Drawing a deep breath he walked on, and in a dozen steps, forcing himself to an even pace, he got to the hotel. He turned in and stopped, leaning weakly against the wall. He looked at the gray-haired clerk. "That," he said, "was close!"

But the situation in the street had not ended. Irritated by his loss of a victim and the inner feeling that he had been tricked as well as frustrated, Todd looked for a new target. He saw a man standing in the center of the street not fifty yards away.

This man was tall, the flat brim of his black hat shaded the upper part of his face. The man wore a sun-faded dark blue shirt, ragged and stained. Twin gun belts crossed his midsection and he wore two guns, low and tied down. His boots were shabby and had seen a lot of weathering since their last coat of polish. He did not recall ever having seen this man before.

As he looked, the silent figure began to move. The tall man walked slowly up the street and Todd, with just enough whiskey in him to be mean, hesitated. There was something about that man that he did not like the looks of. He squinted his eyes, trying to make out the face, and then he heard Peebles.

"Watch it!" Peebles's whisper was hoarse. "That's Utah Blaine!"

Shock stiffened Todd and momentarily he floundered mentally. Todd had never claimed to be a gunfighter of Blaine's class. He was a hired killer, good enough and always ready enough to kill. He was not lacking in courage for all his innate viciousness. On the other hand, he was no damned fool.

Blaine came on, straight toward him, saying nothing. It was Todd who broke first. "What you want? Who are you?"

"You ride with Witter. You've been huntin' me. I'm Blaine."

Todd swallowed. That was the signal, and he should have gone for his gun. Suddenly the sun felt very hot and he began to sweat. Suddenly he wondered what he was doing here in this street. What did he want to start trouble for when he could be in the saloon. Why had he not stayed there?

"I ain't huntin' you."

"Seemed mighty anxious back at the Mud Tank," Blaine said. "Well, you've got a choice. Drop your guns and take the next train out of town—or you can die right here."

There it was, right in his teeth. Somehow he had always known this moment would come: the showdown he could not avoid. Yet it had been a noose he feared more than a bullet. Maybe he was lucky.

Blaine raised his voice. "That goes for you, too, Peebles. Drop your gun belt right where you are and get out of town on the next train."

That did it. Peebles was standing at the door of the saloon. He thought he had a chance. There was no loyalty in the man and if Blaine fired it would be at

Todd. In that split second he might kill Utah Blaine and collect that thousand dollars Nevers offered.

In that stark instant of hesitation before Peebles replied, Todd saw with a queer shock, an intuitive sense that told him what the move would be.

"You don't scare me, Blaine!" Peebles's words rang loud. "I'm not leavin' town an' I'm not droppin' my guns!" As he spoke, his hand dropped to his gun.

Todd had seen it coming. He reached. Both hands dropped...he felt the solid, comfortable grasp of the gun butts...his fingers tightened...something smashed him in the stomach, and for an instant he believed Blaine had swung a fist at him. But there was Blaine, still at least twenty yards away. Another something ran a white hot iron through his body. Todd stared down the street and the figure of the man in the black hat wavered...somewhere another gun blasted...the figure wavered still more and he withdrew his gaze, looking down at the gray dust at his feet. That was odd! There were big, red drops, bright, gleaming drops on the dust...red...blood...but whose...he looked down at himself and a queer, shaking cry went through him. He looked up, staring at Blaine. "No!" he exploded in a deep, gasping cry. "Please! Don't shoot!" And then he fell forward on his face and was dead.

Peebles had snapped a quick shot, missed and lost his nerve. He saw Todd take it in the belly and he wheeled, springing for the door. He would take his second shot from safety, he would...he burst through the doors and stopped.

Ortmann had come in the back door of the saloon. He was standing in the middle of the room with a shotgun in his hands. "Howdy, Peeb!" he said. "You shot at a friend of mine!"

"I got nothin' to do with you!" Peebles said hoarsely. Behind him was Blaine, and Blaine would be coming. Desperation lent him courage and he swung his pistol at Ortmann. His shot missed by a foot, smashing a bottle on the back bar. Ortmann's solid charge of buckshot smashed him in the stomach. Peebles hit the doors hard, spun around them as if jerked by a powerful hand. He hit the boardwalk hard, throwing his gun wide. His eyes opened, closed, then opened again. It was cool in the shadow under the porch. So . . . cool . . .

Padjen mopped his face. Not three minutes had passed since Todd had stopped him, and now two men were dead. He saw Blaine feed shells into his gun and then turn and walk up the street.

Ben Otten was sitting behind his desk. He had heard the shooting but did not get up. He was not anxious to know what was happening right now, the less one was around at such times the better. And someone would come and tell him.

Blaine told him.

When the door closed, Ben Otten looked up. He saw Utah Blaine standing there and he swallowed hard. "What—why—Howdy, Utah! Somethin' I can do for you?"

"Yes. You can pack up an' leave town."

"Leave town?" Otten got up. "You can't be talkin' to me, Blaine! Why, I—you can't get away with that—I own this bank—I've a ranch—I've—" His voice stuttered away and stopped.

"You're in this up to your ears, Ben." Blaine was

patient. "You're a plain damn fool, buckin' a deal like this at your age. You pack up an' get out."

Otten fought for time...time to think, to plan... any kind of time...any amount. "What happened down the street?" he asked.

"Todd and Peebles bucked out in gunsmoke."

"You...you killed 'em?"

"Todd. Ortmann killed Peebles."

"Ortmann?" The banker wiped a hand across his mouth. "What's he got to do with Peebles?"

"Ortmann's with me." Blaine watched Otten take that and was coldly satisfied at the older man's reaction. "And get this straight," Blaine's voice was iron-hard. "When I tell you to leave town, I mean it. When I've straightened things out with Rink Witter, Nevers and Fox, then I'll come for you. I hope you're not here, Otten."

Ben Otten's diplomacy had worn thin. His fear was there, right below the surface. He felt it, knew it for what it was, and was angered by it. He felt his nostrils tighten and knew he would be sorry for this, but he said it. "You've taken on a big order, Utah. Witter, Nevers an' Fox—then me. You may never get to me."

"Don't bank on it." Utah leaned his big hands on the rail. "If there's one thing I've no use for, Ben, it's a man who straddles the fence waitin' for the game to be killed before he rushes in to pick over the carcass—an' all the time hopin' he'll be the only one to get the fat meat.

"You're not a smart man, Ben. I've learned that in just a few days by what I've seen and what I've heard. You've got a few dollars, some mortgages on property and a big opinion of yourself. Don't let that big opinion get you killed. Believe me, a small man enjoys his food just as much—and lives a lot longer."

He turned abruptly and walked from the bank. He was suddenly tired. Pausing on the street he built a smoke, taking his time. He had been left a heritage that made him a wealthy man. But the heritage carried with it the responsibility of holding it together, building something from it. With a kind of sadness he knew his old footloose days were over, yet he accepted the responsibility and understood what it meant.

There could be war here, but there could be peace. But somebody had to accept the responsibility of keeping that peace, and he knew that task was his.

Ortmann was standing down the street, waiting for him. He grinned as Blaine came up. "We do better fightin' together than each other," he said grinning.

Blaine chuckled. "You punch too hard, you big lug. And you sure used that shotgun right."

"I knowed Peebles. He's a sure-thing killer, a pothunter. Killed maybe a dozen men, but maybe one or two had a chance at him." He fell into step with Blaine. "What now?"

Blaine stopped at the newspaper office and Ralston Forbes stepped out to meet him. Padjen was coming down the street. "I want you to get out a paper, Rals," Utah said, "and give me some space on the front page. I'll buy it if need be."

"You won't have to. Anything you say around here is front page news."

"All right." Utah threw his cigarette into the dust and rubbed it out with his toe. "Then say this: As of noon tomorrow I am takin' over the 46 Connected. I'll be hirin' hands startin' Monday an' want twenty men for a roundup. Say that Nevers has ten days to sell out and get out. In that time if I see him, I'll shoot him."

"You want to publish *that*?" Padjen exclaimed.

"Exactly. Also," Blaine continued, "inform Fox that I want any stock of his off 46 range within that same ten days. That so far as I am concerned, he's out of it if he keeps himself out."

"He won't," Ortmann said.

"Maybe, but there's his out." Blaine drew a breath. "Now we've got a job. We're goin' to the 46 tonight."

CHAPTER 19

IT WAS BEN Otten who carried the news to Nevers on the Big N. "So he's goin' back to the 46, is he?" Nevers mused. "Well, he won't last long there."

Ben Otten was heavy with foreboding. He had been given his walking papers by Blaine, but of that he said nothing to Nevers. The only thing that could save him now would be the death of Utah Blaine, and a sense of fatality hung heavily around him. Nevers's confident tone failed to arouse him to optimism.

"Who's on the 46?"

"Turley. Rink and Hoerner are on the girl's place."

Otten got up restlessly. "That's bad! Folks won't stand for any botherin' of women. You know that Nevers. I think some of my own hands would kill a man who bothered her."

"She's safe with Rink. He's mighty finicky around women. But," Nevers looked at Otten, his eyes glistening, "I'm goin' over there myself. That filly needs a little manhandlin'. She butted into this. Now she'll get what she's askin' for."

"Leave that girl alone!" Otten's voice was edged. "I tell you folks won't take it!"

"Once we're in the saddle who can do anythin' about it? Anyway, it'll be blamed on Blaine. Everythin' will."

There was no talk of Angie Kinyon doing any talking herself. Evidently Nevers didn't intend to leave her alive to do any talking. Ben Otten was shocked and he stared at Nevers. How far the man had come! A few weeks ago he had been ranching quietly and looking longingly at the rich miles of 46 grass. First the lynching, then the killing of Gid Blake, and the attempt on Neal. Whose idea had it been? Partly Nevers's and partly Miller's, he seemed to remember. But the step from killing a man and stealing his ranch to murdering a woman was a small one apparently.

He rubbed his jaw, thinking of Angie alone . . . and Nevers. Otten began to sweat.

Nevers went out and slammed the door behind him. Otten looked at the shotgun on the rack . . . Ortmann used a shotgun. He would be blamed . . . He hesitated, remembering the light in the bunkhouse. Anyway, why should he kill Nevers? To protect Angie . . . or to save her for himself?

His mouth grew dry and he gulped a cup of water, then walked to the bunkhouse. A sour-faced oldster whom he knew only by sight sat on the bunk reading. Another man was asleep on a cot. Three bunks within the range of light held no bedding at all. Otten looked at these bunks, then indicated them with a nod of his head. "Some of the hands take out?"

"Yep. Three of 'em pulled their freight this mornin'. Don't know's I blame 'em."

"Why?"

"Big N's finished." There was something fatalistic in the old cowhand's voice. "When Nevers took to buckin' Blaine, he was finished. It's in the wind."

"He's only one man."

"An' what a man. Look what's happened. All of

'em after him. He rides over to Yellowjacket an' whips that big bruiser of an Ortmann. Whips him to a frazzle.

"All of you again' him. Nevers, you, Fox, Miller, Fuller an' Rink Witter. Well, he's out-guessed all of you. Miller's dead. Lud Fuller is dead. Wardlaw is dead. Two, three others are dead. Now Todd an' Peebles are dead—an' they were hard men, believe you me. But is Blaine dead? Not so's you'd notice it."

"He's been lucky."

The oldster spat. "That ain't luck, that's savvy. Once it might o' been luck, twict it might have been, but Blaine has just out-guessed an' out-figured you ever' jump. He just thinks an' moves too fast for you. Besides, this here row's goin' to blow the lid off. Too bloody. The law will come in here an' you fellers ain't got a leg to stand on. Not a bit of it, you ain't."

The truth of this did not make it more acceptable. Otten turned away irritably. Nevers's own hands were deserting him. He walked back to his horse and stood there, weighted down by a deep sense of desolation.

The thought of Nevers alone with Angie came to his mind again. God! What a woman she was! He remembered the easy way she moved, the line of her thigh against her dress when she rode, the whiteness of her throat at her open neck, the swell of her breasts beneath . . . He swung into the saddle and jerked the horse around savagely. Suddenly, he slammed his spurs into the gelding.

He'd get there only a few minutes behind him. He'd stop Rink. He would get Rink or Nevers. He would . . . he would kill Nevers himself. Himself . . .

and then...and then...Viciously he jammed the spurs into the mare and went down the trail with the wind cutting his face.

He took the trail across Bloody Basin at a dead run. He would get there before Nevers could...He settled down to hard, wicked riding. Something warned him he was going to kill the horse, but he was beyond caring.

———

IN RED CREEK Ralston Forbes looked across the restaurant table at Mary Blake. They had been much together these past days. Yet now Forbes was restless. The whole country was alive with suspense and if he ever saw a powder keg ready to blow up, this country was it. Twice within the past hour he had seen men he knew as sober citizens walking down the street, wearing guns and carrying rifles or shotguns. Things were getting stirred up.

"Otten rode out of town," Mary told him.

"He's in it. Right up to his ears. Somebody talked an I've got a list of that lynch crowd. Lud Fuller was the leader, but Otten was with them just before they killed your father. He met them right afterward, too. So soon after that I know he was close by. He was just trying to be smart and keep his skirts clean."

"Dad always thought Otten was his friend."

"The man's money-hungry. It's an obsession now. And there is none worse. It makes a man lose perspective. It's the getting that's important, the getting and having—not how it's gotten."

"What's it come to, anyway, Rals?"

"Honor should mean more." Forbes shrugged.

"Sometimes I think people have gone crazy. The size of this country, the richness of it—it seems to drive them into a sweat to get all they can, to fight, kill, connive—so many have forgotten any other standard. Not all, fortunately, the country breeds good men and it will breed better. All these others, they'll burn themselves out someday, expand so fast they run up against the edges and die there. Then the good men will reconstruct. It's the advantage of having youth in a country, and a government that is pliable and adjustable to change."

Padjen came in as they sat there. He bowed to Mary, then drew up a chair and seated himself. "I've been approached," he said, "by a half-dozen of the townsmen. They want me to help them hold an election and choose a mayor, a city council, and a marshal."

"I'm for it," Forbes slapped his hand on the table. "It's long overdue."

"Who for marshal?" Padjen inquired. "You know these men. I wanted Blaine, but they wouldn't go for that."

"You wouldn't expect them to. He's one side of the argument." Forbes considered it. "I'd roust out Rocky White."

"Wasn't he a Big N cowhand?"

"He's worked for all of them, Neal, Nevers and Otten. But he's a good man, and he's a man who will take the job seriously. And he's not a killer."

"All right."

"What will happen now, Rals? Won't this make trouble for Utah, too?"

"It may, but even he would be for it. There's got to be an end to this shooting and killing."

They were silent, Ralston Forbes staring at the plate before him, his face somber. Mary looked across the table at him, moving uneasily in her chair. "What will they do, Rals?" she asked. "Will they arrest Blaine, too?"

"I don't know. All of them—they are aroused. I could see it coming. They've nothing against Blaine. They know he didn't start it, and they realize his claim to the 46 is just and legal. But his reputation is against him. After all, he's a gunfighter and known as one."

"Have you seen Rip?" she asked then.

"He's a little better. He had his eyes open today and was conscious when they fed him. He went right off to sleep again."

Mary Blake got to her feet. "Rals, I'm worried about Angie. She's out there on that ranch. A few weeks ago I'd not have worried. But the way things are, anything might happen."

He rubbed the back of his neck and nodded. "Yes, we were talking about her. Padjen and I." He walked restlessly down the room while Mary waited. All her animosity for Angie was gone. It had been a transient thing, born of her sudden need for the strong hands and will of Utah Blaine and her need for the ranch— the need for revenge for her father's murder.

Now, since she had been so much with Rals Forbes, her feelings had changed. He was like Blaine, but different. Without Blaine's drive and fury, without some of his strength, but with a purpose behind his will that was equally definite.

"We'll get a posse, Padjen," Forbes said suddenly, "we'll ride out there."

"Wait a minute. No use to go off half-cocked. I've sent for Rocky White."

There was silence in the room. The waiter came in and refilled their coffee cups. Forbes was somber and lonely in his thinking, Padjen absorbed. After a few minutes Kent, who owned a general store, came in. With him was Dan Corbitt, the blacksmith, and Doc Ryan.

Rocky White came at last. He was a tall, rawboned young man with a serious face and strong hands. "This right?" He looked around. "You want me for town marshal?"

"That's right." Forbes did the talking. "We've met and agreed that you're the man for the job. You run things here in town. See the violence stops, guns are checked upon entry of the town limits. No fighting, no damaging of property, protection for citizens."

"How about outside of town?"

"I was coming to that. Angie Kinyon is out there on her place. It isn't safe. We're going out there to get her. If we run into any fighting we'll stop it and make arrests. We'll bring Angie back here."

White nodded slowly. Then he looked around. "My pa was a J.P., and he was sheriff one time. I reckon I know my duties, but you better understand me. I'll kill nobody where it can be avoided. I'll make peaceful arrests when I can—but when I can't, will you back me?"

"To the hilt!" Kent said emphatically. "It's time we had law and order here!"

Forbes nodded agreement as did the others. Then

Rocky White looked around. "One more thing. What about Utah Blaine?"

"What about him?"

"He's right friendly with you, Forbes. An' I understand Padjen here represents him legally. I'll play no favorites. If he has to be arrested, I arrest him, too."

Forbes nodded. "That's right."

White shifted his feet. "Understand me. I've no quarrel with Blaine. I quit my ridin' job because I believed he was right. I still believe it. There was no call to grab all that range, an' Blaine had a right to fight for it. However, if we can make peace at all, it will have to include him."

"Right."

Rocky White shoved back from the table. "Then we'll ride."

———

TURLEY FIXED A meal and ate it, then rousted around until he found a bottle of whiskey. Pouring himself a drink, he walked out to the veranda where he could watch the trail in both directions. He had been on the ranch for several hours and he was restless. He wanted to know what was going on.

He sat on the porch drinking whiskey and smoking, his eyes alert. A thousand dollars for killing Blaine—it was more money than he had ever had in his life. And Blaine would probably come here, to the 46.

Returning to the kitchen, he picked up the bottle and walked back through the house to the porch again. His eyes drifted toward the trail and stopped, his brow puckered. Was that dust?

Rifle in hand he walked to the edge of the porch, then came down the steps. He had heard no sound. If it was dust there was little of it. Maybe a dust devil.

The incident made him nervous. It was too quiet here. He held his rifle in his hands and looked slowly around the ranch yard. All was very still.

"Hell," he said aloud, "I'm gettin' jumpy as a woman."

Rifle in the crook of his arm he strolled down to the corral and forked hay to the horses. He watched them eating for several minutes, then turned and walked lazily back to the shelter of a huge tree. He sat down on the seat that skirted the tree, his eyes searching the edge of the woods, the corners of the buildings—everywhere. Nothing.

It was unlike him to be nervous. He got up again and started for the house. A noise made him turn. Nothing. A leaf brushed along the ground ahead of some casual movement of air. Irritably, he started again for the house and mounted the steps. He opened the door of hide strips and seated himself in the cool depths of the porch.

He poured another drink. Warmth crept through his veins and he felt better. Much better. Suddenly, he got up. Why the hell hadn't they left somebody here with him? It was still as death. Not even a bird chirping...not a quail.

The cicadas were not even singing their hymn to the sun. A horse stamped and blew in the corral. Turley passed his hand over his face. He was sweating. Well, it was hot. He poured another drink...good whiskey...he placed the glass down and looked carefully around, eyes searching the edge of the trees. All was quiet, not a leaf moved.

Suddenly he heard a sound of a horse on the trail. It was coming at a canter. He got up hastily and walked to the edge of the porch, then down the steps. The horse was still out of sight among the trees. Then the horse came nearer, passed the trees and was behind the stable. Then it rounded the stable and rode up in the yard. Turley could not get a glimpse of the man's face under his hat brim. The man swung down and trailed the reins. He stepped around the horse and Turley stared. It was Utah Blaine.

Turley was astonished. He had never for an instant doubted the rider was a friend. No other, he reasoned, would ride into the yard so calmly. But here it was. He had wanted Blaine's scalp, wanted that thousand dollars—Here it stood! A tall man with two good hands and two guns that had killed twenty men or more.

"You're Turley?"

It was an effort to speak. Turley's throat was dry. "Yeah, I'm Turley."

"A couple of friends of yours came out on the short end of a gun scrap in Red Creek, Turley. Todd an' Peebles."

"Dead?" Turley stared uneasily, wishing he was still back on the porch. The sun was very hot. Why had he drunk that whiskey? A man couldn't be sure of his movements when he was drinking. "You kill 'em?"

"Only Todd. Peebles tried to make a sure thing of it from a doorway but there was a man behind him with a shotgun. Ortmann was back there. Nearly tore Peebles in two."

"Why tell me?" Turley was trying to muster the nerve to lift his rifle. Could he move fast enough?

"Figured you'd like to know, Turley," Blaine said softly. "It might keep you alive. You see, Ortmann is behind you right now, an' holding that same shotgun."

Cold little quivers jumped the muscles in the back of Turley's neck as Ortmann spoke. "That's right, man. An' I'm not in line with Blaine. Want to drop your guns or gamble? Your choice."

Turley was afraid to move. Suppose they thought he was going to gamble? Suddenly, life looked very bright. He swallowed with care. "I never bucked no stacked deck," he said. "I'm out of it."

Carefully, he dropped his rifle, then his belt gun. He looked to Blaine for orders.

"Get on your horse, Turley," Blaine said, "an' ride. If you ever show around here again we'll hang you."

Turley was shaken. "You—you're lettin' me go?"

"That's right—but go fast—before we change our minds."

Turley broke into a stumbling run for his horse. Pine...that was where...he would head for Pine... then south and east for Silver City. Anywhere away from here...

CHAPTER 20

ANGIE WAS FRIGHTENED and she was careful. There was an old pistol, a Navy revolver her father had left behind him. It was on a shelf in a closet, in a wooden box, and fully loaded. Her awareness of the gun did a little to ease her fear, yet she made no move to get it. She had no good place to conceal the weapon and did not want to go for it until the move was absolutely essential.

She had taken the measure of Rink Witter within a few hours after his arrival. He treated her with a deference that would have been surprising had she not known western men. Rink was a westerner—utterly vicious in combat, ruthless as a killer, yet with an innate respect for a good woman.

Hoerner was not of this type. Angie also knew that. When she fixed her hair she deliberately dressed it as plainly as possible and did what she could to render herself less attractive. The task was futile. She was a beautiful girl, dark-eyed and full of breast with a way of walking that was as much a part of her as her soft, rather full lips.

Hoerner was a big man, hair-chested and deep of voice. His eyes followed her constantly, but she knew that as long as Rink was present, she was safe. Nor would Hoerner make the slightest move toward her when Rink was around. The gunman was notoriously touchy, and Hoerner was far too wise to risk angering him.

Rink Witter was possessed of an Indian-like patience. Blaine's note had said he would be back and without doubt he would be. Rink sensed that Angie Kinyon was in love with Utah, and he respected her for it. Despite the fact that he intended to kill Blaine, and would take satisfaction in so doing, he was an admirer of the man. Utah Blaine was a fighter, and that was something Rink could appreciate.

When he saw the dust on the trail he did not rise. He sat very still and watched. Yet he knew, long before the man's features or the details of his clothing were visible, that it was not Blaine. This angered him.

Whoever it was, the rider should not be coming here. There was no reason for anyone coming here. The dust or tracks might worry Blaine into being overly cautious. And Rink expected Utah to take no chances, but now he became bothered.

The rider was Nevers. He rode into the yard and swung down from his horse. Rink came to his feet and swore softly, bitterly. Nevers was headed for the door, having left the horse standing there in the open! The fool! Who did he think Utah was, a damn' tenderfoot?

Nevers pushed open the door, looking quickly around for Angie. "Where's that girl?" he demanded.

"Other room." Rink jerked his head. "What's the matter? You gone crazy? If Blaine saw that horse he'd never ride in here."

"Blaine's headed for the 46. That's the place to get him. You and Hoerner get on over there."

Rink did not like it. He did not like any part of it. "He's comin' here. He left a note."

"That doesn't make any difference. Otten saw him in town. He told Ben he was takin' the 46 into camp. That he was movin' on and wasn't goin' to move off."

That made sense, but still Rink did not like the setup. Nor did he like Nevers's manner. What was wrong he could not guess, but something was. Then he thought of another thing. "Otten saw Blaine in town? Where were my men?"

Nevers restrained himself with impatience. To tip his hand now would be foolhardy. Rink would never stand for anything like he had in mind. "Your men?" Despite himself his voice was edged with anger. "A lot of good they did! Blaine an' Ortmann wiped 'em out. Blaine killed Todd an' when Peebles tried to cut in, Ortmann took him."

That demanded an explanation of Ortmann's presence with Blaine. Nevers replied shortly, irritably. Hoerner watched him, smoking quietly. Hoerner was not fooled. He could guess why Nevers was here and what he had in mind.

Rink hesitated, searching for the motivation behind Nevers's apparent anxiety or irritation. He failed. He shrugged. "All right, we'll go to the 46. Turley's there. If Blaine rides in, Turley should get one shot at him, at least."

Rink turned and jerked his head at Hoerner. The big man hesitated, looking at Nevers. "You sure you want me?" he asked softly. "Maybe I'd better stay here."

Nevers's head swung and he glared at Hoerner.

"You ride to the 46!" he said furiously. "Who's payin' you?"

"You are," Hoerner said, "long as I take the wages. Maybe I aim to stop."

Rink Witter stared from one to the other. "You comin' with me?" he asked Hoerner. "Or are you scared of Blaine?"

Hoerner turned sharply, his face flushing. "You know damn' well I'm scared of nobody!" He caught up his hat and rifle. "Let's go!" At the door he paused. "Maybe we'll be back mighty soon," he said to Nevers.

Nevers stood in the doorway and watched them go. Then he turned swiftly. Angie Kinyon stood in the door from the kitchen. "Oh? Have they gone?"

"Yeah." Nevers's voice was thick and something in its tone tingled a bell of warning in Angie's brain.

She looked at him carefully. She had never liked Nevers. He was a cold, unpleasant man. She could sense the animal in it, but it had nothing of the clean, hard fire there was in Utah Blaine. Nevers's neck was thick, his shoulders wide and sloping. He stared across the table at her. "You get into a man, Angie." he said thickly. "You upset a man."

"Do I?" Angie Kinyon knew what she was facing now, and her mind was cool. This had been something she had been facing since she was fourteen, and there had always been a way out. But Russ Nevers was different tonight—something was riding him hard.

"You know you do," Nevers said. "What did you want to tie in with Blaine for?"

"Utah Blaine's the best man of you all," she said quietly. "He stands on his own feet, not behind a lot of hired gunmen."

Red crept up Nevers's neck and cruelty came into his eyes. He wanted to get his hands on this girl, to teach her a lesson. "You think I'm afraid of him?" he demanded contemptuously. Yet the ring of his voice sounded a little empty.

"I know you are," Angie said quietly. "You're no fool, Russ Nevers. Only a fool would not be afraid of Blaine."

He dropped into a chair and looked across the table at her. "Give me some of that coffee," he commanded.

She looked at him, then walked to the stove and picked up the pot. Choosing a cup, she filled it. But instead of coming around the table as he had expected, she handed it across to him. He tried to grasp her wrist and she spilled a little of the almost boiling coffee on his hand.

With a cry of pain he jerked back the hand, pressing it to his lips. "Damn' you! I think you done that a-purpose!"

"Why, Mr. Nevers! How you talk!" she mocked.

He glared at her. Then suddenly he started around the table. "Time somebody took that out of you!" he said. "An' I aim to do it!" Swiftly she evaded his grasp and swung around the table.

"You'd look very foolish if somebody came in," she said. "And what would you do if Blaine rode up?"

He stopped, his face red with fury. Yet her words somehow penetrated his rage. At the same time he realized that he had deliberately separated himself from all help! Suppose Blaine did come?

Coolly, Angie took the note she had picked up from where Rink had thrown it. She tossed it across the table. "How does that make you feel?" she asked. "You know what would happen if Blaine found you trying to bother me."

"He won't find us," he said thickly. "They'll get him at the 46!"

Yet even as they talked several things were happening at once. Ben Otten was racing over the last mile to the cabin on the river, while Lee Fox, with two riders, was closing in from the north. He had left his post, watching for Blaine, and had taken a brief swing around through the hills. Reining in, at the edge of the trees, he looked down and saw the horse standing in the yard. And then he saw a second rider come racing down to the ford and start into the river. Lee Fox spoke quickly and rode down the trail.

In Red Creek six deputies with shotguns were stationed at six points in the town. Their job was to keep the peace. Before the hotel fifteen men were mounted and waiting. And then Rocky White came out, followed by Padjen and Forbes. All mounted.

A tough gunhand who had come drifting into the valley hunting a job, filled his glass. He looked over at the bartender. "One for the road!" he said.

"You leavin'?"

The gunhand jerked his head toward the street. "See them gents ridin' out of town? Those are good people, an' they are mad, good an' mad! Mister, I been in lots of scraps, but when the average folks get sore, that's time to hit the trail! Ten minutes an' you won't see me for dust!"

————

BEN OTTEN RACED up the trail just as Nevers started after Angie the second time. Nevers stopped just as she reached the door into the next room. He stopped and heard the pound of hoofs. His face went blank, then white. He grabbed for a gun and ran to the door. He was just in time to see a man swing down from a horse and lunge at the steps. Nevers was frightened. He threw up his gun and pulled it down, firing as he did so.

Ben Otten saw the dark figure in the door, saw the gun blossom with a rose of fire, and felt something slug him in the stomach. His toe slipped off the first step and he fell face down, and then rolled over and over in the dust.

Russ Nevers rushed out, his gun lifted for another shot. He froze in place, staring down at the fallen man.

Ben Otten!

Angie heard his grunt of surprise, but she was pulling the box down from the shelf of the closet. Lifting out the gun she concealed it under her apron and walked back to the kitchen.

Russ Nevers was on the steps and he heard her feet. He turned, staring blankly at her. "It's Otten," he said dully. "I've killed Ben Otten."

He was still staring when Fox rode into the yard with his men. He looked down at Otten, then at Nevers. "What did you shoot *him* for?" he asked wonderingly.

"He rushed me. I thought he was Blaine."

Fox peered at Nevers curiously, then looked up at Angie. Slowly realization broke over him, and he looked from one to the other, then nodded, as if he had reached a decision.

"Get him out of the way," he said shortly. "Blaine's comin'." He turned to his men. "Gag that girl, but be easy on her."

Angie heard him speak, but not the words. The two men swung down as Nevers caught Otten's body by the arm to drag it aside. The two hands walked toward her, apparently about to help Nevers. She did not suspect their purpose until suddenly they grabbed her. She tried to swing up the gun but it was wrested from her.

"You won't be hurt," Fox said. "We just don't want you to warn Utah."

Helplessly, she watched them scatter dust over the blood where Ben had fallen. She watched them lead the horses away and scatter dust over their tracks. She watched them carefully take their positions.

Russ Nevers inside the house...Lee Fox in the stable...his two riders, one in the corral and one behind a woodpile near the edge of the timber. There they were: five men and all ready to kill. And somewhere along the trails were Rink Witter and Hoerner.

U TAH BLAINE HAD been gone for more than twenty minutes when Ortmann heard the riders coming. He got a glimpse of them right away: Rink Witter and Hoerner.

Taking his time he drew a careful sight on Hoerner and fired. The shot was a miss, but it frightened the two and both of them jumped their horses into the brush. Coolly, using a rifle, Ortmann began to spray the brush, working his way across and then back, and jumping a shot from time to time.

Hoerner was flat on his face in the brush, hugging the ground. The bullets overhead had a nasty sound. "That ain't Utah!" he said. "He'd have let us come closer!"

"I know it ain't. Must be Ortmann."

"What are we waitin' for? Let's get back. Blaine's sure to go gal-huntin' now."

Rink Witter thought it over and decided Hoerner was right. Moreover, he did not like to think of Angie Kinyon alone with Nevers. The more he thought of it, the more he was sure she was not safe, that Nevers had wanted him away.

They worked their way back to their horses and both men mounted and headed away. Ortmann heard them going and swore softly. He hesitated, wanting to follow them, but he remembered Blaine's admonition. No matter what, he was to stay put.

"That way," Blaine had said grimly, "I won't be worried about who I shoot at. I know I won't have any friends out there!"

Ortmann fixed a meal and ate it at a table where he could watch the road. He sat that way until the sun faded and the night crawled down along the mountainsides.

———

NIGHT CAME TO the cabin in the sycamores. It gathered first in the stable, then in the yard under the trees. One by one the men slipped into the rear door of the house, ate and slipped back. Fox came and when he did, he checked the girl's bonds, freed her of the gag and made her coffee.

"You take it easy," he said "an' you won't get hurt."

"Take it easy?" she asked bitterly. "While you kill a better man than all of you?"

The night drew on. A mockingbird spent most of it rehearsing in the sycamore nearest the house. Fox spent it lying on a horse blanket with a gun in his hand. Angie slept, awakened, then slept again.

On the bench among the cedars Utah Blaine was stretched out on his stomach. He had his blanket over him and he was comfortable despite the chill. He was exactly one thousand feet above the little ranch. From his vantage point he could see it plainly except for the places where the thick foliage of the sycamores prevented his getting a view of the yard and the back door.

Angie's mare was in the corral, and his dun was there. Yet he saw nothing of Angie. He had arrived just before night, and after it was dark he could see nothing but the lights and shadows cast by the moon and the mountains. There had been a light in the house, in the kitchen. It continued to be in the kitchen except once when it was carried into another room and then back. Several times he heard a door close.

All the arrivals had reached the ranch before he had a chance to see them. Nevertheless, Blaine knew they would be watching this place. He drew back from the edge and lighted a cigarette. It was growing colder yet he dared not build a fire. Still, he would wait. If she was down there alone, she was all right. If she was not, there would be some sound, some warning.

He would wait until morning. That would be soon enough to go.

———

Fox LIFTED HIS head suddenly. He heard footsteps within the house. He heard the boards creak softly. A door opened. He got to his feet and with a word to his men, moved swiftly.

Like a wraith he slipped into the house. By the shadow on the floor from the dimmed lamp he knew he was right. Nevers was standing over the horrified girl who could only stare at him. He was standing there, leering at her, his eyes wicked.

"This ain't your station, Russ."

Nevers's face twisted with fury. He turned sharply. "Damn you, Lee! Why don't you mind your own business?"

"This is my business." Fox was calm but his eyes had started their queer burning. "I don't want to get hung!"

"You go back where you belong!" Nevers said harshly.

"Not me," Fox grinned. "I'm stayin' here. You go to the stable."

"Like hell!" Nevers exploded.

Lee Fox tipped his rifle ever so slightly until the muzzle was pointing at Nevers's body. "Then shuck your gun, Russ. You go or one of us dies right here!"

Russ Nevers had never known such hatred as he

now felt. He stared at Fox for a long instant. Then he wheeled. "Oh, hell! If you want to be a fool about it!"

He walked from the house and let the door slam behind him. Utah Blaine heard that door slam. It worried him.

CHAPTER 21

I N THE DARKNESS Utah Blaine came down the steep side of the bench. Instinctively, he felt that he was headed for a showdown. When the first gray appeared in the sky, he was standing in the brush not fifty yards from the corral, and no more than eighty yards from the cabin under the sycamores.

He took his time, lighting a cigarette and waiting, studying the house. There was no movement or sign of life for several minutes, and when it did come it was only a slow tendril of smoke lifting from the chimney. He studied it with furrowed brow, trying to recall if Angie had ever said anything about her hour of rising.

There was no wind and the sky was clear with promise of a very hot day. Utah was tired but ready. He could feel the alertness in his muscles, and that stillness and poise that always came to him in moments of great danger.

His wool shirt was stiff with sweat, dust, and dried blood. His body had the stale old feeling of being long without a bath. There was a stubble of coarse beard on his jaws, and as he stood there he could smell the stale sweat of his own body, the dryness of the parched leaves, the smell of fresh green leaves. He could hear the faint rustle of the river, not far off.

The slow tendril of smoke lifted lazily into the sky.

Suddenly, the smoke grew blacker, and his eyes sharpened a little. He drew deep on the cigarette and watched. An oil-soaked cloth—something—suddenly the smoke broke sharply off. There was a puff, a break, another puff, another break!

Someone within the house—it could only be Angie—was signaling, warning him!

There was a sharp exclamation from the corral. A man Utah had not seen suddenly reared from behind the water trough and sprinted for the back door, cursing as he ran.

Utah Blaine smiled bleakly. "Good girl!" he said. "Oh, very good!"

Her ruse had been successful. He heard sharp talk, Angie's voice, then another man interposed. He listened, but could not make out the words. The voice sounded like that of Lee Fox.

The man came out the back door, glanced hurriedly around and went in a crouching run toward the water trough where he vanished from sight. The man was a rider for Fox. Blaine had seen him but once, but had heard the man called Machuk.

Thoughtfully, Utah surveyed the yard. There was a man in the corral. There was a man in the house and there would, without doubt, be one in the stable.

How many in all? Fox did not have as many hands as Nevers, but there could be six or seven men here. More likely there were four or five. And most serious of all, Rink Witter and Hoerner were unaccounted for. Utah finished his cigarette, dropped it and then carefully rubbed it out with his toe.

To hurry would be fatal. First he must find out for sure how many men were here, and unless he was mistaken he would soon have his chance. They had set a trap for him and were waiting, but that fire could only mean breakfast, coffee at least.

Utah grinned wryly, his green eyes lighting with a sort of ironic humor. He could do with some coffee himself. He studied the house speculatively, but the back door was covered by at least one man. Moreover, he could not move to the right because several magpies were scolding around and if he came closer would make enough fuss as to give him away.

There was a deadfall behind him and he sat down on the slanting trunk of the tree and waited. He could hear the rattle of dishes within the house. Had it been Nevers in there he would have gone in. With Nevers there was a chance of bluffing him out of a shooting. If shooting there had to be, killing Nevers would not remain on his conscience. Lee Fox was another thing. There was no chance of bluffing any man on such a hair trigger as Fox. Moreover, Utah understood Fox's position and appreciated it.

He took out the makings and built another cigarette, taking his time. Impatience now would ruin everything. Now that he was here, now that he could see, the waiting would be harder on them than on him. They would break first.

A half-dozen plans occurred to him and were dismissed as foolhardy or lacking in the possibility of a decisive result. He saw Angie come to the door and throw out some water, saw her hesitate just a minute, and then call out to Machuk. The Table Mountain rider got up from behind the trough and went to the house. Utah heard dishes rattle, and the sound spurred his own ravenous hunger. After awhile,

Machuk slipped out and returned to his place behind the trough, calling as he did so to another man. Utah could not distinguish the name.

This man walked with a peculiar droop to one shoulder. He passed the corral, coming from somewhere near the woodpile. That pegged three of them. Where were the others? One in the stable, certainly.

After awhile the man with the drooping shoulder came out of the house. He paused near the trough and Blaine heard his voice clearly. "Lee figures it won't be much longer."

"I hope not. I'm full up to here with settin' here in the dust."

"Gonna be a hot day, too."

"Yeah."

"Well, I gotta call Nevers." The man moved on and paused at the stable.

Nevers crossed the yard to the back door. He looked ugly. His face was black with a stubble of beard and Utah Blaine studied him shrewdly. Nevers was hopping. He was ready to go, just any time. He was a strange combination of qualities. At no time a good man, he had been on the side of decency by accident only. Now he was over the edge. He would not go back.

Nevers entered the house and there was the rattle of dishes again, and then Nevers's voice lifted. "Who's off station now?" he demanded.

Somebody, probably Fox, spoke in a lower tone. Then Nevers replied, "Oh, yeah? You'll butt in the wrong place, sometime, Lee! Damn you, I'll—"

The words trailed off with some kind of an interruption, and then Utah heard an oath from the house. "What is she anyway? Nothin' but a damned—"

"Don't say it!" That was Fox, definitely. The man's voice was sharp, dangerous. Utah tensed, ready to move forward. What was the matter with Nevers? Couldn't he see the man was on a hair trigger? For that matter, Nevers was, too. But not like Lee Fox. In a fight between the two, Fox was top man—any time.

Nevers must have realized it, for he could be heard growling a little. Finally, he came from the house and walked back to the stable, picking his teeth and muttering.

Utah waited . . . and waited. There were no more. Four was all. And he had them all spotted.

This could be the showdown. He knew where Nevers was. If Nevers was out of it he might reach some settlement with Fox. The Table Mountain rancher was rational enough at times. It was Nevers then. Nevers was the man to get.

Angie was safe enough with Lee Fox. His brow furrowed. Where was Ben Otten? In town? On the run?

Utah moved back into the brush, taking plenty of time. He worked his way around through the brush, avoiding the corral, and making for the back of the stable. He was tempted to move up on the man behind the woodpile, but did not. Avoiding him, he finally reached the stable. Here he had to leave the brush and move out into the open. Moving carefully, he made it to the corner. Then he stepped past the corner to merge with the shadow of a giant tree. One more step and he could get inside the stable with Nevers.

The stable was of the lean-to variety: the front

closed across two-thirds of its face, with doors open at each side. It was through one of these doors that Utah expected to step. He knew Nevers was watching from the other door. He could see occasional movement there.

Utah hesitated, then stepped out. Yet even as he stepped he heard a cold, triumphant voice behind him.

"Been watchin' for you, Blaine!"

Utah turned, knowing what he would see. Rink Witter was standing there, not thirty yards away. He had come from the rocks near the trail from the river. Twenty yards farther to the right was Hoerner.

Utah Blaine was cold and still. He was boxed: Nevers behind him, Witter and Hoerner in front; Fox at the house, and his two hands.

Six of them. "This is it, Utah," he whispered to himself. "You've played out your hand."

Yet even as he thought this, his mind was working. There was no chance for him to come out of this alive. The thing to do was take the right ones with him. Rink, definitely. Rink and Nevers. That meant a quick shot at Rink—but not too quick. Then a turn and a shot that would nail Nevers.

After that, if he was still alive, he could get into the stable. But all this meant ignoring the fire of four men, one of them a killer for hire—Hoerner—a man skilled in his business.

Utah Blaine stood beside the tree, his feet apart, his head lowered just a little, and he looked across the hot bare ground of morning at the blazing blue-white eyes of Rink Witter. All was very still. In the house a floorboard creaked. Somewhere a magpie called. And Utah Blaine knew the girl he loved was in that house...depending on him.

Then mounting within him he felt it, the old driving, the surge of fury that came with the fight, the old berserk feeling of the warrior facing great odds. Suddenly doubt and fear and waiting were shed from him, and in that moment he was what he had been created for: a fighting man—a fighting man alone, facing great odds, and fighting for the things he valued.

He looked, and then suddenly he started to chuckle. It started deep down within him, a sort of ironic humor, that he, Utah Blaine, after all his careful figuring had been trapped, surrounded. He laughed, and the sound cracked the stillness like a bullet shattering thin glass.

"Glad to see you here, Rink," he said. "I was afraid you'd be late for the party!"

"I'm goin' to send you to hell, Blaine!" Rink's voice was low, cold.

Utah Blaine wanted to shatter that coldness. He wanted to break that dangerous icy calm. "You?" Utah put a sneer in his voice. "Why, Rink, without help you never saw the day you could send me anywhere! I've seen you draw, Rink. You're a washwoman, so beggarly slow I'd be ashamed to acknowledge you a western man. You—a gunfighter?"

He laughed again. "As for sendin' me to hell, with all this help you might do it. But you know what, Rink? If I go to hell I'll slide through the door on the blood I drain from you an' Nevers. I'll take you two sidewinders right along, I'll—" He had been talking to get them off edge, and now—"take *you*!"

Incredibly fast, his hands flashed for their guns. Rink was ready, but the talk had thrown him off. Yet even without that split second of hesitation he could never have beaten that blurring swift movement of hands, the guns that sprang up. His own gun muzzle was only rising when he saw those twin guns and knew that he was dead.

He knew it with an instant of awful recognition. It seemed that in that instant as if the distance was bridged and he was looking right into the blazing green eyes of Blaine. Then he saw the flame blossom at the gun muzzle and he felt the bullet hit him, felt himself stagger. But he kept on drawing. And then the second bullet, a flicker of an instant behind the first, hit him in the hip and he started to fall.

His gun came out and he fired and the bullet hit the tree with a thud. With an awful despairing he realized he was not going to get even one bullet into Blaine, and then he screamed. He screamed and lunged up and fired again and again, his bullets going wild as death drew a veil over his sight and pulled him down...down...down.

Blaine had turned. Those two shots had rapped out as one and he spun, getting partial shelter from the tree, and in the instant of turning he saw an incredible thing: instead of firing at him, Nevers lifted his gun and shot Lee Fox in the stomach!

Fox stared at him, his eyes enormously wide, the whites showing as he staggered down the steps, trying to get his gun up. "I should—I should have— killed you!" His head turned slowly, with a sort of ponderous dignity and he looked at Blaine. "Kill him," he said distinctly. "He is too vile to live!" And Lee Fox fell, hitting the ground and rolling over.

Hoerner was running and now he was behind Blaine. He fired rapidly into Utah's back. He shot once...twice...three times.

The yard broke into a thunder of shooting and Blaine, shot through and through, staggered out from the tree. He slammed a shot into Nevers that ripped the rancher's shoulder; a second shot that knocked the gun from his hand. Turning, Blaine dropped to one knee, red haze in his eyes, and smashed out shots at Hoerner.

He saw the big body jerk, and he shifted guns and shot again and saw Hoerner falling. Then Utah turned back and he saw Nevers standing there, his right side red with his own blood.

"You're a murderer, Nevers!" Blaine's voice was utterly cold. "You started this! You were there with Fuller when they hung Neal! I heard your voice! You were behind it! Good men have died for you!"

Utah Blaine's gun came up and Nevers screamed. Then Blaine shot him through the heart, and Nevers stood there for an instant, rocking with the shock of another bullet and then fell against the tree. The man with the drooping shoulder was lifting a Winchester and taking a careful sight along it when a rifle roared from the house door.

Amazed, Utah turned his head. Angie stood in the doorway, her father's Spencer in her hands. Coolly, she fired again, and Blaine looked toward the corral. "Come out, Machuk! Come out with your hands up!"

There was a choking cry, then Machuk's voice, "Can't. You—you busted my leg!"

Blaine turned and stared at Angie. One hand clung to a tree trunk. His body sagged. "Angie—you—you—all right?"

Then he heard a thunder of hoofs and he fell, and the ground hit him and he could smell the good fresh dust of the cool shadows. He heard the crinkle of a dried leaf folding under his cheek and the soft... soft...softness of the deep darkness into which he was falling away.

H E OPENED HIS eyes into soft darkness. There was a halo of light nearby. The halo was around a dimmed lamp, and it shone softly on the face of the girl in the chair beside his bed. She was sleeping, her face at peace. At his movement, her eyes opened. She put out a quick hand. "Oh, you mustn't! Lie still!"

He sagged back on the pillow. "What—what happened?"

"You were wounded. Three shots. You've lost a lot of blood."

"Nevers? Rink?"

"Both dead. Rals Forbes was here, and Padjen stayed here. He's sleeping in the other room. Rocky White was here, too."

"White?"

"He's the new marshal of Red Creek."

White, a tall rugged young puncher, looked like a good man. So much the better.

"What happened to Ben Otten?"

"Nevers killed him the night before you got here.

Ben came here—for what I don't know—and Nevers shot him. Maybe he thought he was you. Maybe he didn't care. His body was lying in the stable all night and all the morning before the fight."

Otten...Nevers...Witter. And then Miller and Lud Fuller, and before them Gid Blake and Joe Neal...and for what?

"Country's growin', Angie," he whispered, "growin' up. Maybe this was the last big fight. Maybe the only way men can end violence is by violence, but I think there are better ways."

"They are setting up a city government in Red Creek," Angie said. "All of them are together."

"That's the way. Government. We all need it, Angie." He was silent. "Government with justice... sometimes the words sound so...so damn' stuffy, but it's what men have to live by if they will live in peace."

"You'd better rest."

"I will." He lay quiet, staring up into the darkness. "You know," he said then, "that 46—it's a good place. I'd like to see the cattle growin' fat on that thick grass, see the clear water flowin' in the ditches, see the light and shadow of the sun through the trees. I'd like that, Angie."

"It's yours. Joe Neal would like it, too. You held it for him, Utah."

"For him...and for you. Without you it wouldn't be much, Angie."

She looked over at him and smiled a little. "And why should it be without me?" she asked gently. "I've always loved the place...and you."

He eased himself in the bed and the stiffness in his

side gave him a twinge. "Then I think I'll go to sleep, Angie. Wake me early...I want to drink gallons and gallons of coffee..." His voice trailed away and he slept, and the light shone on the face of the woman beside him. And somewhere out in the darkness a lone wolf called to the moon.

SILVER CANYON

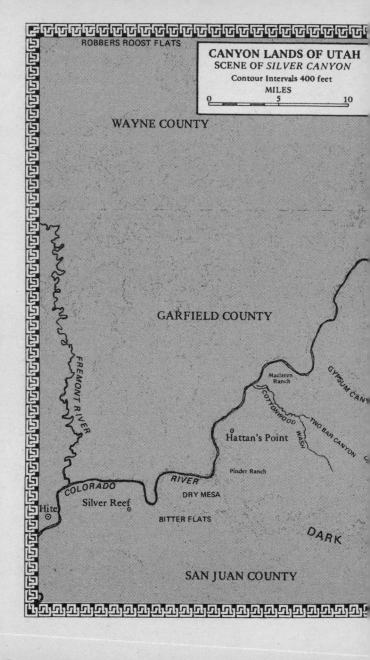

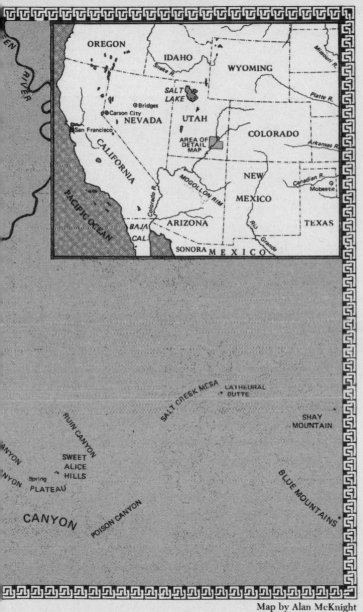

Map by Alan McKnight

CHAPTER 1

I RODE DOWN from the high blue hills and across the brush flats into Hattan's Point, a raw bit of spawning hell scattered hit or miss along the rocky slope of a rust-topped mesa.

This was the country for a man, a big country to grow in, a country where every man stood on his own feet and the wealth of a new land was his for the taking.

Ah, it's a grand feeling to be young and tough, with a heart full of hell, strong muscles, and quick hands! And the feeling that somewhere in the town ahead there's a man who would like to cut you down to size with hands or gun.

It was like that, Hattan's Point was, when I swung down from my buckskin. A new town, a new challenge; and if there were those who wished to try my hand, let them come and be damned.

I knew the raw whiskey of this town would be the raw whiskey of the last. But I shoved open the batwing doors and walked to the bar and took my glass of rye and downed it, then looked around to measure the men at the bar and the tables.

None of them were men whom I knew, yet I had seen their likes in a dozen towns back along the dusty trails I'd been riding since boyhood.

The big, hard-eyed rancher with the iron-gray hair,

who thought he was the cock of the walk, and the lean, keen-faced man at his side with the careful eyes, who would be gun-slick and fast as a striking snake.

And there were the others there, men of the western melting pot, all of them looking for the pot of gold, and each of them probably a man to be reckoned with, and no one of them ready to admit himself second best to any. And me among them.

I remembered then what my old dad told me, back in the hills where I ate my first corn pone. "See it, lad. Live it. There'll never be its like again, not in our time nor any other."

He'd been west, he'd seen it growing out of the days of Bridges and Carson, seen the days of fur change to the day of buffalo, and finally to the day of beef cattle. He sent me west in my 'teens and told me I'd have to walk tall and cut a wide swath.

The big man with the iron-gray hair turned to me as a great brown bear turns to look at a squirrel.

"Who sent for you?"

There was harsh challenge in the words. The cold demand of a conqueror, and I laughed inside me. His voice lifted me to recklessness, for it was here, the old pattern I'd seen before, in other towns, far back down the trail.

"Nobody sent for me." I let a fine insolence come into my voice. "I ride where I want and stop when I wish."

He was a man grown used to smaller men who spoke respectfully, and my reply was an affront. His face went cold and still, but he thought me only an upstart then.

"Then ride on," he said. "You're not wanted in Hattan's Point."

"Sorry, friend, I like it here. Maybe in whatever game you're playing, I'll buy some chips."

His big face flushed, but before he could shape an answer, another man spoke. A tall young man with white hair.

"What he means is there's trouble here, and men are taking sides. A man alone may be any man's enemy."

"Then maybe I'll choose a side," I said. "I always liked a fight."

The thin man was watching me, reading me, and he had a knowing eye, that one.

"Talk to me before you decide," he said.

"To you," I said, "or to any man."

When I went outside the sun was bright on the street. It had been cold on the bench where I'd slept last night, cold under the shadow of the ridge rising above me. The chill had been slow to leave and the sun now was warm to my flesh.

They would be speculating about me back there. I'd thrown down my challenge for pure fun. I cared about no one, anywhere.... And then suddenly I did.

She stood on the boardwalk before me, straight and slim and lovely, with a softly curved body and magnificent eyes, and hair of deepest black. Her skin was lightly tanned, her lips full and rich with promise.

My black chaps were dusty and worn, and my gray shirt sweat-stained from travel. My jaws were lean and unshaved, and under the tipped flat-brimmed hat my hair was black as hers, and rumpled. I was in no shape to meet a girl like that, but there she was, and in that instant I knew she was the girl for me, the only girl.

You can say it cannot happen, but it does, and it did. Back along the road there had been girls. Lightly I'd loved, and then passed on, but when I looked into the eyes of this girl I knew there would be no going on for me. Not tomorrow or next year, nor ten years from now. Unless this girl rode with me.

In two steps I was beside her, and the quick sound of my boots on the boardwalk turned her around sharply.

"I've nothing but a horse and the guns I wear," I said quickly, "and I realize that my appearance is not one to arouse interest, let alone love, but this seemed the best time for you to meet the man you are to marry. The name is Mathieu Brennan."

Startled, as well she might be, it was a moment before she found words. They were angry words.

"Well, of all the egotistical—!"

"Those are kind words! More true romances have begun with those words than with any others. Now, if you will excuse me?"

I turned, put on my hat, and vaulting lightly over the rail, swung into the saddle.

She was standing as she had been, staring at me, her eyes astonished, but no longer quite so angry as curious.

"Good afternoon!" I lifted my hat. "I'll call on you later."

It was the time to leave. Had I attempted to push the acquaintance further I'd have gotten exactly nowhere, but now she would be curious, and there is no trait that women possess more fortunate for men.

The livery stable at Hattan's Point was a huge and rambling structure at the edge of town. From a bin I got a scoop of corn, and while my buckskin absorbed this warning against hard days to come, I curried him.

This was a job that had to be done with care. The buckskin liked it, but his nature was to protest, so I avoided his heels as I worked.

A jingle of spurs warned me and, glancing between my legs as I was bent over, I saw a man standing behind me, leaning against the stall post.

Straightening, I worked steadily for a full minute before I turned casually. Not knowing I had seen him, he was expecting me to be surprised.

The man was shabby and unkempt, but he wore two guns, the only man in town whom I'd seen wearing two guns except for the thin man in the saloon. This one was tall and lean, and there was a tightness about his mouth I did not like.

"Hear you had a run-in with Rud Maclaren."

"No trouble."

"Folks say Canaval offered you a job."

Canaval? That would be the keen-faced man, the man with two guns. And Rud Maclaren the one who had ordered me from town. Absorbing this information, I made no answer.

"My name's Jim Pinder, CP outfit. I'll pay top wages, seventy a month an' found. All the ammunition you can use."

My eyes had gone beyond him where two men lurked in a dark stall, believing themselves unseen. They had come with Pinder, of that I was sure.

Suppose I refused Pinder's offer? Nothing about the setup looked good to me, and I could feel my hackles rising. The idea of him planting two men in the stall got under my skin.

Shoving Pinder aside, I stepped quickly into the open space between the stalls.

"You two!" My hands were over my guns and my voice rang loud in the echoing emptiness of the building. "Get out in the open! Move, or start shootin'!"

My hands were wide, my fingers spread, and right then I did not care which way the cat jumped. There was that old jumping devil in me that always boiled up to fight—not anger, exactly, nor any lust for killing but simply the urge to do battle that I'd known since I was a youngster.

There was a moment when I did not believe they would come out, a moment when I almost hoped they wouldn't. Jim Pinder had been caught flat-footed, and he didn't like what was happening. It was obvious to him that he would get a fast slug in the stomach if anything popped.

They came out then, slowly, holding their hands wide from their guns. They came with reluctance—more than half ready for battle, but not quite.

One of them was a big man with black hair and blue-black jowls. The other had the flat, cruel face of an Apache.

"Suppose we'd come shootin'?" The black-haired man was talking.

"Then they would have planted you before sundown." I smiled at him. "If you don't believe it, cut loose your wolf."

They did not know me and I was too ready. They

were wise enough to see I'd been trailing with the rough-string but they didn't know how far I could carry my bluff.

"You move fast." Pinder was talking. "What if I had cut myself in?"

"I was expecting it." My smile angered him. "You would have gone first, then a quick one for Blackie, and after that"—I indicated the Apache—"him. He would be the hardest to kill."

Jim Pinder did not like it, and he did not like me. Nonetheless, he had a problem.

"I made an offer."

"And I'm turning it down."

His lips thinned down and I've seldom seen so much hatred in a man's eyes. I'd made him look small in front of his hired hands.

"Then get out. Join Maclaren and you'll die."

When you're young you can be cocky. I was young then and I was cocky, and I knew I should be wiser and hold my tongue. But I was feeling reckless and ready for trouble, and in no mood for beating around the greasewood.

"Then why wait," I threw it right in his teeth with a taunt. "So far as I know, I'm not joining Maclaren, but any time you want what I've got, come shootin'."

"You won't live long."

"No? Well, I've a hunch I'll stand by when they throw dirt on your face."

With that, I stepped to one side and looked at Pinder. "You first, *amigo*, unless you'd like to make an issue."

He walked away from me, followed by his two men, and I waited and watched them go. I'll not deny

I was relieved. With three men I'd have come out on the short end—but somebody would have gone with me and Jim Pinder was no gambler. Not right then, at least.

Up the street from the door of the stable I could see a welcome sign:

MOTHER O'HARA'S COOKING
MEALS FOUR-BITS

When I pushed open the door there were few at table—it was early for supper—but the young man with the white hair was eating, and beside him was the girl I loved.

It was a long, narrow, and low-ceilinged room of adobe, with whitewashed walls, and it had the only plank floor among the town's three eating houses. The tables were neat, the dishes clean, and the food looked good. The girl looked up, and right away the light of battle came into her eyes. I grinned at her and bowed slightly.

The white-haired man looked at me, surprised, then glanced quickly at the girl, whose cheeks were showing color.

The buxom woman who came in from the kitchen stopped and looked from one to the other of us, then a smile flickered at the corner of her mouth. This, I correctly guessed, was Mother O'Hara. The girl returned to her eating without speaking.

The man spoke. "You've met Miss Maclaren then?"

Maclaren, was it?

"Not formally," I said, "but she's been on my mind for years." And knowing a valuable friend when I saw one, I added, "And it's no wonder she's lovely, if she eats here!"

"I can smell the blarney in that," Mother O'Hara said dryly, "but if it's food you want, sit down."

There was an empty bench opposite them, so I sat there. The girl did not look up, but the man offered his hand across the table. "I'm Key Chapin. And this, to make it formal, is Moira Maclaren."

"I'm Brennan," I said, "Matt Brennan."

A grizzled and dusty man from the far end of the table looked up. "Matt Brennan of Mobeetie, the Mogollon gunfighter?"

They all looked at me then, for it was a name not unknown. The reputation I'd rather not have had, but the name was mine and the reputation one I had earned.

"The gentleman knows me."

"Yet you refused Maclaren's offer?"

"And Pinder's, too."

They studied me, and after a minute Chapin said, "I'd have expected you to accept—one or the other."

"I play my own cards," I told him, "and my gun's not for hire."

CHAPTER 2

M RS. O'HARA CAME in with my food and I ate and drank coffee and let the others wait and think. Nor could I miss knowing what they were thinking of. In the past it had not mattered. I'd been a drifter, a man riding from town to town.

It was otherwise now...suddenly. And the difference was a girl with green eyes and dark hair. I knew I had been looking for her, for this girl across the table. And what I wanted to give her could not be bought with a gunfighter's wages.

The food was good and I ate heartily. They finished, but they sat over coffee. Finally I finished, too, and began to build a smoke.

Where did I go from here? How did a man turn from the trail and settle down? For this was a girl who had a good home. I could offer her no less.

"What's the fight about?" I asked presently.

"What are most fights about? Sheep, cattle, or grass. Or water...and that's what it is in this case.

"East of here there's a long valley, Cottonwood Wash. Running into it from the east is Two-Bar Canyon. There's a good year-round stream flowing out of Two-Bar, enough to irrigate hay land or water thousands of cattle. Maclaren needs it, the CP wants it."

"Who's got it?"

"A man named Ball. He's no fighter, and he has no money to hire fighters. He hates Maclaren, and he refuses to do business with Pinder."

"And he's right in the middle."

Chapin put down his cup and took out his tobacco and pipe. "Gamblers in town are offering odds he won't last thirty days, even money he'll be killed within ten."

So that was the way of it? Two cow outfits wanting the water that another had. Two big outfits wanting to grow, and a little one holding them back.

No fighter was he? But a man with nerve...it took nerve to sit on the hot seat like that.

But that was enough for now. My eyes turned to the daughter of Rud Maclaren. "You can buy your trousseau," I said. "You'll not have long for planning."

She looked at me coolly, but there was impudence in her, too.

"I'll not worry about it. There's no weddings on Boot Hill."

They all laughed at that, yet behind it they were all thinking she was right. When a man starts wearing a gun it is a thing to think about, but there was something inside me that told me no...not yet. Not by gun or horse or rolling river...not just yet.

"You've put your tongue to prophecy," I said, "and maybe it's in Boot Hill I'll end. But I'll tell you this, daughter of Maclaren, before I sleep in Boot Hill there will be sons and daughters of ours on this ground.

"I've a feeling on this, and mountain people set store by feelings. That when I go I'll be carried there by six tall sons of ours, and you'll be with them, re-membering the good years we've had."

When the door slapped shut behind me I knew I'd been talking like a fool, yet the feeling was still with me—and why, after all, must it be foolishness?

Through the thin panels I heard Mother O'Hara telling her, "You'd better be buying that trousseau, Moira Maclaren! There's a lad knows his mind!"

"It's all talk," she said, "just loose talk."

She did not sound convinced, however, and that was the way we left it, for I knew there were things to be done.

Behind me were a lot of trails and a lot of rough times. Young as I was, I'd been a man before my time, riding with trail herds, fighting Comanches and rustlers, and packing a fast gun before I'd put a man's depth in my chest.

It was easy to talk, easy to make a boast to a pretty girl's ears, but I'd no threshold to carry her over, nor any land anywhere. It was a thought that had never bothered me before this, but when a man starts to think of a woman of his own, and of a home, he begins to know what it means to be a man.

Yet standing there in the street with the night air coming down from the hills, and darkness gathering itself under the barn eaves and along the streets, I found an answer.

It came to me suddenly, but the challenge of it set my blood to leaping and brought laughter to my lips. For now I could see my way clear, my way to money, to a home, and to all I'd need to marry Moira Maclaren...The way would be rough and bloody, but only the daring of it gripped my mind.

Turning, I started toward the stable, and then I stopped, for there was a man standing there.

He was a huge man, towering over my six feet two inches, broader and heavier by far than my two hundred pounds. He was big-boned and full of raw power, unbroken and brutal. He stood wide-legged before me, his face as wide as my two hands, his big head topped by a mass of tight curls.

"You're Brennan?"

"Why, yes," I said, and he hit me.

There was no start to the blow. His big balled fist hit my jaw like an axe butt and something seemed to slam me behind the knees and I felt myself falling. He hit me again as I fell into his fist, a wicked blow that turned me half around.

He dropped astride of me, all two hundred and sixty pounds of him, and with his knees pinning my arms, he aimed smashing, brutal blows at my head and face. Finally he got up, stepped back, and kicked me in the ribs.

"If you're conscious, hear me. I'm Morgan Park, and I'm the man who's going to marry Moira Maclaren."

My lips were swollen and bloody and my brain foggy. "You lie!" I said, and he kicked me again and then walked away, whistling.

Somehow I rolled over and got my hands under me and pushed up to my knees. I crawled out of the street and against the stage station wall, where I lay with my head throbbing like a great drum, the blood welling from my split lips and broken face.

It had been a brutal beating he'd given me. I'd not

been whipped since I was a boy, and never had I felt such blows as those. His fists had been like knots of oak and his arms like the limbs of trees.

Every breath I took brought a gasp, and I was sure he'd broken a rib for me. Yet it was time for me to travel. I'd made big talk in Hattan's Point and I'd not want Moira Maclaren to see me lying in the street like a whipped hound.

My hands found the corner of the building and I pulled myself up. Staggering along the building, using the wall for support, I made my way to the livery stable.

When I got my horse saddled, I pulled myself into the saddle and rode to the door.

The street was empty . . . no one had seen the beating I'd taken, and wherever Morgan Park had come from, now he was nowhere to be seen. For an instant I sat my horse in the light of the lantern above the stable floor.

A door opened and a shaft of light fell across me. In the open door of Mother O'Hara's stood Moira Maclaren.

She stepped down from the stoop and walked over to me, looking up at my swollen and bloody face with a kind of awed wonder.

"So he found you, then. He always hears when anyone comes near me, and this always happens. You see, Matt, it is not so simple a thing to marry Moira Maclaren." There seemed almost a note of regret in her voice.

"And now you're leaving?" she said.

"I'll be back for you . . . and to give Morgan Park a beating."

Now her voice was cool, shaded with contempt. "You boast—all you have done is talk and take a beating!"

That made me grin, and the grinning hurt my face. "It's a bad beginning, isn't it?"

She stood there watching as I rode away down the street.

Throughout the night I rode into wilder and wilder country. I was like a dog hunting a hole in which to die, but I'd no thought of dying, only of living and finding Morgan Park again.

Through the long night I rode, my skull pounding, my aching body heavy with weariness, my face swollen and shapeless. Great canyon walls towered above me, and I drank of their coolness. Then I emerged on a high plateau where a long wind stole softly across the open levels fresh with sage and sego lilies.

Vaguely I knew the land into which I rode was a lost and lonely land inhabited by few, and those few were men who did not welcome visitors.

At daylight I found myself in a long canyon where tall pines grew. There was a stream talking somewhere under the trees, and, turning from the game trail I had followed, I walked my buckskin through knee-high grass and flowers and into the pines. It smelled good there, and I was glad to be alone in the wilderness, which is the source of all strength.

There beside the stream I bedded down, opening my soogan and spreading it in the half sunlight and shade, and then I picketed my horse and at last crept to my blankets and relaxed with a great sigh. And then I slept.

It was midafternoon when my eyes opened again. There was no sound but the stream and the wind in the tall pines, a far-off, lonely sound. Downstream a beaver splashed, and in the trees a magpie chattered, fussing at a squirrel.

I was alone.... With small sticks I built a fire and heated water, and when it was hot I bathed my face with careful hands, and while I did it I thought of the man who had whipped me.

It was true he had slugged me without warning, then had pinned me down so I'd have no chance to escape from his great weight. But I had to admit I'd been whipped soundly. Yet I wanted to go back. This was not a matter for guns. This man I must whip with my bare hands.

But there was much else to consider. From all I had learned, the Two-Bar was the key to the situation, and it had been my idea to join forces with Ball, the man who was stubborn enough to face up to two strong outfits. I'd long had an urge for lost causes, and a feeling for men strong enough to stand alone. If Ball would have my help...

To the west of where I waited was a gigantic cliff rising sheer from the grassy meadow. Trees skirted the meadow, and to the east a stream flowed along one side, where the pines gave way to sycamore and a few pin oak.

Twice I saw deer moving among the trees. Lying in wait near the water, I finally got my shot and dropped a young buck.

For two days I ate, slept, and let the stream flow by. My side ceased to pain except when a sudden movement jerked it, but it remained stiff and sore to the touch. The discoloration around my eyes and on one cheekbone changed color and some of the swelling went down. After two days I could wait no longer. Mounting the buckskin, I turned him toward the Two-Bar.

A noontime sun was darkening the buckskin with sweat when I turned into Cottonwood Wash.

There was green grass here, and there were trees and water. The walls of the Wash were high and the trees towered until their tops were level with them, occasional cattle I saw looked fat and lazy.

For an hour I rode slowly along, feeling the hot sun on my shoulders and smelling the fresh green of the grass, until the trail ended abruptly at a gate bearing a large sign.

TWO-BAR GATE

RANGED FOR A SPENCER .56

SHOOTING GOING ON HERE

Beyond this point a man would be taking his own chances, and nobody could say he had not been warned.

Some distance away, atop a knoll, I could see the house. Rising in my stirrups, I waved my hat. Instantly there was the hard *whap* of a bullet passing, then the boom of the rifle.

Obviously, this was merely a warning shot, so I waved once more.

That time the bullet was close, so, grabbing my chest with both hands I rolled from the saddle, caught the stirrup to break my fall and settled down to the grass. Then I rolled over behind a boulder. Removing my hat, I sailed it to the ground near the horse, then pulled off one boot and placed it on the ground so it would be visible from the gate. But from that far away an observer would see only the boot, not whether there was a foot and leg attached.

Then I crawled into the brush, among the rocks, where I could cover the gate. To all outward appearances a man lay sprawled behind that boulder.

All was still. Sweat trickled down my face. My side throbbed a little from a twist it had taken as I fell from the horse. I dried my sweaty palms and waited.

And then Ball appeared. He was a tall old man with a white handlebar mustache and shrewd eyes. No fool, he studied the layout carefully, and he did not like it. It looked as though he had miscalculated and scored a hit.

He glanced at the strange brand of the buckskin, at the California bridle and bit. Finally, he opened the gate and came out, and as he turned his back was to me.

"Freeze, Ball! You're dead in my sights!"

He stood perfectly still, taking no chances on an itchy trigger finger.

"Who are you? What do you want with me?"

"Not trouble . . . I want to talk business."

"I've no business with anybody."

"With me you've business. I'm Matt Brennan. I've had trouble with Pinder and Maclaren. I've taken a beating from Morgan Park."

Ball chuckled. "Sounds as if you're the one with trouble. Is it all right to turn around?"

At my word, he turned. I stepped from out of the rocks. He moved back far enough to see the boot and grinned. "I'll not bite on that one again."

I sat down and pulled my boot on.

CHAPTER 3

WHEN I WAS on my feet I crossed to my hat and picked it up. He watched me, never letting his eyes leave me for an instant.

"You're bucking a stacked deck," I said. "The gamblers are offering high odds you won't last thirty days."

"I know that."

He was a hard old man, this one. Yet I could see from the fine lines around his eyes that he'd been missing sleep, and that he was worried. But he wasn't frightened. Not this man.

"I'm through drifting. I'm going to put down some roots, and there's only one ranch around here I'd have."

"This one?"

"Yes."

He studied me, his hands on his hips. I'd no doubt he would go for a gun if I made a wrong move.

"What do you aim to do about me?"

"Let's walk up to your place and talk about that."

"We'll talk here."

"All right.... There's two ways. You give me a fighting, working partnership. That's one way. The other is for you to sell out to me and I'll pay you when I can. I take over the fight."

He looked at me carefully. He was not a man to

ask foolish questions. He could see the marks of the beating I'd taken, and he'd heard me say there had been trouble with Maclaren and Pinder. I knew what I was asking for.

"Come on up. We'll talk about this."

And he let me go first, leading my horse. I liked this old man.

Yet I knew the cards were stacked my way. He could not stay awake all night, every night. He could not both work and guard his stock. He could not go to town for supplies and leave the place unguarded. Together we could do all those things.

Two hours later we had reached an agreement. I was getting my fighting, working partnership. One man alone could not do it, the odds were all against any two men doing it . . . but they'd have a chance.

"When they find out, they'll be fit to be tied."

"They won't find out right away. My first job is grub and ammunition."

The Two-Bar controlled most of the length of Cottonwood Wash and on its eastern side opened upon a desert wilderness with only occasional patches of grass. Maclaren's Boxed M and Pinder's CP bordered the ranch on the west, with Maclaren's land extending to the desert at one place.

Both ranches had pushed back the Two-Bar cattle, usurping the range for their own use. In the process, most of the Two-Bar calves had disappeared under Boxed M and CP brands.

"Mostly CP," Ball advised. "The Pinder boys are mighty mean. They rode with Quantrill, an' folks say Rollie rode with the James boys some. Jim's a fast gun, but nothin' to compare to Rollie."

At daybreak, with three unbranded mules to carry the supplies, I started for Hattan's, circling wide around so that I could come into the trail to town from the side opposite the Two-Bar.

It was in my mind that the Two-Bar might be watched, but after scouting the edges of the Wash I decided that they must believe they had Ball safely bottled up and no chance of his getting help. Probably they would be only too glad for him to start to town . . . for when he returned they could be in possession and waiting for him.

Going down the Wash for several miles, I came out by a narrow, unused trail and cut across country, keeping to low country to escape observation.

The desert greasewood gave way to mesquite and to bunch grass. The morning was bright, and the sun would be warm again. Twice, nearing the skyline, I saw riders in the distance, but none of them could have seen me.

The town was quiet when I rode in, and I came up through the shacks back of the livery stable and left my mules tied to the corral near the back door of the store.

Walking out on the street, I smoked a cigarette and kept my eyes open. Nobody seemed to notice me, nobody seemed to know I was in town. There was no sign of Maclaren or Canaval, or of Moira.

Loading the supplies, I broke into a sweat. The day was warm and still, and my side still pained me. My face was puffed, although both my eyes were now open and the blackness had changed to mottled blue and yellow. When I was through I led the mules into the cottonwoods on the edge of town and picketed them there, ready for a quick move. Then I returned to Mother O'Hara's. My purpose was double. I wanted a good meal, and I wanted news.

Key Chapin and Canaval were there and they looked up as I entered. Chapin's eyes took in my face with a quick glance, and there was in his eyes something that might have been sympathy.

Canaval noticed, but it did not show. "That job is still open," he suggested. "We could use you."

"Thanks." There was a bit of recklessness in me. My supplies were packed and ready to go, and there was enough on those mules to last us three months, with a little game shooting on the side and a slaughtered beef or two. "I'm going to run my own outfit."

Maybe I was a fool to say it. Maybe I should have kept it a secret as long as I could. But just as I started to speak I heard a door open behind me and that light step and the perfume I knew. Maybe that was why I was here, to see Moira, and not for a meal or news.

From the day I first saw her she was never to be near without my knowledge. There was something within me that told me, some feeling in my blood, some perception beyond the usual. This was my woman, and I knew it.

She had come into the restaurant behind me and it may have been that that made me say it, to let her know that I had not cut and run, that I intended to stay, that I had begun to build for the future I had promised her.

"Your own outfit?" Chapin was surprised. "You're turning nester?"

Canaval said nothing at all, but he looked at me,

and I think he knew then. I saw dawning comprehension in his eyes, and perhaps something of respect.

"I'll be ranching."

Rising, I faced around. Moira was looking at me, her eyes level and steady.

"Miss Maclaren?" I indicated the seat beside me. "May I have the pleasure?"

She hesitated, then shook her head slightly and went around the table to sit down beside Canaval, her father's foreman and strong right hand.

"You're *ranching*?" Canaval was puzzled. "If there's any open range around here I haven't heard of it."

"It's a place east of here . . . the Two-Bar."

"What about the Two-Bar?" Rud Maclaren had followed his daughter into the restaurant. He rounded the table beside her and looked down at me, a cold, solid man.

Taking a cup from a tray, I filled it with coffee.

"Mr. Brennan was telling us, Father, that he's ranching on the Two-Bar."

"*What?*"

Maclaren looked as if he'd been slapped.

"Ball needed help, and I wanted a ranch. I've a working partnership." Then looking up at Moira, I added, "And a man doesn't want to go too far from the girl he is to marry."

"What's that?" Maclaren was confused.

"Why, Father!" Moira's eyes widened, and a flicker of deviltry danced in them. "Haven't you heard? Mr. Brennan has been saying that he is going to marry me!"

"I'll see him in hell first!" He stared down at me.

"Young man, you stop using my daughter's name or you'll face me."

"I'd rather not face you. I want to keep peace in the family." I lifted my cup and took a swallow of coffee. "Nobody has a greater respect for your daughter's name than I. After all . . . she is to be my wife."

Maclaren's face flushed angrily, but Canaval chuckled and even Moira seemed amused.

Key Chapin put in a quieting word before Maclaren could say what might have precipitated trouble.

"There's an aspect of this situation, Rud, that may have escaped you. If Brennan is now Ball's partner, it might be better to let him stay on, then buy him out."

Maclaren absorbed the idea and was pleased. It was there in his eyes, plain to be seen. He looked down at me with new interest.

"Yes, yes, of course. We might do business, young man."

"We might . . . and we want peace, not trouble. But I did not become a partner to sell out. Also, in all honesty, I took on the partnership only by promising never to sell. Tomorrow I shall choose a building site.

"Which brings up another point. There are Boxed M cattle on Two-Bar range. It should take you no longer than a week to remove them. I shall inform the CP of the same time limit."

Maclaren's face was a study. He started to speak, then hesitated. Finishing my coffee, I got to my feet, I put down a coin and went out the door, closing it softly just as Maclaren started to speak.

There was a time for all things, and this was the time to leave . . . while I was ahead.

Rounding the building, I brought up short. Pinder's black-haired rider was standing beside my horse. There was a gun in his hand and an ugly look in his eyes.

"You talk too much. I heard that you'd moved in with Ball."

"So you heard."

"Sure, and Jim will pay a bonus for your hide."

His finger tightened and I threw myself aside and palmed my gun. It was fast ... the instinctive reaction of a man trained to use a gun. The gun sprang to my hand, it bucked in my palm. I heard the short, heavy bark of it, and between my first and second shots, his gun slammed a bullet that drew blood from my neck.

Blackie turned as if to walk away, then fell flat, his fingers clawing hard at the dirt.

Men came rushing among them those from Mother O'Hara's. "Seen it!" The speaker was a short, leather-faced man who had been harnessing a horse in the alley nearby. "Blackie laid for him with a drawn gun."

Canaval's gaze was cool, attentive. "A drawn gun? That was fast, man."

Maclaren looked at me more carefully. Probably he had believed I was some fresh youngster, but now he knew that I'd used a gun. This was going to change things. Instead of one lonely old man on the Two-Bar there was now another man, a young man, one who could shoot fast and straight.

When I could, I backed from the crowd and went to my horse, leading him around the corner into the street. Stepping into the leather, I looked around and saw Moira on the steps, watching me. I lifted my hat, then cantered away to the cottonwoods and my mules.

Ball was at the gate when I arrived, and I could see the relief in his eyes.

"Trouble?"

My account was brief, and to the point. There was nothing about killing that I liked.

"One more," Ball said grimly, "and one less."

But I was remembering the face of the girl on the steps. Moira knew now that I'd killed a man. How would she feel about that? How would she look upon me now?

CHAPTER 4

DURING THE NEXT two days I spent hours in the saddle going over the lands that lay under the Two-Bar brand. It was even better than I had expected, and it was easy to see why the CP and the Boxed M were envious.

Aside from the rich grass of Cottonwood Wash, and the plentiful water supply, there were miles of bunch grass country before the desert was reached, and even the desert was rich in a growth of antelope bush and wool fat.

It was a good ranch, with several waterholes other than the stream along the Wash, and with subirrigation over against the mountains. Only to the west were there ranches, and only from the west could other cattle get into the area to mingle with the Two-Bar herd.

Ball's calves had largely been rustled by the large outfits, and if we expected to prosper we must rid ourselves of the stock we had and get some young stuff. The cattle we had would never be in any better shape, but from now on would grow older and tougher. Now was the time to sell yet a drive was impossible.

Ball was frankly discouraged. "I'm afraid they've got us bottled up, Matt," he told me. "When you came along I was about ready to cash in my chips."

"Outfit down in the hills past Organ Rock."

Ball's head lifted sharply. "Forgot to tell you. Stay clear of that bunch. That's the Benaras place, the B Bar B. Six in the family. They have no truck with anybody—an' all of them are dead shots."

He smoked in silence for a while, and I considered the situation on the ranch. There was no time to be lost, and no sense in being buffaloed. The thing to do was to start building the outfit now.

An idea had come to my mind, and when I saddled up the next morning I drifted south.

It was a wild and lonely country, toward Organ Rock. Furrowed and eroded by thousands of years of sun, wind, and rain, a country tumbled and broken as if by some insane giant. Miles of raw land with only occasional spots of green to break the everlasting reds, pinks, and whites.

Occasionally, in the midst of a barren and lonely stretch, there would be an oasis of green, with trees, water, and grass. At each of these would be a few cattle, fat and lazy under the trees.

A narrow trail led up to the mesa, and I took it, letting the buckskin find his own way. There were few horse tracks, which told me that even the boys from the B Bar B rarely came this far.

Wind moved across the lonely mesa, the junipers stirred. I drew up, standing in the half shade of the tree and looking ahead. The mesa seemed empty, yet I had a sudden feeling of being observed. For a long time I listened, but no sound came across the silences.

The buckskin walked on, almost of his own volition. Another trail intersected, a more traveled trail. Both led in the direction I was now taking.

There was no sound but the footfalls of my horse, the lonely creak of the saddle, and once, far off, the cry of an eagle. A rabbit bounded up and away bouncing like a tufted rubber ball.

The mesa broke off sharply and before me lay a green valley not unlike Cottonwood Wash, but far wilder and more remote. Towering rock walls skirted it, and a dark-mouthed canyon opened wide into the valley. The trail down from the mesa led from bench to bench with easy swings and switchbacks, and I descended, riding more warily.

Twice antelope appeared in the distance and once a deer. There were tracks of cattle, but few were in evidence.

The wild country to the east, on my left, was exciting to see. A vast maze of winding canyons and broken ledges, of towering spires and massive battlements. It was a land unexplored and unknown, and greatly tempting to an itching foot.

A click of a drawn-back hammer stopped me in my tracks. Buck stood perfectly still, his ears up, and I kept both hands on the pommel.

"Goin' somewhar, stranger?"

The voice seemed to come from a clump of boulders at the edge of a hay meadow, but there was nobody in sight.

"I'm looking for the boss of the B Bar B."

"What might you want with him?"

"Business talk. I'm friendly."

The chuckle was dry. "Ever see a man covered by two Spencers who wasn't friendly?"

The next was a girl's voice. "Who you ridin' fo'?"

"I'm Matt Brennan, half-owner of the Two-Bar."

"You could be lyin'."

"Do I see the boss?"

"I reckon."

A tall boy of eighteen stepped from the rocks. Lean and loose-limbed, he looked tough and wise beyond his years. He carried his Spencer as if it was part of him. He motioned with his head to indicate a trail into the wide canyon.

Light steps came from somewhere behind him as he walked the buckskin forward. He did not turn in the saddle and kept his hands in sight.

The old man of the tribe was standing in front of a stone house built like a fort. Tall as his sons who stood beside him, he was straight as a lodge-pole pine.

To right and left, built back near the rock walls, were stables and other buildings. The hard-packed earth was swept clean, the horses were curried, and all the buildings were in good shape. Whatever else the Benaras family might be, they were workers.

The old man looked me over without expression. Then he took the pipe from his lean jaws.

"Get down an' set."

Inside, the house was as neat as on the outside. The floors were freshly scrubbed, as was the table. Nor was there anything makeshift about it. The house and furniture had been put together by skillful hands, each article shaped with care and affection.

A stout, motherly looking woman put out cups and poured coffee. A girl in a neat cotton dress brought homebaked bread and homemade butter to the table. Then she put out a pot of honey.

"Our own bees." Old Bob Benaras stared from

under shaggy brows. He looked like a patriarch right out of the Bible.

He watched me as I talked, smoking quietly. I ate a slice of bread, and did not spare the butter and honey. He watched with approval, and the girl brought a tall glass filled with creamy milk.

"We've some fat stock," I told him, "but we can't make a drive. What I would like is to trade the grown cattle to you, even up, for some of your young stuff."

I drank half the milk and put the glass down. It had been cold, fresh-taken from a cave, no doubt.

"You can make your drive," I went on, "and you can sell, so you will lose nothing. It would be right neighborly."

He looked sharp at me when I used the word, and I knew at once it had been the right one. This fierce old man, independent and proud, respected family and neighbors.

"We'll swap." He knocked out his pipe. "My boys will help you round up and drive."

"No need—no reason you should get involved in this fight."

He turned those fierce blue eyes at me. "I'm buyin' cows," he said grimly. "Anybody who wants trouble over that can have it!"

"Now, Pa!" Mother Benaras smiled at me. "Pa figures he's still a-feudin'."

Benaras shook his head, buttering a slice of bread. "We're beholden to no man, nor will we backwater for any man. Nick, you roust out and get Zeb. Then saddle up and ride with this man. You ride to his orders. Start no trouble, but back up for nobody. Understand?"

Nick turned and left the room, and Benaras turned to his wife.

"Ma, set up the table. We've a guest in the house." He looked at me, searchingly. "You had trouble with Pinder yet?"

So I told him how it began, of the talk in the stable, and of my meeting with Blackie later. I told that in few words, saying only, "Blackie braced me . . . waited for me with a drawn gun."

That was all I told them. The boys exchanged looks, and the old man began to tamp tobacco in his pipe.

"Had it comin'," that one. Jolly had trouble with him, figured to kill him soon or late."

They needed no further explanation than that. A man waited for you with a gun in hand . . . it followed as the night the day that if you were alive the other man was not. It also followed that you must have got into action mighty fast.

It was a pleasant meal—great heaps of mashed potatoes, slabs of beef and venison, and several vegetables. All the boys were there, tall, lean, and alike except for years. And all were carbon copies of their hard-bitten old father.

Reluctantly, when the meal was over, I got up to leave. Old Bob Benaras walked with me to my horse. He put a hand on the animal and nodded.

"Know a man by his horse," he said, "or his gun. Like to see 'em well chosen, well kept. You come over, son, you come over just any time. We don't neighbor much, ain't our sort of folks hereabouts. But you come along when you like."

It was well after dark when we moved out, taking

our time, and knowing each one of us, that we might run into trouble before we reached home. It was scarcely within the realm of possibility that my leave-taking had gone unobserved. Anxious as I was, I kept telling myself the old man had been on that ranch long before I appeared, that he could take care of himself.

Remembering the sign on the gate, I felt better. No man would willingly face that Spencer.

The moon came out, and the stars. The heat of the day vanished, as it always must in the desert where there is no growth to hold it, only the bare rocks and sand. The air was thin on the high mesa and we speeded up, anxious to be home.

Once, far off, we thought we heard a sound... Listening, we heard nothing.

At the gate I swung to open it, ready for a challenge.

Suddenly, Nick Benaras whispered, "Hold it!"

We froze, listening. We heard the sound of moving horses, and on the rim of the Wash, not fifty yards off, two riders appeared. We waited, rifles in our hands, but after a brief pause, apparently to listen, the two rode off toward town.

We rode through the gate and closed it. There was no challenge.

Zeb drew up sharply. "Nick!"

We stopped, waiting, listening.

"What is it, Zeb?"

"Smoke...I smell smoke."

CHAPTER 5

FEAR WENT THROUGH me like a hot blade.
Slapping the spurs to my tired buckskin, I put
the horse up the trail at a dead run, Nick and Zeb
right behind me.

Then I saw the flicker of flames and, racing up,
drew rein sharply.

The house was a charred ruin, with only a few
flames still flickering. The barn was gone, the corrals
had been pulled down.

"Ball!" I yelled it, panic rising in me. "Ball!"

And above the feeble sound of flames I heard a
faint cry.

He was hidden in a niche of rock near the spring,
and the miracle was that he had lived long enough to
tell his story. Fairly riddled with bullets, his clothes
were charred and his legs had been badly burned. It
took only a glance to know the old man was dying . . .
there was no chance, none at all.

Behind me I heard Nick's sharp-drawn breath, and
Zeb swore with bitter feeling.

Ball's fierce old eyes pleaded with me. "Don't . . .
don't let 'em git the place! Don't . . . never!"

His eyes went beyond me to Nick and Zeb. "You
witness. His now. I leave all I have to Matt . . . to
Brennan. Never to sell! Never to give up!"

"Who was it?"

Down on my knees beside the old man, I came to realize the affection I'd had for him. Only a few days had we been together, but they had been good days, and there had been rare understanding between us. And he was going, shot down and left for dead in a burning house. For the first time I wanted to kill.

I wanted it so that my hands shook and my voice trembled. I wanted it so that the tears in my eyes were there as much from anger as from sorrow.

"Pinder!" His voice was only a hoarse whisper. "Rollie Pinder, he . . . was dressed like . . . you. I let him in, then . . . Strange thing . . . thought I saw Park."

"Morgan Park?" I was incredulous.

His lips stirred, trying to shape words, but the words would not take form. He looked up at me, and he tried to smile. . . . He died that way, lying there on the ground with the firelight flickering on his face, and a cold wind coming along from the hills.

"Did you hear him say that Park was among them?"

"Ain't reasonable. He's thick with the Maclarens."

The light had been bad, Ball undoubtedly had been mistaken. Yet I made a mental reservation to check on Morgan Park's whereabouts.

The fire burned low and the night moved in with more clouds, shutting out the stars and gathering rich and black in the canyons. Occasional sparks flew up, and there was the smell of smoke and charred wood.

A ranch had been given me, but I had lost a friend. The road before me now stretched long and lonely, a road I must walk with my gun in my hand.

Standing there in the darkness, I made a vow that if there was no law here to punish the Pinders, and I knew no move would be made against them, I'd take the law in my own hand. Rollie would die and Jim would die, and every man who rode with them would live to rue that day.

And to the Benaras boys I said as much. They nodded, knowing how I felt. They were young men from a land of feud, men of strong friendship and bitter hatred, and of fights to the end.

"He was a good man," Zeb said. "Pa liked him."

FOR TWO DAYS we combed the draws, gathering cattle. At the end of the second day we had only three hundred head. Rustling by the big brands had sadly depleted the herds of the Two-Bar.

We made our gather in the bottom of Cottonwood Wash, where there was water and grass. Once in that bottom, it was easy to hold the cows.

"Come morning, we'll start our drive."

Nick looked around at me. "Figure to leave the ranch unguarded?"

"If they move in," I told him, "they can move out again or be buried there."

The canyon channeled the drive and the cattle were in good shape and easy to handle. It took us all day to make the drive, skirting the mesa I had crossed in my first ride to Organ Rock. My side pained me very little although it was still stiff. There was only that gnawing, deep-burning anger at the killers of old man Ball to worry me.

They had left a wounded man to burn. They had killed a man who wanted only peace, the right to enjoy the ranch he had built from nothing. He had been an old man, strong for his years, but with a weariness on him and the need for quiet evenings and brisk, cool mornings, and a chair on a porch. And that old man had died in the falling timbers of his burning home, his body twisted with the pain of bullet wounds.

At the ranch we told our story to Benaras, and as he listened his hard old face stiffened with anger.

We ate there, sitting again at that table that seemed always heavy with food, and we talked long, saying nothing of what was to come, for we were men without threats. We were men who talked little of the deeds to be done.

Looking back over the few days since I had first come to Hattan's Point, I knew I had changed.

It is the right of youth to be gay and proud, to ride with a challenge. The young bull must always try his strength. It was always so, the test of strength and the test of youth. Yet when the male met his woman it was different. I had met mine thus, and I had seen an old man die...these are things to bring years to a man.

When day came again to Organ Rock, Jolly and Jonathan Benaras helped me start the herd of young stuff back up the trail. Benaras had given me two dozen head more than I'd asked in trade, but the stock I'd given him were heavy and ready for market as they stood.

Jolly had been at Hattan's when the news of the raid reached the town. The Apache trailer, Bunt Wilson, and Corby Kitchen had been on the raid, and three others unnamed.

"Hear anything said about Morgan Park?"

"Not him. Lyell, who rides for Park, he was along."

Ball might have meant to say it was a rider of Park's rather than Park himself. That was more likely.

Jonathan rode back from the point. He had gone on ahead, scouting the way.

"Folks at your place . . . two, maybe three."

Something in me turned cold and ugly. "Bring the herd. I'll ride on ahead."

Jonathan's big Adam's apple bobbed. "Jolly an' me, we ain't had much fun lately. Can't we come along?"

"Foot of the hill. Right below where the house was.

An idea hit me. "Where's their camp?"

"They got them a tent."

"We'll take the herd . . . drive it right over the tent."

Jonathan looked at Jolly. "Boys'll be sore. Missin' all the fun."

We started the herd. They were young stuff and full of ginger, ready to run. They came out of the canyon some two hundred yards from the camp, and then we really lit into them.

With a wild yell, I banged a couple of quick shots from my gun and the herd lit out as if they were making a break for water after a long dry drive. They hit that stretch with their bellies to the grass and ran like deer.

Up ahead we saw men jumping up. Somebody yelled, somebody else grabbed for a rifle, and then that herd hit them, running full tilt.

One man dove for his horse, missed his grab, and fell sprawling. He came up running and just barely made it to the top of a rock as the herd broke around it.

The tent was smashed down, the food trampled into the dust. The fire scattered, utensils smashed and banged around. The herd went on through, some of them going up the hill, some breaking around it. The camp was a shambles, the gear the men had packed up there was ruined.

One man who had scrambled into a saddle in time swung his horse and came back. He was a big redhead and he looked tough. He was fighting mad.

"What goes on here? What the hell's this?"

He rode a Boxed M horse. Rud Maclaren's men had beaten the CP to the ranch.

Kneeing my horse alongside his, I told him. "I'm Matt Brennan, owner of the Two-Bar, with witnesses to prove it. You're trespassing. Now light a shuck!"

"I will like hell!" His face flushed with anger. "I got my orders, an' I—"

My fist backhanded into his teeth, smashing his lips to pulp. He went back out of the saddle and I swung my horse around and jumped to the ground as he started to get up. I hit him getting off the ground and he went down hard. He started up again, then dove at my feet. I jumped back and as he sprawled out I grabbed his hair and jerked him up. I smashed a fist into his wind, and then shoved him off and hit him in the face with both hands. He went down, and he didn't make any move to get up.

Jonathan and Jolly had rounded up two more men and herded them to me.

One was a slim, hard-faced youngster who looked as if the devil was riding him. His kind I had seen before. The other was a stocky redhead with a scar on his jaw.

"You ruined my outfit," he said. "What kind of a deal is this?"

"When you ride for a fighting brand you can expect trouble. What did you expect when you came up here? A pink tea party? You go back and tell Maclaren not to send boys to do a man's job. I'll shoot the next trespasser on sight."

The younger one was sneering. "What if he sends me?" He put his hands on his hips. "If I hadn't lost my gun in the scramble you'd eat that!"

"Jolly! Lend me your gun!"

Without a word, Benaras passed his six-shooter to me.

The youngster's eyes were suddenly calculating and wary. He suspected a trick, but could not guess what it would be.

Taking the gun by the barrel, I walked toward him. "You get your chance," I said. Flipping it in my hand so the butt was up, I held it out. "Anyway you like. Try a border roll or shoot from where it is. Anyway you try it, I'm going to kill you."

He didn't like it. He stared at me and then at the gun. His tongue touched his lips. He wanted that gun so bad he could taste it, and my gun was in my holster.

He had that streak of viciousness it takes to make a killer, but suddenly he was face to face with killing and right now he wanted no part of it. The thing that bothered him was the fact that I'd gamble. No man would make such a gamble unless he knew ... or unless he was crazy.

"It's a trick," he said. "You ain't that much of a fool."

"*Fool?*" That brought my fury surging to the top. "Why, you cheap, phony, imitation of a badman! I'd give you two guns and shoot your ears off any day you'd like!

"Right now! Shove your gun in my belly and I'll shove mine in yours! If you want to die, let's make it easy! Come on, you cheapskate! *Try it!*"

Crazy? Sure. But right then I didn't care. His face turned whiter and his eyes were hot and ugly. He was trembling with eagerness to grab that gun. But face to face? Guns shoved against the body? We would both die. We couldn't miss. He shook his head, and his lips were dry and his eyes staring.

"No . . . no. . . ."

My fingers held the gun by the barrel. Flipping it up, I caught the gun by the butt and dashed it down across his skull. He hit the dirt at my feet, knocked cold.

The two redheads were both on their feet staring at me, waiting.

"All right," I said. "Pick him up and get off the place."

"It was orders."

"You could quit, couldn't you?"

The stocky redhead stared at me. "He'll be huntin' you now. You won't live long. You know what that is?" He indicated the youngster on the ground. "That's Bodie Miller!"

The name was familiar. Bodie Miller had killed two men. He was known to be utterly vicious, and although he lacked seasoning he had it in him to be one of the worst.

The two redheads picked Miller off the ground and hoisted him into his saddle. Disarmed, they slowly walked their horses out of the Wash and took the trail for home.

The cattle were no cause for worry. They would not leave the good grass of the Wash nor of the feeder canyons from the east.

Jonathan Benaras rolled a smoke and hitched his one gallus higher on his shoulder after he had put the cigarette between his lips. He struck a match and lighted up.

"Well," he said wryly, "they cain't say you don't walk in swingin'. You've tackled nigh ever'body in the country!"

When they were gone, riding home and talking about it, I studied the situation. There was nothing about it that I liked. Maclaren would be back... or the Pinders would come, and I was one man alone.

CHAPTER 6

I T WAS NO longer possible to defend the Two-Bar. No other decision was possible. Reluctantly, I decided that for the time, at least, I must have another place of retreat. Although I might remain at the ranch, I must be prepared to leave at an instant's notice.

Before Ball was killed we had made plans for our last stand, if that became necessary, at an old cliff house in Two-Bar canyon. Ball and I had stored some food there, and now, digging around in the ruins, I found some undamaged canned stuff that I transported up there and concealed near the cliff house.

As I rode I tried to think a way out of the corner in which I found myself.

My only friends were the Benaras family, but this was not their fight, it was mine.

Across the east was broken country of canyons and desert, almost without water, a country brutal and heat-blistered, where a man might die under a blazing sun, choking with thirst... unless he knew the waterholes.

On the west were the holdings of the CP and the Boxed M.

Once, not many weeks ago, I would have been tempted to start hunting down the men who had killed my partner. Now I knew better.

The way to defeat them was to hold the ranch, to keep it for myself, as Ball had wished, to keep them from what they had hoped to gain by murder. To do this I must stay alive, I must think, plan.

Now young cattle ran on Two-Bar grass. They would be growing, fattening up. That much was done. But a new house must be built, new corrals. I must put down such solid roots that I could never be dislodged. And to have roots was a new thing for me.

Maclaren would, when possible, try to give the cover of right and legality to his actions. Pinder was under no such compulsion. Yet they were equally dangerous.

Another thing. I must keep the good will of those few friends I had. The Benaras family were really all. But at Hattan's Point there were people who, if not my friends, were not my enemies either. Key Chapin was not taking sides. Morally at least, I must have him on my side. Mrs. O'Hara was another.

Sheriff Tharp would not interfere in any ranch squabble. That Ball had told me. He would arrest outlaws, killers, and rustlers. It was up to property holders to settle their own arguments, gunplay or not.

Yet if Tharp could find nothing in me to dislike, it would at least help. My fighting must be in self-defense.

All the following day I worked around the place, cleaning up the debris left by the fire, and rebuilding the corral but keeping a careful lookout. Some of the saddle stock had escaped when the corrals were pulled down. These I rounded up and herded back to the corral with my mules.

One young steer had suffered a broken leg in the

drive on the Boxed M camp, so I shot it and butchered the carcass, hanging up the beef until I could jerk it.

I cleaned out the spring near where the house had stood, and built several rifle pits against possible attack. Then, mounting up, I ended my day by scouting the vicinity. No riders were in sight. All was still. The young stock were making themselves happily at home in the knee-high grass.

Three times I spotted good defense areas and mapped out routes that would offer cover in going from one to the other. Being a practical man, I also looked for an escape route.

I slept in a sheltered place near the spring and at daybreak I rolled out of my blankets and saddled up.

The morning was clear and cool. In an hour the sun would be warming the hills, but now a coat was a comfortable thing. Reluctantly, I put out my fire and swung into the saddle. The buckskin was frisky and tugged at the bit, ready to go.

Rounding a bend, I suddenly saw a dozen riders coming toward me at a canter. Wheeling the buckskin, I slapped the spurs into his flanks and went up the Wash at a dead run. A bullet whined past my ear as I swung into a branch canyon and raced to the top of the plateau.

Behind me the racing horses ran past the canyon's mouth. Then there was a shout as a rider saw me, and they turned back. By the time they entered the canyon mouth I was on top of the mesa.

It was the Pinders, and they were out for blood.

I dropped to the ground and took a running dive for a rock, landing behind it and swinging my

Winchester to my shoulder at the same time. The butt settled, I took a long breath, then squeezed off my shot.

A horse stumbled, throwing his rider over his head, and my second shot nailed the rider before he could rise. Firing as rapidly as I could aim, I sent a dozen bullets screaming down the canyon. They scattered for shelter, a wild melee of lunging horses and men.

The man I'd shot began to crawl, dragging a broken leg. He was out of it, so I let him go.

Several horses had raced away, but two stood ground-hitched. On one of these was a big canteen. I emptied it with a shot. A foot showed and I triggered my Winchester. A bit of leather flew up and the foot was withdrawn.

Bullets ricocheted around me, but my position could not have been better. As long as I remained where I was they could neither advance nor retreat.

The sun was well up in the sky now, and the day promised to be hot. Where I lay there was a little shade from a rock overhang, and I had water on my saddle. They had neither. Digging out a little hollow in the sand, I settled down to be comfortable.

Several shots were fired, but they were not anxious to expose their position, and the shots were far off the mark.

Five... ten minutes passed. Then I saw a man trying to crawl back toward the canyon mouth.

I let him crawl.... When he was a good twenty yards from shelter I sighted down the barrel and put one into the sand right ahead of him. He sprang to his feet and ducked for shelter. I splattered rock fragments into his face with a ricochet and he made a running dive for shelter, with another bullet helping him along.

"Looks like a hot day!" I called.

My voice carried well in the rocky canyon, and somebody swore viciously. I sat back and rolled a smoke. Nobody moved down below.

The canyon mouth was like an oven. Heat waves danced in the sun, the rocks became blistering. The hours marched slowly by. From time to time some restless soul made a move, but a quick shot would always change his mind. I drank from my canteen and moved a little with the shade.

"How long you figure you can keep us here?" someone yelled.

"I've got plenty of water and two hundred rounds of ammunition!"

One of them swore again, and there were shouted threats. Silence descended over the canyon. Knowing they could get no water must have aggravated their thirst. The sun swam in a coppery sea of heat, and the horizon was lost in heat waves. Sweat trickled down my face and down my body under the arms. Where I lay there was not only shade but a slight breeze, but where they lay the heat reflected off the canyon walls and all wind was shut off.

Finally, letting go with a shot, I slid back out of sight and got to my feet.

My horse cropped grass near some rocks, well under the shade. Shifting my rifle to my left hand, I slid down the rocks, mopping my face with my right. Then I stopped, my hand belt high.

Backed up against a rock near my horse was a man

whom I knew at once, although I had never seen him. It was Rollie Pinder.

"You gave them boys hell."

"They asked for it."

As I spoke he smiled slowly and dropped his hand for his gun.

His easy smile and casual voice were nicely calculated to throw me off guard, but my left hand held the barrel of my rifle a few inches forward of the trigger guard, the butt in front of me.

As his hand dropped I tilted the gun hard and the stock struck my hip as my hand slapped the trigger guard.

Rollie was fast and his gun came up smoking. His slug struck me a split second after my finger squeezed off its shot. It felt as if I had been kicked in the side and I took a staggering step back, a rolling rock under my foot throwing me out of line of his second shot.

Then I fired again. I'd worked the lever unconsciously, and my aim was true.

Rollie fell back against the rocks. He was still smiling that casual smile. Only now it seemed frozen into his features. He started to bring his gun up and I heard the report. But I was firing . . . I shot three times as fast as I could work the lever.

Weaving on my feet, I stared down at his body. Great holes had been torn into him by the .44 slugs.

I scrambled back to my former position, and was only just in time. The men below, alerted by my shots, had made a break to get away. My head was spinning and my eyes refused to focus. If they started after me now, I was through.

The ground seemed to dip under me, but I raised my rifle and got off a shot, then another. One man went down and the others scrambled for cover.

My legs went out from under me and I sat down hard. My breath coming in ragged gasps, I ripped my shirt and plugged my wounds. I had to get away now. But even if the way were open, I could never climb to the cliff house.

Rifle dragging, I crawled and slid back to the buckskin. Twice I almost fainted from weakness. Pain gripped at my vitals, squeezing and knotting them. Then I got hold of the saddle horn and pulled myself into the saddle. When I finally got my rifle into its scabbard I took some piggin strings and tied my hands to the saddle horn, then across my thighs to hold me on.

The buckskin was already walking, as if sensing the need to be away. I pointed him into the wilderness of canyons.

"Go, boy. Keep goin'."

Sometime after that I fainted.... Twice during the long hours that followed I awakened to find the horse still walking westward. Each time I muttered to him, and he walked on into the darkness, finding his own way.

They would be coming after me. This remained in my mind. Wracked with pain, I had only the driving urge to get away. I pushed on, deeper and deeper into that lonely, trackless land made even stranger by the darkness.

Day was near when at last my eyes opened again. When I lifted my head the effort made it swim dizzily, but I stared around, seeing nothing familiar.

Buck had stopped beside a small spring in a canyon. There was plenty of grass, a few trees, and not far away the ruin of a rock house. On the sand near the spring were the tracks of a mountain lion and of deer, but no sign of men, horses, or cattle. The canyon here was fifty yards wide, with walls that towered hundreds of feet into the sky.

Fumbling at the strings with swollen fingers, I untied my hands, then the strings that bound my thighs. Sliding to the ground, I fell. Buck snorted and stepped away, then returned to sniff curiously at me. He drew back from the smell of stale clothes and dried blood, and I lay staring up at him, a crumpled human thing, my body raw with pain and faint with weakness.

"It's all right, Buck." I whispered the words. "All right."

I lay very still, staring at the sky, watching the changing light. I wanted only to lie there, to make no effort . . . to die.

To die?

No. . . .

There had been a promise made. A promise to Moira, and a promise to a tired old man who had been killed.

Yet if I would live I must move. For they would not let me go now. They would hunt me down. Jim Pinder would want to kill the man who had shot his brother, and there was Bodie Miller, from Maclaren's.

Now . . . I must act now . . . fix my wounds, drink, find a place to hide, a place for a last stand. And it had to be close, for I could not go far.

Nothing within me told me I could do it. My body was weak, and I seemed to have no will, but somehow, someway, I was going to try.

Rolling over, I got my hands under me. Then I started to crawl. . . .

CHAPTER 7

PULLING MYSELF TO the edge of the water hole, I drank deep of the clear, cold water. The coolness seemed to creep all through the tissues of my body and I lay there, breathing heavily.

A sea of dull pain seemed to wash over me, yet I forced myself to think, to fight back the pain. I must bathe my wounds. That meant hot water, and hot water meant a fire.

Yet there was such weakness in me that I could scarcely close my hand. I had lost much blood, I had not eaten, and I had ridden far with the strength draining from my body.

With contempt I stared at my helpless hands, hating them for their weakness. And then I began to fight for strength in those fingers, willing them to be strong. My left hand reached out and pulled a stick to me. Then another.

Some scraped-up leaves, some fragments of dried manzanita ... soon I would have a fire.

I was a creature fighting for survival, fighting the oldest battle known to man. Through waves of recurring delirium and weakness, I dragged myself to an aspen, where I peeled bark to make a pot in which to heat water.

Patiently, my eyes blinking heavily, my fingers

puzzling out the form, I shaped the bark into a crude pot, and into it I poured water.

Almost crying with weakness, I got a fire started and watched the flames take hold. Then I put the bark vessel on top of two rocks and the flames rose around it. As long as the flames stayed below the water level the bark would not burn, for the water inside would absorb the heat. Trying to push more sticks into the fire, I blacked out again.

When next my eyes opened the water was boiling. Pulling myself up to a sitting position, I unbuckled my gun belt and let the guns fall to the ground beside me. Then carefully I opened my shirt and, soaking a piece of the cloth in the hot water, began to bathe my wounds.

The hot water felt good as I gingerly worked the cloth plugs free, but the sight of the wound in my side was frightening. It was red and inflamed, but the bullet had gone clear through and as near as I could see, had touched nothing vital.

A second slug had gone through the fleshy part of my thigh, and after bathing that wound also, I lay still for a long time, regaining strength and soaking up the heat.

Nearby was a patch of prickly pear. Crawling to it, I cut off a few big leaves and roasted them to get off the spines. Then I bound the pulp over the wounds. It was a method Indians used to fight inflammation, and I knew of no other than Indian remedies that would do me here.

It was a slow thing, this working to patch my wounds, and I realized there was little time left to me. My enemies would be working out my trail, and I had no idea how far my horse had come in the darkness, nor over what sort of ground. My trail might be plain as day, or it might be confusing.

There was a clump of amolillo nearby and I dug up some roots, scraping them into boiling water. They foamed up when stirred and I drank some of the foamy liquid. Indians claimed bullet wounds healed better after a man drank amolillo water.

Then I made a meal of squaw cabbage and bread-root, lacking the strength to get my saddlebags. Sick with weakness, I crawled under the brush and slept, awakening to drink deep of the cold water, then to sleep again.

And through the red darkness of my tortured sleep men rode and fought and guns crashed. Men struggled in the shadows along the edge of my consciousness.

Morgan Park . . . Pinder . . . Rud Maclaren, and the sharply feral face of Bodie Miller.

The muzzling of my horse awakened me, and the cold light of a new day was beginning.

"All right, Buck," I whispered. "I'm awake. I'm alive."

And I was . . . just barely.

My weakness frightened me. If they came upon me now they would not hesitate to kill me, nor could I fight them off.

Lying on my back I breathed heavily, trying to find some way out. I had no doubt they were coming, and that they could not be far behind.

They might have trouble with the trail, but they would figure that I was hurt and unconscious, that my horse was finding his own way. Then they would come fast.

High up the canyon wall there was a patch of green, perhaps a break in the rock. My eyes had been on it for some time before it began to register on my awareness. Sudden hope brought me struggling to my elbow. My eyes studied the break in the wall, if that was what it was. There was green there, foothold for a tree or two, and there seemed to be a ledge below.

Rolling over, I crawled along the ground to the water hole and drank deep and long, then I filled my canteen. Now I had only to get into the saddle, but first, I tried to wipe out all the tracks I had left. I knew I could not get rid of all . . . but there was a chance I could throw them off my trail.

Getting to my knees, I caught the buckskin's stirrup and pulled myself erect. Then I got a foot into the stirrup and swung into the saddle.

For an instant my head spun crazily as I clung to the saddle horn. Then my brain seemed to clear and I lifted my heavy head, slowly walking the horse forward. There was a trail, very narrow, littered at places with talus from above, but a trail. Kneeing the horse into it, I urged him forward. Mountain-bred, he started up, blowing a little, and stepping gingerly.

Several minutes passed and I clung to the pommel, unable to lift my head, needing all my strength to maintain my feeble hold. Then suddenly we rounded a boulder and stood in a high, hanging valley.

A great crack in the rock of the mesa, caused by some ancient earth-shock, it was flat-floored and high-walled, but the grass was rich and green. I could hear water running somewhere back in the rock.

The area of the place was not over seven or eight acres, and there was another opening on the far side, partly covered by a slide of rock. What I had found was a tiny oasis in the desert, but I was not the first to use this hideaway. An instant later I realized that.

Before me, almost concealed by the cliff against which it stood, was a massive stone tower. Square, it was almost sixty feet tall, and blackened by age and fire.

The prehistoric Indians who had built that tower knew a good thing when they found it, for here was water, forage, and firewood. Moreover, the place was ideal for defense. Nobody could come up the trail I had used, in the face of a determined defender.

Near the tower grew some stunted maize, long since gone native. Nowhere was there any evidence that a human foot had been here for centuries.

Riding close to the tower, I found the water. It fell from a crack in the rock into a small pool maybe ten feet across and half that deep.

Carefully, I lowered myself to the ground, then I loosened the cinch and let the saddle fall from the buckskin's back. When I had the bridle off I crawled to a place on the grass and stretched out.

There was still much to do, but my efforts had left me exhausted. Nevertheless, as I lay there I found myself filled with a fierce determination to live, to fight back, to win. I was no animal to be hunted and killed, nor was I to be driven from what was rightfully mine.

Regardless of what my enemies might do now, I must rest and regain my strength. Let them have the victory for the present.

There was food in my saddlebags—jerked beef, a

little dried fruit, some hardtack. There was maize here that I could crush to meal to make a kind of pinole. There was squaw cabbage and breadroot. There were some piñons...and I saw signs left by deer and rabbits.

The deer droppings were shiny...evidence of their freshness. Deer still came here then...and I had already seen some of the blue quail that are native to desert country. So I would live, I would survive, I would win.

Near the wall of the ruined tower I made my bed. Working carefully, I erected a crude parapet of stones from which I could cover the trail up which I had come. Near it I placed my rifle and ammunition. At my back would be the spring.

Only then did I rest.

———

SLOWLY A WEEK drifted by. I slept, awakened, cooked, ate, and slept again. Slowly the soreness left my wounds and my strength began to come back. Yet I was still far from recovered. Several times I snared rabbits, and once I shot a deer. Nobody came near, and if they came to the water hole below I did not hear them.

When I was able to walk a few halting steps, I explored my hideaway. While walking through the trees at the far end, I killed a sage hen and made a thick broth, using wild onions, breadroot, and the bulbs of the sego lily.

Several times I found arrowheads. They were entirely unlike any I had seen before, longer in design and fluted along the sides.

But a devil of impatience was riding me. The longer I remained away, the more firmly my enemies would be entrenched. Despite that, I forced myself to wait. The venison lasted, and I killed quail and another sage hen. I ate well, but grew increasingly restless. Several times I managed to climb to the top of the mesa and lay there in the sun watching the canyon up which Buck must have come during the long hours when I had been in the saddle.

The mesa that was my lookout towered above the surrounding country, and below me lay mile upon mile of serrated ridges and broken land. It was a fantastic land of pale pink, salmon, and deep red, touched here and there by cloud shadows. It was raw and magnificent.

But impatience was on me, and the time had come to move. My jerked beef and venison were long since gone. The quail and sage hens had grown cautious.

On the morning of the sixteenth day I saddled my horse. It was time to return.

Reluctantly as I left my haven, I was eager to be back. The deep, slow anger that had been burning in me had settled to resolution. Carefully, I worked my way down the trail.

At the water hole I looked around. There were the tracks of two horses here. They had come this far, given up, and gone back. My trail then, was lost. Knowing nothing of my position, I followed the trail of those searchers as the best way to get back to the Two-Bar.

Before I had ridden three miles down the canyon I began to see how difficult my trail must have been. I knew then that the two riders who had been at the water hole had come there more by chance than by intention.

The canyon narrowed where a stream flowed into it, and following down the canyon the only trail lay in the bed of the stream itself. On both sides the walls lifted sheer. At places great overhangs of rock sheltered the stream and I splashed along in semitwilight. Here and there the canyon narrowed to less than thirty feet, the entire floor covered by water.

Threading the boxlike gorges I came suddenly into a vast amphitheater surrounded by towering rock walls. Drawing up, I looked across the amphitheater toward a valley all of half a mile wide. Buck's head came up and his nostrils fluttered. I spoke to him and he remained still, watching.

Coming toward me, still too far to identify, was a lone rider.

CHAPTER 8

REINING THE BUCKSKIN over into the trees, I drew up and waited. Had I been seen? If so, would the rider come on?

The rider came on . . . studying the ground, searching for tracks. I waited, slipping the rawhide throng from my gun and loosening it in the holster.

The day was warm and the sky clear. The rider was closer now and I could make out the colors in the clothing, the color of the horse, the— It was Moira Maclaren!

Riding out from the shadows I waited for her to see me, and she did, almost at once.

My shirt had been torn by a bullet and by my own hands, my face was covered with a two weeks' beard and my cheeks were drawn and hollow, yet the look of surprised relief on her face was good to see.

"Matt?" She was incredulous. "You're alive?"

My buckskin walked close to her horse. "Did you think I would die before you had those sons I promised?"

"Don't joke."

"I'm not joking."

Her eyes searched mine and she flushed a little, then quickly changed the subject.

"You must go away. If you come back now they'll kill you."

"I'll not run. I'm going back."

"But you mustn't! They believe you're dead. Let them think so. Go away now, go while you can. They've looked and looked, but they couldn't find you. Jim Pinder has sworn that if you're alive he'll kill you on sight, and Bodie Miller hates you."

"I'll be riding back."

She seemed to give up then, and I don't believe she really had thought I would run. And I was glad she knew me so well.

"Jim Pinder has the Two-Bar."

"Then he can move."

She noticed my full canteen, then waved her hand at the valley where we sat our horses.

"Father will be amazed when he learns there is water back here, and grass. Nobody believed anyone could live in this wilderness. I think you found the only place where there was either water or grass."

"Don't give me the credit. My horse found it."

"You've had a bad time?"

"It wasn't good." I glanced back the way she came. "You weren't trailed?"

"No . . . I made sure."

"You've looked for me before this?"

She nodded. "Yes, Matt. I was afraid you'd be dying out here alone. I couldn't stand that."

"Rollie was good. He was very good."

"Then it was you who killed him?"

"Who else?"

"Canaval and Bodie found him. Canaval was sure it was you, but some of the others thought it was the Benaras boys."

"They've done no fighting for me."

We sat there silent for a while, doing our thinking. What it was she thought I'd no idea, but I was thinking of her and what a woman she was. Now that I looked at her well, I could see she was thinner, and her cheeks looked drawn. It seemed strange to think that a woman could worry about me. It had been a long time since anyone had.

"Seems miles from anywhere, doesn't it?"

She looked around, her eyes searching mine. "I wish we didn't have to go back."

"But we do."

She hesitated a little and then said, "Matt, you've said you wanted me. I believe you do. If you don't go back, Matt, I'll go away with you. Now ... anywhere you want to go."

So there it was ... all any man could want. A girl so lovely that I never looked at her without surprise, and never without a quick feeling of wanting to take her in my arms. I loved her, this daughter of Maclaren.

"No," I said, "you know I must go back. Ball told me I was never to give it up, and I will not."

"But you can't! You're ill—and you've been hurt!"

"So ... I have been hurt. But that's over and I'm mending fast. Sixteen days now I've rested, and it's more than time enough."

She turned her horse to ride back with me, and we walked a little in silence. "Tell your father to pull his cattle back," I said. "I want no trouble with him."

"He won't do it."

"He must."

"You forget, I'm my father's daughter."

"And my wife ... soon to be."

This time she did not deny it. But she did not accept it either.

At the edge of the badlands, after miles of argument and talk, I turned in my saddle.

"From here, I ride alone. It's too dangerous for you. But you can tell Morgan Park..."

So I sat and watched her ride away toward the Boxed trail, thinking what a lucky man I'd be to have her.

She sat her saddle like a young queen, her back straight and her shoulders trim and lovely. She turned as if aware of my eyes, and she looked back, but she did not wave, nor did I.

Then I reined my horse around and started for town.

Often I shall live over that parting and that long ride down from the mountains. Often I will think of her and how she looked that day, for rarely do such days come to the life of any man. We had argued, yes, but it was a good argument and without harsh words.

And now before me lay my hours of trouble. There was only one way to do it. For another there might have been other ways, but not for me. My way was to ride in and take the bull by the horns, and that was what I meant to do. Not to the Two-Bar yet, but to town.

They must know that I was alive. They must know the facts of my fight and my survival.

I was no man to run, and it was here I had staked my claim and my future, and among these people I was to live. It was important that they understand.

So I would ride into town. If Jim Pinder was there one or both of us would die.

If Bodie Miller was there, I would have to kill him or be killed myself.

Any of the riders of the Boxed M or CP might try to kill me. I was fair game for them now.

Yet my destiny lay before me and I was not a man to hesitate. Turning the buckskin into the trail, I rode on at an easy gait. There was plenty of time...I was in no hurry to kill or to be killed.

Rud Maclaren was not a bad man, of this I was convinced. Like many another, he thought first of his ranch, and he wanted it to be the best ranch possible. It was easy to see why he wanted the water of the Two-Bar—in his position I would have wanted it, too.

But Maclaren had come to think that anything that made his ranch better also made everything better. He was, as are many self-made men, curiously self-centered. He stood at the corners of the world, and all that happened in it must be important to him.

He was a good man, but a man with power, and somewhere, back in those days when I had read many books, I'd read that power corrupts.

It was that power of his that I must face.

The trail was empty, the afternoon late. The buckskin was a fast walker and we covered ground. Smoke trailed into the sky from several chimneys. I heard an axe striking, a door slam.

Leaving the trail, I cut across the desert toward the outskirts of town, a scattering of shacks and adobes that offered some concealment until I'd be quite close.

Behind an abandoned adobe I drew rein. Rolling a cigarette, I lit up and began to smoke.

I wanted a shave . . . sitting my saddle, I located the barber shop in my mind, and its relationship to other buildings. There was a chance I could get to it and into a chair without being seen.

Once I had my hair cut and had been shaved, I'd go to Mother O'Hara's. I'd avoid the saloons where any Pinder or Maclaren riders might be, get a meal, and try to find a chance to talk to Key Chapin. I would also talk to Mrs. O'Hara.

Both were people of influence and would be valuable allies. I did not want their help, only their understanding.

Wiping my guns free of dust, I checked the loads. I was carrying six shells to each gun. I knocked the dust from my hat, brushed my chaps, and tried to rearrange my shirt to present a somewhat better appearance.

"All right, Buck," I said softly, "here we go!"

We walked around the corner and past a yard where a young girl was feeding chickens, past a couple of tied horses, and then to the back of the barber shop. There was an abandoned stable there, and swinging down, I led the buckskin inside and tied him.

It was a long, low-roofed building, covered with ancient thatch. There was a little hay there, and I forked some into the manger, then stood the fork against the wall and settled my hat lower on my head.

My hands were sweating and my mouth tasted dry. I told myself I was a fool—and then stepped out into the open. There was no one in sight.

Walking slowly so as not to attract attention, I crossed toward the back door of the barber shop.

The grass of the backyard was parched and dry,

the slivery and gray old steps were broken and creaked as I mounted them. I looked through the glass in the door and saw that the only man in the shop was the barber himself. Opening the door, I stepped in.

He glanced up, then got to his feet without interest and went behind the chair.

"Haircut an' shave," I told him, "I been out prospectin'."

"Cowhand?"

"Yeah...an' I'll be glad to get back to it."

He chuckled and went to work. "Missed all the fun," he said. "Been lively around."

"Yeah?"

"Rollie Pinder was killed...never figured the man lived was fast enough. Some folks say it was the Benaras boys, but they use rifles. I figure it was that there Brennan feller."

He snipped away steadily. Then he said, "We'll never know, prob'ly. Dead now."

"Brennan?"

"Uh-huh...folks say Rollie got some lead into him, seems like. They found blood sign."

The chair was comfortable. I closed my eyes. It would be good to sleep, to rest. It had been a long time since I had slept in a bed. With the quiet drone of the barber's voice, the comfort of the chair, I felt myself nodding.

"You'll have to sit up, mister. Can't cut your hair 'less you do."

So I sat up, but when he lay the chair back to shave me, my eyes closed again, and my body relaxed into the comfort of the chair. A hot towel on my face felt good. I listened to the razor stropping, slapping leather. Slapping leather, as I might soon be doing.

Smiling and half asleep, I felt the lather working into my beard under the barber's fingers. I was not quite asleep, not quite awake. A rider went by in the street. The razor was sharp and it felt good on my face . . . I dozed. . . .

A hand shook my shoulder, shook it hard. My eyes opened into the anxious eyes of the barber.

"Look, mister, you better get out of here. Get out of town."

"You know me?" My face was free of the beard now.

"Seen you once . . . at Mother O'Hara's. You better go."

The little rest had left me groggy. I got out of the chair and checked my guns. It was not a time to trust any man.

"Don't want me killed here, is that it? Don't want my blood on your floor?"

"That ain't it. I got nothing against you. Never knowed who you was until you got rid of that beard. No, you just move out. You ain't safe. That Pinder outfit . . ."

My fingers found the money in my pocket.

"Thanks," I said. "I enjoyed the shave."

Then I walked to the front door and looked down the street. Two men sat in front of the store. I put on my hat and lifting a hand to the barber, I stepped out.

It was only sixty feet to Mother O'Hara's, but it was going to be a long walk.

CHAPTER 9

WALKING THAT SIXTY feet, I knew a dozen men might be waiting to kill me. Unconsciously, I guess a little swagger got into me. It isn't every man who is hunted by a small army!

For an instant I paused by the window of Mother O'Hara's and glanced in. Key Chapin was there, and Morgan Park. I could not see who else. Down the street all was quiet. If anyone had identified me they made no move, and the barber had not left his shop.

My hand turned the knob and I stepped in, closing the door behind me.

The smell of coffee was in the air, and the pleasant room was quiet. Morgan Park looked up and our eyes held across the room.

"Next time you won't catch me with my hands down, Park."

Before he could reply I drew back a corner of the bench and sat down, keeping my guns free for my hands. The pot was on the table and I filled a cup.

"Chapin, an item for the press. Something like this: Matt Brennan of the Two-Bar was in town Friday afternoon. Matt is recovering from bullet wounds incurred during a minor dispute with Rollie Pinder, but is returning to the Two-Bar to take up where he left off."

"That will be news to Pinder."

"Tell him to expect me. I'll kill or see hung every man concerned in the killing of old man Ball."

"You know them?"

All eyes were on me now, and Mrs. O'Hara stood in the door of her kitchen.

"I know them . . . all but one. When Ball was dying he named a man to me, only I'm not sure."

"Who?" Chapin was leaning forward.

"Morgan Park," I said.

The big man came to his feet with a lunge. His brown face was ugly. "That's a lie!"

"It's a dead man you're calling a liar, not me. Ball might have meant that one of your riders was present. One was . . . a man named Lyell."

"It's a lie." Morgan Park was hoarse. He looked down at Chapin, who had not moved. "I had nothing to do with it."

This was the man who had struck me down without warning, who had held me helpless while he beat me brutally.

"If it's true," I told him, "I'll kill you after I whip you."

"Whip *me*?"

You could see the amazement in his eyes. He was a man shocked, not by my threat to kill, but by the idea that I, or any man, might whip him.

"Don't be impatient. Your time will come. Right now I need more time to get my strength back."

He sat down slowly and I picked up my cup. Chapin was watching us curiously, his eyes going from one to the other.

"Ever stop to think of something, Park?"

He looked at me, waiting.

"You hit me with your Sunday punch. Right on the chin. You didn't knock me out. You sat on me and held my arms down with your knees and beat me... but you didn't knock me out."

He was staring at me, and if ever I saw hatred in a man's eyes, it was in his at that moment. This was the first time the story of his beating of me had come out. Many believed it had happened in a fair fight... now they would know.

Also he was realizing that what I said was true. He had taken a full swing at my unprotected chin, and I had gone down, but not out. And he did not like the thought.

"Next time I'll be ready."

He got up abruptly and walked to the door. "Get out of here! Get out—or I'll kill you!"

On that he opened the door and went out, yet if he was worried, I was, too. The man was huge. I'd not realized his great size before. His wrists and hands were enormous. Nor was that all. The man had brains. This was something to which I'd not given much thought, but he was shrewd and cunning. He was no hothead. His beating of me had been a carefully calculated thing.

Mother O'Hara brought me food and Key Chapin sat quietly drinking his coffee. Others came in and sat down, stealing covert glances at me.

Rud Maclaren came in, and Canaval was with him. They hesitated then took seats opposite me.

The food tasted good, and I was hungry. Maclaren was irritated by my presence, but I kept quiet, not wanting to bait the man. He irritated me, too, but there was Moira to think of.

Already I was thinking ahead. That amphitheater where Moira had met me ... it would handle quite a number of cattle. It was naturally fenced by the cliffs, and had plenty of water, grass, and shade. And, while it was off the beaten track, it would be good to leave some cattle there to fatten up. With a good, tough old range bull to keep off the varmints.

Some of the men finished eating, and got up and left. I knew that out on the street they would be talking ... about how I'd eaten at the same table with Maclaren and Canaval, how I'd told off Morgan Park—and that I was looking for the killers of old man Ball.

Canaval finished his meal and sat back, rolling a smoke.

"How was it with Rollie?"

So I told him and he listened, smoking thoughtfully. He would fill in the blank spaces, he would see what happened in his mind's eye.

"And now?"

"Back to the Two-Bar."

Maclaren's face mottled. He was a man easy to anger, I could see that.

"Get out ... you've no right to that ranch. Get out and stay out."

"Sorry ... I'm staying. Don't let a little power swell your head, Maclaren. You can't dictate to me. I'm staying ... the Two-Bar is mine. I'll keep it.

"Furthermore, I'd rather not have trouble with you. You are the father of the girl I'm going to marry."

"I'll see you in hell first!" This was what he had said to me before.

I got to my feet and put a coin on the table to pay for my meal. The shave and haircut, the meal and the rest had made me feel better. But I was still weak, and I tired fast.

Katie O'Hara was watching me, and as I turned toward the door she was smiling. It was good to see a friendly smile. Key Chapin had said nothing, just listened and waited.

Outside the door I looked carefully along the street. By now they would know I was in town. I saw no CP horses, but that meant nothing, so turning, I walked up the street, then went down the alley and to my horse.

There was a man waiting for me, sitting on the back steps of the barber shop. He had a face like an unhappy monkey and his head as bald as a bottle. He looked up at me.

"By the look of you, you'll be Matt Brennan."

His shoulders were as wide as those of Morgan Park himself, but he was inches shorter than I. He could not have been much over five feet tall, but he would weigh an easy two hundred pounds, and there was no fat on him. His neck was like a column of oak, his hands and wrists were massive.

"Katie O'Hara was tellin' me you were needin' a man at the Two-Bar. Now, I'm a handy sort. Gunsmith by trade, but a blacksmith, carpenter, holster, and a bit of anything you'll need."

"There's a fight on."

"The short end of a fight always appealed to me."

"Did Katie O'Hara send you?"

"She did that, and she'd be takin' it unkindly of me if I showed up without the job."

"You're Katie's man, then?"

His eyes twinkled. "I'm afraid there's no such. She's a broth of a woman, that Katie." He looked up at me. "Is it a job I have?"

"When I get the ranch back."

"Then let's be gettin' it back."

He led my horse and a mule from the stable. The mule was a zebra dun with a face full of sin and deviltry. He had a tow sack tied before the saddle, another behind. He got into the saddle and sat by while I mounted.

"My name is Brian Mulvaney, call me what you like."

Two gun butts showed above his boot tops. He touched them, grinning wisely.

"These are the Neal Bootleg pistol, altered to suit my taste. The caliber is .35, and they shoot like the glory of God.

"Now this," and he drew from his waistband a gun that needed only wheels to make it an admirable piece of artillery, "this was a Mills .75. Took me two months' work off and on, but I've converted her to a four-shot revolver. A fine gun."

All of seventeen inches long, it looked fit to break a man's wrist with recoil, but Mulvaney had the hands and wrists to handle it. Certainly, a man once blasted with such a cannon would never need a doctor.

Mulvaney was the sort of man to have on your side. I'd seen enough of men to know the quality of this one. He was a fighter...and no fool. As we rode, he told me he was a wrestler, Cornish style.

It would be good to have a man at my side, and a man I could leave behind me on the ranch when we did get it back. How that would be managed I did not know, but somehow, it had to be done.

Yet there was a weariness on me. There had been little sleep or rest in the days since first I'd come to Hattan's Point, except during the sixteen days in the hills, and then I'd been recovering from a wound. And that wound had robbed me of strength I'd need in the days to come.

We scouted the Two-Bar as others had scouted it against me, and there were four horses in the corral. No brands were visible at this distance, and it did not matter. There was a log barricade that looked formidable, and obviously the men had been instructed to lay low and sit tight. They had seen us, and were waiting with their rifles. We saw the reflected light from a moving gun barrel, but we were out of range.

"It'll be a job."

Mulvaney put a hand on the sack in front of him. "What do you think I've got in the sack, laddie? I, who was a miner also?"

"Powder?"

"In sticks, no less. Newfangled, but good."

He rode his mule behind some rocks and as we got down he took the sticks from the sack. "Unless it makes your head ache to handle powder, lend me a hand. We'll cut these sticks in half."

We cut several, slid a cap into each stick, and tied it to a chunk of rock.

Darkness was near. It was time to move. We had waited undercover, but the men behind the barricade knew we were here, and by now they were wondering what we were doing. Perhaps they had seen the tow sacks, and were puzzling over what they contained.

Carefully, we gathered up our bombs and slid over the rim. We were still a good distance from the edge of the barricade. Suddenly, with a lunge, I was running. I had spotted cover just ahead, but a man sprang up from behind the barrier and he snapped a quick shot just as I slid into shelter behind the rock.

Mulvaney was running, too. Another shot sounded, but then I rolled up to my knees and hurled the first bomb.

I'd lit the fuse hurriedly and the flying dynamite charge left a trail of sparks. Somebody let go with a wild yell, and then the bomb hit and exploded almost in the same instant.

Mulvaney's first and my second followed, both of them in the air at once. Another explosion split the night apart and one man dove over the barricade and started running straight toward me. The others charged the corral. The man coming at me glimpsed me then and slid to a halt. He wheeled as if the devil was after him.

Four riders dashed from the corral and were gone.

Mulvaney got up from behind his rock and we walked to the corral. He was chuckling.

"They'd have stood until hell froze over for guns," he said, "but that giant powder got 'em."

Leaving Mulvaney, I returned for my horse and his mule. So again I was on the ranch. . . .

Standing there under the stars, I looked off toward town. They would go there first, or that was my guess. And that meant they would have a few drinks and it would be hours before another attack could be mounted. And Mulvaney had been right, of course. They would have fought it out with guns. The giant powder was frightening and different.

Walking back to the ranch yard, leading the horses, I met Mulvaney gathering wood.

"It's a fine ranch," he said thoughtfully, "and you're a lucky man."

"If I can hold it."

"We'll hold it," he said quietly.

CHAPTER 10

WE HAD EATEN our noon meal on the following day when we saw a plume of dust. It seemed like one rider, at most not more than two.

Mulvaney got up unhurriedly and moved across to the log barricade and waited beside his rifle. He was not a man who grew greatly excited, and I liked him for that. Fighting is a cool-headed business.

Rolling a smoke, I watched that dust. It could mean anything or nothing.

No man likes to stand against odds, yet sometimes it is the only way. No man likes to face a greater power than himself, and especially when there are always the coattail hangers who will render lip service to anyone who seems to be top dog.

It brings a bitterness to a man, and especially when he is right.

Yet this morning I'd no need for worry. The rider came into view, coming at an easy lope. And it was Moira Maclaren.

We had worked all that morning clearing ground for the new house I was to build. Moira drew up and her eyes went to the cleared space and the rocks we'd hauled on a stone boat for the foundation.

The house would stand on a hill with the long sweep of Cottonwood Wash before it, shaded by several huge cottonwoods and a sycamore or two.

"You must be careful. I think you had a visitor last night," she said.

"A visitor?"

"Morgan Park came over this way."

So he had been around, had he? And devilishly quiet or we would have heard him. It was a thing to be remembered, and Moira was right. We must be more careful.

"He's a puzzling man, Moira. Who is he?"

"He doesn't talk much about the past. I know he's been in Philadelphia and New York. And he takes trips to Salt Lake or San Francisco occasionally."

She swung down and looked around, seeing the barricade.

"Were the boys hurt?" I asked her.

"No...but they had a lot to say about you using dynamite." She looked up at me. "Would you have minded if you had hurt them?"

"Who wants to hurt anybody? All I wanted was to get them out of here. Only, that Pinder crowd...I'd not be fussy in their case."

We stood together near her horse, enjoying the warm sun, and looking down the Wash over the green grass where the cattle fed.

"It's a nice view."

"You'll see it many times, from the house."

She looked around at me. "You really believe that, don't you?"

Before I could reply, she said thoughtfully, "You asked about Morgan Park. Be careful, Matt. I think he is utterly without scruples."

There was more to come, and I waited. There was something about Morgan Park that bothered me. He was a handsome man as well as a strong one, and a man who might well appeal to women, yet from her manner I was beginning to believe that Moira had sensed about him the same thing I had.

"There was a young man, Arnold D'Arcy, out here from the East," she said, "and I liked him. Knowing Morgan, I didn't mention him when Morgan was around. Then one night he commented on him, and suggested it would be better for all concerned if the young man did not come back."

She turned around and looked up at me. "Matt, when Morgan found out Arnold's name he was frightened."

"Frightened? *Morgan?*"

"Yes...and Arnold wasn't a big man, or by any means dangerous. But Morgan began to ask questions. What was D'Arcy doing here? Had he been asking questions about anybody? Or mentioned looking for anyone?"

It was a thing to think of. Why would a man like Morgan Park be frightened? Not of physical danger...the man obviously believed himself invulnerable. There must be something else.

"Did you tell D'Arcy about it?"

"No." There was a shadow of worry on her face. "Matt, I never saw him again."

I looked at her quickly. "You mean, he never came back?"

"Never. And he didn't write."

We walked down the Wash, talking of the ranch and of my plans. It was a quiet, pleasant hour, and a rare thing for me, who had known few quiet hours since coming to Hattan's Point, and who could expect few until this was settled and I was accepted as the owner of the Two-Bar, and a man to be reckoned with.

When she was mounting to leave, I asked her, "This D'Arcy—where was he from?"

"Virginia. He had served in the Army, and before coming out here he had been stationed in Washington."

Watching her ride away, my mind turned again to Morgan Park. He might have frightened D'Arcy away, but it was a matter to think about.

Behind Morgan's questions, and behind the disappearance of D'Arcy, there might be something sinister, something that Park did not want known. And yet he had been here during the night and hadn't killed me. Was it because he could not get a good shot? Or for another reason? Did he want me alive?

Mulvaney and I worked steadily around the place, but I rested from time to time, for my strength had not yet returned. We accomplished a lot, and by nightfall our foundation was finished and the shape of my house was plain to see.

Mulvaney was a steady and tireless worker. We each went to the rim of the Wash from time to time to look around the country, although the foundations of the house were almost as high as that rim now.

Toward evening, mounted on a gray horse, I scouted the country with care. I found tracks that must have been those of Morgan Park's horse, for they were the tracks of a big horse, the kind it would take to carry the weight of the man. I studied them, wanting to know them again. For in the back of my mind I had a plan shaping.

There were four sides to the question here at Hattan's. Jim Pinder and his CP, Maclaren and the Boxed M, myself on the Two-Bar, and Morgan Park.

Pinder would understand nothing but force. Maclaren, when he saw he could not win, would back off. He could be circumvented. But Morgan Park worried me.

It would be a good thing to learn something about Morgan Park.

There had been a Major Leo D'Arcy at Fort Concho, in Texas. A sharp, intelligent officer with a good bit of experience. The name was not too uncommon, but Major D'Arcy had, I believed, been from Virginia. He would not be a brother, unless a much older brother. He might be the father, or an uncle. And he might be no relative at all, but it was a chance, and I had to begin somewhere.

We cut hay for the horses that we had to keep in the corral, and by the time the moon was rising we were eating a leisurely supper.

"I'm going to Silver Reef tomorrow, Mulvaney. I'm sending a couple of messages."

"Have yourself a time. I'll be all right."

He looked down at the Wash in the moonlight. "It's a fine place this. I'd like to stay on."

"And why not? I'll be needing help."

I told Mulvaney about Morgan Park being near us in the night, and I could see he did not like it. We would have to be careful.

Rolled in my blankets I lay long awake, looking at the stars. The fire burned low . . . a coyote yammered at the moon, and somewhere a quail called inquiringly into the night.

Mulvaney turned and muttered in his sleep. And nothing moved along the western rim.

Into my mind came again the face of Morgan Park, square, brutal, and handsome. It was a strong face, a powerful face, but what lay behind it? What was there in the man? Who was he? Where had he come from? What was his stake here?

And what had become of Arnold D'Arcy?

Far off, the coyote called... slow smoke lifted from the embers, and my lids grew heavy....

CHAPTER 11

SKIRTING WIDE, I had left Hattan's Point to it-self, and cutting through the broken land of bare rock and sand, I'd come to the trail to Silver Reef, and had seen no man during my riding.

It was very hot, and it was still. Jagged ridges thrust themselves from the earth, their crevasses and deep-furrowed sides filled with blown white sand. A dust devil danced before me and I pushed on, seeing the roofs of the town take shape.

There was no sound but that of my horse's hoofs on the hard-packed trail as I walked him down the last slope to Silver Reef.

The town lay sprawled haphazardly along the main street. There were the usual frontier saloons, stores, churches, and homes. The sign on the Elk Horn caught my attention, so I swung my horse into the shade in front of the saloon and dismounted.

"Rye?"

At my nod, the bartender served me. He was a bald-headed man with narrow eyes.

"How's things in the mines?"

"So-so. But you ain't no miner." His eyes took in my cowhand's clothing, and I knew he had seen my two tied-down guns when I came in.

"This here's a quiet town. We don't see many gun handlers around here. Place for them is over east."

"Hattan's?"

"Uh-huh. I hear both the Boxed M and the CP are hirin' fightin' men."

"Have one with me?"

"Don't drink. Seen too much of it."

My rye tasted good and I asked for another. That one I held in my fingers, stalling for time and information. It was cool inside the saloon, and I was in no hurry. My messages I would send in a few minutes. Meanwhile it was good to relax.

"Couple fellers from Hattan's in town the other day. Big man, one of them."

Inwardly, I poised, waiting. Somehow I knew what was coming.

"Biggest man I ever saw."

Morgan Park in Silver Reef....

"Did he say anything about what was going on over at Hattan's?"

"Not to me. The feller with him was askin' after the Slade boys. They're gunmen, both of 'em."

"Sounds like trouble."

I tossed off my drink and refused another when he gestured with the bottle. "Not a drinking man myself. Maybe a couple when I come to town."

"Could be trouble over there at Hattan's." The bartender put his forearms on the bar. "That big feller, he went to see that shyster, Jake Booker."

"Lawyer?"

"An' a crook."

The bartender was not disposed to let me go so easily. The saloon was empty and he felt like talking. Pushing my hat back on my head, I rolled a smoke, and listened.

Morgan Park had visited Silver Reef several times, but had not come to the Elk Horn. He confined his visits to the office of Jake Booker or to the back room of a dive called The Sump. The only man who ever came with him was Lyell, and the latter occasionally came to the Elk Horn.

The bartender talked on, and I was a good listener. He was no well of information, but the little he did know was to the point, and it helped to make a picture for me.

Morgan Park did not want to become known in Silver Reef. In fact, nobody knew his name. He had his drinks in the back room of The Sump, and if he was known to anyone aside from Booker, it was to The Sump's owner. He rarely arrived during the day, usually coming in before daylight or just after dark. His actions were certainly not those of a man on honest business.

When I left the saloon I went to the stage station and got off my message to Leo D'Arcy. Then I took pains to locate The Sump and the office of Jake Booker.

Night came swiftly, and with darkness the miners came to town and crowded the streets and the saloons. They were a rough, jovial crowd, pushing and shoving but good-natured. Here and there during the early evening I saw big-hatted men from the range, but they were few.

Silver Reef was booming, and money was flowing as freely as the whiskey. Few of the men carried guns in sight, and probably the majority did not carry them at all. Several times I saw men watching me with interest, and it was always my guns that drew their attention.

One hard-faced young miner stopped in front of me. His eyes looked like trouble, and I wanted no action with anyone.

"What would you do without those guns?" he asked.

I grinned at him. "Well, friend, I've had to go without them a time or two. Sometimes I win ... the last time I got my ears beat down."

He chuckled, his animosity gone. "Buy you a drink?"

"Let's go!"

He was urging a second one on me that I didn't want, when a group of his friends came in. Carefully, I eased away from the bar as they moved up, and lost myself in the crowd. I went outside and started up the street.

Turning at Louder's store, I passed under a street lamp on the corner, and for an instant stood outlined in all its radiance. From the shadows, flame stabbed. There was a tug at my sleeve and then my own gun roared, and as the shot sped, I went after it.

A man lunged from the shadows near the store and ran, staggering, toward the alley behind it. Pistol ready, I ran after him.

He slipped and went to his knees, then came up and plunged on, half running, half falling. He brought up with a crash against the corral bars and then fell, rolling over. Apparently he had not even seen the corral fence.

He got his hands under him and tried to get up,

then slipped back and lay still. His face showed in the glow of light from a window. It was Lyell.

His shirt front was bloody and his face had a shocked expression. He rolled his eyes at me and worked his lips as if to speak. He had been hit hard by my quick, scarcely aimed shot.

"Damn you . . . I missed."

"And I didn't."

He stared at me, and I started to move away. "I'll get a doctor. I saw a sign up the street."

He grabbed my sleeve. "Don't go . . . no use. An' I don't want to . . . to die alone."

"You were in the gang that killed Ball."

"No!" He caught at my shirt. "No, I wasn't! He . . . he was a good old man."

"Was Morgan Park there?"

He looked away from me. "Why should he be there? Wasn't . . . his play."

He was breathing hoarsely. Out on the street I could hear voices of men in argument. They were trying to decide where the shots had come from. In a matter of minutes somebody would come down this alley.

"What's he seeing Booker for? What about Sam Slade?"

Footsteps crunched on the gravel. It was a lone man coming from the other direction and he carried a lantern.

"Get a doctor, will you? This man's hurt."

He put down the lantern and started to run. I took the light and began to uncover the wound.

"No use," Lyell insisted, "you got me." He looked

at me, his eyes pleading for belief. "Never ambushed a man before."

I loosened his belt, eased the tightness of his clothing. He was breathing hoarsely and his eyes stared straight up into darkness.

"The Slades are going to get Canaval."

"And me?"

"Park wants you."

"What else does he want? Range?"

"No."

He breathed slowly, heavily, and with increasing difficulty. I could hear the boots coming, several men were approaching.

"He... he wants money."

The doctor came running up. In the excitement I backed away, and then turned and walked off into the darkness. If anybody would know about Park's plans it would be Booker, and I had an idea I could get into Booker's office.

Pausing in the darkness, I glanced back. There was a knot of men about Lyell now. I heard somebody call for quiet, and then they asked him who shot him. If he made any answer, I didn't hear it. Either he was too far gone to reply, or had no intention of telling. Standing there in the darkness, I studied the situation.

The trip had been valuable if only to send the message, but I had also learned something of the plans that Morgan Park was developing.

But why... *why?*

He wanted to be rid of Canaval. That could only indicate that the Boxed M gunman stood between him and what he wanted.

That could mean that what he wanted was on the Boxed M. Was it Moira? Or was it more than Moira?

Park had seemed to be courting Moira with Maclaren's consent...so why kill Canaval?

Unless there was something else, something more that he wanted. If he married Moira, Maclaren would still have the ranch. But if Maclaren were dead...? Lyell had said, though, that what Morgan Park wanted was money.

———

Booker's OFFICE WAS on the second floor of a frame building reached by an outside stairway. Once up there, a man would be trapped if anyone mounted those stairs while he was in the office.

Standing back in the shadows, I looked up. I never liked tight corners or closed places...I was a wide open country man.

It was cooler now and the stars were out. There was no one in sight. Now was my chance, if there was one for me once I started up those stairs.

Up the street a music box was jangling and the town seemed wide awake. In a saloon not many doors away a quartet was singing, loudly if not tunefully, but in the streets there was no movement.

Booker had friends here and I had none. Going up those steps would be a risk, and I had no logical story. He was an attorney I had come to consult? But the lights in his office were out.

Yet, waiting in the shadows, I knew that I had to go up those stairs, that what I needed to know might be found there.

Glancing up the street, I saw no one. I crossed to

the foot of the steps and, taking a long breath, I went up swiftly, two at a time. The door was locked, but I knew something of locks, and soon had the door opened.

It was pitch dark inside and smelled of stale tobacco. Lighting my way with a stump of candle, I examined the tray on top of the desk, the top drawer, and the side drawers. Every sense alert for the slightest sound, I worked quickly and with precision. Suddenly, I stopped.

In my hand was an assayer's report. No name was on the report, no location was mentioned, but the ore that had been assayed was amazingly rich in silver. Placing it to one side and working swiftly through the papers, I came suddenly upon a familiar name.

The name was signed to a letter of one paragraph only . . . and the name was that of Morgan Park.

You have been recommended to me as a man of discretion who could turn over a piece of property for a quick profit, and who could handle the negotiations with a buyer. I am writing for an appointment and will be in Silver Reef on the 12th. It is essential that my visit as well as the nature of our business remain absolutely confidential.

It was very little, yet a hint of something. The assayer's report I copied swiftly, and put the original back in the desk. The letter I folded and placed carefully in my pocket. Dousing the candle, I returned it to the shelf where I had found it.

The long ride had tired me more than I had

realized, and now I suddenly knew what I needed most was rest. Before anything else, I must conserve my strength. The wounds had left me weak, and although the good food, the fresh, clear air, and the rugged living were quickly bringing back my vitality, I still tired easily.

Turning toward the door, I heard a low mutter of voices and steps on the stair.

Swiftly I backed away and felt for the knob of a door I had seen that led to an inner room. Opening it, I stepped through and drew the door softly closed behind me. I was barely in time.

My hand reaching out in the darkness touched some rough boards stacked against the wall. The room had a faintly musty smell as of one long closed.

Voices sounded closer by and a door closed. Then a match scratched and a light showed briefly around the door. I heard a lamp chimney lifted and replaced.

"Probably some drunken brawl. You're too suspicious, Morgan."

"Lyell didn't drink that much."

"Forget him. . . . If you were married to the girl it would simplify things. What's the matter, Brennan cutting in there, too?"

"Shut up!" Park's voice was ugly. "Say that again and I'll wring you out like a dirty towel, Booker. I mean it."

"You do your part, I'll do mine. The buyers have the money and they're ready. They won't wait forever."

There was silence, the faint squeak of a cork turning in a bottle, then the gurgle of a poured drink.

"It's not easy . . . he's never alone." It was Morgan Park's voice.

"You've got the Slades."

A chair scraped on the floor. A glass was put down, and then the door opened and both men went out. Listening, I heard their descending footsteps. From a window I saw them emerge into the light and separate, one going one way, one the other.

At any moment, Booker might decide to return. Swiftly opening the door, I went down the steps two at a time. When I came back to the street it was from another direction, and only after a careful checkup.

There was nothing more for me in Silver Reef. I must be getting home again. Only when I was in the saddle did I sort over what I had learned. And it was little enough.

Nobody knew who had killed Lyell, but Morgan Park was suspicious. Yet he had no reason for believing that I was even in the vicinity.

Lyell had denied his presence at the killing of Ball, which might or might not be the truth. Dying men do not always tell the truth, but his manner when questioned about Park's presence caused me to wonder.

Morgan Park and Booker had some sort of an agreement as to the sale of some property that Park could not yet deliver.

When he had said, "He's never alone" he could not have meant me. I was often alone.

It was not much to work with, and riding along through the night I told myself I must not jump to conclusions, but the man who was never alone could easily be Maclaren.

Or it might be someone else. It might be Key

Chapin. Yet the remark about being married to the girl would not fit Chapin...or would it? Certainly. Maclaren's son-in-law would be a protected man in a well-nigh invulnerable position.

The more I thought of it, however, the more positive I became that the man must be Maclaren. That would be why the Slades were to kill Canaval.

When I was six miles from Silver Reef I turned off the trail into a narrow-mouth draw and rode back up some distance. There, under some mesquite bush, I made a dry camp.

It was after midnight...something stirred out in the brush.

This was lonely country, only desert lay to the north, and south the country stretched away, uninhabited, clear to the Canyon of the Colorado. It was a rugged country, split by great canyons, barred by pinnacled backbones of sandstone, a land where even the Indians rarely roamed.

In Silver Reef, I had stocked a few supplies, and over a tiny fire I fried bacon and a couple of eggs, then cut grass for Buck, and bedded down for the night.

In the moonlight the bare white stones of the draw bottom stood out clearly. The mesquite offered some concealment, and I was safe enough while the night lasted.

There was a tough sheriff in Silver Reef who might put two and two together if he talked to the bartender to whom I had talked.

When I awakened it was cold and gray in the earliest dawn-light. The clumps of brush were black against the gray desert...the sky was pale, with only a few stars. Over coffee I watched the stars fade out, then saddled up.

Buck moved out, eager to be on his way, and swinging wide of the trail I rode toward the ridge that followed the trail but lay half a mile away from it. Morgan Park would be riding that same trail. I did not want him to know I had been in Silver Reef.

There was no sound but that of the horse's hoofs and the creak of saddle leather. The black brush turned to green, the last stars faded, and the ridges stood out sharp and clear in the morning light. Great boulders lay scattered in the desert beyond the mountain's base, and here there were occasional stretches of sparse grass.

Once, looking toward the trail, I saw a faint plume of dust . . . a rider passing there.

Morgan Park?

It could be . . . and he might have seen my tracks.

CHAPTER 12

SEVERAL TIMES I drew up, looking off toward the trail. That lone plume of dust seemed to be keeping pace with me, yet I doubted if the rider was aware of my presence.

Where I rode there was little dust. We circled and climbed and dipped, and we had the rocky face of the mountain in back of us. Against that background I could not be outlined nor easily seen, but I held to low ground.

The wall of the mountain grew sheer, reaching high and straight up, its face without crack or crevice. At the base were heaps of talus, the scattered fragments of rock falling from the eroded sandstone. At noon I made camp at a small seep among a clump of trees. There was no sound . . . I picketed the buckskin on a patch of grass and rested, chewing on a chunk of jerked beef.

Resting by the water, I tried to plan. If Park was actually plotting some move against Maclaren, I should warn him, but he would not listen to me. Nor would Moira . . . she had known Morgan Park for some time, while I was a new and troublesome visitor. Such a story coming from me, and without proof, might do more harm than good.

Canaval . . . Canaval was the man.

He might not believe me, but he would be cautious, for he was a naturally cautious man and, like most gunmen, he trusted no one.

I must warn him of the Slades.

When I came back to Cottonwood Wash and the Two-Bar, the wind was whispering among the cottonwood leaves and stirring the tall grass. It was good to be home, and under me I felt the buckskin's gait quicken as he stepped into a trot despite his weariness.

Mulvaney stepped into sight as I rode past the boulder where I had waited on that day that now seemed so long ago, the day when I first saw old man Ball and waited for him to approach me.

"Any trouble?" I asked.

"No ... some men came by, but the sound of my Spencer moved them along." He turned back to the cabin. "There's grub on the table."

Stripping the saddle from the buckskin, I looked around. Mulvaney had not let up on the work while I was gone, and what he had done was a day's work for two men. He was a good man, Mulvaney, and I owed a debt to Katie O'Hara for sending him to me.

"Trouble in Silver Reef?"

"A man killed."

"Be careful, lad. There's too many dying."

So as I curried the buckskin, I told the story, leaving nothing out, and Mulvaney listened, watching me. He was a good man and I had respect for his judgment.

"Right," he said, at last. "You'd best talk to Canaval."

Turning away from the corral I looked off down the length of Cottonwood, looked at the white-faced cattle grazing there, and at the water flowing through the ditch to irrigate the vegetable garden we'd planned. It was something begun. I was no longer dreaming. I was putting down roots.

Mulvaney had been watching me as we ate, sitting back from the fire and sheltered so no shot could reach us. "You're tired," he said. He had lighted his pipe, and he smoked quietly, then went on, "You'll back up that challenge to Morgan Park?"

"I will."

"He's a power of man, lad. I've seen him lift a barrel of whiskey to the length of his arms overhead."

He need not tell me that, me who had felt the weight of his fist. But how would Morgan Park be with a man who stood up to him? And one hard to hit? I was thinking that such big men rarely have to fight. Their size is an awesome thing and most men draw back. Had he fought much? Or had he always won easily and by bluff? I meant to see.

"Have you boxed any, Mulvaney? You told me you'd wrestled, Cornish style."

"What Irishman hasn't boxed? If it's a sparrin' mate you want, you've picked your man. It would be good to get the leather on me maulies again."

There followed a week at the Two-Bar that was uninterrupted, and it was a week of work, but a week of sparring, too. Only sometimes we went at it hot and heavy, and Mulvaney was a brawny man, a fierce slugger and powerful in the clinches. On the seventh day we did a full thirty minutes without a break; my strength was nearly back, and my side hurt hardly at all.

The rough and tumble part of it . . . let Morgan

choose the way. I'd grown up in wagon camps and cow camps. I knew my way around as a fighting man. After our tenth session with the gloves, Mulvaney stripped them from his hands.

"It's a power of muscle behind that wallop, lad! That last one came from nowhere, and I felt it to my toes!"

"Thanks . . . I'll be riding to town tomorrow."

"To fight him?"

"To see Moira, to buy supplies, and to talk to Canaval. It is late for that. I've been worried."

On the day after my return two of the Benaras boys had stopped by on a rare trip to town, and I'd sent them to Canaval with a message from me—and to be given only to him. What might have happened since then, or what Canaval had thought of my message, I had no idea. And I was worried. Canaval could care for himself, but could Maclaren?

In my message to Canaval I had said there was some plot against Maclaren. I'd dared to say no more.

"And Morgan Park," I told Mulvaney, "I want the man mad. I want him mad and wild before we fight."

"It'll help . . . but be careful, lad."

Hattan's Point lay still under a noonday sun when my buckskin shambled down the street. When he'd been watered I walked into the saloon. It was not a drink I wanted so much as conversation. I wanted news.

Key Chapin was there, and as always, I wondered about the man. Where did he stand? What did he want?

"You've been making a name for yourself," Chapin said.

"All I want is a ranch."

"Lyell was killed . . . over in Silver Reef."

His eyes measured me, searching, but asking no question.

I shrugged. "You know there's a saying, 'If you live by the sword—' "

"They've got a sheriff who's serious about his business. They say he's asking questions."

Ignoring that, I asked one of my own.

"You said when I first came here that the town was taking sides. On which side are you?"

He hesitated, fiddling with his glass.

"That's harder to say since you came. I'm against the CP because they are essentially lawless men."

"And Maclaren?"

"Stubborn, and sure of himself. But at times he can be reasoned with. He has an exaggerated view of his own rightness."

"And Morgan Park?"

He glanced sharply at me, then looked out the door. He was frowning. "Morgan is generally believed to see things as Maclaren does . . . you don't believe that?"

"No . . . unless it so serves his interest. Morgan Park does anything to get the coon. He could choose any side if it would further his own interest."

At that, Chapin was silent, and I could see he was disturbed by what I had said, although for what reason I could not guess. He was Maclaren's friend, I believed, but he had also seemed friendly to Morgan Park.

"Look, Chapin," I said leaning toward him, "you're the press. I've seen a dozen frontier towns tougher than this one—and all of them were tamed. To get law and order meant a fight, but they got it. You more than anyone could lead such a fight here. And I'll help."

"Even to stopping this war?"

"What war? A peaceful old man had a ranch that two big outfits wanted. They tried to get it. They failed. He left that ranch to me. If protecting one's property is war, then settle down for a long fight."

"You could sell out."

"No...." I took my hat from the table and was about to leave. "What you should do is start examining motives. How'd the fight start? Why not look into the background of some of the people around? And I don't mean Maclaren or Pinder."

"You haven't gotten over being sore at Morgan."

Standing up, I put on my hat. "Ever hear of a lawyer at Silver Reef named Booker?"

"He's an unmitigated scoundrel."

"Ask yourself why Morgan Park is meeting him in secret. And when you see the Slade Boys in town, ask yourself why they are here."

He looked up at me, definitely startled, and then I turned and walked outside.

Moira was not in town, so I turned the buckskin toward the Boxed M.

When I rode into the ranch yard the first person I saw was a cowhand with a bandaged foot. He started up, then realizing he was far from a gun, settled carefully back in place.

"Howdy...if you want to know, I'm visiting,

not hunting trouble." I grinned at him. "I've no hard feelings."

"You've no hard feelin's? What about me? You darned near shot my foot off!"

"Next time keep your foot under cover. Anyway, why gripe? You haven't done a lick of work since you were hurt. Just sittin' around eating your head off!"

Somebody behind me chuckled and I turned in my saddle. It was Canaval.

"Did it for an excuse, Brennan."

"Excuse?" The injured man came to his one good foot, his face flushed. Then he saw we were grinning and, disgusted, he limped away.

Canaval turned to me. He took out his tobacco and began to build a cigarette.

"What do you want, Brennan?"

"Courting... you mind?"

"None of my business. Rud may not like it. He may have me order you off."

"If you tell me to go, Canaval, I'll go. Only one thing. If Park is here, you keep him off me. I'm not ready for him, and when I *am* ready I'd rather she didn't see it."

"Fair enough." His eyes twinkled a little and he looked up at me, only his eyes smiling. "You might be wrong about Moira. She might like to see it."

Swinging down, I loosened the girth a little and tied my horse to the corral. Canaval stood by, watching me.

"The Benaras boys were here."

"You got the message?"

He was alert and interested now. "Yes... I got it.

Why would the Slades come here? Who would want to kill Rud Maclaren?"

"You figure it out...maybe somebody wants you dead so Rud will be alone."

He was not disbelieving me. I could see that, and I saw it with surprise. Did Canaval know something I did not? Or had something happened since my warning?

On the steps I stopped and looked back. "That same gent is saving me for dessert...and his own special attention."

He was standing there smoking when I knocked, and inside a voice answered that sent my blood pounding. It was a voice that would always have that effect on me, a voice that I would never hear too often.

As I entered there was an instant when my reflection was thrown upon a mirror beside hers. Seeing me gazing over her shoulder, she turned.

We stood there looking at ourselves. A tall, dark young man with wide shoulders in a dark blue shirt, a black silk handkerchief, black jeans, and tied down holsters with their walnut-stocked guns; and Moira in a sea-green gown, filmy and summery-looking, a girl with a lovely throat and shoulders, with soft lips....

"Matt! You shouldn't have come! Father will be—"

"He'll have to get over it sometime, and it might as well be now."

"That's foolish talk!"

She said it, but her eyes didn't seem to say it was foolish. Yet right at that minute, looking as lovely as she did, and surrounded everywhere by evidences of wealth and comfort, it may have sounded foolish even to me.

"You'd better start buying your trousseau. I won't have much money for a year or two, and—"

"Matt"—her eyes were anxious—"you'd better go. I'm expecting Morgan."

I took her hands. "Don't worry, Moira. I promised Canaval there'd be no trouble, and there will be none."

She was unconvinced and tried to argue, but I could only keep thinking how lovely she was. Poised, a little angry, her lovely throat bare, she was enough to set any man's pulse to pounding.

"Matt!" She was really angry, and a little frightened by the thought of Morgan Park coming. "You're not even listening! And *don't* look at me like that!"

"How else would a man look at a woman?"

She gave up then and we walked inside. The living room was comfortable, not in the ornate, overdecorated manner of the eastern cities, but with a simplicity bred by the frontier. Rud Maclaren was obviously a man who loved comfort, and he had a daughter who could shape a house to beauty even in this harsh land.

"Matt...how do you feel? Those wounds, I mean. Are you all right?"

"No...but much better."

We sat down, and for the first time she looked a little uncomfortable, and would not let her eyes meet mine.

"Where were you before you came here, Matt? Canaval said you were marshal of Mobeetie once."

"Only a short time." So I told her about that, and

then somehow about the rest of it, about the long nights of riding, the trail herds, the buffalo, the border *cantinas*. About the days in Sonora when I rode for a Mexican hacienda, and about prospecting in Baja, California, the ruins of the old missions, and much more.

And somehow we forgot where we were and I talked of the long wind in the vast ocean of prairie east of the Rockies, how the grass waved in long ripples. About the shrill yells of the Comanches attacking...and about nights under the stars, lonely nights when I lay long awake, yearning into the darkness for someone to love, someone to whom I belonged and who belonged to me.

We were meeting then as a man and woman must always meet, when the world and time stand aside and there is only this, a meeting of minds and of pulsing blood, and a joining of hands in the quiet hours.

And then we heard hoofs in the yard, the coming of horses.

Two horses...two riders.

CHAPTER 13

MOIRA GOT UP quickly, tendrils of dark hair curled against her neck, and there were tiny beads of perspiration on her upper lip, for the day was very hot.

"Matt, that's father. You'd better go."

She had stepped toward me and I took her elbows and drew her to me. She started to draw away, but I took her chin and turned her face toward me. She was frightened and tried to draw back, but not very hard. Her eyes were suddenly wide and dark ... and then I kissed her.

For an instant we clung together, and then she pulled violently away from me. She stood like that, not saying anything, and then moved quickly to kiss me again. We were like that when we heard footsteps outside.

We stepped apart just as Rud Maclaren and Morgan Park came through the door.

Park saw us, and something in Moira's manner must have given him an idea of what had taken place. His face went dark with anger and he started toward me, his voice hoarse with fury.

"Get out! Get *out*, I say!"

My eyes went past him to Maclaren. "Is this your home, Maclaren, or his?"

"That'll do, Morgan!" Maclaren did not like my

being there, but he liked Morgan Park's usurping of authority even less. "I'll order people from my own home."

Morgan Park's face was ugly. He wanted trouble, but before he could speak Canaval appeared in the door behind them.

"Boss, Brennan said he was just visitin', not huntin' trouble. He said he would go when I asked him and that he would make no trouble for Park."

Moira interrupted quickly. "Father, Mr. Brennan is my guest. When the time comes he will leave. Until then, I wish him to stay."

"I won't have him in my house!" Maclaren declared angrily. "Damn you, Brennan! You've got a gall to come here after shootin' my men, stealin' range that rightly belongs to me, and runnin' my cows out of Cottonwood!"

"We've no differences we can't settle peaceably," I told him quietly. "I never wanted trouble with you, and I think we can reach an agreement."

It took the fire out of him. He was still truculent, still ready to throw his weight around, but mollified. Right then I sensed the truth about Rud Maclaren. It was not land and property he wanted so much as to be known as the biggest man in the country. He simply knew of no way of winning respect and admiration other than through wealth and power.

Realizing that gave me the opening I wanted. Peace I had to have, but peace with Maclaren especially. And here it was, if I made the right moves.

"Today I had a talk with Chapin. This fighting can only be stopped through the leadership of the right man. I think you are that man, Maclaren."

He was listening, and he liked what he heard. He could see himself acting in the role of peacemaker. And he was a shrewd man who could not but realize that every day of this war was costing him men, cattle, and money. While his men were fighting or riding the country they could not attend to ranch business.

"You're the big man around here. If you make a move, the others will follow."

"Not the Pinders. You killed Rollie, and they'll not rest until you're dead. And he hates me and all I stand for."

Morgan Park was listening, suddenly hard and watchful. This was something he had never expected, that Maclaren and I would actually get together and talk peace. If we reached an agreement, any plans he had would be wasted, finished.

"If the CP try to continue the fight," I suggested, "they would outlaw themselves. In the eyes of everyone they would have no standing.

"Moreover, if this fight continues all the rustlers in the country will come in here to take advantage of the situation and steal cattle."

Moira was listening with some surprise and, I thought, with respect. My own instinct had always been toward fighting, yet I had always appreciated the futility of it. If we could settle our difficulties, the CP would be forced to restrain themselves. The joker in the deck was Morgan Park. If, as I now believed, he had reason to want to continue the fight in order to complete his plans, then an end to hostilities would be a death blow for his arrangements with Booker.

Rud was impressed, that was obvious to Morgan Park as well as to me. Maclaren rubbed his chin thoughtfully, seeing the logic of the situation as I expressed it.

Rud Maclaren was a careful man who had come early, worked hard, and planned well. It was only now in these later years that he had become acquisitive of power. But he could not help but realize that he was looked upon without affection by many of his neighbors. While he affected no interest, it was obvious that my suggestion offered an opportunity for that.

Park interrupted suddenly. "Don't trust this talk, Rud. Brennan makes it sound all right, but he has some trick in mind. What's he planning? What's he covering up?"

"Morgan!" Moira protested. "I'm surprised at you! Matt is sincere, and you know it."

"I know nothing of the kind. Yet you defend this— this killer."

He was staring right at me when he said it, as if daring me to object. That he wanted trouble, I knew. A fight now would ruin all I had been saying.

It came to me then, and I said it, not without doubt.

"At least, I've never killed a man who had no gun. A man who would have been helpless against me in any case."

When I said it I was looking right at him and something changed in his eyes, and into his face there came something I had not seen there before. And I knew now that I was marked for death. That Morgan Park would no longer wait.

It was D'Arcy I had in mind...for, playing a hunch only, I believed D'Arcy had been murdered.

Yet it was more than a hunch. D'Arcy was a man who would never have neglected to thank his hostess. He would never have left without paying his respects. Something had happened to prevent it. But I had no evidence. Only that flimsy hunch, and the fact that D'Arcy had vanished suddenly after Morgan Park had shown an interest in him.

Now that I had started I did not intend to hold back. As best I could, I intended to put Rud Maclaren on his guard.

"It is not only rustlers," I said, "but those who have other schemes as well, schemes they can only bring to success under the cover of this fighting."

Morgan Park's features were stiff. Actually, I knew little or nothing, yet somehow I had touched a nerve, and Morgan Park was a worried man. If my guess was correct, he now knew that I knew something and he would suspect me of knowing much more than I actually did.

"I'll think this over," Maclaren said finally. "This is no time to make a decision."

"Sure." I turned toward Moira and took her arm. "And now if you'll excuse us?"

We moved toward the door, and Morgan Park's fury suddenly snapped. His face livid, he started forward. Putting Moira quickly to one side, I was ready for him.

"Hold it!"

Canaval stepped between us, stopping Morgan Park in his tracks.

"That's all Park. We'll have no fighting here."

"What's the matter? Brennan need a nursemaid now?"

"No." Canaval was stiff. "Brennan promised me there would be no trouble. I'm not going to let you cause any."

There was a moment of silence, and Moira moved back to my side. What Morgan Park might have done or said, I do not know, but whatever it was, I was ready. Never before had I wanted to smash and destroy as I did when I faced that man. All I could remember was him sitting astride me, swinging those huge, methodical fists.

"Brennan," Maclaren spoke abruptly, "I've no reason to like you, but you talk straight from the shoulder and you are my daughter's guest. Remain as long as you like."

Later, I understood that right at that moment Park must have made his decision. There could be no other alternative for him. He drew back and slowly relaxed, and he did not say another word.

Moira walked with me to my horse, and she was worried. "He's a bad enemy, Matt. I'm sorry this happened."

"He was my enemy, anyway. That he is a bad enemy, I can guess. I believe another friend of yours found out about that."

She looked up quickly, real fear in her eyes. "I don't understand you."

"Did you ever have a note of acknowledgment from D'Arcy?"

"No . . . but what has that to do—"

"Strange, isn't it? I'd have thought a man of his sort would not neglect such an obvious courtesy."

There had been, I think, some similar thought in her mind. I had sensed it when I first mentioned that other friend. It was inexplicable that a man like D'Arcy should drop so suddenly from sight.

We stood there without talking, no more words between us for several minutes, but needing none. Our hearts were beating together, our blood pulsing together, our faces touched by the gentle hand of the same wind.

"This will pass," I said, "as the night will pass, and when it is gone, I shall take you back to Cottonwood Wash to live."

"You're a strange man. You look like an ordinary cowhand, but you talk like a man of education."

"I read a book once." I grinned at her. "A couple of them, in fact. And don't fool yourself about cowhands."

Tightening the cinch, I swung my horse for mounting.

"But could you settle down? Could you stay?"

My foot went into the stirrup and I swung into the leather.

"On the day I rode into Hattan's Point and saw you, I knew I would stay. Why does a man drift around? Only because he is looking for something. For money, for a home, for a girl."

Night had closed in from the hills, moving its dark battalions of shadows under the trees and in the lee of buildings, then reaching out to cover the ranch yard. A few stars had come out.

Reaching down, I caught Moira's hand and swung her up, her foot slipping into the stirrup. Her breath caught as I pulled her into my arms, then came quickly and deeply, her lips parting slightly as she came into my arms. I felt her warm body melt against mine and her lips were seeking, urgent, passionate. My fingers went to her hair, and all the waiting, all the fighting, all our troubles dissolved into nothingness.

She pulled back suddenly, frightened and excited, her breasts rising and falling as she fought for control.

"This isn't good, Matt! We're too—too violent. We've got to be more calm."

I laughed then, full of the zest of living and loving and holding the beauty of her in my arms in the early night.

"You're not exactly a calm person."

"I?" She seemed to hesitate. "Well, all right, then. Neither of us is calm."

"Need we be?"

And then we heard someone coming down from the house, someone whistling lightly. Boots grated off the gravel path and I let Moira down to the ground quickly.

It was Canaval.

"Better ride ... Morgan Park will be leaving soon. Might be trouble."

I gathered the reins. "I'm practically gone."

"Mean what you said back there? About peace and all?"

"What can we gain by fighting?"

Canaval turned to Moira. "Let me talk to Brennan alone, will you? There's something he should know."

When she had gone back to the house, Canaval said quietly, "She reminds me of her mother."

Surprised, I looked down at him. "You knew her mother?"

"She was my sister."

"But . . . does Moira know?"

"Rud and I used to ride together. I was too fast with a gun and killed a man with too many relatives, so I left the country we came from. Rud married my sister after I left, and from time to time we kept in touch. Then Rud needed help against rustlers, and sent for me. He persuaded me to stay." He hesitated, then added, "Moira doesn't know."

We were silent, listening to the night, as men of our kind would. I knew then that Canaval liked me or he would never have told me this.

CHAPTER 14

I T WAS AFTER midnight when finally I rode away from the Boxed M, leaving the main trail and cutting across country to the head of Gypsum Canyon.

Before leaving I had told Canaval what I had heard about the Slades, and he had listened, without comment. Whether he believed me I could not say, but at least he had been warned. Each of us knew all there was to know about Slade. The man was a killer for hire, a cold-blooded and efficient man with a gun.

There is a magic about the desert at night. Until you have seen it, stood alone in the midst of it, you cannot know what enchantment is. There is a stillness there and a nearness of stars such as no other place on earth offers.

I rode quietly and steadily, not hurrying, but feeling the coolness of the night, and remembering the girl I had left behind me, remembering Moira.

Mulvaney was waiting for me. "Knew the horse's walk." He nodded toward the hills. "Too quiet out there."

We turned in then, and rested, but during the night I awakened with the sound of a shot ringing in my ears. Mulvaney was sleeping soundly so I did not disturb him, nor was I even sure that I had heard it. A real shot? Or something in a dream? All was quiet, and after listening for a while I crawled back into the warmth of my blankets, of no mind to go exploring in the middle of a chill desert night.

In the morning I mentioned it to Mulvaney.

"Did you get up?"

"Yes, but I didn't hear anything. It might have been one of the Benaras boys. Sometimes they hunt at night."

Two hours later I knew better. Maverick Spring lay in that no man's land where the Boxed M bordered the Two-Bar, and I had ridden that way, for there was bog on one side of the spring and twice I'd had to pull steers out of there.

The morning was fresh and clear as I was coming up out of the Wash. Heading across for the spring, I saw a riderless horse.

He was standing his head down and, suddenly worried, I picked my horse up to a canter.

Drawing near, I saw that a dark bundle lay on the ground near the horse. The dark bundle was a man, and he was dead. Even before I turned the body over, I knew it was Rud Maclaren.

He had been shot twice from behind, both times in the head.

He was sprawled on his face, one knee drawn up, both hands lying in sight, on the sand. His belt gun was tied down. Rud Maclaren had been shot down from behind without an instant of warning.

After that one quick look, I stepped back and, drawing my rifle from the scabbard, I fired three quick shots as a signal to Mulvaney.

When he saw Maclaren his face went three shades whiter.

"This is trouble, lad. The country respected him. A man will hang for this."

"Feel of him, Mulvaney. The man's cold. It must have been that shot I heard last night."

Mulvaney nodded. "You'd best rig a story, Matt." It was the first time he had ever called me by name. "This will blow the lid off."

Of that there was no doubt, and I needed no argument to convince me that I was the logical suspect.

"No rigging. I'll tell the truth."

"They'll hang you. He's on your place, and the two of you had been feuding."

Standing over the body with Mulvaney's words ringing in my ears, I could see with clarity the situation I faced. Yet why had Maclaren come here? What was he doing on my ranch in the middle of the night? And who could have been riding with him?

Somebody wanted Maclaren dead badly enough to shoot him in the back, and had lured him here on some pretext. He certainly was not a man given to midnight rides. It had been late when I left his ranch and at that time he had been there. But so had Morgan Park.

The morning was cool, with a hint of rain. Mulvaney started for the Boxed M to report the killing to Canaval. It would be up to Canaval to break the news to Moira. And I did not want to think of that.

My luck broke, in one sense, Jolly Benaras came riding up the Wash, and I sent him off to town to report the shooting to the sheriff and to Key Chapin.

When they had gone, I mounted my horse and, careful to obscure no tracks, scouted the area. There was a confusion of hoofprints where his horse had moved about during the night, and at that point the sand was soft and there was no definition to any of the tracks.

One thing puzzled me. I had heard only one shot, yet there were two bullet holes. Crouching beside the body, I studied the setup. Strangely enough, only one bullet hole showed evidences of bleeding.

There were no other tracks that I could identify. They were mingled and overlapped each other, and all were indefinite because of the soft sand.

When I saw riders approaching I walked back to the body. The nearest was Canaval, and beside him, Moira. The other three were Boxed M cowhands. One glance at their faces and I knew there was no doubt in their mind as to who had killed Rud Maclaren.

Canaval looked at me, his eyes cold, calculating, and shrewd. Moira threw herself from the horse and ran to the still form lying on the sand. She had not looked at me or acknowledged my presence.

"This looks like trouble, Canaval. I think I heard the shot."

"Shot?"

"Only one ... and he's been shot twice."

Nobody said anything, but all kept their eyes on me. They were waiting for me to defend myself.

"When did he leave the ranch?"

"No one knows, exactly." Canaval sat very still in the saddle, and I knew he was trying to make up his mind about me. "He turned in after you left—it must have been around two. Maybe later."

"The shot I heard was close to four o'clock."

The Boxed M riders had moved out, casually, almost accidentally it seemed, but shutting me off from any escape. Behind me was the spring, the bog, and a shoulder of rock. Before me, the riders formed a semicircle.

These were men who rode for the brand, men loyal, devoted, and utterly ruthless when aroused. The night before they had given me the benefit of the doubt, but now the evidence seemed to point at me.

"Who was with him when you last saw him?"

"He was alone. And if it's Morgan Park you're thinking of, forget it. He left right after you did."

Tom Fox, a lean, hard-bitten Boxed M rider, took his rope from his saddle.

"What're we waitin' for, men? There's our man."

"Fox, from all I hear you're a good hand, so don't throw your loop over any quick conclusions. I didn't kill Rud Maclaren, and had no reason to. We made peace talk last night and parted on good terms."

Fox looked over at Canaval. "Is that right?"

"It is—but Rud changed his mind afterward."

"What?"

That I could not believe, yet Canaval would not lie to me. Rud Maclaren had been only half won over to my thinking, I knew. But that he could have changed his mind so fast I was not willing to believe.

"Anyway, how could I know that?"

"You couldn't," Canaval agreed, "unless he got out of bed and rode over to tell you. He's the sort that might do just that—I can think of no other reason why he would ride out durin' the night."

The one thing I had been telling myself was that I'd

be in the clear because I had no motive. And here it was, the perfect motive. My mouth was dry and my hands felt cold . . . sweat broke out on my forehead.

Fox began to shake out a loop. I tried to catch Moira's eye, but she refused to look at me. Canaval seemed to be studying over something in his mind.

Nobody had drawn a gun, yet that loop in Fox's hand could snake over me quicker than I could throw a gun and fire. And if I moved toward a gun, Canaval would also. I didn't know whether I could beat Canaval or not . . . and he was a man I didn't want to kill.

Fox moved his horse a step forward, but Moira stopped him.

"No, Tom. Wait for the men from town. If he killed my father I want him to die, but we'll wait."

Reluctantly, Fox waited, and then we heard the horses coming. There were a dozen riders, with Key Chapin in the lead.

He threw me a quick, worried glance, then turned to Canaval. Briefly and to the point, the foreman of the Boxed M explained the situation.

Maclaren and I had talked, we had made a tentative peace agreement. Then Rud had changed his mind. Now he was dead, and I had been found with the body.

The evidence as he summed it up was damning. There was motive and opportunity for me, and for no other known person.

Looking at their faces, I felt a sinking in my stomach. You are right up against the wall, Matt Brennan, I told myself. You've come to the end, and you'll hang for another man's crime.

Mulvaney had not returned after informing the Boxed M of Maclaren's death. And there was no sign of Jolly Benaras.

"One thing," I said suddenly, "I'd like to call to your attention."

There were no friendly eyes in those that turned to me.

"Chapin," I said, "will you turn Maclaren over?"

He looked from me to the body, then swung down and walked over. In looking at Maclaren's face, I had lifted the body but had let it fall back in place. I heard Moira's breath catch as Chapin stooped to turn the dead man. He rolled him over, then straightened up.

He looked at me, puzzled. The others simply waited, seeing nothing, understanding nothing.

"You accuse me because he is here, on my ranch. Well, he was not killed here. *There's no blood on the ground!*"

Startled, their eyes turned to the sand upon which Maclaren had been lying. The sand was ruffled, but there was no blood.

"One wound bled badly and there must have been quite a pool where he was lying because his shirt is covered with it. The sand would be bloody if he was killed here.

"What I am saying is that he was killed elsewhere, then carried here and left."

"But why?" Chapin protested.

"You suspect me, don't you? What other reason would there be?

"Another thing," I added, "the shot that I heard was fired into him after he was dead!"

"How d'you figure that?" Fox was studying me with new eyes.

"A dead man does not bleed. Look at him! All the blood came from one wound."

Suddenly, we were aware that more horsemen had come up behind us. It was Mulvaney and the Benaras boys, all of them.

"We'd be beholden," Jolly said, "if you'd all move back. We're friends to Brennan and we don't believe he done it. Now move back."

The Boxed M riders hesitated, not liking it, but they had been taken from behind and there was little chance to even make a fight of it if trouble started.

Carefully, the nearest riders eased back. The situation was now at a stalemate and I could talk. But it was Moira I most wanted to convince, and how my words were affecting her I had no idea. Her face was shadowed with sadness, nothing more.

"There are other men who wanted Maclaren out of the way. What had I to fear from him? I had already showed I could hold the ranch...I wanted peace."

Then more horses came up the trail and I recognized the redhead with whom I'd had trouble before. With him was Bodie Miller.

CHAPTER 15

B ODIE MILLER PUSHED his horse into the inner circle, and I could see that the devil was riding him again. His narrow, feral features seemed even sharper today; his eyes showed almost white under the brim of his tipped down, narrow-brimmed hat.

Bodie had never shaved, and the white hair lay along his jaws mingled with a few darker ones. These last, at the corners of his mouth, lent a peculiarly vicious expression to his face.

He was an ugly young man, thin and narrow-shouldered, and the long, bony fingers seemed never still.

He looked up at me, disregarding the body of Maclaren as if it was not there. I could respect the feeling of Tom Fox, for his eagerness to destroy me was but a reflection of his feudal loyalty for Maclaren. There was none of that in Miller. He just wanted to kill.

"You, is it? I'll kill you, one day."

"Keep out of this, Bodie!" Canaval ordered, stepping his horse forward. "This isn't your play!"

Miller's hatred was naked in his eyes. In his arrogance he had never liked taking orders from Canaval, and that fact revealed itself now.

"Maclaren's dead," he said brutally. "Maybe you

won't be the boss any more. Maybe she'll want a *younger* man for boss!"

The leer that accompanied the words gave no doubt as to his meaning, and suddenly I wanted to kill, suddenly I was going to. In the next instant I would have made my move, but it was Canaval's cool, dispassionate voice that stopped me.

"That will be for Miss Moira to decide." He turned to her. "Do you wish me to continue as foreman?"

Moira Maclaren's head came up. Never had I been so proud of anyone.

"Naturally." Her voice was level and cold. "And your first job as my foreman will be to fire Bodie Miller."

Miller's face went livid with fury, his lips bared back from his big, uneven teeth, but before he could speak I interfered.

"Don't say it, Bodie. Don't say it."

So there I stood in the still, cool morning under the low gray clouds, with armed men around me in a circle, and I looked across the body of Rud Maclaren and stood ready to draw. Within me I knew that I must kill this man or be killed, and at that instant I did not want to wait for the decision. I wanted it now...here.

The malignancy of his expression was unbelievable. "You an' me are goin' to meet," he said, staring at me.

"When you're ready, Bodie."

Deliberately, I turned my back on him.

Standing beside the spring, I rolled a smoke and watched them load the body of Maclaren into the buckboard. Moira was avoiding me, and I made no move to go to her.

Chapin and Canaval had stood to one side talking in low voices, and now they turned and walked over to me.

"We don't think you're guilty, Brennan. But have you any ideas?"

"Only that he was killed elsewhere and carried here to throw suspicion on me. And I don't believe it was Pinder. He would not shoot Rud Maclaren in the back. Rud was no gunman, was he?"

"No...definitely no."

"And Jim Pinder is...so why shoot him in the back? The same thing goes for me."

"You think Park did it?"

Again I repeated the little I had learned from Lyell, and those few words in Booker's office.

The Slades were to kill Canaval—and why, except that Canaval was Maclaren's strong right hand? And it was Park who was hiring them.

This information they accepted, as I could see, with reservations. For Morgan Park had no motive that anyone could see. When I mentioned the assay report, they turned it off by saying simply that there was no mineral in this area, and there had been nothing to connect the report with Park. Nor did Morgan Park have anything to fear from Maclaren otherwise, for Maclaren had looked favorably upon Park's visits, had welcomed him, even treated him as a son-in-law to be. Maclaren had several times asked Moira, Canaval said, why she did not marry Park. All I had was suspicion and a few words from a dying man... no more.

Smoking my cigarette, I watched them start off with the buckboard. The Boxed M riders bunched around it, a silent guard of honor. Only then did I start toward Moira.

Whether she saw me coming, I did not know. Only she chose that moment to start her horse and ride quietly away, and I stayed behind, surrounded by my little guard, Mulvaney and the Benaras boys.

Bob Benaras had stayed behind to protect the ranch, and he was waiting for me when we rode into the yard.

"We'll be heading home," he said, "but Jonathan an' Jolly, they can stay with you. I ain't got work enough to keep 'em out of mischief."

He was not fooling me in the least, but I needed the help, as he knew.

————

AND THEN FOR a time, nothing happened.

With four men to work, the walls of the house mounted swiftly. All of us were strong, and Mulvaney was a builder. He was the shaper of the house, the planner of all our work. Forgetting everything, we worked steadily for two weeks. My side lost its stiffness and my muscles worked with their old-time smoothness. I felt better, and I was toughening up again.

There was an inquest over the body of Rud Maclaren, but no new evidence turned up. Despite the reports by the sheriff who rode out to investigate two days after the killing, many people still believed me guilty. To all appearances, there was not even another suspect. Jim Pinder had not even been in the county, and had a solid alibi, for on that night he had been in a minor shooting over a card game at Hite.

There had been no will, so the ranch went to Moira. Yet nothing was settled. Only, the Boxed M withdrew all claims upon the Two-Bar and any Two-Bar range or waterholes.

Jim Pinder remained on the CP and was not seen at Hattan's Point.

Of Bodie Miller we heard much. He killed a man at Hattan's in a saloon quarrel. Shot him down even before he could get a gun drawn. Bodie and Red were reported to be running with a lot of riffraff from Hite, many of them men from Robber's Roost. The Boxed M was missing cattle, and Bodie was reported to be laughing at the reports. He pistol-whipped a man in Silver Reef and was rapidly winning a name as a badman.

And during all this time I continued to think about Moira. Once I rode over to the ranch, and Canaval met me in the yard. Moira would not see me.

Oddly enough, I thought there was real regret in Canaval's voice when he told me.

He was a quiet man, stern, yet not unfriendly. His hair was prematurely gray, and he had an easy way about him that drew friendships that he rarely developed. He was a lone wolf, never mingling with the men of the ranch, usually riding alone.

He said nothing about the Slades, nor did I ask him. I knew that he was closer to Moira than ever before. She relied on his judgment, although she knew more than a little of how to handle a cow ranch.

Maclaren had wanted more land. She began within two weeks after his death to make the most of what they had. For the first time in Boxed M history, hay was cut and stacked, and grain was planted for feed for the horses.

A fence without a gate was run along the line between the Boxed M and the Two-Bar.

The day they finished it, I was riding over that way. Tom Fox was in charge.

He rode out to meet me as I came near. His animosity had died, and we sat our horses, watching the fencing.

"No gate?" I asked.

"No...no gate."

She was shutting me out, cutting me off. Whatever might have been, had Rud Maclaren lived, his death seemed to have ended it, once and for all.

My thoughts returned to Morgan Park. He had gone back to his ranch and was not seen around, but he was never really out of my mind. There had been no sign of the Slades, and I could imagine what Canaval would be thinking.

There were changes with me, too. The old devil-may-care spirit was there, but it rarely came out. The work was hard and I kept at it steadily. My house was completed, and the garden we had planted was showing signs of coming up. We had even transplanted several trees and moved them up to the ranch yard.

We built furniture and we bricked up the water hole. We planted vines around the house, and one day we drove to town and loaded up household things to carry back.

That was the day I saw Moira.

She had come from the post office in the stage station and she was waiting for her buckboard, which was coming up the street from the general store.

She came out of the building into the sunlight just as our wagon came by. I was behind, just putting my foot in the stirrup, and looked over my saddle at her, almost a block away.

I could not see her eyes, but as our wagon drew abreast I saw her turn to look at the pots and pans, at some rolled-up Indian rugs. Her face turned with the wagon and she watched it out of sight, and then I swung my leg over the saddle. As I turned the buckskin, she saw me and turned quickly away. Before I could reach her she got into the buckboard and was driving off.

It was a slow ride back to the Two-Bar, for wherever I looked I saw the pale, lovely features of Moira, saw her standing alone before the stage station, watching my wagon go by. These household things, these might have been ours. I wondered if she thought of that?

Jolly Benaras was waiting for me when I rode into the yard.

"Nick was over. Said he seen tracks over east of here. Three, four men."

Three or four men ... in the broken, lonely country to the east, the land where no man rode willingly.

"Where'd he see them?"

"Plateau above Dark Canyon ... mighty wild country."

"Might be Bodie Miller."

"Might ... he didn't think so. Bodie sticks close to towns. He likes to brag it around, playin' big-man."

Who then?

The Slades ...

"Thanks," I said, "tomorrow I'll ride that way. I'll have a look. There's a valley over there where we could run some cows, anyway. I'll check it."

If it was the Slades, what were they waiting for? Had the killing of Rud Maclaren made it seem too risky to take a chance on more killings? It could be ... and if anyone wanted what Maclaren had, Canaval still stood between them.

We moved the rugs into the house, put the pots and pans in the cupboards. I walked in the wide living room and looked around. It looked bare, cold. It was a house, but it was not yet a home.

At night I was restless. So much was left unfinished. Bodie Miller was around, rustling Boxed M cattle, no doubt. Sooner or later the Boxed M hands would meet him, and from talk I heard around, the least he could expect was a rope.

And there were the unknown riders east of us, lurking back in those mysterious, unknown canyons near the Sweet Alice Hills.

Saddling up a tough bay pony, I rode out toward the Maverick Spring where Rud Maclaren had fallen. In the darkness my horse made little sound as he cantered over the bunch grass levels.

We stopped at the spring and I drank, then watered my horse. It had been hours later than this when Maclaren was killed. . . . Suddenly my horse jerked up his head.

Instantly I was alert, and spoke softly to the bay. He had swelled his sides for a whinny but my low word stopped him. He looked off in the darkness toward the boxed M.

Moonlight silvered in faint strands, stretching

away. The fence . . . Stepping into the saddle, my right hand resting on my thigh near my gun butt, I rode toward the fence, walking my horse from shadow to shadow.

Suddenly, I drew up.

There was a horse standing there in the darkness, a horse with his head toward me.

And in the night I heard a muffled sob . . . and my bay started walking again.

We were nearing the fence when the other horse whinnied. Instantly, a dark form sat erect in the saddle.

"Moira!"

An instant she sat stiff and still in the saddle, then with a low cry she wheeled her horse and spurred him into a run.

"Moira!"

Her horse ran on, but once I thought I caught the white flash of a face turned back.

"Moira, I love you!"

But there was no sound save the echo of my own voice and the pounding of hoofs, fading away.

For a long time I sat there beside that twin strand of wire, staring off into the night and the darkness, listening, hoping I'd hear those hoofs again, bringing her back.

But there was no sound . . . only a quail that called inquiringly into the night.

CHAPTER 16

JOLLY BENARAS HUNKERED down and drew with his finger in the sand. His bony shoulders hunched against the morning chill, his right eye squinted against the tobacco smoke.

"Sure, that place you call the amphitheater, that's here. Now right back of this here cliff is a trail. You can make it with a good mountain horse. When you get on top, that's the mesa above Dark Canyon. The trail I seen was over across, nigh six mile. There's a saddle rock over thataway, an' when you sight it, ride for it. On the north side you'll find that trail if the wind ain't blowed it away."

Jonathan had bunched forty head of cattle for me, and I walked to the buckskin and shoved my Winchester in the bucket. Then I stepped into the leather.

We started the cattle, but they had no mind to hit the trail. They had found a home in Cottonwood Wash and they aimed to stay, but we finally got them straightened out and pointed for the hills. Jonathan was riding along, but he would leave me when we got into the canyon.

He carried his Spencer in his hand, a lean, tall boy, narrow-hipped and a little stooped in the shoulders. His face looked slightly blue with the morning chill, and he rode without talking.

As for myself, I was not anxious to talk. My mind was not on my task. Herding the cattle up the canyon was no problem, for they could not get back past us, could only move forward. Nor was I thinking of the mission that lay ahead of me, the scouting of the group of men Nick Benaras had seen near Dark Canyon.

Had it really been Moira I'd seen? And if so, had she heard my call? Restlessly, I stepped up my pace. I was angry with myself and half angry with her. Why should she act this way? Did she really believe I'd kill her father? Both Canaval and Chapin had disclaimed any suspicion of me, although there were others who still believed me guilty.

Irritably, I watched the moving cattle, pushing them faster than was wise. Jonathan glanced back, but said nothing, moving right along with me.

At the amphitheater the cattle moved into the grass, lifted their heads and looked around. We swung away from them and slowly they began to scatter out, already making themselves at home.

There was no sound but that of water running over stones. Jonathan put his rifle in the boot and hooked a leg around the saddle horn. He rolled a smoke and glanced at me.

"Want company?"

"Thanks ... no."

He touched a match to the cigarette. "I'll stay with the cows for a while, then. Maybe some of 'em will take a notion to head for home."

He swung his legs down and shoved his boot into the stirrup.

I was thinking of Moira.

"You take it easy, Matt. You're too much on the prod."

"Thanks...I'll do that."

He was right, of course. I was irritable, upset by Moira's action the night before, and I was in no mood for scouting. What I really wanted was a fight.

The trail that Jolly had told me about was there. Looking up, I backed off a little and looked again.

At this point the red sandstone cliff was all of seven hundred feet high. The trail was an eyebrow skirting the cliff face, and one which a spooky horse would never manage. But I was riding Buck, who was far from spooky, mountain-bred, and tough. He could have walked a tight wire, I think.

We started up, taking our time. It was nearing noon and the sun was hot. The cliff up which the trail mounted was in the mouth of a narrow canyon. The wall across from me was not fifty feet away, and as I mounted the distance grew less and less, until it was almost close enough for me to reach out and touch the opposite wall. I penetrated almost a thousand yards deeper into the canyon, then emerged suddenly on top.

Here the wind blew steadily. The terrain here was flat as a floor, tufted with sparse grass, and in the distance a few dark junipers looking like upthrust blades from a forest of spears.

Sitting very still, I scanned the mesa top with extreme care. From now on I would be moving closer and closer to men who did not wish to be seen. No honest men would gather here, and if these were the Slades, then they were skilled manhunters, and dangerous men.

Nothing moved but the wind. Overhead the sky was wide and blue, with only a few tufts of lonely cloud.

I walked my horse forward, looking out for the saddle rock. In every direction the mesa stretched far, far away. I could smell sagebrush and cedar. Here and there on top of the mesa were tufts of desert five-spot, a rose-purple flower with flecks of bright red on the petals, and scattered clumps of rabbit bush.

My horse walked forward into the day. The air was clear and the chill was gone.... Suddenly ahead of me I saw the dark jut of the saddle rock, and closed the distance, keeping my eyes roving, wary of any rider, any movement.

At the saddle rock I dismounted to rest the buckskin, and let him crop some sparse grass. There was a niche in the black lava of the rock, and I led Buck back into it and out of sight.

Trailing the reins, I stretched out on the grass in the shade. It had been a long ride, and I had been late to bed and up early. After a few minutes, I dozed. Not asleep, nor yet awake. Several minutes must have passed, perhaps as much as half an hour, when suddenly I heard the sound of a trotting horse.

Instantly I was on my feet and, moving swiftly to Buck's side, I spoke softly. He eased down, waiting. The rider came nearer and nearer. I slid my Winchester from the scabbard and waited, holding it hip-high.

Then I realized the rider would pass on the far side of the rocks, where Jolly had told me I'd find the trail. Swiftly, careful to make no noise, I climbed up among the jumbled rocks toward the saddle itself. When able to see the mesa beyond, I settled down and looked past a round rock.

For a minute, two minutes, I saw nothing. Then a horse came into view, now slowed to a walk. A horse ridden by a huge man, and there could be but one man of that size.

Morgan Park!

Where he rode I could see the dim tracks of other horses. After a moment of watching, I drew back and slid down off the rocks. Leading the buckskin, I walked around to where I could stand concealed, yet could see the trail ahead.

Morgan Park rode on until he turned, over a mile away, to the edge of the cliff. There he disappeared.

Waiting, for he might have stopped to watch his back trail, I let three, four, five minutes pass. Then I mounted and rode out to parallel the trail he had taken. The hoofprints of his big horse were plain, and I studied them. Also, the other prints that were several days old.

The day was hot. A film of heat daze obscured the horizon. Shimmering heat waves veiled the Sweet Alice Hills in the distance, the hills that seemed to end the visible world. From time to time the trail neared the lip of the mesa and I could look out over an infinity of canyons.

Yet when I reached the place where Park had disappeared, instead of the trail going over the edge of the mesa as I had expected, it merely dropped to a lower level and continued on.

Before me the mesa stretched ahead, apparently to the foot of the Sweet Alice Hills. But knowing that country, I knew half a dozen canyons might cut through the mesa before those hills were reached. There was no sign of Morgan Park. He had vanished completely.

Riding on, I came to a fork in the trail. Here there was only flat rock, and, look as I might, I could find no indication of which way Park had gone.

Finally, taking a chance, I held to the trail that kept closest to the mesa's edge.

Suddenly the edge of the cliff broke sharply back into the mesa and showed a steep slide. From talks with the Benaras boys I knew this was Poison Canyon. So I went down the slide and ended in the bottom of a narrow canyon.

If I met a rider here, there would be nothing to do but shoot it out. No man could get back up that slide under fire, and one could only go along the canyon's bottom. I slid my rifle out of the boot and rode with it in my hand, ready to shoot.

The canyon bottom was sand littered with rocks of all sizes and shapes. The walls rose sheer on either side. There was little vegetation here, but many tumbled and dried roots washed down in the freshets that swept these canyons after rains.

Suddenly, I smelled smoke.

Drawing up, I listened, waiting, sniffing the air again. After a moment I got a second whiff of woodsmoke.

There was no cover here, so I walked my horse on a little farther. A brush-choked canyon opened on my right, filled with manzanita. Swinging down, I led my horse back into it, pushing through the brush until I found an open spot with a little grass. I tied the buckskin to a bush and worked my way back, then slipped off my boots and continued on in my sock feet.

No air stirred in the canyon. It was hot, stifling hot. Sweat trickled down my body under my shirt. The hand that clutched the rifle grew sweaty. Careful to avoid thorns, I worked my way out through the manzanita and in among the rocks.

Here I hunched down behind a clump of mixed curl-leaf and desert apricot. Then, working forward on my knees, I crept deeper into the thicket.

The air was motionless...the heat was heavy... the leaves of the curl-leaf had a pleasant, pungent, tangy smell. I lay still, listening.

The smell of woodsmoke again...then a faint rattle of rocks, and the *chink* of a tin pan on rock.

Keeping inside the thicket of curl-leaf, I crawled forward. A lizard lay on a rock staring at me. His lower lids crept up, almost closing his eyes, his sides throbbed. My hand moved and he fled away over the sand. I crawled on, then waited, hearing a low mutter of voices.

Nearer, I could distinguish words. Settling down in the thickest part of the tangle of brush, with a rock in front of me, I listened.

"No use to shave. We won't get to Hattan's now."

"Him an' Slade are makin' medicine...we'll move."

"I don't like it."

"Nobody ast you. Slade, he'll decide." Tin rattled again. "Anyway, what you beefin' about? Slade will have the worst of it done before we move in. They's two, three men on the Two-Bar, that's all. 'Bout that on the Boxed M."

"Big feller looks man enough to do it himself."

"Then you an' me wouldn't have the money."

There was silence. Sweat trickled down my spine. My knee was cramped, but I did not dare to move. I could see nothing, for the curl-leaf thicket reached right to the edge of their camp.

I dried my hands on my shirtfront, and took up the rifle again.

"Pinder'll raid today. Maybe that'll take care of it."

Pinder . . . raid.

My place? Where else but my place? While I lay here in this thicket, Mulvaney and the Benaras boys might be fighting for their lives. I started, then relaxed. I could not get there in time now, and the Benaras boys were no chickens. Neither was Mulvaney. Their position was strong and they had food and water.

"Who gets Brennan?"

"How should I know? Big feller maybe."

"He's welcome."

"Finish that coffee. I want to wash up."

"You can't. Slade ain't et yet."

There was silence then. Cautiously I straightened my leg, then eased away from the rock. Carefully, I began to retreat through the thicket.

A branch hooked on my shirt, then whipped loose, a dry, rasping sound in the thicket.

"What was that?"

I held very still, holding my breath.

"Aw, you're too jumpy. Settle down."

"I heard somethin'."

"Coyote, maybe."

"In this close to us? You crazy?"

Footsteps sounded, and I eased my rifle into position, mentally retracing my steps to my horse. Where were Morgan Park and Slade? I might have to ride in a hurry and I knew no way out but up the slide, which would be impossible under gunfire.

"You goin' in there? If you do, you're crazy." The speaker chuckled. "You got too much imagination. An' if there was anybody in there, what would happen to you? He'd see you first."

The footsteps stopped...hesitated. A sound of brush against leather came to me, and I put my thumb on the hammer of the Winchester. I knew right where the man was standing and at this distance with a rifle I could not miss. Whatever happened afterward, that first man was as good as dead.

He didn't like it. I could almost see his mind working. He suddenly decided he had heard nothing.

He still stood there, and I gambled and eased back a little farther. There was no sound, and I withdrew stealthily to my horse.

Mounting, I walked the horse out of the brush-choked canyon and started back toward the slide. But when I reached it I went on past.

Around a bend I drew up and taking out a handkerchief, mopped my face.

Then I walked my horse deeper into the unknown canyon. I'd found what I wanted to know. Slade and his gang were here. They were waiting to strike. Even now they were meeting with Morgan Park....

Tomorrow?

CHAPTER 17

I

T WAS MIDAFTERNOON before I found a trail out of Poison Canyon. It was at the head of the canyon, and I came up out of it heading almost due east. Rounding the end of the canyon, I started back along Dark Canyon Plateau.

At sundown there still was far to go, and when my horse began to tug the bit toward the north, I let him have his head. Ten minutes later we had come up to a spring.

My horse was dead beat and so was I. It would soon be dark, and the trail was only vaguely familiar to me. The spring stood in a small grove of aspens over against the mountain. There were tracks of deer and wild horses, but no tracks of shod horses, nor of men.

Stripping the saddle from the buckskin, I gave him a hurried rubdown with a handful of dry grass, and picketed him out on a patch of grass. Impatient as I was, I knew better than to arrive home on a worn-out horse.

Behind me the Sweet Alice Hills lifted their rough shoulders, all of a thousand feet higher than the spring where I was camped. The sun was setting over the Blue Mountains and, hunkered down over a tiny fire, I prepared my supper, worried and on edge because of all that might be happening.

Yet, as the evening drew on, my anxiety left me. The hills were silent and dark. There was only a faint trickling of water from the spring, and the comfortable, quieting sound of my horse cropping grass.

Putting on more coffee I sat back, watching the fire, but far enough away from it to be out of sight. But I was not worried. I had strayed well away from the trail across the plateau, and if Morgan Park elected to return that night, there was no danger that he could find me.

Finally, banking my fire, I rolled in my blankets and was ready to sleep. But in those last minutes before I slept I decided what to do. Up to now we had been attacked; now I would stage a one-man counterattack. I would strike at the home ranch of the CP.

At daybreak, when long streamers of mist lay in the canyons, I was up and making coffee. As soon as I had eaten I saddled up and started back, and I rode swiftly.

The CP lay among low, rolling hills covered with sparse grass and salt-bush. Here and there were clumps of snowberry. Along the slopes were scattered piñon and juniper, and weaving among them I worked my way close to the ranch.

It lay deserted and still. A windmill turned lazily, and there were a few horses in the corral. Watching, I saw a big-bellied, greasy cook come to the door and throw out a pan of water.

He stood on the steps, mopping his face with a towel, then turned back inside. When the door closed, I swung to the saddle again, rode close, then suddenly spurred my horse and went into the yard on a dead run.

As I had planned, the sound of the racing horse brought the cook running to the door. He rushed outside and I slid my horse to a stop, with my gun on him.

His face went pale, then red. He started to speak but I dropped off my horse, turned him around, and tied him up. Then I grabbed him by the collar, dragged him inside, and rolled him under the bed. He promptly began to yell so I rolled him out and gagged him solidly.

Outside once more, I took down the corral bars and hazed all the fresh horses out and drove them off. Rummaging around in the tool shed, I found some giant powder that had been used to blast rock. I went back into the house and raised up a stone in the back wall of the fireplace and put the can of powder in the hole, then trailed a short fuse from it into the fireplace itself.

Finding several shotgun shells, I scattered them around and brushed ashes over them. Then I placed a few logs carefully over them, and filled a can with water for coffee and placed it on top.

Returning to the brush on a little bench overlooking the ranch, I settled down for a long wait.

A slow hour passed. The leaf mold upon which I lay was soft and comfortable. Several times I dozed a little, weary from my long ride. Once a rattler crawled by within a few feet of my head. A packrat stared at me, his nose twitching. He came closer and looked again. Crows quarreled in the trees above me. . . .

And then I saw the riders. One look was enough. Whatever had happened at the Two-Bar, these men were not victorious. There were nine in the group and two were bandaged, one with his skull bound up, the other with an arm in a sling. Another was being brought home tied over his saddle, head and heels hanging.

Lifting my rifle, I waited until they were down the hill and close to the house. Then I put my rifle to my shoulder and fired three times as fast as I could trigger the rifle.

A horse screamed and leaped into the air, half-turning and scattering the group. A man grabbed at his leg, lost balance and fell, his foot catching in the stirrup. His horse raced fifty yards, then stopped.

As one man they had scattered, some for the barn, others for the main house or the bunkhouse.

Two bullets I put into the barn wall, and then turned and shot at the hinges on the kitchen door. Two bullets in the lower hinge, then two in the upper. Taking time out, I reloaded.

The door hung in place, but I was sure the shots had gone true. Shifting my aim I smashed a window, holding the sight just above the sill where a head would be apt to be. Then I shifted and broke another window, swinging the rifle farther to fire at an ambitious cowhand who was trying to get a shot at me from the barn door.

I took aim at the top hinge again, and taking up the slack of the trigger, eased back. The rifle leaped in my hands and the door sagged. Hastily I shifted my aim to the lower hinge and finished it off with two more shots.

My position was perfect. I lay among rocks and brush on a bench overlooking the ranch yard, where the barn door, the rear of the house and every inch of the space around the bunkhouse door were visible. Nor was there any way for a man to slip out and get into the brush without exposing himself. There was no cover away from the ranch buildings.

The door was open now, and I put two rifle bullets through the opening, heard a startled yelp from one of the men, then fired again, knocking more glass out of the window. Although I still had shells in the rifle, I took time out to refill the magazine.

Several minutes passed. I put the rifle down and rolled a smoke. Shifting my position to one more comfortable, I waited. A couple of tentative shots were fired from the house, both wide of my position.

One man suddenly ducked from the barn and darted toward a heavily planked water trough. I let him run, then as he dove behind the trough I put two bullets through it, right over his head, letting the water drain out over his head and shoulders. When he made a move, I put a bullet into the dirt beside him.

Waiting, I saw his rifle barrel come up. His position was a little better, but obviously he was trying to reach the corner of the corral from which he might outflank me. His rifle barrel was steadied against the post at the end of the trough. Taking careful aim at the edge of the post just above the rifle, I fired.

The rifle fell and the man slumped to the ground, whether dead or merely grazed, I could not tell. After that there was no more effort to escape from either barn or house.

The afternoon wore on. It was time I was moving, but I waited, wanting to see what would happen when they started a fire to make coffee.

Once I put a shot through the door to let them know I had not gone.

Crawling back to my saddlebags, I took a piece of jerked beef and my canteen from the saddle. Then I returned and settled into place again.

It was almost evening before a slow trail of smoke began to lift from the fireplace. Chuckling with anticipation, I waited. There was very little time left to me. Once it was dark I could not keep them undercover; and my position would speedily become untenable.

Now the smoke was lifting. Easing back to my saddle, I replaced the canteen and got my horse ready for a fast leave-taking. A shot through the barn door was enough to let them know I was still there.

The smoke increased, and suddenly there was an explosion within the house.

A shotgun shell...suddenly three others went, one, two, three! There were startled yells within the house and one man sprang for the door, but a bullet into the step nearly tore his toe off, and he ducked back into the house. Running back, I swung into the saddle, and almost at the same instant there was a heavy concussion and flame blasted out of the chimney. The chimney sagged, and smoke and fire burst from a hole at ground level.

It was enough for me. I swung the buckskin and took to the hills. Behind me there were shouts and yells, but they had not seen me. Then another crash...from the ridge I looked back, and saw that the chimney had fallen. There was a hole in the end of the house where the roof had been smashed in, and smoke was coming out.

Jim Pinder knew now it was no longer a battle in

which he did all the striking...his opponent was striking back.

Avoiding the usual trails, I started for the Two-Bar. They would be worried about me, and they themselves might have suffered from the attack. But my day-long siege of the CP had given me satisfaction, if nothing more.

Mulvaney saw me coming and walked down to open the gate. A quick look showed me he was uninjured. The Benaras boys came out when I swung down from my horse and both of them were grinning.

Jonathan told me of the fight. The two boys had gone out from the ranch when they first spotted the approaching riders. Fighting as skirmishers, they had retreated steadily until in position to be covered by Mulvaney.

They had wounded one man and killed another before the attack even began. Then they fought it out from the bunkhouse, with all the weapons on the place loaded and at hand.

The CP had retreated, then tried a second time and been beaten off again. After that they listened and could hear an argument among the raiders. Pinder wanted another attack, but he was getting no support. Finally they had picked up the dead man and, mounting, they'd retreated down the Wash.

We talked it over, discussing a new plan of defense. Then suddenly Jonathan turned around.

"Say! I been forgettin'. Bodie Miller shot Canaval!"

"Canaval? . . ."

"Took four bullets before he went down."

"Dead?"

"Not the last we heard."

"Miller?"

"Not a scratch."

Canaval ... beaten by Bodie Miller.

Canaval had been a man with whom I could reason. He had a cool, dispassionate judgment, and dangerous as he undoubtedly was in any kind of a fight, he never made a wrong or hasty move. Moreover, with Canaval on hand there was always protection for Moira. And I had an idea that now she was going to need it.

Jonathan talked on. There was strong feeling against me in town, and it had grown since he was last in. Undoubtedly somebody was stirring it up. It was even said that Miller and I, despite our reported trouble, were working together, that I had instigated Miller's shooting of Canaval.

The firelight flickered on our faces ... Jolly was out on guard, the night was still. It is a lonely business when one fights alone, or almost alone. It is not easy to stand against the feelings of a community.

Bodie Miller would not rest with this. Canaval had been a big name where men talked of gunfighters and gunmen, and now he was down and might be dying. Bodie's hatred of me would feed upon this triumph, it would fatten, and he would want a showdown.

There was little time. I must see Canaval if he was alive. I must talk to him. He must know of Slade and his gang, and what their presence implied.

Miller would not wait long to try to kill again. At any time we might meet, and win or lose, I might be out of the fight for weeks to come.

I would ride to the Boxed M. I would ride tonight.

CHAPTER 18

KEY CHAPIN WAS dismounting at the veranda of the ranch house when I rode into the yard at the Boxed M. He turned toward me, then stopped. Fox was walking across the yard and in his hands he held a Winchester.

"Get off the place, Brennan!"

"I've got business here."

"You get! You're covered from the bunkhouse an' the barn, so don't start for a gun."

"Don't ride me, Fox. I won't take it."

The buckskin started on toward the house and Fox stepped back, hesitated, then started to lift his rifle. Although I wasn't looking at him, I could sense that rifle coming up, and debated my chances, remembering those guns behind me.

"Fox!" It was Moira, her voice clear and cool. "Let the gentleman come up."

Slowly the rifle lowered, and for an instant I drew rein, "I'm glad she stopped you, Fox. You're too good a man to die."

The sincerity in my voice must have registered, for he looked at me with a puzzled glance, then turned away toward the bunkhouse.

There was no welcome in Moira's eyes. Her face was cool, composed.

"Was there something you wanted?"

"Is that my only welcome?"

Her gaze did not flicker or change. "Had you reason to expect more?"

"No, Moira. I guess I didn't."

The lines around her mouth softened a little, but she merely waited, looking at me.

"How's Canaval?"

"Resting."

"Is he conscious?"

"Yes ... but he will see no one."

From the window Canaval's voice carried to me. "Brennan, is that you? Come in, man!"

Moira hesitated, and for a minute I believed she would refuse to admit me. Then she stepped aside and I went in. She followed me, and Chapin came behind her.

Canaval's appearance shocked me. He was drawn and thin, his eyes huge against the ghastly pallor of his face. His hand gripped mine hard.

"Watch that little demon, Matt! He's fast! He had a bullet in me before my gun cleared. He's a freak! Nerves all wrapped up tight, then lets go like a tight-coiled spring."

He put a hand on my sleeve.

"Wanted to tell you. I found tracks not far from here. Tracks of a man carrying a heavy burden. Not your tracks. Big man ... small feet."

We were all thinking the same thing then. I could see it in Moira's startled eyes. Morgan Park had small feet. Chapin let his breath out slowly.

"Brennan, I was going to ride over your way when I left here. A message for you. Picked up in Silver Reef yesterday."

It was a telegram, still sealed. I ripped it open and read:

My brother unheard of in many months. Morgan Park answers description of Park Cantwell, wanted for murder and embezzlement of regimental funds. Coming West.
> *Lep D'Arcy,*
> *Col., 12th Cavalry.*

Without comment I handed the message to Chapin, who read it aloud. Moira's face paled, but she said nothing.

"I remember the case," Chapin said. "Park Cantwell was a captain in the cavalry. He embezzled some twenty thousand dollars, and when faced with the charge, murdered his commanding officer and escaped. He was captured, then broke jail, and killed two more men getting away. He was last heard of five or six years ago in Mexico."

"Any chance of a mistake?"

"I don't think so."

Chapin glanced down at the message. "May I have this? I'll take it to Sheriff Tharp."

"What is it Park and Booker want?" Canaval said.

"Lyell said Park wanted money, quick money. How he planned to get it . . . that's the question."

Moira had not looked at me. Several times I tried to catch her eye, but she avoided my glance. Whether or not she believed I had killed her father, she obviously wanted no part of me.

Canaval's hoarse breathing was the only sound in

the quiet room. Outside in the mesquite I could hear a cicada singing. It was hot and still. . . .

Discouraged, I turned toward the door. Canaval stopped me.

"Where to now?"

Back to the Two-Bar? There was nothing there to be done now, and there were things to be done elsewhere. Then, suddenly, I knew where I was going. There was a thing that had to be done, and had to be done before I would feel that I could face myself. It was a thing that must not be left undone.

"To see Morgan Park."

Moira turned, her lips forming an unspoken protest.

"Don't . . . I've seen him kill a man with his fists," Chapin protested.

"He won't kill me."

"What is this?" Moira's voice was scathing. "A cheap, childish desire for revenge? Or just talk? You've no right to go to town and start trouble! You've no reason to start a fight with Morgan Park just because he beat you once!"

"Protecting him?" My voice was not pleasant. I did not feel pleasant.

Did she, I wonder, actually love the man? Had I been that mistaken? The more I thought of that, the angrier I became.

"No! I'm not protecting him! From what I saw after the first fight, it is you who will need protection!"

She could have said nothing more likely to bring all my determination to the surface.

Her eyes were wide, her face white. For an instant

we stared at each other, and then I turned on my heel and went out of the house, and the door slammed behind me.

Buck sensed my mood, and he was moving even as I gathered the reins. When my leg swung over the saddle he was already running.

So I would need protection, would I? Anger tore at me, and I swore bitterly as the buckskin leaned into the wind. Mad all the way through, I was eager for any kind of a fight, wanting to slash, to destroy.

And perhaps it was fortunate for me that I was in such a mood when I rounded a bend and rode right into the middle of Slade and his men.

They had not heard me. The shoulder of rock and the blowing wind kept the sound from them. Suddenly they were set upon by a charging rider who rode right into them, and even as their startled heads swung on their shoulders my horse smashed between two of the riders, sending both staggering for footing. As the buckskin struck Slade's horse with his shoulder, I drew my gun and slashed out and down with the barrel. It caught the nearest rider over the ear and he went off his horse as if struck by lightning. Swinging around, I blasted the gun from the fist of another rider with a quick shot. Slade was fighting his maddened, frantic horse, and I leaned over and hit it a slap with my hat.

The horse gave a tremendous leap and started to run like a scared rabbit, with Slade fighting to stay in the saddle. He had lost a stirrup when my horse struck his and hadn't recovered it. The last I saw of him was his running horse and a cloud of dust.

It all had happened in a split second. My advantage was that I had come upon them fighting mad and ready to strike out at anything, everything.

The fourth man had been maneuvering for a shot at me but was afraid to risk it for fear of hitting a companion in the whirling turmoil of men and horses. As I wheeled, we both fired and both missed. He tried to steady his horse. Buck did not like any of it and was fighting to get away. I let him have his head, snapping a quick backward shot at the man in the saddle. It must have clipped his ear, for he ducked like a bee-stung farmer, and then Buck was laying them down on the trail for town.

Feeding shells into my gun, I let him go, feeling better for the action, ready for anything. The town loomed up and I raced my horse down the street and swung off, leaving him with the hostler to cool off and be rubbed down.

One look at me and Katie O'Hara knew I was spoiling for trouble.

"Morgan Park is in town," she warned me. "Over at the saloon."

It was all I wanted to know. Turning, I walked across the street. I was mad clear through, stirred up by the action, and ready for more of it. I wanted the man who had struck me down without warning, and I wanted him badly. It was a job I had to do if I was going to be able to live with myself.

Morgan Park was there, all right. He was seated at a table with Jake Booker. Evidently, with Maclaren dead and Canaval shot down, they figured it was safe to come out in the open.

I wasted no time. "Booker," I said, "you're a no

account, sheep-stealin' shyster, but I've heard you're smart. You should be too smart to do business with a thief and a murderer."

It caught them flat-footed, and before either could move I grabbed the table and swung it out of the way, and then I slapped Morgan Park across the face with my hat.

He came off his chair with an inarticulate roar and I met him with a left that flattened his lip against his teeth. Blood showered from the cut and I threw a right, high and hard.

It caught him on the chin and he stopped dead in his tracks.

He blinked, and then he came on. I doubt if the thought that he might be whipped had ever occurred to him. He rushed, swinging those huge, iron-like fists. One of them caught me on the skull and rang bells in my head. Another dug for my midsection, but my elbow blocked the blow. Turning, I took a high right over my shoulder, then threw him bodily into the bar rail.

He came up with a lunge and I nailed him with a left as he reached his feet. The blow spatted into his face with a wicked sound, and there was a line of red from the broken skin. He hit me with both hands then and I felt that old smoky taste in my mouth as I walked in, blasting with both fists.

He swung a right and I went under it with a hooked left to the belly, then rolled at the hips and drove my right to the same spot. He grunted and I tried to step back, but he was too fast and too strong. He moved in on me and I hit him a raking blow to the face before we clinched. His arms went around me but I dug my head under his chin and bowed my back. It stopped him, and we stood toe to toe, wrestling on our feet. He got his arms lower and heaved me high. I smashed him in the face with my right as he threw me.

Just as he let go I grabbed a handful of hair with my right hand and he screamed. We hit the floor together, and rolling over, I beat him to my feet.

There was a crowd around us now, but although they were yelling, I heard no sound. I walked in, weaving to miss his haymakers, but he jarred me with a right to the head, then a short left. He knocked me back against the bar and grabbed a bottle. He swung at my head, but I went under it and butted him in the chest. He went down, and my momentum carried me past him.

He sprang up and I hit him. He turned halfway around, and when he did I sprang to his shoulders and jammed both spurs into his thighs. He screamed with agony and ducked. I went over his head, landing on all fours, and he kicked me rolling.

Coming up, we circled. Both of us were wary now. My hot anger was gone. This was a fight for my life, and I could win only if I used every bit of wit and cunning I possessed.

His shirt was in ribbons. I'd never seen the man stripped before, and he had the chest and shoulders of a giant. He came at me and I nailed him with a left and then we stood swinging with both hands, toe to toe. His advantage in size and weight was more than balanced by my superior speed.

I circled, feinted, and when he swung, I smashed a right to his belly. An instant later I did it again. Then

I threw a left to his battered features, and when his arms came up I smashed both hands to the body. Again and again I hit him in the stomach. He slowed, tried to set himself, but I knocked his left up and hit him in the solar plexus with a right. He grunted, and for the first time his knees sagged. Standing wide-legged, I pumped blows at his head and body as hard as I could swing. He tried to grab at me. Setting myself, I threw that right, high and hard.

My fist caught him on the side of the chin as he started to step in. He stopped, swayed, then fell, crashing through the swinging doors and rolling over to the edge of the porch, where he lay, sprawled out cold.

Turning from the door, I took the glass of whiskey somebody handed to me, and gulped it down. My heart was pounding and my body was glistening with sweat and blood. My breath came in great gasps and I sagged against the bar, trying to recover.

Somebody yelled something, and I turned. Morgan Park was standing there, his feet spread. As I turned, he hit me. It was flush on the chin and it felt like a blow from an axe. I fell back against the bar, my head spinning, and as I fought for consciousness, I stared down at his feet, amazed that such a huge man could have such small feet.

He hit me again and I went down, and then he kicked at my head with those deadly, narrow-toed boots. Only the roll of my head saved me as the kick glanced off my skull.

It was my turn to be down and out. Then somebody drenched me with a bucket of water and I sat up. It was Moira who had thrown the water.

I was too dazed to wonder how she came to be there, then somebody said, "There he is!" I saw Park standing there with his hands on his hips, leering at me through his broken lips.

We went for each other again and how we did it I'll never know. Both of us had already taken a terrific beating. But I had to whip Morgan Park or kill him with my bare hands.

Toe to toe we slugged it out, then I took a quick step back and when he came after me, I nailed him with a right uppercut. He staggered, and I hit him again.

"Stop it, you crazy fools! Stop it or I'll throw you both in jail!"

Sheriff Will Tharp stood in the door with a gun on us. His cold blue eyes meant what he said.

Around him were at least twenty men. Key Chapin was there ... and Bodie Miller.

Park backed toward the door, then turned away. He looked punch drunk.

After that I spent an hour bathing my face in hot water.

Then I went to the livery stable and crawled into the loft, taking with me a blanket and my rifle. I had worn my guns all along.

Outside somebody moved and murmured in the street. Below me the horses stamped and chomped their feed. Slowly, my exhausted muscles relaxed, my fists came unknotted, and I slept ...

CHAPTER 19

WHEN I AWAKENED, bright sunlight was filtering through a couple of cracks in the roof, and I lay there, feeling soreness in every muscle. I watched the motes dancing in the stream of light and then rolled over.

The loft was like an oven. Sitting up, I gingerly touched my face with my fingers. It was swollen and sore. Working my fingers to loosen them up, I heard a movement on the ladder. Looking over my shoulder, I saw Morgan Park staring at me. And I knew that I looked into the eyes of a man who was no longer sane.

He stood there, his head and shoulders visible above the loft floor, and I could see the hatred in his eyes. He made no move, just looked at me, and I knew then he had come to kill me.

I could have knocked him off the ladder. I could have cooled him, but I could not take that advantage. This was one man, sane or insane, whom I had to whip fairly or I would never be quite comfortable again. There was no reason in it. He had taken advantage of me . . . it was simply the way I felt.

Poised for instant movement, I knew I was in trouble. I knew now what enormous vitality that huge body held, and that he could move with amazing speed for his size.

When he came off the ladder, I got to my feet. When he moved I could see he was stiff, also. Yet I was in better shape. My workouts with Mulvaney had prepared me for this.

He did not rush me when he had his feet on the loft floor. He just stood there with his hands on his hips, looking at me. And the advantage was with him.

One side of the loft, where the ladder was, opened to the barn. A fall from there would cripple a man. The rest of the loft, except for a few square feet, was stacked with hay. With his size and weight, in these close quarters, the advantage was on his side.

My mouth was dry and I dearly wanted a drink. He faced me, and I knew at the instant when he was going to move. He came toward me, not fast, taking his time. Morgan Park had come for the kill.

He moved closer, and I struck out. He took the blow on his shoulder and kept coming in, forcing me back into the hay. Suddenly he lunged and swung. I rolled inside the punch but his weight knocked me back into the hay, for I could put no power into my punches.

With cold brutality he began to swing, his eyes lit up with sadistic delight. Lights exploded in my head, and then another punch hit me, and another.

Deliberately I slid down the side of the hay, and threw my weight against his legs. He staggered and, unable to reach me, backed off a step and swung his leg to kick. I threw my shoulder into him, and he fell back to the floor. Jumping past him, I grabbed a rope and slid down to the barn floor.

He turned and started down the ladder. Near the

door I heard someone yell, "They're at it again!" And then Morgan Park came for me.

Now it had to be ended, once and for all. Moving away from his first punch, I stabbed a left to his cut mouth, starting the blood again. He was slower than he had been yesterday, and the blood seemed to bother him. I feinted, then hit him solidly in the ribs. Rolling at the hips, I threw three solid punches to the midsection before he grabbed me, then I twisted away and hit him in the face.

He seemed puzzled. He wanted to kill, but I was being careful to avoid his hands. He swung, and I slipped inside the punch with a right to the chin.

He stopped, and I stepped in wide-legged and hit him with both fists on the chin, and he went down. I stepped back and allowed him to rise.

Behind me a crowd had gathered, but it was a silent crowd this time, a crowd awed by what they were seeing.

Morgan Park got up, and when he came off the floor he rushed, head down and swinging. Side-stepping swiftly, I thrust out a foot and he tripped, falling heavily. He got up again, stolidy, with determination. When he turned toward me, I hit him.

The blow struck his chin solidly, like the butt of an axe striking a log. He fell, not backwards, but on his face. He lay there quiet and unmoving, and I knew my fight was over.

Sodden with weariness and for once fed up with fighting, I picked up my hat and walked by the silent men. I got my rifle again and shoved it in my saddle boot. Nobody said anything, but they stared at my battered face and torn clothing.

At the door I met Sheriff Will Tharp coming in. He stopped, measuring me. "Didn't I tell you to stop fighting in this town, Brennan?"

"What am I to do? Let him beat my head off? He followed me here."

"Better have some rest," Tharp said then. "When you're rested, ride out of town for a while."

When I was in the doorway, he stopped me again. "I'm arresting Park for murder. I have official confirmation on your message."

All I wanted just then was a drink of cold water. Gallons of it.

Yet all the way to Mother O'Hara's I kept remembering that bucket of water dashed over me in the saloon. Had that really been Moira, or had it been an illusion?

When I had washed my face and patched my shirt together I went into the restaurant. Key Chapin was there.

He said little, watching me eat, passing things to me. My jaw was sore and I ate carefully.

"Booker's still in town," Chapin said. "What's he want?"

Right then I didn't care. But as I drank my coffee, I began to wonder. This was my country now, my home. It did matter to me, and Moira mattered.

"Was I crazy, or was Moira in there last night?"

"She was there, all right."

Refilling my cup, I thought that over. She was not entirely against me then.

"You'd better get over to Doc West's. That face needs some attention."

Out in the air I felt better. With food and some black coffee inside me I felt like a new man. The mountain air was fresh and good to the taste, and even the sun felt good.

I walked along the street. Out of the grab bag of the world I had picked this town. Here in this place I had elected to remain, to put down my roots, to build a ranch. Old man Ball had given me a ranch, and I had given my word. Here I could cease being a trouble-hunting, rambunctious young rider and settle down to a citizen's life. It was time for that, but I wanted one more thing. I wanted Moira.

Doc West lived in a small white cottage surrounded by rose bushes. Tall poplars stood in the woodyard and there was a patch of lawn inside the white picket fence. It was the only painted fence in town.

A tall, austere man with a shock of graying hair answered the door. He smiled at me.

"No doubt about who you are, Brennan. I just came from treating the other man."

"How is he?"

"Three broken ribs and a broken jaw. The ribs were broken last night, I'd say."

"There was no quit in him."

"He's a dangerous man, Brennan. He's still dangerous."

After he had checked me over and patched up my face, I got back on my feet and buckled on my guns. My fingers were stiff. I kept working them, trying to loosen up the muscles. What if I met Jim Pinder now? Or that weasel, Bodie Miller?

Picking up my sombrero, I remembered something. "Have Tharp check Morgan Park's boots with those tracks Canaval found. I'm betting they'll fit."

"You think he killed Maclaren?"

"Yes."

On the porch I stopped, gingerly trying to fit my hat over the lumps on my skull. It wasn't easy.

Scissors snipped among the rose bushes. Turning I looked into the eyes of Moira Maclaren.

Her dark hair was piled on her head, the first time I had seen it that way. And I decided right then it was much the best way.

"How's Canaval?" I asked.

"Better. Fox is running the ranch."

"He's a good man."

My hat was back in my hands. I turned it around. Neither of us seemed to want to say what we were thinking. I was thinking that I loved her, but I was afraid to say it.

"You're staying on at the Two-Bar?"

"The house is finished." When I said that, I looked at her. "It's finished . . . but it's empty."

Her voice faltered a little, and she snipped at a rose, cutting the stem much too short.

"You . . . you aren't living in it?"

"Yes, I'm there, but you aren't."

So there it was, out in the open again. I turned my hat again and looked down at my boots. They were scuffed and lost to color.

"You shouldn't say that. We can't mean anything to each other. You . . . you're a killer. I watched you fight. You actually *like* it."

Thinking it over, I had to agree.

"Why not? I'm a man...and fighting has been man's work for a long time on this earth."

"It's bad...it will always be bad."

I turned my hat, then put it on. "Maybe...but as long as there are men like Morgan Park, Jim Pinder, and Bodie Miller, there must be men to stand against them."

She looked up quickly. "But why does it have to be you? Matt, don't fight any more! Please don't!"

I drew back a little, though I wanted to go to her and take her in my arms.

"There's Bodie Miller. Unless someone kills him first, I'll have to face him."

"But you don't have to!" Her eyes flashed angrily. "All that's so silly! Why should you?"

"Because I'm a man. I can't live in a woman's world. I must live with men, and be judged by men. If I back down from Miller, I'll be through here. And Miller will go on to kill other men."

"You can go away! You can go to California to straighten out some business for me! Matt, you could—

"No, I'm staying here."

There were more words, and they were hard words, and then we parted, no better off.

But she had started me thinking about Bodie Miller. He was riding his luck with spurs, and he would be hunting me. Remembering that sallow-faced killer, I knew we couldn't live in the same country without meeting. And my hands were bruised, my fingers stiff.

Bodie Miller was full of salt now. I'd have to ride the country always ready. One moment off guard and I would have no other moments, ever.

How could I live and not kill?

Yet when I rode up to the ranch I was thinking of a dark-haired girl tall among the roses....

CHAPTER 20

JONATHAN BENARAS STARED at my face, then looked away, not wanting to embarrass me with questions.

"It was quite a fight . . . he took a licking."

Benaras grinned in his slow way, and a sly humor flickered in his gray eyes. "If he looks worse'n you do, he must be a sight."

While I stripped the saddle from the buckskin I told them what had happened, as briefly as possible. They listened, and I could see they were pleased. Jolly hunkered down near the barn and watched me.

"It'll please Pa . . . he never set much store by Morgan Park."

"Wish I'd been there to see it," Mulvaney mused. "It must have been a sweet fight."

We went inside where supper was laid, and we sat at a table and ate as men should—for the first time, not around a campfire. But I was thinking of the girl I wanted at this table, and the life I wanted to build with her, and how she would have none of me.

Nobody talked. The fire crackled on the hearth, and there was a subdued rattle of dishes. When we had eaten, Jolly Benaras went out into the dark with his rifle. Walking to the veranda, I looked down the dark valley.

The first thing was to find out what Booker and Morgan had been up to, and the only possible clue I had was the silver assay.

The place to look was where the Two-Bar and the Boxed M joined, I decided. The next day I would ride that way, and see for myself. If it was not there, then I must swing wide and heed tracks, for tracks there must be.

Mulvaney rode with me at daybreak. The Irishman had a facile mind, and a shrewd one. He was a good man to have on such a search, and also, he had mined and knew a little about ore.

The morning fell behind us with the trail we made across the Dark Canyon Plateau, and we lost it at Fable Canyon's rim. Off on our right, but far away, lay the Sweet Alice Hills.

Heat waves danced....I mopped my face and neck. We saw no tracks but those of deer, and once those of a lobo wolf.

We rode right and left, searching. More deer...the spoor of a mountain sheep, the drying hide of an antelope, with a few scattered bones, gnawed by wolf teeth. And then I saw something else....

Fresh tracks of a shod horse.

Turning in my saddle, I lifted my hat and waved. It was a minute before Mulvaney saw me, and then he turned his mule and rode toward me at a shambling trot. When he came closer I showed him the tracks.

"Maybe a couple of hours old," he said.

"One of the Slade gang?" I suggested, but I did not believe it.

We fell into the trail and followed along, not talking. At one place a hoof had slipped and the torn earth had not yet dried out. Obviously then, the horse had passed after the sun had left the trail, possibly within the past hour. The earth had dried some, but not entirely.

We rode rapidly, but with increasing care. Within an hour we knew we were gaining. When the canyon branched we found where the rider had filled his canteen and prepared his meal.

We looked at his fire and we knew more about him. The man was not a Slade, for the Slades were good men on a trail, and their gang were men on the dodge who had ridden the wild country. The maker of the fire had used some wood that burned badly, and his fire was in a place where the slightest breeze would swirl smoke in his face.

The boot tracks were small. Near by there was the butt of a cigar, chewed some, and only half smoked through.

Cowhands rarely smoke cigars, and they know which wood will burn well and which will not. And they have learned about fires by building many.

When we started to go, we suddenly stopped. For there were no tracks.

He had come here, watered his horse, prepared a meal, then disappeared.

The rock walls offered no escape. The earth around the spring was undisturbed beyond a few square yards. The tracks led in . . . and none led out.

"We've trailed a ghost," Mulvaney said, and I almost agreed.

"We'd best think of him as a man. What would a man do?"

"Not even a snake could mount those cliffs, so if he rode in, he rode out."

There were no tracks, nothing had been brushed out. We scouted up the canyons, but we found nothing. Mulvaney tried one branch, and I the other.

Walking my buckskin, I studied the ground with care. Wild horses had fed up this canyon, browsing along slowly, evidently at least twenty in the group. Suddenly the character of the tracks changed. The horses had broken into a wild run!

Studying the hoofprints, I could see no indication of any tracks other than those of the wild horses.

What was likely to frighten them? A grizzly? Perhaps, but they were rarely seen this far south. A wolf—no. A wild stallion was not likely to be disturbed by a wolf, even a large one. Nor was a wolf likely to get himself into a fight with a wild stallion in such close quarters. A lion then? Certainly, a lion perched on one of these cliffs might make an easy kill. Yet no lion would make them run as they had. The horses would move off all right, but not in such wild flight.

Only one thing was likely to make them run as they had . . . a man.

The tracks were only a few hours old at most. They might even be less than an hour old.

And then I saw something that alerted me instantly. In tracking, what the tracker seeks for is the thing out of place, the thing that does not belong. And on a manzanita bush was a bit of sheep's wool!

Dismounting, I plucked it from the bush. It was

not the wool from a wild sheep, not from a bighorn. This was wool from a merino, a good sheep, too.

No sheep would ever find their way into this wild canyon alone, and who would bring them in and why?

The whole situation became suddenly plain. The man we had followed had tied sheepskin over his horse's hoofs so they would leave no tracks.

Mulvaney was waiting for me when I rode back. I showed him the wool and explained quickly.

"A good idea ... but we'll get him now."

The way out through the branch canyon led northeast, and finally to a high, windswept plateau unbroken by anything but a few towering rocks and low-growing sagebrush. We sat our horses, squinting against the distance.

Far off the Blue Mountains lifted their lofty summits ten thousand feet into the sky, but even those summits gathered no clouds. And between us and the mountains was a Dante's *Inferno* of unbelievable grandeur, arid and empty.

"We may never find him," Mulvaney said at last. "You could lose an army out there."

"We'll find him."

Taking my hat from my head, I mopped my brow, then wiped the hatband. My eyes squinted against the glare. Sweat got into the corner of one eye and it smarted. My face felt raw and sore. We rode on into the heat, the only sounds those made by our walking horses; the only change, the distant shadows in the canyon and hollows of the distant hills.

Some of this country I had known, much of it had been described to me by old man Ball or the Benaras boys, who were among the few white men to have ridden into this desolate waste. Far away, between us and the bulk of the mountains, I could see a rim. That would be Salt Creek Mesa, with the towering finger above it, Cathedral Butte. Far beyond, and even higher, but not appearing so at this distance, was Shay Mountain.

The man we were searching for was somewhere in the maze of canyons between us and those mountains. And he could not be far ahead.

With the sheepskin on his horse's hoofs he would leave no trail but, knowing what to look for, we might find some indication of his passing. And his horse could not move fast.

We rode on, walking our horses. The heat was deadening, the plodding pace of the horses almost hypnotic. I shook my head, and dried my hands on my shirt.

Mulvaney's face was hard and sweaty. There was deep sunburn along his cheekbones and jaw. He rolled a smoke and lighted it, clipping the cigarette tight between his flat lips, marked with old scars.

"Hell of a country!"

His eyes flickered at me. "Yeah." He shook his canteen to gauge the amount of water remaining, then rinsed his mouth, holding the water a while before he swallowed. My own thirst seemed intensified by hearing that slosh of water in his canteen. I took a long swallow from my own.

After I replaced the cork my eyes swept the country, searching it far away, then nearer, nearer.

Nothing. . . .

We went on, seeing another bit of wood, and later a smudged place in the dust.

"Not far . . . he ain't far."

Mulvaney was right. We were closing in. But who were we following? What manner of man was this? Not a plainsman, not a cowhand. Yet a man who knew something of the wilds, and a man who was cunning and wary.

I mopped my face again, and swore softly at the heat. Sweat trickled down my ribs and I rubbed my horse's neck and spoke reassuringly.

"We'll need water," Mulvaney said.

"Yes."

"So will he."

"Maybe he knows where it is. He isn't riding blind."

"No."

Our talk lapsed and we rode on, our bodies moving to the rhythm of the walking horses. . . . The sun declined a little. It must be midafternoon, or later. I wanted another drink, but did not dare take it. I wanted to dismount for a pebble to put in my mouth, but the effort seemed too much.

Our senses were lulled by the heat and the easy movement. We rode half dozing in our saddles.

And then there was a shot.

It slapped sharply across our consciousness, and we reined wide, putting our mounts apart.

We had heard no bullet, only the flat, hard report, not far away. And then another.

"He ain't shootin' at us."

"Let's get off the flat . . . *quick!*"

The shots had come from the canyon, the trail led

there, so we went over the edge into the depths, and swung, right, always right, down the switchback trail.

If we were seen here we were dead, caught flat against the mountainside like paper ducks pinned to a wall.

CHAPTER 21

A T THE BOTTOM we swung our horses in a swirl of dust and leaped them for cover in a thick cluster of trees and brush. Even our horses felt the tension as they stood, heads up and alert.

All was still. Some distance away a stone rattled. Sweat trickled behind my ear and I smelled the hot aroma of dust and sunbaked leaves. My palms grew sweaty and I dried them, but there was no further sound.

Careful to let my saddle creak as little as possible, I swung down, Winchester in hand, and with a motion to Mulvaney to stay put, I moved away through the brush.

From the edge of the trees I could see no more than thirty yards in one direction, no more than twenty in the other. Rock walls towered and the canyon sand lay still under the blazing sun. Close against the walls there was a thin strip of shadow.

Somewhere nearby water trickled, aggravating my thirst. My neck felt hot and sticky, my shirt clung to my shoulders. Shifting the rifle in my hands, I studied the rock wall with misgiving. I dried my hands on my jeans and, taking a chance, moved out from my cover, and into that six-inch band of shade against the wall. Easing along to a bend in the wall, I peered around the corner.

Sixty yards away stood a saddled horse, head hanging. My eyes searched and saw nothing more, and then just visible beyond a white, water-worn boulder, I saw a boot and a leg as far as the knee.

For a space of a minute I watched it. There was no movement, no sound. Cautiously, wary for a trick, I advanced, ready to fire. Only the occasional chuckle of water over rocks broke the stillness. And then I saw the dead man.

That he was quite dead was beyond doubt. His skull was bloody and there was a bullet hole over one eye. He probably never knew what hit him. It served also as a warning. A man who could shoot like that was nobody to trifle with.

There was a vague familiarity to him, and moving nearer, I saw his skull bore a swelling. This had been the rider with Slade whom I had slugged on the trail.

The bullet had struck over the eye and ranged downward, which indicated he had been shot from ambush, perhaps from somewhere on the canyon wall. Lining up the probable position, I sighted a tuft of green on the wall that might be a ledge.

At my low call, Mulvaney approached. He studied the man.

"This wasn't the man we followed."

"One of the Slade crowd," I told him.

We started on, but no longer were the tracks disguised. The man we followed was going more slowly now.

Suddenly, there was a boot print, sharp and clear. Something turned over inside me.

"Mulvaney, that's the track of the man who shot Maclaren!"

"But Morgan Park's in jail," he protested, studying the track. He knew that I had ridden by to see the track Canaval had mentioned.

"He was—"

My buckskin's head came up, his nostrils dilated. Grabbing his nose, I stifled the whinny. Then I followed his gaze.

Less than a hundred yards away a strange dun horse was picketed near a clump of bunchgrass.

"You know," I said thoughtfully, "whoever we followed may think he has killed whoever followed him. He may think he's safe now."

We hid our horses in a box canyon and climbed the wall for a look around. From the top of the mesa we could see all the surrounding country. Under the southern edge of the wall opposite was a cluster of ancient ruins, beyond them deep canyons.

I studied the terrain ahead, and suddenly saw a man emerge from a crack in the earth, carrying a heavy sack. He placed it on the ground and removed his coat, then with a pick and a bar he began working at a slab over the crack from which he had come.

Mulvaney could see the man, but not what he was doing.

Explaining as I watched, I saw him take the bar and pry hard at the slab. The rock slid, then came all the way, carrying with it a pile of debris. The dust rose, settled. The crack was invisible.

After carefully looking to either side, the man concealed his tools, picked up his rifle and the sack, and started back toward us. Studying him as he walked, I could see he wore black jeans, very dusty now, and a small hat. His face was not visible, but he bore no resemblance to anyone I knew.

He disappeared from sight, and for a long time we heard no sound.

We had been concealed from sight, or so we believed, but now we climbed back down to the canyon floor. We were turning toward the box canyon where our horses were hidden when we heard two shots in quick succession.

We stared at each other, puzzled. But there was no other sound as we uneasily worked our way back to the box canyon.

Mulvaney saw it first, and he swore viciously. It was the first time I had ever heard him swear.

My horse and his mule lay sprawled in pools of their own blood. Our canteens had been emptied and smashed with stones. We were thirty miles from the nearest ranch, and our way lay through some of the most rugged country on earth.

"There's water, but no way to carry it. Do you think he knew who we were?"

"If he lives in this country he should know that buckskin of mine," I said bitterly. "He was the best horse I ever owned."

It told me something else about our man, whoever he was. He was utterly ruthless. This man had not driven the horses off, he had shot them down. He was cautious, too. To have hunted us down might have exposed himself to danger.

"We'll have a look at the place he covered up. No use leaving without that."

It was almost dark before we had dug enough behind the slab of rock to get at the secret. Mulvaney cut into the rock with his pick. Ripping out a chunk he showed it to me, his eyes glowing with excitement.

"Silver! The biggest strike I ever saw! Better than Silver Reef!"

The ore glittered in his hand as he turned it. This was what had killed Rud Maclaren and the others.

"It's rich," I said, "but I'd settle for the Two-Bar."

"But it's a handsome sight!"

"Pocket it then. We've a long walk."

"Now?"

"Tonight . . . while it's cool."

The shadows grew long while we walked, and thick blackness came down to choke the canyons and cover the mountains. We walked on, with little talk, up Ruin Canyon and over a saddle of the Sweet Alice Hills and down to a spring on the far side.

There we rested and drank, and I was remembering, and thinking ahead.

The camp where I had seen Slade's gang was not many miles away, it had water and shelter, and so far as they knew only Morgan Park knew about it. Outlaws are rarely energetic men, and I doubted that they had moved. Where outlaws were, there would be horses also.

It had taken us five hours to walk ten miles, and it was well into the night. Most of our walking had been along the canyon's bottom. Now we would be crossing Dark Canyon Platau . . . but no, *this* was the canyon they were in!

Dark it was as we walked, doing no talking. There was water rustling over stones and the dampness in the canyon was good after the heat of the long day.

We heard singing before we saw the light of the

fire. The canyon walls caught and magnified the sound. A few yards farther along, we spotted the fire, and the reflection of it on a face.

Three men were there, and one sang as he cleaned his rifle.

We were at the edge of the firelight before they saw us, and I had my Winchester on them, and Mulvaney his cannon-like four-shot pistol.

Slade was no fool. He sat very still, with his hands in sight. His face was pale, as well it might be, with a hanging waiting for him.

"Who is it?"

Our faces were shielded by the brims of our hats, and we stood partly concealed by the brush.

"The name is Matt Brennan, and I'm not asking for trouble. We want two good horses. You can lend them or we'll take them.

"Our horses," I added, "were shot by the same man who killed your partner."

"Lott killed?"

Slade studied me, absorbing that news. None of them seemed in the mood for trouble. Nevertheless I discouraged any such idea with my Winchester.

"He met up with a man we were trailing. He caught a slug between the eyes." I pushed my hand up and moved my hat back. "Then he shot both our horses."

"Damn a man who'll kill a horse. Who was it?"

"He leaves a track like Morgan Park, but Park's in jail."

"Not now," Slade said. "He broke jail within an hour after dark last night. Pulled an iron bar out of that old wall, stole a horse, and disappeared."

But the man we had seen had not been big enough for Park. Nevertheless, it was a thing to remember.

"How about the horses?"

"Take them. We're clearing out."

"Are they spares?"

"We've got a dozen extras. In our business it pays to keep fresh horses." He grinned up at me and slowly leaned back on his elbow. "No hard feelin's, Brennan?"

"None . . . only be careful."

"With two guns on us? Sure. . . . What kind of a cannon is that your partner's got? A man could ride into that barrel with his hat on."

Mulvaney went after the horses, then returned with them. They were saddled and bridled.

Slade's mouth twisted when he saw the saddles. But he had nothing to say.

"Any other news?"

He smiled maliciously at me. "Yeah. Bodie Miller's talking it big around town. Says you're his meat."

"He's a heavy eater, that boy. Hope he doesn't tackle anything that'll give him indigestion."

We mounted up. "The horses will be at the livery stable in town."

"Better not," Slade said. "There's a corral in the woods back of Armstrong's. You might leave them there."

The horses were fresh and ready to run, and we let them go. It was good to be in the saddle again, but both of us were hanging heavy before many miles.

We rode and we did not talk, for neither of us had words to say. The stars faded and the sky turned gray in the east, and then a pale yellow showed above the mountains behind us. The rosy color of dawn tipped the mountains before us, and we slowed our pace and cantered down the trail and watched the sun pick out the roofs ahead of us.

Daylight saw us riding down the street at Hattan's Point.

CHAPTER 22

WE FOUND A town that was silent and waiting. But the loft was full of hay and both of us needed sleep. And what was to come would wait.

Two hours later, as if by signal, I awakened suddenly. Leaving Mulvaney to his needed rest, I splashed water on my face and headed for Mother O'Hara's. The first person I saw when I came through the door was Moira. And the second was Key Chapin.

"Sorry," Chapin said. "We just heard the news."

My blank expression must have told him. I knew of no news, but I didn't want to wait to hear it.

"You're losing the Two-Bar."

"What are you talking about?"

"Jake Booker filed a deed to the Two-Bar. He purchased all rights from a nephew of old man Ball's. He had laid claim to the Boxed M, maintains it was never actually owned by Rud Maclaren, but belonged to his brother-in-law, now dead. Booker found a relative of the brother-in-law, and bought the property."

"It's a steal."

"If he goes to court he can make it very rough."

He went on to explain that Booker was a shrewd lawyer, and despite my two witnesses, could go far toward establishing a solid claim.

He went on to say that Booker had turned up the fact that a few years before, while suffering from a gunshot wound, Maclaren had deeded the ranch to his brother-in-law and it had apparently never been deeded back to himself.

Moira's face looked pale, and I could understand why. If Booker could make his claim hold good, then Moira, instead of being an independent young lady with a cattle ranch, would be broke and hunting a job. I knew that Maclaren had spent cash in developing the place and actually had little money on hand.

"What's more important right now," Chapin added, "Booker has a court order impounding all bank deposits, stopping all sales, and freezing everything as is until the case is settled."

I sat down. Swiftly, I ordered my thoughts. Booker would have paid out no money for claims he did not think he could substantiate in court. The man was shrewd.

There was no attorney within miles capable of coping with Booker. What had begun as a range war had degenerated into a grand steal by a shyster lawyer. And neither of us would have the money to fight him.

A thought occurred to me. "Has Canaval been told?"

Chapin gestured impatiently. "There's nothing he can do. He's only a foreman."

Katie O'Hara brought me coffee and it tasted good.

Sheriff Will Tharp had left town, accompanied by the recently arrived Colonel D'Arcy. They had gone to Morgan Park's ranch, searching for him.

"They should have gone to Dark Canyon," I said.

"Why there?" Chapin looked at me curiously. "What would take a man there?"

"That's where he'll be."

When Katie O'Hara brought my breakfast I ate in silence. Morgan Park was free and would be wanting a shot at me. Bodie Miller was probably in town. Whatever was to be done would have to be done fast, and however good I might be with gun or fists, I had no experience with the intricacies of the law. I could not hope to meet Booker on his own ground.

Moira did not look at me. She talked a little with Key Chapin, who had been her father's friend.

"Moira," I said, "you better send a messenger to the ranch to tell Canaval what's happened."

Still she did not look at me. "What can he do? It would only worry him."

"No matter—take my advice."

She tightened a little, resenting the suggestion. "Better still, have Fox and some of your boys bring him into town in a buckboard."

"But I don't—

"Do what I say." My abruptness seemed to shock her. She looked up, and our eyes met. Hers fell swiftly, but for an instant I thought . . .

"Moira," I said gently, "you want your ranch. It can be saved. Get Canaval in here and tell him what's happened. Have witnesses, take a statement from him, and have it signed by the witnesses."

"What are you talking about? What statement?"

"Do what I advise."

Finishing my coffee with a gulp, I picked up my hat and put it on the back of my head. Then I rolled a smoke. While I was doing it, my eyes were studying the street outside. There was no sign of Miller.

But then I saw something else. A weary dun horse was tied to the side of the corral. It was barely visible between the buildings.

"Who owns that horse?"

Chapin came to the window to look. He shook his head. "I've no idea."

Katie was picking up the dishes, and she glanced out the window. "Jake Booker rides it. He did this morning."

And Jake Booker had small feet.

Mulvaney was crawling down from the loft when I got to him. He listened, then ran to the stable office and got a fresh horse.

Key Chapin was in the door of the restaurant when I walked by.

"Get Canaval in here. We're having a showdown. Send for Jim Pinder, too."

He studied me. "Matt, what do you know?"

"Enough . . . I think. Enough to save the Boxed M and probably to find the man who killed Maclaren."

Without waiting, I went through the town, store by store, saloon by saloon. I was looking for Bodie Miller, but there was no sign of him, nor of his partner.

At Mother O'Hara's, Key Chapin and Moira were waiting. I sat down and without giving them a chance to talk, I outlined my plan in as few words as possible. Moira listened with surprise, I thought, but she shouldn't have been surprised, for I had said much of this before. Chapin nodded from time to time.

"It might work," he agreed at last. "We can try."

"What about Tharp?"

"He'll stand with us. He's a solid man, Matt."

"All right, then. Showdown in the morning."

The voice came from behind me. It was a voice I knew, low, confident, a little mocking.

"Why, sure! Showdown in the morning, I'd like that, Brennan."

It was Bodie Miller.

He was smiling when I looked at him, but his eyes did not join in the smile.

This was Bodie, the man who wanted to kill me.... Bodie the killer.

———

THE SUN IN the morning came up clear and hot. At daybreak the sky was without a cloud, and the distant mountains shimmered in a haze of their own making. The desert lost itself in heat waves, and a stillness lay upon both desert and town, a sort of poised awareness that seemed to walk on tiptoe as if the slightest sound might shatter it."

When I emerged on the street I was a man alone. The street was empty as a town of ghosts, silent except for the sound of my own boots on the boardwalk. Then, as if that sound had broken the spell, the bartender came from the saloon and began to sweep off the walk in front.

He glanced at me, bobbed his head in recognition, then hastily completed his sweeping and ducked back inside.

A man carrying two wooden buckets emerged from an alley and looked cautiously around. Assured there was no one in sight, he started across the street, glancing apprehensively first one way, then the other.

Sitting down in one of the pants-polished chairs in front of the saloon, I looked at the far Blue Mountains. In a few minutes I might be dead.

It was not a good morning to die—but what morning is? Yet in a short time two men, myself and another, would meet somewhere in this town and one of us, perhaps both of us, would die.

Mulvaney rode into the street and left his horse at the stable. He walked over to me, carrying enough guns to start a war.

"The whole kit an' kaboodle. Be here within an hour. Jolly's already in town."

A woman stood at a second-floor window looking down. She turned suddenly and left the window as if called.

"If Red cuts into this scrap," Mulvaney said, "he's mine."

"You can have him."

The man with the two buckets hurried fearfully across the street, slopping water at each step.

Sheriff Tharp had not returned. There was no sign of Pinder, Morgan Park, or Bodie Miller.

Mother O'Hara had a white tablecloth on the table and the meal looked impressive.

"You should be ashamed!" she said severely. "That girl lay awake half the night, worryin' her pretty head over you."

"Over me?"

"Worried fair sick, she is. About you and that Bodie Miller!"

The door opened then and Moira entered. Her dark hair was tied in a loose knot at the back of her neck, and her eyes looked unusually large in her pale face. She avoided my glance and it was well for me she did. It was a day when I could show no weakness, not even for her.

Chapin came in, and after him, Colonel D'Arcy. I knew him at once. Right behind them was Jake Booker. He looked smug around the eyes.

They had scarcely seated themselves when Jim Pinder came in.

"Glad to see you, Jim," I said, and could see the shock of the words reflected in his eyes. "We've been fighting somebody else's battle."

He stood with his hands on his hips, looking around the room. Chapin he knew, D'Arcy he had heard about. If he knew Booker there was no evidence of it.

Turning my head, I looked at Booker. "This is a peace conference, Booker. The fighting in this area ends today."

He looked at me, his eyes blinking slowly. He was a thin-faced man with the skin tight across his cheekbones. He was disturbed, I could see that. He was a man who liked to know a little bit more about what was happening than anyone else. And this was a surprise, and as yet he had not decided what to make of it.

"I ain't said nothing about peace," Pinder said flatly. "I come in because I figured you were ready to sell."

"No—no sale. The ranch is mine. I mean to keep it. But we are organizing a peace move. Key Chapin and Sheriff Tharp are in it. Chapin has lined up the town's merchants and businessmen.

"You can come in or you can stay out, but if you

don't join us you'll have to buy supplies in Silver Reef. This town will be closed to you. Each of us in this fight will put up a bond to keep the peace, effective at daybreak tomorrow."

"You killed my brother."

"He came hunting me. That makes a difference. Look," I said, "this fight has cost you. You need money, so do we all. You sign up, or you can't ship cattle. Everybody knows you've nerve enough to face me, but what will it prove?"

He stared stubbornly at the table, but what I had said made sense, and he knew it. Finally he said, "I'll think it over. It'll take some time."

"It will take you just two minutes."

He lifted his eyes and stared hard at me. Of the two of us, he knew I was the faster man with a gun. And yet it was I who was talking peace. I knew this war had cost him heavily and no sane man would want to continue it.

Suddenly his mouth twisted in a wry sort of grin. Reluctantly, he shrugged. "You ride a man hard, Brennan. But peace it is."

"Thanks." My hand went out. He looked at it, then accepted it. Katie O'Hara filled his cup.

He looked at the coffee, then at me. "I've got to make a drive. The only way with water is across your place."

"What's wrong with that? Just so it doesn't take you more than a week to get 'em across."

The door opened and Fox came in, supporting Canaval. He was pale and drawn, but his eyes were alert and interested.

"Miss Moira could sign for me. She's the owner," he said. "But I'm for peace."

"You sign, too," I insisted. "We want to cover everything."

Jake Booker had been taking it all in, wary and a little uncertain of what to think.

Now he decided to speak. "This is utter nonsense, as you all know. Both ranches belong to me. You have twenty-four hours to yield possession."

Sheriff Tharp had come into the room as Booker spoke. He sat down, saying nothing. He took out his pipe with deliberation. He was an old man, but a careful man, and shrewd.

"We aren't moving, Booker. And you'll never move us."

"Are you threatening me?" He was vastly pleased that the sheriff had heard.

Ignoring the question, I made a point of filling my cup, stalling a little.

"On what basis does your claim to the Boxed M rest?"

"Bill of sale," he said promptly. "The ranch was decded to Jay Collins, the gunfighter. Collins was killed. Collins's nephew inherited. I bought the Boxed M from him, and all appurtenances thereto."

Canaval looked at me. He smiled a little, and nodded, "So that was why."

"Jake," I said, "let me introduce you to Jay Collins."

Booker looked at Canaval as I gestured toward him. He looked and his face went two shades whiter. He started to speak, but the words stumbled and took no form. He tried to find the words and they would not come out. But anyone could see that he did not doubt what I said was true. Undoubtedly Canaval tied in with what he had known of Collins.

Moira was staring at Canaval, and he looked over at her and smiled. "That's why I knew so much about your mother. She was the only person I really loved—until I met my niece."

"Mother told me about you, but I never thought—"

Turning my eyes away from her, I looked across the table at Booker. In a matter of minutes half his plan had come to nothing, and I knew that in this case half was almost as good as all.

Yet Booker was searching desperately for a way out. He knew we would not be bluffing, that if the claim we made for Canaval was tested in court it would stand up.

He looked down at his hands, and I could almost feel his thoughts.

Now where? Now what?

CHAPTER 23

IT WAS A showdown, but from here on I was working in the dark. Counting on the shock of what I had just told him, I hoped he would believe that I knew more than I did. What I was about to say I was sure was true, but I had no proof.

"As for the Two-Bar, I've witnesses and my claim will stand in court." So much was possible, at least. Now—"Not that it will matter to you, Booker."

He was worried now, as I wanted him to be. He was not sure what I was holding back. The fact that Jay Collins was alive was an eventuality to which he had given no thought.

He looked up at me, his eyes veiled. But there was a little tic at the corner of his eye that betrayed his nervousness.

"What do you mean by that?"

"You'll hang, Booker. For murder."

Nobody said anything. Booker inhaled sharply, but he gave no other indication. He did not even protest, he just waited.

"You killed Rud Maclaren because Park's way was too slow for you. You also killed one of Slade's men from ambush.

"We can trail your horse to the scene of that crime, Booker, and if you believe the western jury won't take the word of an Apache tracker, you're wrong."

Jake Booker straightened in his chair. He glanced around the room and found no friendliness there, but he was not a man who relied on friendships.

"Lies," he said, with a wave of dismissal, "all lies. I knew Maclaren only by sight. I had no reason to kill the man—and no opportunity."

Canaval looked doubtfully at me. Tharp was merely waiting, but a little impatiently now. If there was anyone there who believed in me it was only Mulvaney.

The room was still. I could hear the clock ticking, and Katie O'Hara was standing in the door of her kitchen listening.

I felt their eyes on me, and knew the spot I was in. Yet I was sure. Carefully, I began to build. I knew that if they were to be convinced, it must be now. If Booker left this room he would escape. If I failed to prove my point, the peace we had planned would fall through.

"How Booker got him out of the house, I do not know. Probably on some pretext. Perhaps to show him the silver, perhaps to show him something I was planning.

"The mere fact that Booker, whom Maclaren knew only by reputation, would ride all that way to talk in secret would be enough to get Maclaren out.

"It does not matter what excuse was used. Booker shot him, loaded him on a horse and carried the body to my place. Then he shot Maclaren again, hoping the shot would draw me into the vicinity so I would leave tracks around the body."

Moira was watching me closely now, and Tom Fox had moved up beside me, looking across the table at

Booker. Two other Boxed M hands had shifted, one to the outer door, one to a place behind Jake Booker.

Nobody seemed aware of the moves but Booker and myself. Sweat broke out on his brow. His eyes shifted to Will Tharp, but if the sheriff noticed he did not indicate it.

"Arnold D'Arcy had found the silver lode and filed a claim. Morgan Park trailed D'Arcy to kill him. He was fiercely jealous, as we all know, but that was the least of it. Sooner or later Arnold D'Arcy would see him and would realize who he was.

"To be recognized meant arrest and trial. Following D'Arcy led him to the silver, and after the murder Morgan Park stood within reach of enough money to take him to South America to live in style.

"But he must have realized that he dared not connect his name with that of D'Arcy. Arnold had filed on the claim. He could do nothing until the assessment work lapsed, and even then to take up the claim of a man who had disappeared, and when investigation might establish a connection, was a risk he dared not take."

Supposition, much of it, but the only logic that would fit the facts.

So as the hot morning drew on into a hotter day, I built the case I had. Not much evidence, but logic enough.

Unable to make use of his discovery, Morgan Park had gone to Booker. The lawyer could find a buyer, keep Park's name out of it, and if the two ranches could be obtained, the claims might even be worked in secret. D'Arcy had evidently bribed the recorder to let out no word of the discovery.

Morgan Park had been content to work along with Rud Maclaren, believing he would sooner or later win out. But he had kept in touch with Jim Pinder.

To this Pinder acknowledged with a short nod.

And then into this stewing pot of conflicting issues and desires, I stepped.

By joining Ball I had upset the balance of power and made the certainty of the Two-Bar falling into other hands extremely doubtful.

Morgan Park still believed he could win. He was a man who had not been beaten, and he was confident. Jake Booker had been less so. Although Booker had, in my presence, doubted any belief that I had been implicated in the shooting of Lyell, he actually believed I had. The idea was upsetting.

Booker wanted the claims for himself. There was a chance that Morgan Park might be killed or arrested. Booker was already delving into Park's past, knowing there must be some reason for his great secrecy.

The assessment work D'Arcy had done on the claims had long since lapsed, but Morgan Park had dared not file on them and risk questions. The silver claims lay on land claimed by both the Two-Bar and the Boxed M, but if both ranches could be had . . .

"Lies." Booker was composed now. He was fighting for his life and he knew it, yet he was lawyer enough to see that I had little evidence.

Tom Fox was a lean, tough man. He leaned over the table.

"Some of us are satisfied, Booker," he said quietly. "Have you got any arguments that will answer a rope?"

Booker's face thinned down. "The law will protect

me. Tharp's here ... and no jury on earth will convict me on that evidence. As for the track you say you found? How do you know it hasn't been wiped out?"

I didn't know. Neither did anybody else. Canaval looked at me, and so did Tharp. There was nothing I could say to that.

"Aw, turn him loose!" Fox said carelessly. "We all know he's a crook. But turn him loose. Rud Maclaren was a good boss, and I was with Canaval when he found that track. I ain't no 'Pache, but I can read sign. Just you turn him loose. There's a mighty nice pin oak down the road a piece."

Jake Booker spread his fingers on the table. He was a frightened man. Argument and evidence might stand with Tharp, with Chapin, with Canaval, and with me. He knew he had no argument to reply to Fox.

Fox turned to the man at the door. "Joe, get an extry horse. We'll be needin' it."

Tharp began to fill his pipe. Nobody else said anything or moved. Then Key Chapin leaned back in his chair. The chair creaked a little, and Booker shifted his weight, looking up quickly at Fox.

Nothing I had said had moved Booker to more than contempt. For nothing I had said would stand up in court against the artifice Booker could bring to bear. But Fox was doing what I could not have done. Booker had looked into the eyes of Fox and there was certainty there.

A boot track to a skilled reader of sign is as good as a signature.

Jake Booker was a plotter and a conniver. He was not a courageous man. Will Tharp has said nothing.

Chapin had obviously washed his hands of the situation. I was letting Fox do the talking. And Jake Booker was frightened.

The rest of us might bluff, but never Fox. The rest of us might relent, but not Fox. Booker's mouth twitched and his face was wet with sweat.

"No...no."

He looked around at us. He looked at me. "You can't let him hang me. Not without a trial."

"Did Maclaren have a trial?"

Booker shifted his hands on the table. He knew there was a man behind him. And Fox was across from him. And nobody was doing anything.

"Morgan Park killed him," Booker said. "It wasn't me."

He was talking. Once started, he might continue. It had not been Park, and we all knew it now.

"Where is Park?"

"Dead...Park killed his horse getting away. He came up to that Apache tracker of Pinder's. The Apache had a good black. Morgan Park knocked him off the horse when the Apache wouldn't trade...the Indian shot him out of the saddle."

"You saw it?" D'Arcy asked.

"Yes...you'll find his body in a gully west of Bitter Flats. Park had started for the Reef."

Booker sat very still, waiting for us, but we did not speak. He shifted uneasily. Tharp would say nothing, and Booker knew that if he left here now he would be taken by Fox and the Boxed M riders. After that there was only the short ride to a tree.

"Tell us the truth," Chapin said finally. "If you get a trial you will have a chance."

"If I confess?" His voice was bitter. "What chance would I have then?"

"You'll live a few weeks, anyway," I said brutally. "What chance have you now?"

He sat back in his chair. "I've nothing to confess," he said. "It was Morgan Park."

Will Tharp got up from his chair. "You asked me here to conclude a peace meeting. The Boxed M, Two-Bar, and CP agree on peace, is that right?"

We all assented, and he nodded with satisfaction. "Good...now I've some business in the northern part of the county. I'll be gone for three days."

It took a minute for Booker to grasp the idea that he was being abandoned. He looked up, his eyes shifting quickly. The man behind him eased his weight and a board creaked.

Key Chapin got up. He extended a hand to Canaval. "Be glad to help you across the street, Canaval." He turned his head to Moira. "Coming?"

She got up. Katie O'Hara had disappeared. Jim Pinder, a wry grin on his face, got up, too.

They started for the door and Jake Booker looked wildly about. Fox was across from him, smiling. Behind him was the other Boxed M hand. Outside the door with an extra horse was still another.

"*Wait!*"

Booker jumped to his feet. His face was yellow-white and he looked ghastly.

"Tharp! You can't do this! You can't leave me!"

"Why not? I've no business with you!"

"But...but the trial? What about the trial?"

Tharp shrugged. "What trial? We haven't evidence

enough to hold you. You said that yourself." He turned away. "You're not my business now, Booker."

Fox had drawn his gun. The Boxed M hand behind Booker grabbed him suddenly. I stepped back, my hands at my sides.

"Wait a minute! Tharp—"

The sheriff was outside, but he was holding the door open. The others were on the walk near him.

"Tharp! I did it. I'll talk."

There was a tablet on which Katie O'Hara wrote up her menus. I took it down, and put the inkwell beside it, and a pen.

"Write it," I said.

He hesitated, looking down. His hands trembled and he looked sick.

"All right," he said.

He sat down when the Boxed M hand released him, and Tharp returned to the room. He looked over at me and we waited, standing around, while the pen scratched steadily.

Jonathan Benaras appeared in the door. "Bodie Miller's gone," he said. "Left town."

Moira was still standing on the walk outside. The others had gone. I opened the door and stepped out.

"You're going back to the Two-Bar?" she asked.

"Even a killer has to have a home."

She looked up quickly. "Matt, don't hold that against me."

"You said what you thought, didn't you?"

I started to put my foot in the stirrup, but she looked too much like a little girl who had been spanked. "Did you ever start that trousseau?" I asked suddenly.

"Yes, but—

I dropped the reins of the horse Benaras had led up for me.

"Then we'll be married without it."

Suddenly we were both laughing like fools and I was kissing her there on the street where all of Hattan's Point could see us. People had come from saloons and stores and they were standing there grinning at us, so I kissed her again.

Then I let go of her and stepped into the saddle. "Tomorrow noon," I said, "I'll be back."

And so I rode again from Hattan's Point.

CHAPTER 24

DID YOU EVER feel so good the world seemed like your big apple? That was how I felt then.

We had our showdown, and we had peace between the three ranches. We could live together now, and we could make our acres fertile and make our cattle fat.

There was grass on the range, water in the creeks, and the house I had built would have the woman it needed to make it home. From the smoke of battle I had built a home and won a wife. The world was mine.

Morgan Park was dead... he had died in violence as he had lived, died from striking the wrong man, heedless of others, believing that his strength would pull him through. Only an Apache had fired from the ground and the bullet had torn through his skull.

I would go home now. I would make ready the house for the wife I was to have, I would care for my horses in the corral, and I would change my clothes and ride back to town to become a bridegroom.

The trail to the Two-Bar swung around a mesa and opened out on a wide desert flat, and far beyond I could see the pinnacles of the badlands beyond Dry Mesa.

A rabbit burst from the bush and sprinted off across the sage, and then the trail dipped down into a hollow, with junipers growing in and around it. And there in the middle of the road was Bodie Miller.

He was standing with his hands on his hips laughing, and there was a devil in his eyes. Off to one side of the road was Red, holding their horses.

Miller's hair was uncut and hung over the collar of his shirt. The hairs at the corners of his upper lip seemed longer and darker. But the two guns tied down to his thighs were nothing to smile about.

"Too bad to cut down the big man just when he's ridin' highest."

The horse I rode was skittish and unacquainted with me. I'd no idea how he'd stand for shooting, and I wanted to be on the ground. But there was little time. Bodie was confident, but he did not know that I might have company farther back along the road.

Suddenly I slapped spurs to the gelding and when he sprang at Bodie, I went off the other side. Hitting the ground, I ran two steps and drew as I saw Bodie's hands blur.

His guns came up and I felt mine buck in my fist. Our bullets crossed each other, although mine got off a shade the faster despite that instant of hesitation to make sure my bullet would shoot true.

His slug ripped a furrow across the top of my shoulder that stung like a million needles, but my own bullet struck him in the chest and he staggered, his eye wide and shocked.

Suddenly the devil of eagerness was in me. I was mad, mad as I had never been before. Guns up and blasting, I started for him.

"What's the matter ? Don't you like it?"

I was yelling as I walked, my guns blasting and the lead ripping into and through him.

"Now you know how the others felt, Bodie. It's an ugly thing to die because some punk wants to prove he's tough. And you aren't tough, Bodie, just a mean, nasty kid."

He swayed on his feet, bloody and finished. He was a slighter man than I, the blood staining his shirt crimson, his mouth ripped wider by a bullet. His face was gray and slashed across by the streak left by the bullet.

He stared at me, but he did not speak. Something kept him upright, but he was gone and I could see it. He stood there in the white hot sunlight and stared into my face, the last face he would ever see.

"I'm sorry, Bodie. Why didn't you stick to punching cows?"

He backed up a slow step and the gun slid from his fingers. He tried once to speak, but his lips were unable to shape the words, and then his knees buckled and he went down.

Standing over his body I looked at Red. The cowhand seemed unable to believe his eyes. He stared at Bodie Miller's used-up body, and then he lifted his eyes to me.

"I'll ride . . . just give me a chance."

"You've got it."

He swung into the saddle, then looked back at Bodie. He studied him, as if awakening from a dream.

"He wasn't so tough, was he?"

"Nobody is," I said, "especially with a slug in his belly."

He rode away then and I stood there in the lonely afternoon and saw Bodie Miller dead at my feet.

It wasn't in me to leave him there, and I did not want to find him there when I returned. There was a gully off the trail, a little hollow where water had washed before finding a new way. So I rolled him in and shoved the banks in on top of him and then piled on some stones.

Sitting in the shade of a juniper I put together a cross, and on an old wagon tailgate that had laid beside the road for a long time, I carved out the words:

HE PLAYED OUT HIS HAND
1881

It was not much of an end for a man, but Bodie was not much of a man.

Beside some campfire Red might talk, someday, somewhere. Sooner or later the story might travel, but it would take time, and I wanted no more reputation as a gunfighter. There had been too much of that.

There was a stinging in my shoulder, but only from cut skin. At the ranch I could care for that. And it was time I was getting on.

Ahead of me the serrated ridges of the wild lands were stark and lonely against the late afternoon sky. The sun setting behind me was picking out the peak points to touch them with gold. The afternoon was gone and now I was riding home to my own ranch, riding home with the coolness of evening coming on . . . and tomorrow was my wedding day.

About Louis L'Amour

*"I think of myself in the oral tradition—
as a troubadour, a village taleteller, the man
in the shadows of the campfire. That's the way
I'd like to be remembered—as a storyteller.
A good storyteller."*

IT IS DOUBTFUL that any author could be as at
home in the world re-created in his novels as
Louis Dearborn L'Amour. Not only could he physically fill the boots of the rugged characters he wrote
about, but he literally "walked the land my characters walk." His personal experiences as well as his
lifelong devotion to historical research combined to
give Mr. L'Amour the unique knowledge and understanding of people, events, and the challenge of the
American frontier that became the hallmarks of his
popularity.

Of French-Irish descent, Mr. L'Amour could trace
his own family in North America back to the early
1600s and follow their steady progression westward,
"always on the frontier." As a boy growing up in
Jamestown, North Dakota, he absorbed all he could
about his family's frontier heritage, including the
story of his great-grandfather who was scalped by
Sioux warriors.

Spurred by an eager curiosity and desire to broaden

his horizons, Mr. L'Amour left home at the age of fifteen and enjoyed a wide variety of jobs, including seaman, lumberjack, elephant handler, skinner of dead cattle, miner, and an officer in the transportation corps during World War II. During his "yondering" days he also circled the world on a freighter, sailed a dhow on the Red Sea, was shipwrecked in the West Indies and stranded in the Mojave Desert. He won fifty-one of fifty-nine fights as a professional boxer and worked as a journalist and lecturer. He was a voracious reader and collector of rare books. His personal library contained 17,000 volumes.

Mr. L'Amour "wanted to write almost from the time I could talk." After developing a widespread following for his many frontier and adventure stories written for fiction magazines, Mr. L'Amour published his first full-length novel, *Hondo,* in the United States in 1953. Every one of his more than 120 books is in print; there are 300 million copies of his books in print worldwide, making him one of the bestselling authors in modern literary history. His books have been translated into twenty languages, and more than forty-five of his novels and stories have been made into feature films and television movies.

His hardcover bestsellers include *The Lonesome Gods, The Walking Drum* (his twelfth-century historical novel), *Jubal Sackett, Last of the Breed,* and *The Haunted Mesa.* His memoir, *Education of a Wandering Man,* was a leading bestseller in 1989. Audio dramatizations and adaptations of many L'Amour stories are available on cassette tapes from Random House Audio publishing.

The recipient of many great honors and awards, in

1983 Mr. L'Amour became the first novelist ever to be awarded the Congressional Gold Medal by the United States Congress in honor of his life's work. In 1984 he was also awarded the Medal of Freedom by President Reagan.

Louis L'Amour died on June 10, 1988. His wife, Kathy, and their two children, Beau and Angelique, carry the L'Amour publishing tradition forward with new books written by the author during his lifetime to be published by Bantam.

LOUIS L'AMOUR

AMERICA'S FAVORITE FRONTIER WRITER

Be sure to read all of the titles in the Sackett series: follow them
from the Tennessee mountains as they head west to ride the trails,
pan the gold, work the ranches, and make the laws.

JUBAL SACKETT

SACKETT'S LAND

TO THE FAR BLUE MOUNTAINS

WARRIOR'S PATH

RIDE THE RIVER

THE DAY BREAKERS

SACKETT

LANDO

MOJAVE CROSSING

THE SACKETT BRAND

THE LONELY MEN

TREASURE MOUNTAIN

MUSTANG MAN

GALLOWAY

THE SKYLINERS

RIDE THE DARK TRAIL

LONELY ON THE MOUNTAIN

Ask for these titles wherever books are sold,
or visit us online at *www.bantamdell.com*
for ordering information.